THE GOALKEEPER

THE GOALKEEPER

SEAN WHITE

For Jenny and Joshua,
with all my love xxx

British Kingdom
REGIONAL LEAGUE

SyBall World Cup: Men's Final Starting Elevens

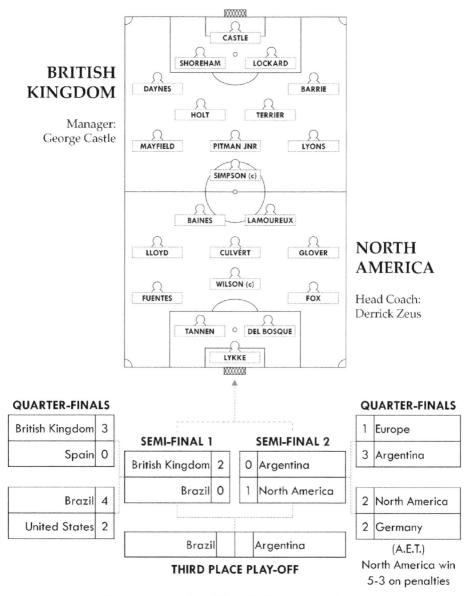

BRITISH KINGDOM

Manager: George Castle

CASTLE
SHOREHAM   LOCKARD
DAYNES   BARRIE
HOLT   TERRIER
MAYFIELD   PITMAN JNR   LYONS
SIMPSON (c)

BAINES   LAMOUREUX
LLOYD   CULVERT   GLOVER
WILSON (c)
FUENTES   FOX
TANNEN   DEL BOSQUE
LYKKE

NORTH AMERICA

Head Coach: Derrick Zeus

Route to the Final (Last 8 of 64)

QUARTER-FINALS

British Kingdom	3
Spain	0

Brazil	4
United States	2

SEMI-FINAL 1

British Kingdom	2
Brazil	0

SEMI-FINAL 2

0	Argentina
1	North America

QUARTER-FINALS

1	Europe
3	Argentina

2	North America
2	Germany

(A.E.T.)
North America win 5-3 on penalties

THIRD PLACE PLAY-OFF

Brazil	Argentina

Prologue
Mary-Jane Castle

In Manchester, the referee blew the whistle and the match was over. Brazil had won.

I was in my room at the time. I laid back on my bed and took a few deep breaths to calm myself down. My heart was pounding, the blood was rushing to my head. I felt dizzy. The room spun and when I closed my eyes, I saw these little blue stars floating in the darkness.

Crazy what you remember, isn't it? The tiny details.

I laid still for a moment trying to figure out what happened. It wasn't the match. I'd watched it, obviously, but it was the third-place play-off and we were already in the Final, so it wasn't like I really cared.

I thought instead it might be the reality of the situation finally hitting me. This was it. Nothing else left to think about. The juncture point of my entire life, and I had absolutely no control over which way it went. Enough to make anyone have a panic attack, right? Except it wasn't like that. It was warm and comforting and,

I don't know... freeing, I guess. Like that moment when you wake up from a bad dream and you're so grateful it wasn't real that everything seems that little bit fresher. You feel like you've been given your life back.

Does that make sense?

Maybe I was trying to tell myself not to worry. I was still young, still had time to shape my own destiny. And surely things couldn't change that much, anyway. People already looked at me like I had two heads as soon as they found out who my brother was.

'Ben Castle?' they'd say.

'Yes.'

'*The* Ben Castle?'

'Yes.'

Don't get me wrong, I was always very proud of my big brother. That same tormentor who used to backwash my drink and steal my toys and bury them in the garden was now one of the best players in the world. Two regional titles with Northumbria and the only goalkeeper ever to win the SyBall Player of the Year Award.

Ben was my hero.

God how I miss him.

And yes, you've guessed it – if Ben was my brother, then blah-de-blah-de-blah, that must mean George was my dad.

The George Castle.

What's strange is I still remember a time, before the merger of the Home Nations, when Dad was managing at club level and he took a lot of crap in the papers for trying to sign Ben at the outset of his career. Just shows how quickly things changed. By the time the national team job rolled around, there would have been lynch-mob fury if the press had dared question my father or the decisions he made.

Dad didn't care about that stuff anyway. He was what you'd call 'old school'. Bovril and rattles, that sort of thing. They threw around all kinds of terms to describe him. A master tactician. A fiery mentor. Unconventional. Unpredictable.

'Pfft! Is that what they think?' he once said. 'What a load of old codswallop. There's nothing the least bit 'unpredictable' about it, Mary Jane.'

To him, every game of football ever played followed a unique pattern that could be broken down and analysed like a series of equations. Nothing was random. Every team had a structure – every structure had weakness.

Why did I care about that? Because one of my favourite things to do was sit next to him on the sofa as he replayed hour upon hour of footage of upcoming opponents, scribbling notes on a scrap a paper, cracking the code. I never even looked at the screen, just at the determination behind those clever eyes.

God, how I miss him.

All the enduring memories from when I was a kid are infused with the same two elements – my love for my family, and their love for football. The only problem was whatever magic Dad passed onto Ben had missed me completely. A ball arriving at my feet would immediately become possessed of a life of its own and, once kicked, would go off in a direction of its choosing rather than the direction I intended.

'You're not practicing enough,' was the usual response.

Maybe they were right. But the truth is I didn't want to practice. Like I said, I never looked at the screen. Football was their thing, not mine. And if you think that's me telling you why I survived – because I was one of those weirdos who didn't 'get it' – then you're wrong. I was ready to roar my heart out that day when... well, you know, the day they were meant to lift the trophy, and I wouldn't be sitting here now if...

If I hadn't met...

I guess it started with my mum.

She was a ballet dancer, years ago, then had this brief stint playing a murderous housewife on a soap opera before marrying my dad. She was wise and she was beautiful; but whenever she talked to me about the ups and downs of a life in showbusiness, there was always a tinge of sadness that her own career never quite worked out the way she'd hoped. I was determined to do better. And while I'm not saying my family's wealth or fame wouldn't have helped, I was going to do it the right way. Training first, then fringe shows, Edinburgh, transfer to the West End and finally across to Broadway, where once established I could make the flight to Hollywood.

You know, usual stuff.

So, this is the story: it's my final year at drama school, and it all comes down to this one last show – the one where all the agents get invited, and you either graduate as their client or your career is over before it starts.

That year it was *A Midsummer Night's Dream*, and, out of nowhere, the school decided to bring it forward a few months to early spring. Why? To give everyone – me in particular – the freedom to enjoy the World Cup without the pressure of worrying about anything else. One tutor even likened football to a sort of epic melodrama – thrilling battles played out every weekend before a captive audience.

Perhaps this was why they decided to set a fantastical love story against a footballing backdrop, as some kind of weird tribute. It was a simple idea: Lysander and Demetrius, rival suitors for the hand of Hermia, were also the star strikers for two rival teams, Athens City and Athens United, separated only by the magical forest between their stadiums.

I can't really say how well I auditioned, but I have never quite shaken the feeling that they only asked me to play Helena, Hermia's best friend, because they wanted my name high up on the cast list. The character, so they said, had the most emotional complexity; her deconstructive dialogue on the act of falling in love came from her desperation to be loved by Demetrius. Then later on, when the fairy potion had bewitched Demetrius and Lysander to finally look her way, she just thought they were making fun of her. Helena was the narrative heart of the story – troubled at the beginning, her eventual happiness, above the happiness of all others, felt the most satisfying for the audience.

Was I being taken advantage of? Were there other girls in the class whose families weren't famous, who were more deserving of the role? Probably. Okay, definitely. But I was over the moon; conveying my love for Demetrius would be the easiest thing in the world – because he was being played by my boyfriend. Asher Bloom. To this day I still can't decide if that were his real name or not.

Asher was stylish, articulate, with smooth skin, sharp features and a far-off gaze that made him look old and young at the same time. (I worked on that description a lot). I'd been infatuated with him from the moment we met on induction day; his voice when he told me his name was like a matinee idol. He looked like a high school bad boy in an old black-and-white movie, mature yet dangerous. He even slicked back his long hair into a giant quiff like a true greaser.

From then on, we spent every possible moment together. In class we would pair up to perform silly skits, over-playing the melodrama until we fell about in fits of giggles. In the evenings we'd head off to an all-night café where we'd read our lines to each other over an endless cup of coffee.

He even liked football too, which was great – I guess – although I never really thought it suited him, and he was about as good at it as I was. That didn't matter – an interest alone was enough to seal the approval of my dad, who took an unexpected shine to Asher and was even happy to have him round for dinner every so often.

Once – it must have been December because I remember there were Christmas decorations in the living room – I came home to find Asher already there, talking tactics with the most powerful coach in the country, who was wagging his finger in his face and saying, 'you make a very good point there, lad'.

There was a brooding, anguished quality to Asher that I found simply irresistible. He never said much about his home life, and I got the impression his parents weren't around much, so I didn't like to press the issue. Rainy days made him sad, but then he'd go out for long walks in the downpour, sometimes in nothing more than just a t-shirt. No wonder he was ill all the time – every two months, like clockwork, he'd call in sick to college and I'd hear from him only by text. Then a few days later he'd be back with a spring in his step and ready to take on the world.

People who didn't understand Asher often thought of him as rude or arrogant, but there's nothing wrong in having the courage of your convictions. That, to me, was the mark of a genius. I was in awe of the way he insisted, despite his football kit costume, on always wearing his favourite hat – a black trilby with a feather in the band – whenever he was onstage as Demetrius. He argued his character was a prisoner by the end of the play, shackled by false emotion and who married Helena because he was still brainwashed under the fairies' spell. The hat was an act of defiance, a symbol of Demetrius' true self as well as – and this is the sticking point – a reflection of Asher's own personality.

He told the director: 'If, as Shakespeare tells us, the purpose of playing is to hold a mirror to nature, then what is the nature of performance, if not to hold a mirror to oneself?'

He was wearing his hat that day in my bedroom. I can't tell you how long it took for the room to stop spinning and my mind to clear, but when I lifted my head Brazil were receiving their bronze medals, so it couldn't have been more than a few minutes. Asher was perched on the end of my bed, staring blankly at the screen.

I waited for him to ask if I was okay, but he didn't even look at me. His expression was pained; I think he might have been shaking a little. Before I could say anything, the doorbell rang. Pizza delivery. I could hear the journalists shouting questions and the cameras clicking as the door opened and shut. They'd been camped out there for weeks. Pleasant enough, most of the time, stayed off the lawn – but that evening they seemed, I don't know... ravenous, I guess. Then as we headed downstairs to the kitchen, I heard the phone ringing.

I've never enjoyed a pizza less. Asher was in such a funny mood, eating really slowly, studying the cheese and toppings before each bite. All the while Mum was pacing the floor with the phone against her ear.

'What do you mean you can't tell me?'

She leant on the counter and took one of those long, meditative breaths of hers; an artist finding their centre.

'Okay, fine. I won't push it. Just look after yourselves, promise? Don't let this distract you. Get a good night's sleep and we'll see you all tomorrow.'

I asked her what was wrong.

'Oh, nothing, nothing,' she said. 'There was an intruder at the training ground. Police are there.'

Asher suddenly looked up, alarmed; the slice of pepperoni he'd been examining fell to his plate.

'An intruder? What kind of intruder?'

I could tell this caught my mum by surprise. He didn't usually blurt things out like that.

'George wouldn't say, darling. Look, it doesn't matter – he's fine, Ben's fine, we'll still be champions by this time tomorrow.'

Her smile might not have been real, but it was unfaltering. The picture of poise and sophistication.

'Now, are you going to save some of this for me or not?'

God how I miss her.

Asher then threw his half-eaten slice back into the box and stared down at the table, his face all scrunched up. He said he didn't feel well.

'Oh, Asher, not again…'

I was a little annoyed at him if I'm honest. My head was fuzzy still, swirling with memories of those wonderful little moments we'd shared together and a breathless excitement of more to come… and I just… I just wanted him to look at me, to show me that desire I felt for him.

'Do you want Mum to drive you home?' I offered, only to realise I still had no idea where he lived. I laid my hand on his arm and he leapt out of his chair.

'No! Thanks. It's a bad headache, that's all. I just need to walk it off.'

Asher slunk out the room and out of the house without saying goodbye. That was the last time I ever saw him.

Later that night my phone went off. It was him. It said: *Farewell Helena – Demetrius is free.*

Smug prat.

But I was distraught; blinded by the fear I might never set eyes on him again. A flame in my heart had gone out.

God how I would miss him.

Or so I thought.

That is why I survived.

The First Eleven

'1

Test Run

The Vessel hovered, still and silent in the low evening light.
Lexa repositioned the tripod for a better angle, placing each foot gently on the muddy ground in hope that they wouldn't start to sink. The picture on the viewfinder was grainy and distorted, damaged pixels flashed here and there, but still the great machine dominated, puffing its chest in the centre of the frame.

Lexa watched as the Captain negotiated his way through the bog, his notebook held tightly against his chest. The sight of him, with his long, scraggly grey hair, his gaunt, scarred face and his filthy blue overalls, was no different to any other day, but the lens seemed to accentuate the ravages of age and circumstance and she felt a well of bitterness fill inside her. No man like him should have to stand there, among the dirt and debris, the twisted metal and the rotting wood, breathing in the stench of decay that constantly lingered.

In an otherwise darkened landscape, the only source of light was a single ray of sun streaming through a rare gap in the thick black clouds. Through it the shadows of desolated buildings and their exposed frames rose from the ground like the grasping hands of monsters pushing out through the rubble. The surrounding silence was as dense as the atmosphere; the far-off sounds of human activity fading slowly into nothing over the course of her life. There was no whistle of the wind, no call of a bird. Everything was frozen, trapped inside a moment and unable to move on.

He squinted at the camera. 'Is it on?'

'The light's red, isn't it?' Lexa replied. 'I thought you were a scientist?'

The Captain's laugh crackled through the microphone. It was heartening to hear his daughter joke again. A sign, perhaps, that things were really about to change. His nerves settled. He'd been feeling sick to his stomach, too ashamed to admit his hope for a last-minute malfunction to allow him a little extra time to compose himself. He took another step closer, squelching through the mud, then stopped as he felt that radiating warmth, so dangerous and inviting. Even now, after so many years of deconstructing, paring down and rebuilding, he was still intimidated by its presence, even though the coppery tones of the outer shell were less vivid than they'd once been, and his own crude additions had stripped away its other-worldly elegance. Like him, the craft had been forced into unwelcome changes, and now, with one last mission to complete, both were nearing the end.

'Do you want to say anything?'

The Captain turned back and nodded. He cleared his throat and adjusted the collar of his boiler suit as though straightening an imaginary tie. Rogue hairs had fallen across his eyes and nose, and his fingers shook as he pushed them away. He looked down into the lens.

'As you can see, the modifications have, at last, been completed and we are in a position to commence the primary test of the Core's temporal upgrade.'

He paused, and saw his own reflection in the underside of the tapered fins bolted onto the sides, amazed that they were still holding firm. He'd long since come to terms with his fate and his only fear was that he might be the first in the loop to have got the mechanics wrong. So far everything had followed the path, but he had never felt anywhere near as smart as people believed, and he knew better than anyone how even the smallest of errors could have the greatest of impacts.

'We can't be out here too long.'

The Captain didn't move.

'Dad?'

The urgency in his daughter's voice pulled him back.

'Yes, of course. Forgive me. The computer, if you please.'

Lexa stepped from behind the camera and into shot as she approached her father with an open laptop in her hands. The top half of her overalls were tied around her waist, the black t-shirt underneath freely exposing the cuts and bruises that were the honour badges of her life. Her shoulder-length hair was tied into a ponytail with a purple band belonging to her mother, though a few loose strands were dangling down or stuck to her skin with sweat.

The Captain took hold of the laptop, but it wouldn't move. Lexa was still gripping it tightly, squeezing her fingers around the edges. It had often been remarked by the collective members of their extended family how strong his daughter was, despite her size and piecemeal diet. He, on the other hand, was tired and weak, and he understood how hard this must have been for Lexa to use her physical advantage against him.

'What do we do if it's not us?' she said.

There was no trace of pity in her voice, and for that the Captain's heart burst with admiration and shame. The cloud-filled sky was clear all the way to the fractured horizon, but he knew better than to be fooled by the appearance of calm.

'Then we run,' he said. 'We accept our fate and keep going until we find somewhere safe.'

'Nowhere is safe. And you, you're too –'

'What? Old?'

Lexa shook her head. 'I've changed my mind. I don't know the programmes as well as you, we should travel back *together* –'

'Lexa, Lexa – stop.'

A memory suddenly came to the Captain's mind of Lexa, no more than six years old, running off and playing with the other children in the passageways, before falling on a gantry and twisting her ankle. He remembered cradling her and kissing her forehead as she cried through the pain. She had been in pain her whole life, and he wanted nothing more than to give in to her demand.

'It's too risky, sweetheart. If we're both in there and the test fails, then that's it. Chance over. Everything we have worked for is lost.' He kissed her forehead. 'You deserve better than this.'

Feeling her grasp weaken, the Captain took the laptop and in return handed her his notebook. On screen, the co-ordinates were locked in and waiting – she had executed the sequence perfectly.

His heart was thumping now, so hard he could feel the reverberations through his whole body. Every word, every movement, was an act of surrender. If there was one chance to abandon the plan, this was it. The final doubts leapt through his mind, subjugators pinning back his arms and covering his mouth as he tried to speak.

'The process is simple but fragile,' he said to the camera. 'With every trip we are reliant on the Core's continued understanding – and acceptance – of our requests. There is simply no telling how long that partnership may last.' He smiled. 'More than twice, one hopes.'

He listened out for a derisive scoff, but nothing came. Her initial cheeriness had abated and instead she stood aside from him, chewing on the edge of a fingernail. Whenever she slipped into those habits the Captain was reminded of how much Lexa looked like her mother; how sadness and frustration couldn't mask how beautiful they both were.

He turned to face her. Adrenaline coursed through his veins and he was overcome by a cocktail of fear, panic and hope, blindsiding him to the point he struggled even to raise his finger. He struck the return key and felt his breath turn cold. Around his feet the wet mud began to ripple across the surface. Broken rubble tumbled and clattered over the blocks of fallen masonry. Tree branches creaked and splintered as they were bullied by the growing wind in cruel, relentless beats.

In every single contemplation of this moment, over so many years, the Captain always imagined his first impulse would be to check that Lexa was still holding onto his notebook. But despite all the preparations, the careful calculation, the best guesses and the decisions based on logic and reason as to what this moment was *expected* to look like, nothing had prepared him for the sensory barrage of what was happening:

The Vessel, spinning.

Very, very fast.

Lexa winced in the face of the wind as she struggled to face forward. The ground disturbance trembled up through her legs and down her arms. She could feel the shock waves pulse through the air, as though they were sucking the breath straight out of her lungs. A moment later and the coolness of the waves became interspersed with gusts of heat that grew quickly in speed and temperature, paired with electrifying slashes of white light.

There was a crash and a clatter behind her, and she spun to find the camera and its tripod lying sideways on the ground. But as she turned, she was thrown off balance by the wind whipping around her body and she fell into the mud. Her hands, held out to break her fall, landed first, the greasy wet dirt oozing between her fingers. She crawled along, propelled by the artificial storm, and, still struggling to her feet, reached out towards the tiny red light.

'Lexa! Look!'

The Captain was barely audible over the thrum, but his voice travelled far enough to turn Lexa back. The speed and noise were incredible, and the light so dazzling it hurt their eyes, but still they watched, as the Vessel began to move. It hovered above the ground, travelling steadily across the pre-programmed distance of ten metres before coming to an unhurried stop. A sonic boom hit them both with a sucker punch as a veil of light shrouded the Vessel.

And then in a flash, it was gone.

'2

The Away Team

'Pass the ball! Quick!'

Matthew Blaumann grunted with despair. On screen, the North American full-back, who spoke only Spanish and couldn't hear through Matthew's television, obliged in any case and chipped the ball across the width of the pitch to his teammate. Taking the pace out of the pass with a deft touch, Tom Glover, the winger, surged forward, cutting in towards the Argentinian penalty area, and went for the shot, the ball nutmegging one defender, striking the backside of another and flying off past the wrong side of the post.

Matthew slumped back onto the sofa, took a swig of beer and grabbed a handful of popcorn before offering the bowl to Miguel.

'Lykke, right?'

A hand poked out from under the Puerto Rican flag wrapped around Miguel's shoulders and waved away the offer.

'Three minutes left,' said Matthew, 'and he's still playing out from the back. And always to your guy, too! No offence but Fuentes spends too long on the ball, it's like he's gotta do a little flamenco dance before he makes the pass.'

Miguel smiled awkwardly; he had become immune to his friend's wayward generalisations. They only came out when Matthew was nervous, and right now there was reason to be. One-nil up in the last minute of a major semi-final, and North America were defending their lead with the ill-discipline and slow reactions of a tired team on the receiving end of a thrashing. It was typical of their seat-of-the-pants progress through the tournament, but no less frustrating. Argentina had sensed the opportunity and were pushing hard for the equaliser that would send the match to extra time.

Miguel moved a pizza box with his foot to obscure his view of a blob of tortilla dip on the carpet, as once again the Argentines flowed through the gears of another excellent passage of play, only to see the striker's volley smack the palm of Jesper Lykke's outstretched glove and fly over the crossbar. Matthew hissed though his teeth as the replay showed the ball inches off target as it rose through the air. On the other side of the room, Eric and Claudia, the Canadian couple from work, had taken the near-miss as confirmation of the result and were already up and dancing.

Lykke rose to greet the corner cross, pushing off the shoulders of an opponent, and punching the ball clear of the box into the path of Emmett Baines, whose counterattack cleared the danger but ultimately came to nothing.

'Lorraine Browne would've caught that, you know.'

Catie's long arms had coiled around Matthew's neck from behind the sofa and her cheek rested softly against his as she delighted in ruffling his feathers.

'What is it now, Claudia, eleven clean sheets in the past fifteen games for Canada?'

'Twelve!' Claudia shouted, jumping up and down on an armchair that didn't belong to her.

'Cate, please,' said Matthew as he fidgeted his way out of her arms and reached for some more popcorn. 'Why you gotta ruin this for us, huh?'

By 'us', he meant 'me'.

'I'm serious,' she said. 'Put Browne in for you, put Christine Crawford up front with PJ – drop Troy, he's useless – and *that's* the Final I want to see.'

Matthew took two pieces of popcorn and shoved them into her mouth. 'Stop, alright? Show a little compassion.'

A wide grin passed between them as she chewed. Catie was as funny as hell and he loved it.

'You're my boyfriend. Compassion doesn't come into it.'

'Is that what your Principles say?'

'They sure do.'

The match had evaporated almost entirely from Matthew's mind. That was her power; to make him forget it all, just for one moment, by losing himself in those big blue eyes. But then:

'What about Miguel?'

The bubble burst. Matthew's habit of bringing their flatmate into their flirtations was immensely irritating and both Catie and

Miguel knew why he did it – to solidify Miguel's role as the third wheel of the relationship and secure the couple's place at the top of their little group's hierarchy

If only Matthew knew, like they did, that after the swift and upsetting end to his previous relationship (for which Catie felt partly responsible), Miguel had been dating the same guy for months now and they were even thinking about moving in together.

'Miguel's like my brother, isn't that right?' said Catie. The Puerto Rican replied with a coy smile. 'What goes for you, goes for him.'

One minute.

Catie moved around the sofa and, in the name of fun, knelt down between the coffee table and the television and began clearing up the leftovers. The remonstrations were music to her mischievous ears.

'What's more, my darling,' she went on, 'I haven't said anything that isn't true. You can't know much about football if you think Lykke's better than Browne – who is, by the way, an *actual* North American. And the reason you're playing poorly and will be torn apart in the Final, is because your friend the Prime Minister –' Catie jabbed a derisive finger at every boy in the room. '– copped out of his promise to normalise unisex football.'

'Oh, come on...'

But there was no stopping her now. 'And why? For money. Why have one World Cup when you can have two at twice the profit? The effects are proven and if the Prime Minister hadn't been such a chicken, then we'd have a *real* Grand Unifier, not this sausage party.'

Something on screen made the crowd cheer. Matthew slammed his bottle down.

'That's enough! Get out of the way and let us enjoy this!'

There was a palpable sense around the room that it had all gone too far. The plates and glasses balanced precariously on her forearms as Catie left for the kitchen muttering her complaints about all the mess.

Twenty seconds.

A free kick had been awarded near the centre circle for an ugly challenge on Chris Wilson, the captain. Argentina knew it was over and were lashing out. Now all North America needed to do was keep the ball at their feet, pass it between them and resist the urge to attack and invite pressure. Eric joined Claudia up on the armchair and hugged her tight.

The referee looked at his watch – this was it, the moment. Matthew looked at the faces around him and saw the same expectant expression of terrified glee. The United States had already been knocked out of the competition, Puerto Rico hadn't qualified and neither, surprisingly, had Canada, and so this continental cluster of rejects would have to do.

And yet somehow, as the seconds ticked agonisingly towards victory, he couldn't remember ever feeling happier. Catie's outburst had already evaporated from his mind. He could barely remember she had left the room. That was the game's power; to make him forget it all, just for a moment, by losing himself in that big green field. Once it was over, they could travel across London and spend the evening in one of the bars surrounding the stadium celebrating with their compatriots.

Funny how things changed.

Growing up thousands of miles away, in a quiet Wisconsin suburb on the banks of Lake Michigan, Matthew had given little consideration to the rain-soaked island he now called home much beyond a peripheral awareness with all the associated stereotypes: ousted rulers turned to grateful allies; lazy assumptions of eccentric, castle-dwelling tea-drinkers with bad teeth, stiff lips, and a far-reaching history which served primarily to provide the attractions for their 600-mile long amusement park off the coast of France.

Then one spring, when he was still in high school, something strange started to happen. The British were due to vote in a General Election and Matthew had *paid attention to it.* Teachers talked about it in class and a mock election was held in the gymnasium, with Union Jacks hanging from the ceiling and cardboard cut-outs of double-decker buses, black cabs and all the familiar landmarks stuck up on the walls and along the bleachers (his contributions had been to paint the numbers on Big Ben and stand as the MP for Hull, wherever that was).

Outside of school, coverage of the impending vote dominated every paper and every news channel, his father switching indiscriminately between stations in search of a new angle; an interview with a candidate, perhaps, or a flashy-graphic analysis of the most recent polls.

By the time the new Prime Minister walked through Number 10's sleek black door, Matthew was hooked. The man himself looked a little like his grandpa, only when he spoke there was no smoky rasp but instead the eloquent infusion of someone who was determined and forthright, yet still found every moment of his life to be something of a lark.

Matthew had struggled to understand why, but it really did feel like the promise of companionship, of making friends with the world and ushering in a new era of Joy and Compassion, was made just for him, as though the Prime Minister were calling out to him across the ocean:

Come, young Blaumann, you're one of us now.

And if Matthew could infer anything from this message, it was that it had something to do with soccer. The British Kingdom's Department of Footballing Activities had already made big strides in reinvigorating the world's passion for the sport with outreach programmes, a careful language of cultural unity and the global popularity of its own Regional League; twelve elite franchise teams that sat above the hegemony of club football, without the threat of relegation to put off its growing fanbase. Each season culminated in a spectacular championship game, held at the kingdom's jewel in its crown: the BK Stadium, an enormous oblong amphitheatre, with 150 thousand seats for the chosen few and, for everyone else, a huge radial antenna that swept upwards from the roof and broadcast every match without charge or interruption to every television, tablet and smartphone in the world.

But for Matthew Blaumann, who had been beckoned by the call, this hadn't been enough.

26

'Mom, Dad, I don't want to go to college,' he'd announced the day after receiving his high school diploma. 'I want to move to London.'

'Outstanding!' his father had replied, the accompanying backslap painful and impassioned. 'When are you leaving?'

'Well, I'd been thinking... wait, don't you want to know why?'

'What's to know? The BK is a great place – beautiful scenery, exciting cities. I mean, why have Milwaukee when you can have Milton Keynes? And, if you think the Rockies are impressive, wait until you see Mount Snowdon!'

'Yes, you're right, and the government have this overseas internship –'

Matthew would always remember the way his mother had lowered the crumpled pamphlet in his hand and cupped his cheek with her own; how her eyes had searched his face, overwhelmed with pride.

'We're just so glad you've made such a sensible decision.'

'Your mom's right. Start getting ready. I'll transfer what money you need in the morning.'

And with that, Don Blaumann had winked at his son and then ambled out of the house to water the roses in the front yard.

A couple of months later, Matthew had said his goodbyes and never looked back, arriving the same week it was announced that the British Kingdom had been selected, by a unanimous vote of the sport's governing body (who were by ways and means employees of the DFA), to host the men's and women's SyBall World Cups – the world's first fully inclusive international football tournaments – beating off rival bids from Russia, China and Australia.

London was everything he'd hoped for and more. The buzz, the activity and the general air of serenity and good humour enthralled and beguiled him from the start. But this sense of blissful immersion, based on evidence shown on television and through online channels, was to be expected. What Matthew hadn't prepared for was the deeper feeling of just being *so* alive.

He threw himself into his job in the Office for Culture and the Online Society (COSY) and became close with Eric and Miguel, two fellow apprenticeship programmers from across the Atlantic. Then, at a point when he felt as though he couldn't get any higher, Claudia brought a friend along to the overloud bar in Camden Town one Friday evening. In an instant Catie turned a sublime experience into a perfect one, and from that night onward Matthew knew he wasn't just happy, he was home.

What's more, it hadn't rained once since he arrived.

Ten seconds to go.

As Catie scrubbed the plate, she could hear them dancing and singing and cheering. Even Miguel was joining in as best he could.

The referee blew his whistle. The crowd roared and the flat erupted.

Then... nothing.

Catie waited for over a minute before coming back in. Perhaps they had stopped to listen to a post-match interview, but still it seemed odd. She returned and noticed the tortilla dip on the floor next to the pizza box. The popcorn bowl lay upturned on the sofa. The North America players were in the midst of their wild celebrations.

When later questioned by police, the other tenants in the block who had heard Catie's screams would claim not to have seen anything unusual that day.

Except for one witness, who had happened to glance out of her window a few minutes before and noticed a man, looking a little worse-for-wear and dressed in unseasonably warm clothing, hobbling along the pavement outside. Regrettably, she was unable to offer much of a physical description, as from her angle up on the top floor the man's face had been obscured in its entirety by the wide rim of his old-style hat – a trilby or fedora, she couldn't quite tell.

'3

The (Reserve) Goalkeeper

Josh pulled the glove over his hand and tightened the strap around his wrist. It had been a while, but it was just as uncomfortable as he remembered, the added weight and the loss of dexterity making him feel even more unsure of himself than usual. They were like gauntlets from a suit of armour; he couldn't imagine how a knight managed to swing his mace, duck the blade, swish his sword, and come out the end of it in one piece, when the battle gear was so damn inhibiting.

He opened and closed his fist a couple of times – that was what the professionals probably did – and then repeated the process with the other hand; only this time he became distracted by the Velcro and how the sound of the rip rose and lowered in pitch from one end of the strap to the other.

A shadow passed in front of him; a teammate brushing against his knees as he took a seat on the bench nearby. Josh wasn't sure who it was, but it wasn't Callum, and that was all that mattered. He hung his head and looked down to the floor, his eyes gliding helplessly over his all-green kit.

All-green?

Maybe he'd blend in with the grass and the other team would shoot straight at him. Maybe that was the plan. He'd need all the help he could get.

'Alright,' said Tony, the manager, 'settle down.'

Around him the cacophony of bullish conversation died down and the team turned to the track-suited man with the clipboard under his arm. Josh lifted his head. A harsh light was streaming in through a grimy window, illuminating the flecks of dust drifting through the stagnant air.

'Now, I know many of you are aware of this –'

Josh felt an enormous lump rise in his throat. He was *very* aware.

'– but for those of you who aren't, I have some sad news. Martin Bannick was involved in a motorbike accident yesterday and is currently in intensive care.'

The room filled at once with the players' gasps of shock and horror and demands for more information.

'Not again?' said one.

Josh knew it was who was without looking.

'Yes, Callum, again; but I'm afraid it's a little more serious than his last one. To be truthful with you all, he hasn't woken up yet.'

More gasps. The thought crossed Josh's mind that this might be the worst team talk in the history of football.

'So, I am sure,' Tony continued solemnly, 'you will join me in wishing Martin a speedy recovery and that the thoughts of the club are with Gillian and the rest of his family at this difficult time. Moving on...'

Instantly rallied, Tony swung the clipboard out from under his arm and rapped on the team sheet with his knuckles. The lump in Josh's throat dropped like a lead weight and nestled as a ball of dread in the pit of his stomach.

'...this of course means that today Josh Pittman will be in goal.'

It might have been his insecure imagination, but Josh was convinced this particular bombshell had drawn the biggest gasps of all. This was the reaction he had feared; the reaction that had him shamefully thinking of Martin's accident only in terms of what it meant for him.

'What!?' Callum spluttered, showering the floor his spit. 'Are you joking? I'm a better keeper than him!'

Josh was spared the full view of Callum's ugly smirk as the forward pointed vaguely in his direction with his tattooed, sunburnt arm.

Tony retorted. 'And you're a better striker than you are a keeper, so I'd rather have you up the front scoring goals than at the back saving them.'

'It'll have to be loads with the amount he'll let in.'

'Callum, please,' said Tony, a placating hand gently raised, 'our Principles –'

'Oh my God, here we go again!' Callum threw his arms up in the air with frustration. 'What is with you people? No disrespect to you, Tone,' he said, disrespectfully, 'but you're driving me mad. All of you. Like the other night, everyone going on about the Brazilians, and how well they played, and how proud they must be to get to the semis, I mean *for God's sake!* What about us? We stuffed 'em! Big Troy, top corner – *doof!*'

The sound effect was accompanied by an energetic reconstruction in mime of the British Kingdom's second semi-final goal two nights earlier.

'And now we're gonna stuff this bloody lot, right, boys? That is if butterfingers over there doesn't bottle it.'

'I said that's enough!' Tony barked. 'Mind your filthy language.'

The changing room fell silent. Callum recoiled in what was probably one the greatest sights of Josh's life so far. Managers these days weren't supposed to shout at their players, but Callum was one of those who just pushed and pushed until even the meekest of men would snap.

Tony swept a few loose strands over his balding head. 'I don't care how talented you are, Mr Owens, there's always room for you on the bench. Josh is our reserve and today he will play. That is the end of it.'

Callum said nothing more but threw Josh a seething glance of contempt. For the past year and a half, their relationship had operated on an unspoken jock-and-nerd assumption of school-ground dislike; of Josh because he was talentless, and of Callum because he was an arrogant, red-faced twit with more air in his head than the ball.

But if there were any common ground between them, one that might possibly light a fire of conversation, it was that neither quite understood why people talked about football in such spiritual terms. Sure, it brought everyone together as a kind of cohesive glue for society, but why get so silly about it? Ask anyone – *anyone* – for the reason why the game was so important, and the answer would be *exactly* the same:

It is the national pastime; the Great Unifier through which we, the people of the British Kingdom, can achieve peace and prosperity in mutual respect and healthy competition through the Guiding Principles of Joy and Compassion.

Every time, without fail.

But for some, like Josh and Callum, the mass acceptance of these ideals seemed unsettling. There was a cultish, glossy-eyed quality, as though people didn't really know what they were saying as they recited the words and then adhered to them, strictly, in the everyday course of their lives.

This, however, was where the similarity ended, as Josh and Callum's reasons for feeling unease with the world were entirely opposite. While Callum vehemently maintained that, instead of some open-armed cultural exchange, every match ought to be a battle, with blood and spit and sweat all thrown in, Josh simply thought participation ought to be voluntary, and wished he had a socially-acceptable reason to be anywhere else in the world except this rank changing room with its putrid odour of wet socks and mud.

'If you go a goal down,' Tony was now saying, 'then deal with it – but be consistent! Keep a strong backline, mark your players and push, push, push! When you get the ball, possess in midfield for as long as possible and then get it out to the wingers. These Marsham Fields guys are fast, and they've got two big, burly centre-backs, but they don't press quick enough and they're too eager to jump, especially in set pieces. So, forwards, when those crosses come in,

34

take a touch and strike low, try to get in under their feet. Callum, you got that?'

'Yes, boss,' Callum replied, still smarting.

'Good. Right then, Rovers, on your feet!'

The entire team stood, with most taking the chance to begin their warm-up – rolling their heads from side to side, shaking out their arms and legs and filling their lungs with long, loud sniffs of the air. Callum went one better and jumped a couple of times, tucking his knees into his chest mid-air, and power-sprinting on the spot. Then, as they settled, each player laid a hand over the Belmont Park Rovers crest sewn into their shirts.

Josh stood last and did nothing.

Only when Tony looked poised to speak again did he join in. Even through the glove he could feel the bumps and ripples of the rough-hewn stitching goading him into allegiance.

Normally the squad would stand for a minute or more, listening to some variation of Tony's standard speech (*'we stand for Belmont Park; we play for the British Kingdom; we work for each other'*) but today the manager took a slow, composing breath and, looking like he was about to cry, simply said: 'For Robohand.'

In unison the team repeated Martin Bannick's nickname back at Tony, who a second later shattered the moment by slapping his chest so hard Josh thought he was going to topple over.

'Now let's get out there and show them who we are!'

Roars of pumped-up enthusiasm filled the air as the team filed out of the changing room. Josh couldn't move. Nothing about the squad's excitement, the chants and the high-fives and the clatter of hundreds of boot studs on the tiled floor, had been enough to spur him into action. There was no rush of panic, no queasiness, no nerves. Nothing.

He was empty.

He let his arms slump and gazed down at the crest; a red circle surrounding the letters BPR in a bland serif font. The kind used in newspapers. It repulsed him. A white or yellow tincture might make it stand out, but in reality, the whole thing was unfit for purpose; cheap, lazy, ill-considered and in need of an entire redesign to elevate it beyond the standard of a stylistic outrage. Where was the composition? Where was the symbolism? Didn't this entire park lie on the site of an old hospital – what about a nod to that?

'Josh?'

A hand had landed on him. Josh looked up at Tony, who was so close he could see the yellow teeth and the tufty flecks of white stubble around his chin.

'What are you just standing there for? Come on!'

Tony shoved his shoulder from behind, half-supportive, half impatient. With an effort, Josh turned and headed out of the door.

It was a large crowd for a weekday, but this came as no surprise. The happy hangover from the national team sealing their place in the SyBall World Cup Final meant people were more ready than ever to lose their minds over the next ninety minutes of this amateur league rubbish.

The weather was bright and cloudless, and Josh squinted as he emerged through the players' tunnel. He felt like a prisoner in Ancient Rome being dragged into the arena by a chain of expectation to face the lions. The rest of the team were already on the pitch, passing balls back and forth, skipping along the perimeter lines or sprinting in short, zig-zagging bursts. Marsham Fields – today's lions – were there too, performing similar rituals. Josh saw none of this activity as a reason to rush. The crowd in their numbers were loud and encouraging, but still he heard the voice calling to him over the barrier of the seating stand as he ambled alongside.

'Oi! Where have you been?'

Out of nothing but obligation, Josh stopped and looked up at the middle-aged man with the flaring nostrils.

'I was just getting ready.'

Frank Pittman stroked his chin in the usual way whenever his son did something to frustrate him. His face was round and weathered and seemed to exist in a continual screwed-up state of disapproval.

'I see,' he said, 'getting into the zone, were you? Great. Their keeper was the first one out – he's been doing chin ups on the crossbar for the past ten minutes.'

Josh shrugged. 'Well then, he's probably done his arms in for the match.'

'Don't get snarky with me, mister.'

'Stop it you two!' Caroline snapped. 'Why can't you say something supportive for once?'

Frank looked to his wife on the next seat, her eyes peering at him over the top of her prescription sunglasses. Josh could always recognise his mother in a crowd, in her gingham dress and sunhat, looking as though she'd gotten lost on the way to a picnic.

'What I mean to say,' said Frank, 'is this might be your chance. Now you'll never be as good as Martin –'

Caroline tutted. 'Frank!'

It was sweet, Josh thought, but even she couldn't defend him from the truth.

'What? The bloke's got studs in his hand and he still gets picked over him.'

'They're pins, dad. They hold his bones in place'.

Frank sneered. *'Does it matter?'*

A few heads in the crowd turned. Was someone angry at a football match?

'Now you've got three games – three *games* – to show yourself off. I've heard...'

The barrier creaked a little as Frank leant forward and rested his broad chest on the metal frame. His eyes shifted from side to side to ensure no-one was eavesdropping.

'...there's a scout here today from the South-East. They're in the market for a new keeper. Do well and they might sign you up for the academy, at least. You don't know what it could lead to.'

Frank let this vital information sink in for a moment. Part of Josh wished he could tell his father what he wanted to hear. But there was a lesson to be learnt, a point of fact that Josh wasn't happy with the decisions being made on his behalf.

'I really hate this badge,' he said, tugging on his shirt. 'I think I might ask Tony if I can change it. I'll draw something up, more like a proper crest, see if he likes it.'

The rugged old hand rubbed the chin again, continuing up over Frank's face and all the way back down again.

'This is your first start since you joined and all you want to talk about is the *bloody badge?*'

'Oh, let him do it if he wants,' said Caroline.

'He's not a kid anymore,' Frank spluttered, the exasperation a chokehold around his throat, 'he should be past bloody doodles in his bedroom. Didn't you hear me? A scout, Josh. You can't keep plodding through life like a sloth with a headache.'

Josh resisted the urge to tell his father to get stuffed.

'You know what, Dad,' he said, 'while I appreciate this rousing pep talk, it isn't going to do any good – I am useless. You should just accept that and move on.'

Frank clenched his eyes and gulped as though he had swallowed something vile.

'Now, don't say that. That's not the attitude. You've got to believe in yourself. All I'm asking is you try; can you promise me that? Then whatever happens, I...' He paused and leant away from Josh. 'Whatever happens after that doesn't matter.'

The sincerity in his voice stabbed at Josh's sense of guilt. It had been so long since father and son had connected over anything – maybe this was all Frank really wanted.

'Fine. I promise. Just don't expect miracles.'

'Good luck, son.'

Josh crossed the touchline onto the pitch was greeted by a smattering of applause and a general hubbub of conversation, more curious than scandalised; the crowd eager to see what the understudy could bring to the performance.

Frank sat back down and sighed. The stadium's plastic fold-down chairs were too small for him and his arms were wedged between the barrier and his wife.

'You put too much pressure on him,' Caroline said, as he fidgeted around in his seat.

'You mollycoddle him too much,' Frank replied, as he found a position on the approach to comfort.

He could feel the look she gave him. Then she turned and watched her eldest child make his way towards the goalposts.

'I shouldn't wonder,' she said airily, 'if you didn't *push* poor Martin off his motorbike.'

Caroline could feel the look he gave her, but she didn't care.

Josh's parents weren't the only ones conscious of how directionless their son's life was. He was acutely aware of it too. He felt it every single day, particularly during the hours spent immobile on the substitutes' bench, or lying on the bed he had long since outgrown, staring up into the darkness.

Days like today, according to the perceived wisdom of everybody except him, were meant to be thrilling. In nearly two decades of life his total achievements amounted to precisely zero, with little outsider enthusiasm for the 'doodles' he wearily occupied himself with. Even his passion for that was starting to wane, eroded by the constant rejection and disinterest in his solo expressions. Football, he'd been told, was different. There was always a target to aim for. Every match was an opportunity to remind the world you were alive.

But the very idea of going out and playing was burdened by an apathy Josh simply couldn't control, which acted as both the cause and effect of his listlessness. It wasn't the parental pressure that bothered him, nor his place in the pecking order. The fire was just missing.

Still, it wasn't all bad. If there was one thing to be said about peoples' overly jolly demeanour as they skipped and tra-la-lalled from one game to the next, it was that they didn't hold grudges. What was done was done. Unless, of course, those people took the form of either Frank or Callum, but the Bovill Arms, their local pub and the Rovers' unofficial clubhouse, had enough nooks and crannies and tables tucked into darkened corners that both could be easily avoided when the time came for the mandatory post-match drink later that evening. He just had to get there first. And now that he was finally in position within the goalframe, it seemed all of a sudden wrong to blame a lack of effort on shoulder-shrugging indifference.

Union JAC, Josh told himself. *Union JAC.*

The stadium itself appeared much larger from this new vantage; or if not larger, then higher, as though his sense of impending doom had been shrinking him with every step closer to the posts. Then he realised; never before had he stood in a spot where he couldn't see the trees rising above the seating bowl. It felt apt – the tranquillity of the park's surrounding landscape was the only thing he enjoyed about the place.

Once little more than some white lines painted on the grass with a set of goalposts at each end, the Belmont Park Rovers home ground had evolved quickly over the past few years into the fully equipped, five-thousand-seat stadium that stood today. The pitch was remarkably flat for an amateur club, but such was the rush for completion that the architect's plans had failed to account for the parkland's imperceptibly shallow downhill slope, and as a result the entire venue was off-kilter.

Martin would often play this to his advantage. An engineer with a mind as quick and strong as his body (including the metal-infused hand), his keen mathematical eye could not only calculate the necessary length and speed to ensure his goal-kicks met their intended targets, but the wayward angles he employed to offset the narrow gradient would often bamboozle the opposition into running the other way.

Josh, on the other hand, could not do any of this. His only surprise was that after seventeen minutes of game time, he had yet to be tested. Marsham Fields were camped in their own half and unable to get out, and even Josh couldn't deny the tingle of excitement he felt as the pressure paid off and his team took the lead.

It was Callum, of course; his clean strike had cut beneath the sluggish defence and nestled into the bottom corner of the net, just as Tony told him. During the celebrations, in which Callum sparred like a boxer with the corner flag, then roared at the crowd with a guttural war cry and shook off the arms of his congratulating team mates as though he hated them, Josh noticed his dad in the crowd, punching the air in delight.

'*Yeeeaaahh!* Get in there, my son! Alright!'

He clenched his fists. But no, the parental pressure did not bother Josh at all.

Marsham Fields responded with a swagger, pegging the home side back into their own half with quick, short passes. Their first shot came from range, in the style of the Hitman but with none of the accuracy, the ball drifting so far wide even Josh knew it wasn't worth the bother. A moment later, he held the ball in his hand for the goal kick, buckling under the pressure over which teammate to pass it out to.

'Hey, Josh. Mate, to me.'

Decision made. David McCrea, the right-back, was the nearest player to him and a decent enough sort; the very idea that someone in the squad knew his name and could unquestionably call him 'mate', represented the kind of camaraderie and respect so often talked about but never felt.

And then it happened.

Opting to roll the ball out, Josh underthrew it completely and could only watch as it trickled down the slope away from McCrea and into the path of a greasy-haired opponent in a shirt two sizes too big, who swept in from nowhere and sliced the ball past Josh's midriff and into the goal.

Somewhere in the distance Josh could hear Callum's angry grunts, swearing, shouting and spitting, a wave of abuse that showered indifferently over him, its collective mass absorbing any specific detail.

The rest of the half meandered away in a despondent blur, and following a half-time team talk in which Tony had not spoken to him once, Josh found himself back in goal at the opposite end of the pitch for another arduous forty-five minutes of his life he would never get back.

To make matters worse, Callum had made the clear decision that Josh wasn't to be trusted and would have to fall back and spend more time in the defensive third than either of them liked. Conceded goals were like kryptonite to Callum, who frothed at the mouth in his feral determination to prevent them, enormous pearls of slobber flying out from the corners of his lips, and before long he had launched himself across the ground with a leg in the air and dug his studs deep into an opponent's thigh.

The referee blew his whistle, pointed to the penalty spot and held a red card in front of Callum's equally red face. Disbelieving gasps rang out from the stands as Callum offered a colourful counterpoint to the official's decision and then lumbered over to Josh.

'Alright, ginger-nut's going to take it,' he whispered, his hot, wet breath wafting into Josh's ear.

The Marsham Fields captain, a handsome attacking midfielder with a neat crop of red hair, placed the ball on the spot.

'Now he'll look like he's going right, yeah? But *he thinks* that *you think* he's gonna dummy and strike left. Nah, he won't, he'll stick and go right. And don't forget your left is his right, right?'

'Right,' said Josh. 'Didn't you just get sent off?'

Callum Owens narrowed his eyes and spat on the ground before walking away. With him gone, attention turned to the spot kick. The thump of Josh's heart drowned out the noise of crowd. Five thousand pairs of eyes stared at him. The oblong shape of the stadium bowl stretched into the distance, warping impossibly as the stand seemed to rise and tower over him; the emptiness inside him felt sharper now than ever, and such was the cacophony of silence pounding in his ears that Josh didn't even hear the referee blow for the kick.

The red-head fired the ball straight down the middle. The ball seemed to travel in slow motion and Josh found he was able to react, forgoing all Callum's advice, and take two steps forward; his arms were moving, his hands were outstretching...

I am going to catch this!

But he had planted his foot too far forward; his ankle twisted, his head dipped and his arms flayed as he tried to stay upright, but the momentum was taking him down. The ball struck the tip of his forehead and deflected upwards, giving him an immediate, intense headache.

If it hadn't been for David McCrea offering a hand, he might never have got back up. Against the backdrop of Marsham Fields' celebrations, Josh had taken a breather from the game to lie in the mud and look up at the beautiful blue sky. The ground was hard and cracked, it really could do with some rain.

I miss clouds.

David smiled but said nothing, no words of recrimination or comfort. Just quiet acceptance.

The defender ambled back into position ready for the restart, and while waiting for the whistle, Josh glanced unthinkingly over at the front row of the stands, not far from the corner flag. It seemed his mother's mantle as the most inanimate spectator was being challenged by a young girl, around his age perhaps, but difficult to tell at this distance, who sat motionless and staring straight at him. She was on her own, so it appeared, unengaged with the fans immediately around her. Josh wondered at first if this were the

45

scout his dad mentioned, but he would have expected an on-duty professional to still be enjoying the game. This girl looked how he felt; nervous and withdrawn, her body closed in on itself as she bit anxiously on her fingernails.

All this Josh had to discern in an instant, for as soon as his eyes caught hers the girl stood up and left, barging past the spectators and heading out through the exit tunnel where she disappeared from sight.

The oddness of the encounter played on Josh's mind for the remainder of the match, and it was for this reason alone, so he told himself, that he allowed his concentration to dip and went on to concede three more goals before full-time.

Final score: Belmont Park Rovers one, Marsham Fields five.

'4

Albright

The Prime Minister of the British Kingdom leant back in his seat and rubbed his eyes. His ear felt hot and greasy from having the receiver pressed unwillingly against it for the best part of an hour.

Ugh.

Everything here was tactile; everything had to be touched. Even their way of talking was like a mid-air exchange programme for each other's germs. It confirmed Ray Albright's opinion that people were, frankly, disgusting, and he felt dirtied by his own attraction towards them. He often wondered if mammals who ate insects ever found insects repulsive.

It was a puzzle too, how so many humans, while wallowing in the filth of their existence, could have consciously put pen to paper to vote for *that man*; the one who'd just spoken to him like a bear with a sore throat as he listed his demands for the Final (150 complimentary tickets, a public relations visit to the North American team camp and a private meeting after the match with the other heads of state to discuss the Anti-Ballistic Treaty). It was almost laughable, the way the President acted as though by gracing these shores he was doing Albright – indeed, the whole country – a great personal favour.

Apple Blossom was sniffing around his leg. At the sound of the receiver returning to the handset, the White Highland Terrier had sat up from her favoured spot under the desk and waited at the feet of her master. He looked down at the little shaggy-haired creature, and noted, as he often did, the subtle flecks of pink fur in her ears and the wet, dark strands around her mouth, a mixture of saliva and dirt. Her nose was black, her eyes were brown, and she'd never been to the Highlands. The description was ill-fitting, and yet there had once been a time when Albright had been mocked in the national newspapers for daring to name her 'Apple Blossom'.

Thankfully those days were over. He smiled and ruffled her head with his thick fingers.

'Insufferable man. Hair like candy floss. Still, done now. We'll plonk him next to the Queen and maybe he'll collapse on top of one of the corgis.'

Grunting considerably, with one hand on the armrest and the other on his cane, he lifted himself from the chair and leant against the desk to steady himself. He was old – much older than he looked – but Albright refused to accept any bearing this might have on his ability to manage both his jobs; the one he appeared to be doing and the one he was actually doing.

His private office was large by Parliamentary standards. The walls were covered by green flock wallpaper, split through the middle by a varnished oak dado rail, and an ornate glass lampshade hung from the ceiling above a dusty space full of faux-antique furniture embossed with the Portcullis; unnecessary embellishments, he thought, if the room existed only for him.

Shaking off the wobbliness, Albright stepped across to where a free-standing mirror was set between two arch windows overlooking the courtyard. The sun streamed through the glass, illuminating his reflection. His ear was still red and he was sweating a little, but in all other ways he looked as composed and assured as ever.

He had no particular love for his appearance, but appreciated its value; where once he would have been labelled 'short and fat', he was now 'round and cuddly'. His speech was clipped but full-bellied, like a great blunderbuss actor who had chosen to dabble in politics. Theatricality and eccentricity were deliberate catchpoints of Albright's public persona; he was ruddy-cheeked and hyperbolic and had become renowned for his colourful collection of woollen cardigans (mustard yellow today, with a black zig-zag around the cuffs), which he wore in place of a suit in the House of Commons. His indifference to the dress code seemed hardly to matter given so much of the cardigan would always be obscured by his enormous white beard, which spread from down his thick sideburns, under his nose, around his mouth, and over his chin, leaving just his eyes and arms as the only uninvaded territory anywhere above his naval.

He lowered his head towards the mirror and picked at what he called his 'toothpaste stripes'; thin strands of auburn that appeared occasionally among the dense thicket of white hair around his skull. Follicle birthmarks. That was the official line, but recently he had started to worry the truth was slowly revealing itself, his hair becoming darker, redder, thinner even. In a few days it wouldn't matter if the whole lot fell out – but there was plenty that could go wrong before then.

He straightened.

Stop fannying about, you old fool. You're only going to the tower. No-one's going to inspect your scalp on the way there.

The whole charade was easier at Christmas, when he get away with wearing his big Santa hat throughout December as he offered glad tidings outside Number 10 with Apple Blossom looking adorable in an elf costume.

Blasted creature.

She was only meant to be an accessory, a crucial element in his carefully constructed image. This Prime Minister didn't have a wife, or children, or grandchildren, because he was *everyone's* husband, or father, or grandfather. But he did have a dog; a sweet, yappy little thing with a memorable name and a resemblance to his beard. Pictured together they gave the impression of warmth and homeliness, far removed from the usual mean-spirited perception of politics.

But it was part of the act. Albright wasn't supposed to actually *feel* anything for her.

'Bugger it,' he said. 'You *are* only a dog, I suppose. But consider yourself lucky: if you were any other mutt then your days would be well and truly numbered.'

Apple Blossom barked happily in response, enjoying the familiarity of the old man's voice.

After his routine struggle with the heavy door leading out onto the Palace of Westminster's central service road, Albright gave a cheery wave to the security guard nestled in his booth. The guard smiled back, perplexed as usual at how the Prime Minister, in that cardigan, with that beard, could cope with the heat.

Better than you, my friend. Better than you.

Passing into Speaker's Court, with the sun framed perfectly within the four high walls of sand-coloured limestone, carved into a Gothic fantasy and crumbling with age, Albright felt rejuvenated. His stagger became a skip and with every step he swung out his cane with a histrionic flick. The courtyard had once been a very functional entity; a parking area for MPs' cars and a smoking area for their drivers, whose capacity for witless chat outside his window spurred Albright into measuring the space up for Parliament's first five-a-side football pitch. The Speaker's constituency offices on the Thames side had made perfect changing rooms.

As he approached, a Commons library research assistant tore down the opposing flank with impressive speed, side-stepping one defender, then another, the ball a magnet at her feet. Her manager raised his arm pleadingly, looking for the cross, but instead she curled a low shot pass the goalkeeper and into the bottom corner.

The lunchtime crowd reacted with a polite chorus of low-level cheers and gentle applause. The aftertaste caught Albright by surprise and he stopped suddenly, squeezing his eyes and concentrating hard on the cognitive equivalent of holding his breath. How could this be happening? The pitch had been laid outside his window so he could condition himself to *resist* temptation, not give into it.

– *Blow the whistle, damn you!*

The referee blew his whistle and at once the celebrations ended. Albright breathed again and feigned the reason for his discomfort by placing a hand on his lower back and wincing. They were all looking at him now, the referee with the ball under his arm in his DFA regulation black-and-white striped shirt and baseball cap.

– *Screw you. You look ridiculous.*

The referee averted his eyes sheepishly. A fairer leader might have been sympathetic – the shirts were, after all, Albright's design.

'Excellent strike, miss,' he called, his voice full of affection.

The research assistant smiled timidly.

'Oh, don't look so worried, my dear, just my age. Nothing untoward. I could still run rings around your superior. Don't blame you for not passing to that boss-eyed old codger. My dog's got a better chance of finding the net!'

A smattering of laughs. In general, laughter had little effect on him – humour was not the same as rapture – especially when it was awkward laughter, as this certainly was.

For heaven's sake, man, just shut up and leave.

'Carry on!' he said, and lifted his cane to signify his approval. The sunlight caught the handle; his beautiful custom-made orb of multi-coloured, translucent gems fused together and smoothed into shape and which, as he rolled the cane between his fingers, refracted the light like a kaleidoscopic disco ball. A constant reminder, he claimed, of the rich diversity of life.

Apple Blossom tottered behind him as at last Albright left the courtyard and turned onto the colonnade, the long thoroughfare which led to the base of the tower. It was one of his favourite features of the building; a series of interconnected archways which had been around almost as long as him. In his mind he had only to strip away the statues, spires and criss-cross patterns of heraldic masonry for the architecture to remind him a little of home.

The two-way traffic of purposeful-looking individuals, checking their phones as they paced towards their next meeting, slowed considerably at the sight of their Prime Minister. Smart young things, dressed to impress with papers they didn't intend to read tucked under their arms, all pausing to bid him good morning with as much hidden sycophancy as they could muster. Further along, a tall woman with a wild, frizzy perm thundered down the colonnade towards him, the rhythmic click-clack of her high heels on the flagstones echoing beneath the archways.

– *Good day, Temperance.*

– *And you, Prime Minister.*

– *Don't call me that.*

The entrance to the tower was boarded off by a temporary wooden wall and a door with a keycode lock. Black-and-yellow tape ran around the frame; in the centre, a sign had been nailed into the wood at head height:

Sorry folks, the tower is closed for repairs!
Come back in a couple of months once we've got everything looking spick and span!
But if you are coming in – *don't forget your hard hat!*
Have a great day!

Apple Blossom pawed at the door, running her claws over the scratch marks she'd made the day before, and the day before that.

The long-running restoration project had been beset by budgetary and practical difficulties. The general scrub-up of the clock was straightforward enough, but the challenge of putting a lift in the disused ventilation shaft running the length of the tower had never resolved the issue of the Victorian era bells taking up the space where the counter-weight mechanism would need to be.

'No trouble, all good things happen in 'time',' had been Albright's last words on the matter, humorously received in the Commons, immediately before he'd given the entire restoration workforce time off to enjoy the World Cup.

He tapped in the code (the date of the Final) and gripped the turn-screw handle.

– *Sir?*

Albright gritted his rotten teeth.

So close.

He turned to his Defence Secretary, who stood before him like a timid schoolboy about to ask if he could get out of detention.

– *Yes, Felix?*

Felix Gently was the closest Albright had come to making a mistake. The idea had been to put a friendly, youthful face in the role as the government pursued its policy to move the military away from combat roles and focus on peacekeeping, humanitarian aid and the development of football-based community projects in the far-flung corners of the world. The figurehead therefore had to take on a more liberal, academic persona – a university graduate with dreams of global harmony and an ill-fitting suit.

But choosing Gently had come at an irritating price. The man was like a bag of gold with fleas inside.

Apple Blossom scratched behind her ears.

– I just wondered if you had a chance to read my last email?

Albright puffed his chest.

– No, I bloody well didn't. I can only presume it contained the same load of old balls as all the others?

– Except this one is my final plea, Prime Minister. I am running out of time.

– Out of time?

– To save her.

Albright chuckled derisively, startling a nearby intern who scurried off in embarrassment. The silent conversation between Albright and Gently was unfolding much faster than if they were saying the words out loud, which meant from an outsider's point of view, Gently had arrived beside the Prime Minister and a second later the Prime Minister had looked up and laughed in his face.

Albright opened the door.

– Go away, Felix.

He could sense a quivering act of defiance coming his way and it was all he could do not to snigger again.

– I can't. Sir, I'm begging you. She will not be a nuisance, I promise… but if I am forced to leave her behind… I will –

A pudgy hand grabbed Gently by the lapel of his jacket, pulled him through the doorframe and shoved him against the wall. Albright lifted his cane and pinned him across his chest, leaning in close enough for Gently to see (and smell) the wrinkled orifice beneath his beard and the rotten rows of vestigial teeth.

– What? What will you do? Hmm? Try to hurt me? Don't be ridiculous. What do you think would happen if I gave in to your absurd

demands? You truly believe your wife will want to remain with you once she knows the truth?

Gently tried to answer, one way or another, but his struggle for breath was hampering the attempts.

– Precisely. So now, you listen to me, you snivelling wretch. I have suffered your whiney presence until now because you once had something of value. But it is quite foolish of you to choose the point at which you have outgrown your usefulness to start disobeying orders. Do you know what happens to superfluous little buggers who don't do as they're told?

Albright saw the look of fear in Gently's eyes as they ran along the rosewood cane to the glass handle at its end. He held the moment a second longer and released him. Gently gasped for breath.

– Be there on Sunday or face the consequences. Do I make myself clear?

– Yes, sir

– Good. Now sod off.

The wooden wall swayed as Felix Gently used it to steady himself before skulking away through the door. In an instant all thoughts of the obstinate minister were gone from Albright's mind and his attention turned to the second door – the permanent one, the one made of oak, with wrought iron hinges, set into the grand stone façade at the base of the tower. Inside, the spiral stairwell looked as intimidating as ever. It was infuriating the way age cancelled out the comfort of familiarity. Albright placed a foot on the first step and looked back, as always, at his dog.

'Come along, old girl.'

The first stop on the climb was roughly a third of the way up – 114 steps to be exact. Albright waited for Apple Blossom to skip inside the room to her water bowl before he hauled his bulk through the door and sat himself down in the recess of the nearest window.

The tower was full of these square U-shaped rooms, which wrapped around the central weight shaft that ran down from the mechanism room above and to a pile of sandbags at ground level. Most of the rooms were disused dumping grounds for broken bits of machinery, reclaimed furniture (deck chairs mainly) and mini-fridges for the clockmakers. All were 'scheduled' for refurbishment but only Albright's room had been shown any attention. Carpets had been laid, the walls repainted, and a lock fitted on the door. A plush leather bench had also been installed beneath the western windows overlooking the river, opposite a large flat-screen television on the weight-shaft wall.

The remote control was where he had left it the night before, but he wanted to savour the silence and stillness a little longer. With his eyes closed the sound of Apple Blossom's drinking was like the lapping of water against an empty shore.

A few more days, then it will all be yours. You'll never have to watch football again.

The thought was invigorating, but it hadn't been a total masquerade. There was a time when the idea of his own personal man-cave had been quite exciting; a place where he could abandon his responsibilities for an hour or so and immerse himself in some Regional League highlights. Albright was no unthinking robot, there was still nuance to his expressions, and it was easier to talk hyperbole about the game if he believed a little of it himself.

But with the end in sight, he'd begun to self-medicate against the disease of fandom by stripping away much of the paraphernalia – the framed shirts, the honorary trophies, the autographed balls – and leaving only a large tournament wall chart, which he filled in with each new score-line in much the same way a prisoner might tick off the days on a calendar towards his release date.

Having regained his breath, Albright hobbled over to the chart and took a pen from the pocket of his cardigan.

'North America one, Argentina nil,' he intoned as he filled in the box. 'Bloody boring, wasn't it?'

Apple Blossom ignored him, too thirsty from the climb. He stood back and marvelled at the organisational beauty of it all. The flowing symmetry of a sixty-four-team, 128 -match tournament, the largest ever conceived, all mapped out on a single sheet of paper.

Around the edge the sixteen groups were detailed in sixteen tables with match-ups, dates, locations and a bespoke flag icon next to each team. Between them, the bow-shaped knockout bracket depleted inwards from the Round of Thirty-Two on either side to the last two matches in the centre, the only ones left to be played: The third-place play-off and the Final.

The excess space on the sheet was occupied with various action shots of the national team players pointing, running, kicking, shouting, laughing. Except, of course, for Nathan, the adolescent youth upon whose shoulders all hope rested in ways he'd never live to understand, who was pictured with his arms crossed above the title, written in large chunky lettering:

SyBall World Cup

'5

The Bovill Arms

L exa had never seen cars quite like this before. Through the
stories her father had told and the pictures he'd shown, she
was prepared for things being a little more intact than she was used
to; the buildings had roofs, the roads were paved and the bridges
that crossed them were navigable – you could get from one side to
the other without the need for a running jump. All these oddities
she could adapt to, but there was something about the vehicles of
this time that refused to settle with her.

It might have been because in her world cars were purely
functional. They were utilities; used for cargo transports, as a
means of escape, or if the need arose, a bed for the night. As long
as the bio-fuel smugglers could keep up with their supply, cars
were valuable assets in a time when currency had been rendered
meaningless.

They were not, by any means, there to look good. A new car
would come bashed, broken and pierced with shrapnel; but if it had
at least one working door, then it was considered a fortunate
acquisition. Here, each one was pristine – even the ones that

weren't. Passing a garage, she had seen a sign for a 'car wash' – the idea that a machine built entirely for purpose could engender such care and attention was mystifying.

Lexa pushed these distractions from her mind as she walked through the car park towards the entrance of the pub. She squirmed inside her stolen clothes, hoping to shrug off her discomfort before she went inside. But the jeans were too tight, and the hoodie was too baggy – neither much use if she had to make a run for it.

She stopped by the last car, at the end of the row next to some dumpsters. It was certainly more in keeping with what she knew; a small, squat, dark-green thing, with a broken wing mirror, a bent aerial and four mud-soaked wheels. It was parked in the bay at a severe angle, which allowed her to see the big dent in the driver's door. But the rust-bucket familiarity was not what appealed to her. It was that the car would be lightweight, fast, and easy to break into; her first choice tonight for a quick getaway.

The evening was warm, and the last remnants of the setting sun had turned the sky a hazy, light orange. The air was clear and in a few hours the stars would be out. The light beyond the windows was bright and golden and the muffled sound of music and buoyant conversation disturbed the tranquillity of the surrounding village.

The Bovill Arms was set on the opposite side of the Belmont Park estate and occupied a large, Tudor-style cottage with white limestone walls and an exposed black timber frame. Lightbulbs in the old iron lanterns above the windows flickered like candle flames, illuminating the ivy that sprawled its way up to the thatched roof.

She had stood on this spot before, years into the future, when the small pond across the road was a diseased bog and precisely nothing of this ornate building was left to be found among the mud and filth.

Nearby, someone was giggling. A girl with long chestnut hair and a boy with none were perched on a wall on the other side of the carpark, inspecting the inside of each other's mouths with their tongues. Lexa stopped and looked – she had seen bald heads before, but never without the markings.

Very strange.

The boy's eyes shifted and caught her staring. Without breaking his rhythm or disturbing his partner, he winked at Lexa.

She dashed inside, but was so startled by the sudden increase in noise her heart skipped a beat. Further passage into the pub was blocked by a throng of people having the time of their lives; drinking, talking, shouting and shuffling past one another with their glasses held above their heads. High in one corner, a large television screen showed three people sitting on a sofa in the middle of a patch of grass, their voices inaudible. Next to this, above an enormous fireplace big enough for someone to fall into, hung a portrait of an imperious-looking man holding the lapel of his huntsman's coat and staring out into the distance, a dog at his feet and a dead pheasant over his arm.

The mass of people was too heavy for Lexa to pick her target out by sight, but seeing the bar ahead, she stepped forward, moving shoulder first and squeezing her way through. Behind the mahogany counter four bartenders were serving drinks, ducking and weaving around each other in well-practiced fashion. After a number of attempts Lexa managed to grab the attention of the oldest and the slowest.

'Yes, love, what can I get you?'

'I'm looking for a football player,' Lexa replied, raising her voice above the noise.

The man leaned forward and shut one eye, as though this might help him hear better. He smelled of tobacco and old books.

'Say that again?'

'A footballer. I need to find one.'

He let out a phlegmy chuckle and rested on the bar. 'You and half the girls in here, love. Take your pick.'

Lexa's nails dug into the wood. It was all she could do to keep her cool with this slimy old man.

'*Joshua Pittman,*' she said, shouting now. '*Do you know where I can find him?*'

'Who?'

This time Lexa leant forward, going as far as she dared without feeling sick.

'*Josh-u-ah-pit-mun,*' she said a final time, punctuating each syllable.

'Oh, Josh, the keeper, yeah – he's sitting over by the telly. One second, I'll call him.'

The barman trotted off to the opposite end of the bar, pulled up the wooden hatch and disappeared into the crowd. Lexa's mouth went dry and her heart rate increased. It was stupid – she was finally about to meet him and there were butterflies in her stomach.

As she waited, Lexa spotted something familiar. A large flag was pinned up on the wall above the hatch. It had a distinctive, geometric design of interlocking crosses in three different colours – red, white and yellow – set against a dark blue field. She had seen one before, filthy and with torn, frayed edges, and without the badge in the middle that this one had: twelve bulbous petals curling out from the centre, alternating black-and-white on a green shield the shape of an inverted teardrop. Lexa stared at the words in the scroll beneath and became lost in the bitter memory of everything they had cost her.

'Hello?'

The genial voice of the young man standing next to her snapped her out of her sad reminiscence. Blood rushed to her head. Up close he was much less athletic than she'd been expecting. Tall and gangly, with a lopsided stance and hardly any muscle; his long-sleeved top hung off him like a rag.

'Hi. I'm Josh. Mick said you were looking for me?'

The girl turned as white as a sheet. As Josh arrived beside her, she'd been staring into the middle distance, lost in thought, and for a moment he thought he'd got the wrong person. But then she turned, seemingly dumbfounded by the sight of him, and straight away he recognised her.

'I saw you today, didn't I? At the stadium?'

Again, there was no reply. Her dark eyes were a vivid contrast against her pale skin. Curling strands of loose hair framed her face perfectly and a smattering of freckles accentuated the contours of her cheeks, which rose gently as at last she spoke.

'Joshua Pittman,' she said, 'nice to meet you.'

'Uh – you too. And please, call me Josh – I hate Joshua.'

'Oh,' said the girl. She glanced around the room, twitching nervously under her baggy red hoodie. 'Why's that?'

Josh shrugged. 'People make jokes – and they're never funny.'

'Right.'

It was clear from her face she had no idea what he was talking about. He decided not to press it. Josh had never been very good at talking to strangers and this conversation felt particularly laboured.

'And you?'

'Me?'

'What's your name?'

'Oh, it's…' Her eyes shifted, as though the answer were a closely guarded secret she'd rather not disclose. 'Lexa.'

'Lexa,' Josh repeated, smiling at the very sound. The name settled like a feather in his hand and he felt suddenly at ease with this odd encounter. 'That's unusual. Is that short for Alexa? Or Alexandria?'

'No.'

'Oh, right. Can I get you a drink?'

He raised his own pint glass of Coke. Lexa peered at it with an expression wavering somewhere between confusion and disgust.

Damn it, Josh, you idiot.

'Oh, this is nothing,' he said quickly, covering the glass with his hand. 'I can't drink tonight, that's all. I'm driving. But I am old enough, so have what you like.'

'Water,' she said.

'Water? Um, okay… Mick?' Josh turned to the ageing barman, who was watching all this with a raised eyebrow. 'A glass of water, please.'

The old man took a glass from the shelf above his head, poured some water from the tap and set it on the bar. Josh reached for his wallet, imploring Mick with his eyes to charge him something, but the barman was having too much fun and waved away the suggestion.

Lexa took three quick gulps, one after the other. Then, with about an inch of water left, she paused, took a breath and finished the rest.

'Would you like another?'

Lexa set the glass back down on the bar.

'No,' she said. 'Let's go outside.'

Mick smiled creepily.

An hour later Lexa found herself sitting on the wall outside the pub, listening to Josh talk while he took painfully small sips of the fizzy black liquid he was drinking tonight even though he 'wasn't drinking tonight'.

There was no way she could've completed her mission inside. Too many people around to hold her back. She had started to feel a little edgy too; it was clear her behaviour at the bar had been uncustomary. Why else would the old barkeeper have looked so bewildered at someone's natural thirst for water?

But now she and Josh were out in the open, with no-one else about, and yet still she hadn't taken her chance, as though the risks of further delay were failing to have the required impact on her. Instead they floated somewhere in the recesses of her mind for over an hour as she allowed Josh to garble on about his day; a goalkeeper falling off his bike, a dislike for a badge and a tip-off about a talent scout were some of the highlights Lexa had vaguely tuned in on.

'That wasn't you then, I take it?'

'Uh, no,' she said.

Josh shrugged. 'So why did you run off like that? I didn't save the penalty, I know, but...' He stopped and shook his head. 'It was my sisters, wasn't it?'

Before Lexa could make up a lie, Josh had sunk his face into his hands, and when he removed them his cheeks were flushed.

'God, this is so embarrassing. They're always trying to set me up. If you want to go, I understand. It's been very nice to meet you, honestly, I've enjoyed it, but as you've probably guessed I'm not very good at... well, you know...'

Lexa didn't know, but she certainly wasn't about to leave him.

'No, no, it's fine,' she reassured him. 'I'm enjoying myself too.'

It was surprising how sincere she had managed to make that sound. Perhaps she owed him this much, to get to know him a little bit and offer him some time. And he could blame what was coming on these sisters of his too. A chance to spread the fault around a bit.

Josh smiled, but his demeanour had changed. He had shrunk into himself and spoke into his glass rather than at her.

'Good. I'm glad,' he said. 'Still, I bet I'm not what you were expecting. I bet they told you about this hotshot young keeper, just broke into the first team, not some guy who gets face-palmed by the ball and still lets it in. If you came here to meet a player, you've got the wrong guy.'

Alarm bells were ringing.

'I thought you were very good,' Lexa said as she tried to withhold the quiver of growing concern.

'You don't have to say that, we both know it isn't true. But it doesn't matter anyway; I could be the most talented player in the world and it wouldn't make a difference.'

'Why not?'

'Because...' His eyes shifted and he whispered, as though the answer were a closely guarded secret he'd rather not disclose. 'I don't *like* playing football.'

 The quiver was now a full-blown tremor of fear and she bit her thumb to calm herself.

'So why do you?'

'Because my dad makes me.'

'I see. Well, I can understand that. We all want to please our fathers, don't we?'

Josh scoffed. 'Not really. If anything, the more I do it, the more it seems to annoy him.' He was becoming bullish now, wagging a finger in the air. 'Turns out I don't *think* about football the way I'm supposed to, the way others do. And the only reason I went along with it is because I thought there might be something nice about being part of a team, you know?'

Lexa was confused. 'But you *are* part of a team, aren't you?'

'I'm the *goalkeeper*. The outcast. The one with the different coloured shirt. I get the blame if we lose and forgotten about if we win. And that's only if I actually play – but I don't, because I'm the *reserve* keeper. Second choice to a guy with a broken hand.'

Josh slumped on his perch with an exhaustive grunt, then lifted his chin and closed his eyes as the cool evening breeze swept around them. Lexa hadn't noticed the fall of the night or the full moon's shimmer reflecting off the surface of the pond.

'Sorry,' he said. 'I know I shouldn't complain. Poor guy. He could've turned pro if it weren't for the hand. But me, I... I just feel trapped by it all, you know?'

Lexa nodded. This guy would not have lasted five minutes in her world; there was no time for inner pain when worse horrors waited for you just around the corner.

Who was this guy?

She was forced to consider the possibility that something had gone horribly awry. If it hadn't, then the fate of the world rested on the shoulders of this lanky, awkward kid with patchy stubble, floppy hair and a severe inferiority complex. He had neither the physicality nor the swagger and apparently hated the game that would make him famous.

She thought back to the Vessel. The predictions could never to be truly relied upon, but they still gave the advantage, a head-start from which to plan and make changes. They were erratic, yes, but never *wrong*. That was impossible.

Wasn't it?

Her head spun with doubt and confusion as she recalled the details given to her by the Captain: a strike towards the goal in the ninety-first minute. A man named Joshua Pittman playing for a team in blue.

It had to be him, surely?

Perhaps it wasn't so unlikely. Josh just said he felt trapped. What if she had come all this way to interrupt the freeing of his potential? Maybe one of these 'scouts' was in the stadium today, and tomorrow Josh would receive a phone call telling him to ditch the goalkeeper thing and try scoring the goals instead. Then his talent would shine, and like some modern fairy tale he becomes a national hero overnight...

It seemed unlikely, but far-fetched scenarios were all in a day's work for Lexa, and with this one she couldn't take the risk. Her hand reached into the pocket of her hoodie and her fingers wrapped around the glove, feeling around the leathery material, moving slowly and gently so as not to cut herself on the razor-sharp blades, only to let go a second later. She'd changed her mind. The thought of using the glove was easy when it was only a thought, but now felt like a step too far in light of the mounting uncertainty.

In the gap left by her hesitation, Josh downed his drink and stood up.

'I can give you a lift home, if you like?' he said, fumbling for the keys in his pocket.

'What? No, I can't!'

Lexa had already put it off for long enough, she couldn't allow for any more distractions. But her panic was obvious, having been caught off guard, and now Josh looked panicked too.

'No, I didn't mean, you know, anything funny or anything, I just thought you might...'

He held up his keys and pressed the button on a small black fob. Behind him orange lights flashed on the little green car Lexa had noticed earlier. She wouldn't have to break in and hot wire it after all.

'You can phone ahead if you want, tell someone you're coming, give them my details... but only if, you know, you want to. You don't have to, probably a bit weird... I don't even know where –'

'Okay, yes,' Lexa said, 'a lift would be great, thank you.'

'Okay,' Josh said, beaming.

The distance between the wall and the car couldn't have been more than fifteen metres or so, yet Josh strolled beside Lexa as though the pair were ambling slowly along a wide sandy beach (in his head they were). For the most part he looked down at his feet, or over to the trees, or back to where the light through the windows spilt onto the tarmac, hoping beyond hope that no-one was watching. But when he did turn to the mysterious girl who had entered his life from nowhere, he found her staring into the sky. Without speaking he followed her gaze.

The night was crystal clear and even through the turbulence of artificial light around them, the stars were out in their millions, scattered across the black vista like silver dust. Some, he knew, were planets, orbiting the Sun as his own world did, passing through the seasons one after the other in a never-ending loop. He often felt that his life followed a similar cycle; a yearly repetition in which so little changed it was negligible – he aged, he grew, he could buy a drink, he could a drive a car; but these were nothing more than fluctuations within an eternal pattern of boredom. He was a planet without its star, orbiting an empty black mass, wondering where its beacon of light had gone.

Yet tonight had felt like he was being treated to a rare cosmic event, a meteor shower or a solar eclipse, or something even closer to home he had never before appreciated, like that one day in winter when the snow no longer falls but hasn't yet begun to thaw.

He could even forgive Sophie and Jessica for setting him up, which in itself was extraordinary. Most of their aspirations for their big brother were cocktail-drinking party girls who lauded their own 'lovely, bubbly personalities', especially when drunk, as if this somehow made them unique.

Lexa, on the other hand, was as genuinely unique a person as he could ever imagine; curious but detached, quiet but outspoken, every guarded word laced with apprehension. He couldn't presume to have got the full measure of her; it was impossible when she had offered so little of herself during their conversation – not because she found him captivating, but because she was trying to protect herself. Against what, Josh had no idea.

'Well, here it is,' he said as they arrived beside his car. The smell of the dumpsters pervaded the air. 'The Lock Niss Monster.'

Lexa looked blank. 'Excuse me?'

'It's a Nissan,' Josh said, apologetically. 'And, I have to lock it, so… it's not much to look at, I know. But I'm going to do it up one day. When I know how.'

Josh opened the door for her but Lexa didn't move.

'Is there something wrong?'

'I'm just trying to understand,' she said. 'I'm worried things aren't what they ought to be. So, I have to ask; if you don't like football, what do you like?'

This was it. The moment when Lexa was finally going to get the measure of him. She'd used the words 'ought to be', which could only mean that she too found his indifference to the game to be a blemish on his character. He leant against the door. There was no way she was getting in now. He might as well be honest.

'I like drawing,' he said. 'I want to go to art college, to do graphic design. I was gonna go this year, but I...' He didn't have an ending to that sentence. He hadn't gone because he thought he shouldn't. 'And I like films, too.'

'Films?'

'Yeah, mostly eighties and nineties. I don't like modern stuff. Too much world-building. So concerned with setting up the sequel they forget to tell a decent story. And I can't be doing with all those stupid football subplots.'

'I see,' said Lexa. 'You should leave.'

'Excuse me?'

'Your team. Quit and go to art college if that's what you want.'

It was like being spoken to by his mother. He thought back to earlier in the day and the conversation with his parents and the 'doodles in his bedroom,' then later the sight of his dad cheering Callum's goal. He scrunched up his face, embarrassed by his own cowardice.

'I can't do that. It's not worth the hassle.'

'So, you're not going to give up?' she asked, the tone of disappointment so crushing he could only offer another meek shake of the head.

'Are you sure? Final chance, Josh.'

That was odd.

'What does that mean?'

Lexa, the girl who'd come from nowhere to make him feel as if he'd never been alone, gently closed her eyes and took a long, slow breath. In through her nose and out through her mouth. She re-opened her eyes; they were beautiful and determined and regretful all at the same time.

'You have to understand,' she said. 'I wasn't expecting it to be like this. You're not the kind of person I thought you'd be. So... I apologise.'

A fearful flutter rose in his stomach. 'For what?'

And then it began.

Josh didn't even see Lexa's fist swinging towards him before he felt the contact with the side of his face. His head jerked with the force, but it wasn't until he could smell the blood starting to trickle down the inside of his nose that he realised how much it had hurt. He tried to say something, but Lexa struck again, harder and more direct, catching his lower jaw. The pain spread immediately to the other side of his mouth and down the back of his neck. In the space of a few seconds, he had developed the sort of migraine that would normally take a whole day to come. He thought he might be sick.

After the first hit he had stumbled but stayed on his feet, but this second time he fell. His keys flew out of his hand and landed with a jangle nearby. He hit the ground with a thud, the tarmac ripping the skin on his palm as he stretched out his hand to break his fall. His first instinct was to show the injury to her, an unwitting plea for mercy, but as Josh held up his hand, Lexa kicked it back down, pinning his arm to the ground with the sole of her boot and snapping the strap of his wristwatch. With her other foot, she stamped down on the bloody hand, and with his scream came the first real attempt to defend himself, reaching his free hand across to her leg, but not finding the strength to twist his body on its side and grab it.

'Please, stop –'

Lexa kicked him in the face and the blood sprayed from his mouth. Then she landed a boot square in the middle of his chest, crushing any further resistance. He wheezed and struggled for breath and moments later heard his car door opening, the engine starting and tyres crunching along the gravel. He lay motionless on the ground; his whole body felt heavy and contorted. The pain alternated with every heartbeat between the sharp and the aching. Above him, the stars spiralled uncontrollably.

Josh rests his hands on the windowsill and sees that it's a beautiful day; the sun is bright, and the butterflies are out. There is a silky feel to the air. A bird whistles in the tree and he follows its flight as it swoops down and perches on the sundial. Josh spots his toys all out on the lawn.

To one side there is the low but constant whir of a miniaturised motor. Josh looks and sees his little model of the Solar System on the shelf above his headboard. He's shocked. The model had broken years ago, Jupiter having snapped off its thin plastic stem, and yet here it was, good as new, each and every planet present and correct and orbiting around the sun in perfect synchronicity.

There's a noise coming from downstairs.

Josh climbs off the bed and walks over to the door. It's the television in the living room, with the match-day commentary and a cheering crowd blaring through the speakers. A moment later footsteps pass the bottom of the stairs and disappear off down the hall.

If I go down, will they recognise me?

Josh turns back into the room and looks around. In one corner sits his desk, at the moment a place to pile dirty clothes, schoolbooks and a day-old glass of raspberry squash. On the walls are his collection of old scrappy film posters, ripped out of magazines and stuck up at jaunty angles with Sellotape. Movies he was once too young to fully understand but loved nonetheless: Indiana Jones, Jurassic Park, Back to the Future.

But there is something different here too. Something out of place with the time. Nestled amongst the posters is a single sheet of white paper with a pencil drawing he can't make out from across the room. He creeps forward and the picture starts to come into focus, but then...

'Remember when I said, "don't cross the streams"?'

The voice is coming from outside. Josh rushes back to the window and gasps in shock. Outside on the lawn, a little boy, about ten years old, is playing with his toys.

'Cross the streams!'

Four action figures stand in a row, their feet wedged into the soil, the grass up to their knees, staring determinedly at the ghost disguised as a garden gnome. The heroes fire their weapons and the little boy shakes them two at a time.

'Uuuugggghhh... release the trap!'

Directly below, Frank Pittman walks out of the conservatory door and towards the boy. Josh has a great view of the sun glinting off his father's head. Frank stands in front of the boy, who in turn offers up one of the plastic figurines for him to play. Frank refuses and walks back inside, rubbing his brow.

The little boy's face changes from hope to disappointment and for a second Josh thinks he is going to cry. He knows he should go out there and try to make him feel better, but before he can move, he notices the sheet of paper has appeared on the windowsill. Josh looks back to the wall above and sure enough, it's not there anymore. It's in front of him. He takes the chance for a closer look.

The drawing is of a squirrel, dressed as a superhero, holding a football.

'6

The SyBall World Cup

If ever there were a reason for Ray Albright to keep the chart tacked to the wall, it was the sight of these three words. The first, with its upper-case S and B, was one of his own creation. His election platform had been built, to all appearances, on a new vision for the country, one of boundless optimism, naive positivity and a blind eye to the dreary injustices of daily life. The people were to be fuelled by the power of a cheery smile, with the source of this energy arising from a culture beholden to the game of football.

But he had realised early on that if the country were to change, the sport would need to too. While practical methods had centred around the success of the Regional League, it was the introduction and influence of SyBall as a byword for compassionate, joyful and inclusive football support that had been the real game-changer.

'Mr Speaker, can the new Prime Minister tell us,' the Opposition Leader had asked, shortly before the post ceased to exist, 'if he is intent on rebranding all our national pastimes and what this "SyBall" of his actually means?'

The question had been met with the usual sycophantic howls and jeers, but the response had come with a ruddy-cheeked smile beamed directly into the overhead camera angled towards the government front bench.

'A fair question indeed, one I think my handsome friend across the table already knows the answer to, but I thank him anyway for the opportunity to make my answer a matter of public record. It stands for Society Football.'

The House fell silent in an instant. For that was Albright's power – to look down a camera lens and with a few simple words plant an idea directly, without scrutiny, hesitation or discussion, into the minds of those watching.

And watch they did, for the more he spoke the more the people slipped under his trance. And why not? Who would object to being told that the 'rebranding' was about 'warmth, community and the cosy feeling that comes from sharing your passion with other people'?

Even 'Sunny', the World Cup mascot (supposedly the winning entry in a nationwide competition, but in truth designed by a Cabinet committee chaired by Albright himself) was an anthropomorphic sun, with arms, legs and a jolly little face encircled by beams of light radiating away from him. A representation of great untruths in cartoon form.

Albright hated him.

The little figure was there now, staring at him from his perch atop a group table (Group J – Europe, Nigeria, Nicaragua and Yemen), the effervescent smile somehow reproving of his creator. Albright sensed a troubled soul beneath that perky exterior;

ashamed of his existence, forever frozen in his resentful stance, hands waving, with his chest puffed out to accentuate the tournament logo emblazoned on his shirt.

From a distance the impression was of a football spinning on a grass pitch, but with no other references to the countries taking part or the trophy up for grabs, the spiral crest served equally as that of the Department for Footballing Activities and its national and regional teams. It had felt logical to keep things consistent ever since his administration had taken over the worldwide governance of the game from that fusty old consortium of wealthy businessmen.

The only change for the World Cup had been in the scroll at the bottom, where the national motto 'Joy and Compassion', had been replaced with the far more succinct *#UnionJAC*, a call-to-action which at this very moment was connecting people in feverish discussion on the SyBall App, the government's online service for live match streaming, betting and social media. Undoubtedly vulgar, the hashtag hammered home the key message that the British were at the heart of football's reinvention as the planet's Grand Unifier. Global adoration of 'his' country was key; without it all was lost.

A rush of blood stole the focus from Albright's vision; the colours and shapes on the wallchart merged together and threatened a headache that would rule out the rest of the climb. He sat on the nearest chair and tapped his leg.

Apple Blossom skipped across the room at once and leapt onto her master's lap. The velvety fur around her ears was his favourite place to stroke, up and down with his thumb, a soft comfort that brought him back to himself. The dog liked it too. She sniffed his beard and then sneezed as the strands of her companion's hair tickled her nose. This was why he kept her – he needed the innocence and the smallness of her life. At times he thought so hard about where he was and what he was doing that he felt overwhelmed and melancholy, which for a being like him left a sour taste in his mouth.

'Am I ready, Apple Blossom?'

The dog whined, either with sympathy or boredom.

'Quite right, my lovely. Time to get going.'

But as soon as he lifted from the seat and Apple Blossom leapt to the ground, he heard a guttural clack of twisting metal from somewhere far above him, followed by a hollow rumble that grew quickly in volume. The mechanism had engaged. High up in the belfry, the Westminster Chimes rung out, followed by the morbid peal of the hour bell.

The Prime Minister checked his watch – eleven o'clock – and scratched the beard around his chin. The door of the sideboard beneath the television had been left invitingly ajar, the brandy and tumbler waiting inside.

'To hell with it,' Albright said, jabbing the remote with his forefinger. 'Let the buggers wait.'

It had been a good few days since he last watched an episode of *SyBall Daily*, a conscious effort on his part, but he reasoned with himself that it was a necessary ill to relieve a little of the pressure, and perhaps he had subconsciously known this when choosing to climb the tower at this time in the morning.

As the first warm taste reached his tongue and slipped like molten gold down his throat, the flashy titles faded and the screen settled on the face of the *SyBall Daily* host. Geoffrey Sterling was in his sixties, handsome even without the tanned skin and dyed hair, and bore the expression of a mischief maker continually on the verge of revealing a juicy secret.

'Good morning and welcome,' Sterling began, his voice as smooth as the drink in Albright's hand. 'Thank you for joining us, the sun is shining, the birds are singing, and the Final...' he leant into the camera and whispered '...is just two days away.' Sterling summed up the excitement of millions with a single raise of an eyebrow. 'Here to brighten up to your day – don't worry, they won't be singing! – are my guests; former East Country defender Mark Kemp and captain of the British Kingdom's national women's team, Christine Crawford! Hello to you both, glorious, isn't it?'

Mark wiped his sleeve across his brow. 'Bit hot for me, Geoff.'

Albright sneered and took another sip. Mark Kemp could act about as well as he could comb his hair without looking like he'd spent the night in a ditch.

Christine Crawford, sat at the far end away from the other two in a long summer dress, smiled unconvincingly and twitched her hand, as though she were about to fan her face but thought better of it.

Albright knew a thing or two about illusion, but he wondered if these little theatrics were really necessary when everyone watching knew the open stadium around them wasn't real. *SyBall Daily* was filmed on an old motion picture soundstage in west London and

81

had a budget to match. Green-screen effects, computer-generated imagery and virtual reality rendering abound to give the impression that the plush curved sofa and oversized coffee-table were, in fact, positioned in the centre circle of the BK Stadium pitch. The shadow of the antenna fell across the grass as Sterling ran through the programme's schedule.

Sterling continued. 'And of course, we'll be looking ahead to tomorrow night's third-place play-off. Now, Mark,' he said, not to Mark, but into the camera, 'you may be wondering why you're on today. Is it your insight, your analysis, your boyish good looks? No. It's because today we're talking a little about 'firsts' – and you, of course, hold the record for being the first player to concede a penalty *and* be sent off in a Regional League match!'

Mark burst into laughter and slapped his thigh. Christine applauded.

'Things were different back then, Geoff.'

'Indeed. But a slightly more honourable first occurred on Wednesday, when, of course, North America became the first continental team to reach the final of a World Cup, thanks to their one-nil win over Argentina. Now, here are the line-ups…'

On Sterling's word, the camera pulled back to reveal twenty-two full size static footballers in their starting positions across the length of the pitch. North America in red, Argentina in their famous blue and white stripes.

'We've mentioned this before Christine, but look…' Sterling spun in his seat and out of the sky a series of spotlights illuminated several of the players '…*eight* of the starting eleven last night were

Canadian. How important has that been to North America's success in the tournament?'

'Yes, hugely important,' Christine said with a shrug.

Albright liked her. There was something about the way she responded, as though it were a tiny insult to her intelligence to be asked to point out the obvious. The camera swung away from the sofa and focused in on the two spot-lit players nearest the sofa.

'Emmett Baines and Corentin Lamoureux in particular, the forwards, they've been playing together for a long time, their link-up play is probably the best we've seen in this World Cup.'

Mark held up a hand to stop her. 'Aside from Troy and the Hitman, you mean?'

Albright raised his glass. That was Mark Kemp's worth; to butt in with a statement of blind patriotism to keep the priorities clear. Christine Crawford looked caught for a moment – clearly, she didn't agree, and Albright didn't expect her to, not really. But she was a guest on *SyBall Daily* and a DFA employee, so:

'Uh… yeah. Yes. I think they're on a par, which makes it so interesting. It was a shock, obviously, when Canada failed to qualify. But for these players it's come as a blessing in disguise, because look where they are now, preparing to face the British Kingdom in the final.'

The camera cut quickly back to Mark Kemp.

'You gotta give the gaffer credit too,' he said. 'Derrick Zeus. The continental managers, they've got it tough Geoff, they really have – don't know where the players are coming from, not much time to prepare… but the way he's got 'em playing, Geoff…'

Kemp puffed out his cheeks and shook his head, as though there were no words to describe the way the manager had got them playing.

Sterling agreed. 'Yes, they're all doing fabulously. And we have to include the keeper in that too, don't we? He made some fantastic saves in that second half to keep Argentina out.'

As Sterling spoke, the pitch began to roll away beneath their feet like a magician pulling a tablecloth from under the crockery. The sofa zoomed across the turf, passing through the outfield players and coming to a stop in front of the goalposts. Jesper Lykke stood behind them, his gloved hands held out ready to catch. He was short and stocky with pale-blonde hair cropped in militaristic fashion.

'Oh, I like the lad, Geoff, I really do. Look at him. Couldn't get in the Danish squad, got picked for Greenland through his...' Mark looked to Christine, '...what was it, his Grandma?'

'Grandma.'

'Grandma, which put him in the frame for North America. He's not at the level of Big Ben –'

The Prime Minister gritted his teeth and pulled unwittingly on Apple Blossom's fur, barely noticing as she whimpered and scurried away under a seat.

Big bloody Ben? I'll kill the bugger!

'– I mean, who is? But still, top keeper. Pleased for the lad.'

'Hmm. Christine?'

Christine paused before answering. 'I agree with Mark. I don't think Lykke is quite the finished article. He rides his luck sometimes with those aerial battles. If we take a look, this is in stoppage time, the game is almost over…'

The three of them rose in unison and walked towards the goalposts. Once the sofa was out of shot, the players suddenly came to life, running around the pundits in a three-dimensional replay of the match. Lykke side-stepped like a crab along his goal-line, shouting and pointing at his defenders as the camera turned and focused in on Adriano Flores, an Argentinian winger tearing down the flank. Two North Americans were crowding him from either side, looking for the tackle. But Flores' feet proved too quick for them and he cut in between, curving towards the corner of the penalty area and striking the ball in a single fluid motion. The ball shot through the air, rising up and over the box, the players scrambling, the goalkeeper jumping –

The action paused.

The players were frozen again in an array of contorted statues. The ball was stuck mid-air above Mark's head, who looked up at it grinning. Lykke was off the ground, caught in a diagonal leap across the goalmouth, his arm outstretched towards the top corner. Christine walked over to him and looked along the length of his extended body.

'You see how far his feet are off the ground here and how far he still has to go before he gets to that corner. He's not as tall as a lot of goalkeepers. Fortunately for him, Flores doesn't get enough height and the ball is already starting to dip...'

The game sprung back into life; the ball skimmed Kemp's greasy, dishevelled hair, smacked into Lykke's palm and rebounded over the bar.

'Unbelievably last night was North America's first clean sheet since the group stages. It's testament to their attacking threat that they've got this far – but I think George Castle will have noted that vulnerability in Jesper's game and will be looking to exploit.'

Sterling grinned. 'Exciting times. Thank you very much for that, Christine. Mark. Right, after the break…'

Albright smacked his withered old lips. Never before had a glass of brandy tasted so good. It was surely the closest humanity had come to replicating itself. Apple Blossom was back by his side, his outburst forgiven in exchange for a biscuit from the zip-lock bag in his pocket. All was well – a moment ago he was overwhelmed with anxiety and now he felt in awe of his own genius. His plan had ripened to perfection.

A tournament featuring all 200-odd national teams was unrealistic, but his masterstroke had been the inclusion of six continental teams, featuring the best players from respective countries that had failed to qualify. It had been easy to promote as an opportunity for every single person on the planet to have a team to support, but Albright had been careful to ensure the notion of a multi-national squad actually winning the SyBall World Cup remained an unpopular one.

There was little doubt which of the six would be chosen to reach the final. The populations of Africa and Asia were too spread out; Europe and South America had too much talent; Oceania too little. But North America, with their diminutive Dane in goal, treaded the line rather nicely. Their ascent to the final looked unexpected, rather than unrealistic. The Canadian element added depth and drama to the idea; without those key players it was a leap to imagine the team going any further than the group stages. The USA and Mexico had already crashed out, and with the majority of the region's supporters being from Central America and the Caribbean, reports suggested that worldwide support for North America wavered at about twelve per cent. Lop off another billion, say, for the elderly, the infirm, the squitty little pre-schoolers and other assorted lost causes (there were those on whom the mass hypnosis simply did not work), then Ray Albright could reasonably expect around eighty-six percent of the global population to be cheering the British Kingdom come the Harvest.

And that, at least, deserved one more glass.

Albright poured freely, doubling the shot from last time. He closed his eyes to savour the aroma wafting up his nose, and when he opened them again, he saw the boy darting around in front of him.

The advert went like this:

A suburban household. A perky woman with tight blonde curls and a polka dot dress opens a door into a messy bedroom with twelve bunk beds. She shakes her head, opens the curtains to let in the sunlight and says, 'Wake up, boys!'

There is a chaotic flurry of bedsheets as twelve teenage boys leap out of bed. They are all the same person, replicated with the use of special effects, wearing different sets of pyjamas, one for each of the twelve Regional League teams.

The boys run downstairs and out into the back garden and launch into a lively game of football. A montage of close-up shots shows the boys becoming caked in mud, getting dirtier with every kick, header and tackle.

The woman stands at the back door, sighs with a smile and then whistles with her fingers. The boys race into the kitchen and throw their filthy clothes into the washing machine. The woman shows the detergent brand to the camera and throws in a capsule.

The twelve identical young men eat breakfast in their underpants as the washing machine rumbles away. Later, the woman hangs the beautifully clean pyjamas on the line in the garden.

The brand logo appears again on screen next to the tagline: 'Perfect for getting the mud off your PJs.'

Albright choked on the brandy with the glass in his mouth, spilling the golden-brown liquid over his hand and down his beard. Apple Blossom ducked for cover. Though she couldn't hear it, her master swore as he wiped his mouth with his sleeve and shook the drops from his fingers over the carpet. He reached into his cardigan pocket (blue with a bronze plaid), pulled out the dog-biscuits, threw them on the floor, knocked over his cane, picked it up again, reached into his other pocket and took out his phone. Holding it lengthways, he tapped the SyBall App and said:

– *Temperance Newhart.*

Newhart answered the call in her office with that same saccharine smile she wore whenever she was in front of a camera or a superior. In this case it was both.

– *Good morning, Prime Minister.*

Newhart tucked a curled lock behind her ear. She was clearly leaning over the phone at her desk, which angered Albright even more because the shadow of her perm was covering too much of her face.

– *Did you authorise the boy's advert?*

He was doing his best to appear intimidating, showing his teeth like he had to Felix Gently, but he knew it wouldn't work. It never did. Losing her cool was just not her thing.

– *No.*

– *But you knew about it?*

– *Winsome...*

– *Winsome! Of course!*

– *...told me about it last month. You were overseeing a rehearsal for the opening ceremony and had said you weren't to be disturbed. It came from her office, so perhaps you should –*

Albright balked at her impertinence, though it hardly surprised him.

– *I don't give a damn whose office it came through! Winsome Free is your subordinate, you should have pressed her for full details and passed them onto me. I hope Max didn't pay for this?*

– *The Treasury split the budget with the detergent company.*

The temptation to throw the phone across the room was almost irresistible.

– You reckless bloody fools! How on earth do we expect people to idolise him if we go about cheapening his image with some half-arsed pun on his name?

– On the contrary, Prime Minister, Winsome thought it would be a last-minute opportunity to raise his profile.

– A wretched sodding soap advert?!

– Detergent, Prime Minister.

Apple Blossom had ripped open the bag of biscuits and was nosily tucking into the unexpected treat. The crumbs around her mouth were adorable. He calmed – a little.

– Does Strong know?

– I'm not sure. We haven't heard from Ernie in a while.

– Nothing new there, then. And it's 'Ernest'. Use it properly or don't use it at all.

– Of course, Prime Minister.

Her composure was unfaltering.

– Would you like to send Nathan a letter of reprimand from your office?

– What ruddy good would that do? We can't risk unsettling him. No, I shall speak to the noble Baroness myself, remind her of her responsibilities. If there are no adverse repercussions, then that will be the end of it. If problems do occur, however, I shall be holding you both responsible. Is that clear?

– Crystal, Prime Minister.

– You could at least pretend to care, Temperance. When are you visiting the training ground next?

– Later today. I'm attending a joint press conference with the managers, but we have agreed the players need to maintain their focus in a distraction-free environment. No more visitors, not even from the

Department. So, I'll touch base with Ernie – Ernest – while I'm there, but after that I won't be returning.

Albright tutted.

– 'Touch base'… fine. But on the subject of distractions, when you do go down there, for goodness' sake try and make yourself appear less attractive. Troy Simpson won't score a bloody thing if goes into the Final in a sulk because you won't go on a date with him.

Breakthrough.

Temperance shifted in her seat and looked around the edges of her screen.

– Actually, I've been thinking about that. If he does make his proposal – for the fifth time – I think it sensible to accept.

– Oh?

– Yes. It can only buoy his spirits and any such arrangement wouldn't be made until after the tournament – by which time he'll be dead.

There was something desultory about her tone. With their long journey together drawing to a close, Albright thought maybe he should indulge his second-in-command's rare flight of fancy.

– Indeed, he will. As you were, Temperance.

– Thank you, Prime Minister.

– Stop calling me that.

Albright ended the call and threw his phone on the sofa where it clattered against the remote. The sound startled Apple Blossom, who had closed her eyes in the comforting silence of the last few moments. His glass refilled, Albright sat back as he replayed the advert in his mind.

Get the mud off your PJs?

Tortuous.

What was Winsome trying to do to him? 'Hitman' was bad enough, and that had already taken plenty of convincing. When it came to the thorny issue of names, Baroness Free had persuaded Albright that the boy was to be the exception. The country, the sport, the Principles, were all perhiperary to that single, solitary moment he would provide. People had to feel as though they knew him personally, that they – in some small way – had some kind of influence on that final strike of the ball. Familiarity, nicknames, it was all supposedly key in grounding the boy with those around him. Idolisation was too detached. It wasn't enough. The people had to –

No.

Albright couldn't even bring himself to *think* the word. Winsome was probably the only member of his Cabinet who came close to matching the intelligence of his own, but sometimes he wondered if her radical ideas wouldn't end up sabotaging the whole project.

And to think I gave her a peerage.

Perhaps he ought to use today's broadcast to subtly remind everyone – and therefore *her* – of the precarious nature of what they had put in place. Perhaps, he ought to have one more glass and try a little something out on Apple Blossom.

'Nicknames,' he began, alerting the dog's attention with his oratorial tone and taking a sip for dramatic effect, 'when carelessly handled, breed confusion. Confusion breeds division. This very tower is testament to that; the country's singular landmark, recognised across this planet as a beacon of Britishness.'

Albright raised a finger, a little drunkenly, as though struck by a unique thought.

92

'A timepiece, no less, that once spoke to the heart of a nation's industrious outlook, yet through lazy mismanagement of information, was allowed to become a paradigm of awkward dinner conversations with smug gits leaning forward and saying things like *"I think you'll find that's the name of the bell, actually"*. And what does that lead to? Embarrassed hosts and a future of passive-aggressive friendships that simmer with unspoken hatred for one another.'

He allowed his excellent point to hang in the air for a moment. Apple Blossom cocked her head at him, then licked her lips when she noticed his hand resting inside the pocket which had once contained the biscuits.

'Hatred is antithesis of our goals. It is a disease that will see the end of all of us if we don't take care. Contentment is our bread and butter, and in order to breed contentment among the rabid horde to whom we are unfortunately and inexorably linked, we must offer stability and simplicity.'

She was licking his hand now. Her tongue felt moist and warm on his skin.

'You don't understand a bloody word I'm saying, do you?'

Apple Blossom scooted away for another drink from her bowl. Albright necked his glassful in one, and as the tumbler lowered, he saw that Christine Crawford had returned to the screen, standing next to a superimposed image of a footballer with long dreadlocks. She looked as though she hadn't a care in the world, talking enthusiastically and intelligently on a subject she felt so passionately about.

With the tumbler set on the cabinet at the second attempt, Albright opened the door again and reached into the recess beyond a second, unopened bottle. There he rummaged around the stash of memorabilia he meant to throw out – the framed shirts, the honorary trophies, the autographed balls – until…

Aha!

The photograph had been set into a thick wooden frame with a gilt edge. Albright felt the weight of it in his hands and tutted at his younger self for being so sentimental. There he stood with Christine Crawford in the centre of the pitch, the cane under his hand, Apple Blossom at his feet and the women's team in their bright blue kits flanking them on either side in two neat lines. It had taken seventeen attempts to get the damn dog to look at the camera, but still Albright's smile was full of warmth and sincerity. What an actor he was. But then, he'd had plenty to be happy about.

A year ago the women's SyBall World Cup had proved an excellent test event of the ship's technical systems in preparation for Sunday's Harvest, as well as an opportunity to gauge the extent of the world's footballing mania. Work had still needed to be done, but the results were promising. The photo had been taken inside the BK Stadium a week before the opening match, but even then, he had been precise with his adjustments and already knew exactly what was going to happen. Crawford's team had torn their group stage opponents apart and then been paired with Iceland in the first knockout game. An early penalty had given British Kingdom the lead, but they were then 'stunned' by two lazy goals minutes afterwards and never recovered.

Albright chuckled at the memory.

'Am I ready, Apple Blossom?'

He lifted his cane and peered at the distorted figures on the screen through the colours of its handle.

'Of course, I'm bloody ready!'

The luxurious warmth of the brandy had now spread evenly throughout his body. Feeling satisfied and secure, the Prime Minister drifted off to sleep with the television still on.

'7

George & Derrick

Josh woke with his head still pounding. It was a headache in the fullest and truest sense of the word, unlike anything he'd felt before; a nauseating throb that journeyed up from his forehead, across and over his cranium, around past his temples and beneath his eyes to the point of greatest intensity in the dead centre of his face. His nose was inexplicably sore and heavy and tender to the touch, and whenever he looked down, he could see the raw mass of tissue that hadn't been there before.

The harsh light of the room wasn't helping matters either. The strobe lighting beat down on him like two iron weights resting on his eyebrows, reflecting unwelcomely off the white walls and the white ceiling and the white cotton sheets covering his legs.

Without looking, he fumbled around until he located the small plastic button at the end of a long cable, which snaked along his covers and off the edge of his bed. He pressed it and at once the machine next to him whirred into life. Josh felt the warmth of pain relief course through him.

If he didn't know any better, then he might have suspected that Lexa had actually succeeded in killing him last night, clocking off his meaningless existence early, and he had now entered into an endless white expanse. But as the pain continued to ease, he could recall more clearly being given the button by a nurse, and not an angel. The feathered wings cushioning his back were a pair of propped-up pillows and the angelic robe wrapped around his bare skin was nothing more than a hospital gown of unremarkable cotton.

There were other clues too; the beeps and the boops of the observation monitors, the soft shuffle of the nurses' plimsolls along the floor, the swish and swoosh of sky-blue curtains, like the one around his own bed, being constantly opened and closed, and the combined odour of filter coffee and disinfectant wafting through the air. As he took in his sterile surroundings, Josh at last became aware of the two hazy lumps either side of him, and could now feel the cold hand resting on top of his own.

'Mum, is that you?' he croaked.

'There, there, now,' she said softly, 'Just relax. You've been asleep for almost three hours now.'

Josh saw their faces as they came into focus; his mother forcing the smile, his father glum and anxious, sitting slumped with his forearms resting on the bed and his hands clasped, as though he were about to either address a committee or start praying.

'I had a horrible nightmare,' Josh said as he tried to sit up, struggling with the heft of his own body. 'Dreamed I was in the garden, when I was little, but then I got lost, and...' The pain was casting shadows over his memory. He shook his head. 'It was terrible.'

'Well, you're safe and sound on the ward now, sweetheart. How are you feeling?'

Like I've been punched in the face.

'Better than earlier.'

'Good. Take it slowly, though, won't you?'

A sharp twinge shot across his chest.

'I will, Mum, I promise.'

Frank sneered. 'For God's sake, it ain't like he's going anywhere, is it?'

It was remarkable to witness how quickly Caroline could shoot her husband down with the filthiest look Josh had ever seen in his life, and then retract it just as fast when she saw the group of five or six people approach the foot of his bed. Among them, a short, blonde nurse in a sister's uniform grinned as though she were about to congratulate him for something. Next to her, a couple of students with stethoscopes around their necks took the folder hanging off the end of the bed and huddled over the paperwork with great interest, occasionally flicking their eyes up towards him.

At the head of this group was a tall, clean-shaven doctor with a salesman's smile. He wore a salmon pink shirt with sleeves rolled up to the elbows and was resting his fists on the nape of his thighs. A cape and a leotard and he might have been the leader of a league of superheroes.

'So then, Mr Pittman,' the doctor began. His voice was charming and assured and unnecessarily loud, as though he were about to announce his candidacy for political office to the entire hospital. 'Feeling better this afternoon, I hope?'

Caroline dived in before Josh could answer. 'He keeps falling asleep, doctor, that was the third time today. And now he says he's having nightmares. I think he's given himself too much.'

The doctor raised a hand in front of her. 'Don't be alarmed, Mrs. Pittman, that is quite normal. Your son is on a strong anti-inflammatory, he's bound to be a little drowsy, but I promise you there is no chance of overdose.' He then turned and said 'Fiona, check the pump, would you?'

'Yes, doctor.'

The sister, still beaming, stepped forward and took the button from Josh's hand and wrapped the cable around a hook below the machine as she inspected its settings. She caught him looking and winked.

The doctor went on. 'Now then, I've been monitoring your progress throughout the day, and all in all I'd say you've been a very lucky boy.'

Josh didn't feel particularly lucky.

'The CT scan revealed no signs of concussion, compression on the brain or any internal bleeding. Heart healthy, lungs healthy, normal brain function, which in short means what we see is what we've got.'

Caroline rubbed the tops of Josh's fingers. Behind her, Frank nodded gently to himself and mumbled 'That's great, that's great' so quietly Josh struggled to hear it.

'Now let's see...'

The doctor took the folder from the curious students and consulted the notes, clicking his tongue and then whispering into the sister's ear. Josh noticed how Fiona's face changed, the smile shifting from her professional bedside manner to something more mischievous. She bit her lip, said 'Yes, doctor,' and then left.

'Broken nose,' the doctor resumed. 'A bit wonky. We'll speak to our friends down in rhinoplasty about having it reset at some point down the line. Swelling's too big to do anything now.' He sighed as if the rest were boring: 'Lacerations to the lip, cheek and palm of the hand. All superficial, all will heal. Compound bruising to the wrist, again the hand, two beautiful shiners around both eyes, top of the forehead –'

'He already had that one', Frank chipped in, helpfully.

'– and on your chest.' The doctor closed the folder and placed it back inside the metal cubby. 'What's it like to breathe?'

'Hurts a little.'

'Hmm, yes, it will do for a day or two. Those intercostal muscles are probably a little tender, but really, your assailant could have done a lot worse.'

Assailant.

It was the first time the subject of Lexa had really come up since he'd arrived in hospital. He objected to the term. She wasn't a thug; she had done a thuggish thing, but there had clearly been a reason.

His mother naturally opened the questioning. 'Do you remember anything at all, sweetheart?'

'No, not much.'

'Did you get a good look at his face, at least?'

Josh paused. He might have let the error slide if he thought there were anything to be ashamed about.

'*Her* face, Mum.'

She lowered her head and whispered, 'Oh yes, I forgot.'

Frank shook his head, his cheeks flushing with embarrassment.

'And no, I didn't. It was too dark.'

It was an insufficient lie, but as he watched his father turn to face the curtain, it was satisfying, nonetheless. Plenty of people had seen Lexa with him at the brightly lit bar, and many – not least Mick the landlord – could easily have given the police a description of her. But now, at least, he felt in control of the situation. And besides, they'd been alone in the darkened car park; just because Josh had spoken to a girl *inside* doesn't mean it was the same girl who assaulted him *outside*.

Or something.

He'd figure out the detail later, when his head wasn't thumping.

'Well, the police want to talk to you,' Caroline said. 'They want you to make a statement. Do you feel up to it?'

The doctor intervened. 'I think we should hold off just for the moment, Mrs. Pittman. Let's keep him one more night and then see where we are.'

Josh had to be grateful. He'd quietly planned to evade the police for as long as possible, and it seemed as though the young doctor was about to provide him with a postponement, if not an excuse.

'Your son's been through quite a traumatic experience and it's going to take some time for him to process his thoughts. He'll be better equipped to deal with what's happened once he's out of the ward environment.' He smiled a silky smile. 'I understand you're a goalkeeper, Mr Pittman?'

Josh nodded reluctantly.

'Terrific stuff. Well, get plenty of rest and we'll have you back between the sticks in no time.'

Great.

The doctor patted Josh on his shin, either knowing or guessing the area was injury free. He leant casually towards Frank and said with a wink: 'I play centre-midfield at the weekend.'

Frank pulled an expression which successfully conveyed his feeling that in any other situation, he would have been impressed.

Everything changed after 8pm. The six-hour visiting period ended, the day nurses went from bed-to-bed on handover to the night shift, and the patients' dinner plates were cleared away. He hadn't felt much like eating, but still had ordered a chicken curry from the limited menu – a mild, soggy korma of tiny meat pieces and congealed brown rice. Josh ate less than half before moving onto the carton of orange juice and the pot of red jelly.

There was still plenty of motion and activity; the catering staff who had brought him his meal came again with cups of tea and biscuits; the nurses popped in to change bags of fluid on the intravenous lines, and their station out in the corridor was a hive of phone-calls and endless paperwork. But most of the doctors had left and the decisive noise of the day was replaced by the general chit-chat of the early evening. The whole emphasis of the ward had shifted from treatment of injuries to the comfort of guests.

Josh found it strangely cosy. His bed was positioned by the window at the far end of a room branching off the ward's central corridor, and with the changing of the day outside closer than the hustle and bustle inside, he felt comfortable occupying the middle ground in the kind of secluded bubble he generally preferred.

Patients in the other three beds had come and gone throughout the day, and by the time the sun had set Josh was bunking with two other young men, both fresh out of surgery. Scott Baker, on his right, was a strapping, stubbled firefighter, who'd just returned from a year out spent travelling the globe in search of the most extreme thrills the human body could endure, and had been preparing for his return to work by doing keepie-uppies on the summit of the North Downs, only to slip, fall and land face-down on a cluster of rocks. Having been airlifted to the hospital with his femoral artery crushed, Scott had awoken from the operation as though he'd slept on a bed of feathers and spent the evening happily reading a thriller novel entitled *The Defender* (a disgraced former ACA agent tries to put his chequered past behind him and start a new life as a centre-back).

Opposite Scott was Brian Kelly, himself a paramedic, barely out of his teens, who that morning had broken 'the third, the fourth, the fifth metatarsals' in his foot right outside the hospital's A&E unit; a full oxygen cylinder had tumbled out the back of the ambulance when he and his colleague pulled out the gurney with a little too much gusto.

While they seemed nice enough, sharing the room with the pair left Josh with that familiar sunken feeling he got whenever he was with Belmont Park Rovers, surrounded by real men. He couldn't have cared less what his father thought, but in front of these strangers, Josh felt the first rumblings of wounded pride at being hospitalised by a girl.

Luckily, Brian's fondness for talking (mostly about other injuries sustained throughout his life that he had either ignored or treated himself) had spared Josh the chance to tell his story. The pair didn't even know his name until the nurse who'd popped in to change the dressing on his nose asked if he were looking forward to going home.

'Josh,' Brian mused. 'What's that short for?'

There was no way out of this now.

'Joshua,' said Josh.

Brian considered the name for a moment, rolling it around his tongue and saying it out loud in a variety of annunciations.

'Joshua... Joh-shu-ah... Josh-u-ah...'

The childish parroting reminded him of his school days and how older kids felt the need to weigh up his name as though it required their approval.

'Hehe! Josh-You-Are!' Brian chortled and began jabbing a finger in Josh's direction. '*Josh-you-are, Josh-you-are!*'

Trapped by his injuries and unable to hide, Josh tried to filter the noise of Brian's voice as best he could.

Maybe I ought to reveal my surname... couldn't be worse than this.

Scott lifted his eyes from the book and confirmed his appreciation of the joke with a grin. Catching this, Josh smiled in return and nodded in time to the air pokes, the pain in his head rising again. Weak attempts at ending conversations by feigning amusement had been the order of the day at school; there was no reason not to try it here.

'Heh, yeah,' Josh mumbled, 'it's why I don't use it. I always think it sounds a bit like Yoda.' And then, going for broke, he offered his best worst impression. *'Mmm... Josh, you are!'*

Brian broke off mid-chant and his face went blank. 'Who?'

Mission accomplished.

An hour later and Josh still couldn't settle. The ease of sleep that had washed over him periodically throughout the day was gone, and in the relative quiet of the early night he found himself staring up at the darkened squares of the paneled ceiling. His whole face ached, and an aggravating itch had developed under the latest round of dressing on his nose; his gown was baggy and misshapen and kept exposing parts of his body to the whole ward. He didn't like the feel of his bare buttocks on the sheet below him and he wondered where his clothes had disappeared to. Either the police had bagged them as evidence or, far more likely, Caroline had taken them home to wash.

Already he was bored; bored of the hospital, bored of the pain and bored of Brian's prattling, now an incessant and incoherent whine in the background, like a bee no one could be bothered to catch. He reached up with his strongest hand and pulled down his personal television set, mounted to the wall by a long arm which craned over his bed. Josh tapped the screen and groaned when he saw the only free channel was the SyBall App live stream. But it was better than nothing.

Today was Friday, the last of a two-day break between the second semi-final and the third-place play-off between Brazil and Argentina the following evening. It was the first real gulf in live action for weeks, and people had acted as though they were being asked to live underwater for two days, with the only bubbles of air provided by the SyBall App's endless match reruns, previews and breaking news-style reports.

Josh had tuned in around halfway through a repeat of the press conference held earlier that day between the managers of the final two teams.

George Castle was as familiar as anyone in the British Kingdom's national squad or its government; full-faced and round-bellied, but possessing neither a beard nor a sense of humour, he had once been described by the press as the 'Tweedle-Glum to the Prime Minister's Tweedle-Glee' – brash, grumpy, outspoken, decidedly old-school, and seemingly the only person in the country allowed to be any of those things. Even now he was sitting with his arms folded in front of the cameras, listening with old-fashioned disdain to his opponent's impassioned appraisal of North America's journey to the Final as though he'd just been served a plateful of foreign muck.

Derrick Zeus, on the other hand, was a far more emotional character. Springy and buoyant, with a shock of grey-black hair and wrinkle lines around his face from a lifetime of smiling, Zeus never spoke about his tactics or style of play or team selection in front of the cameras; instead, he would ramble on about the boundless pride he felt coaching his 'home continent' and how humbled he was by the team's success in the tournament. Josh often wondered if Derrick Zeus actually knew anything about football, and whether, in fact, the reason his team was playing so well was because they knew how much it would break his heart if they didn't.

The picture cut to a close-up of the tall woman sat between them. Temperance Newhart. The prim and self-satisfied Secretary of State for Footballing Activities was on full display with her public relations smile and careful nods at the important points in Derrick Zeus' speech, her straight back and her accessorised outfit that was all business and all style, the perfect blend of confidence and control. Though today Josh did note one chink in her armour – her hair, the usually immaculately coiffed perm, was looking a little disheveled.

Josh switched off the screen with Derrick and Brian both in full flow. The latter was halfway through a story about the time he'd ridden on his neighbour's quad bike and was such a natural the neighbour couldn't believe he'd never been on one before; a tale peppered with so much detail that during its course Josh came to the horrifying realisation that Brian too lived on the Belmont Park Estate.

He briefly considered calling Brian out on his alleged exploits with the local football team, given that Josh was the current first-team goalkeeper and had never met Brian before in his life, but decided instead the best thing to do was to say absolutely nothing until the moment he was discharged and then promptly persuade his parents to sell the house.

Scott slammed his book shut, his tolerance for the jabbering having reached its limit.

'Shall we play a game?'

Josh groaned in his head, but as the patient with the greatest mobility, he soon revelled in his usefulness as the one to place the wastepaper bin in the middle of the floor and then retrieve and distribute the balls of rolled up tissue after each round. Each player sat upright in bed as they threw, Josh's cautious arcs landing clear of the target every time, Scott's strongarm flicks spinning inside the bin as they landed and Brian's casual, yet accurate, lobs piling up and sending him into a shock early lead. It was a small mercy, for when he did miss, there was usually some technical excuse along the lines of:

'Problem is with the foot, I can't grip into the mattress, so I can't get the right leverage on the throw.'

The lead proved unassailable, however, and it was almost funny – sweet, even – to see how a genuine achievement had such a humbling effect on Brian. No need to elaborate when the triumph spoke for itself, and in thinking back over the evening Josh realised the paramedic had never once spoken about the people he helped, the daily victories that were clearly too personal to talk about.

After the game, conversation between the three relaxed and evolved into easy-going chatter on subjects ranging from the last time anyone played basketball to who would win the Golden Boot (Emmett Baines, Josh's choice, was apparently the wrong answer). As they chatted, Scott fashioned a trophy for Brian out of a paper coffee cup, some plastic spoons and the lid of a jelly pot.

Josh carried the cup from one man to the other and began the applause. Though he'd lost the game, for once it didn't matter; instead, he was laughing and embracing the company of men his age for the first time in his life. He couldn't imagine a friendship with either of them outside these walls, but the hospital environment introduced handicaps that upset the usual pecking order. It was also taking his mind away from the pain in his face and from any lingering thoughts of the girl.

Yet once the game was over and Brian and Scott were both sound asleep, the pain resurfaced and the image of Lexa in those final moments in the car park returned to haunt him.

She hadn't wanted to do it. Given the choice she would have backed out. At the bar Lexa had looked panicked, scared even, by the sight of him and the water she'd ordered went down like a soldier necking a shot of rum before going over the top.

Their conversation in the car park, to Josh at least, had seemed genuine, if a little one-sided. He had talked and responded to questions about himself, but had asked her practically nothing in return.

He really was terrible at dates.

But then something must have struck a chord; why else would she carry on a conversation if not to stall herself? And then, immediately before the attack, there'd been that moment of reluctance and a regretful plea to take it out her hands:

'So, you're not going to give up? Are you sure? Final chance, Josh.'

Lexa had wanted him to walk away from Belmont Park Rovers to spare them both the pain, but once the first hit landed, she was committed and determined to keep going.

Was this really about *football?*

Josh grimaced in the dark of the room. Nothing about it made sense. His sisters had denied any involvement, so she must have sought him out herself. She knew his name, but not much else, and yet it was obvious that she had targeted him specifically for an attack. The next match was against Hurley Athletic, three places behind Rovers in the league. Could Josh really believe that an amateur village team would consider taking a hit out on the division's worst goalkeeper, then go and hire a contrite professional who gets to know him first before beating him half to death and stealing his watch?

At last the tiredness washed over him and the repetitive rhythm of beeps and twangs from the observance monitors filled the deep recesses of his mind, mixing surreally with his eager need to see Lexa again, before sending him slowly into a light, dreamless sleep.

'8

Casey

'I need to get some coffee. 'Scuse me.'

Jaitley leant precariously over the back of his chair and pointed. 'Just there in the corner.'

'No, I'll try the machine. Thank you.'

Special Agent Jen Casey, of the American Crime Agency, Washington, DC, nodded her thanks and headed out the door. Once out of sight, she let out an exasperated sigh and headed down the corridor. When first told of the 'machine' out front, she had hoped for some sort of barista machine perched on the desk sergeant's counter; but on entering the foyer, as she did again now, Casey had grimly discovered the sepia-coloured vending machine positioned near the station entrance. Another addition to the day's long list of disappointments – and this one she had to pay for.

Rooting through her loose change, she tried to pick out the correct coins, studying each one back and front. It was her third day in London, and still she couldn't get used to the money. How could anyone? The sizes weren't proportionate to the value. They were British, and therefore deliberately confusing.

Casey pushed a couple of coins through the slot and selected a double-shot Americano, the name fondly reminding her of home. The vending machine whirred unconvincingly as two streams of white and brown liquid spluttered into the little plastic cup that had dropped onto the dispensing tray.

It tasted disgusting.

Exactly what she imagined hot brown river water would taste like. Back home, a percolator would be switched on in the office at the start of the day and constantly topped up until nightfall. The ground coffee inside might be a sweet Colombian or a smooth Kenyan, but whatever the flavour, there was always a fresh pitcher of cold cream to top it off. This place, however, in supposedly the birthplace of civilisation, took the same idea and de-evolved it, providing only a small kettle, a jar of instant granules and a round tin overflowing with tea bags in a variety of shapes.

It would have been better than nothing, but without proven ownership of a 'mug', even these luxuries were contraband. In her house, an ocean away, there were plenty of flasks and reusable cups good enough for the job, and she would have given anything to drop by over lunch, grab one from the cupboard, and then on her way back out leave a note for Mike and the boys telling them she'd be home for dinner.

Instead, all she had was the vending machine. Still, if the scalding filth in her hand contained any shred of caffeine, it might just be enough to get her through the day.

The smell of her drink was also a welcome distraction from the dim reception's stagnant odour that she couldn't decide was either melted chocolate or sweaty feet. Above her a strobe light flickered and hissed, while a noisy and ineffective air conditioner hummed and rotated in irregular rhythm next to a dying bamboo palm. The empty lounge chairs were torn and annoyingly non-uniform and the linoleum floor was streaked with various marks of indeterminate colours. The whole place was in need of a thorough sprucing up.

Scratch that – what it actually needed was tearing down and starting again. And that included the workforce.

As Casey sipped and grimaced at the heat, she looked over at the two uniformed police officers on the other side of the wire-glass service hatch. One edge of their small television monitor was just visible, attached to the wall on an extendable bracket; the screen usually displayed the CCTV feeds – but nothing about the deserted parking lot or the vacant holding cells could have excited them this much.

'Go on, fella!' shouted one of them, a stocky moron barely out of high school.

'That's it, round you go!' exclaimed the second, the higher ranked of the two, with scraggly hair and a goatee. 'Pass it, pass it, and again…'

'Here it comes, here it comes…'

The pair leant forward in unison, their eyes wide with expectation. The moment of silence ended with their cheers, accompanied by the faint sound of thousands of other people doing exactly the same thing.

'Oh my God, oh my God,' said the moron. 'I could watch that all day!'

'Switch over to SyBall, semi-final's on repeat.'

Happily obeying his order, the first officer reached up to change the channel, and, as he did, briefly caught Casey's eye. She kept watching them, and in desperate need of a sweetener, found herself willing the young men to invite her over and join them.

'*Soccer?*' she would finally have the opportunity to say. '*You want me to watch soccer with you?*

'*Let me tell you guys something. The major themes in my household are law, order and sports. My sons are in Little League. My husband was a wide receiver for his college football team – real football, I mean. Now he's a DA. I played basketball in high school and coached the Academy team before my last promotion.*

'*Those are sports. Soccer is not a sport.*

'*It's a disease; spreading across the planet from the furthest reaches of Outer Nowheresville, right past this counter and straight into my goddamn living room. Even my own family have been suckered in.*

'*Does that scare me? Sure as hell does, but that ain't nothing new. I've been scared to death since my first day on the job. The only difference is now I don't have the first damn clue what it is I am meant to be afraid of.*

'*So thanks for the offer, but no, I'm not gonna watch the game with you. Your coffee goes down better than that crap. I'm gonna finish my cup and go back to work. How about you boys do the same?*

But the offer never came, and the words went unsaid. And so, Casey stood alone in the reception, questioning her place in a world that had left her behind, exhausted by the weight of the investigation that had consumed her life.

Nonetheless, she would carry on. The five deaths bearing the hallmarks of the case that had brought her to this country gave Casey little other option. Perseverance was draining, but that was what coffee was for. She crushed the empty cup in her fist, revelling in the satisfying crunch of the plastic, and tossed it into the trash can. Walking back towards the CID room, she mustered the depths of her resolve to give Jaitley one last try.

'Vik', she said, twitching at the discomfort of using his first name, 'I'm sorry I yelled, alright? I just... I just got a little worked up.'

It might have been the first time in her career she'd apologised to a junior officer, but she was willing to try anything to get this guy on the same page.

Detective Sergeant Vikram Jaitley, a short, scruffy-haired man with sweat patches seeping through his flannel shirt, looked up from his desk with a pencil in his mouth and stared blankly.

'Um... no problem,' he mumbled. 'I didn't realise you had, sorry. What were we talking about again?'

'The suspect.'

'Ah, yes!' Jaitley proudly held up his drawing, on the back of an accident report form, like a school kid showing his teacher. 'I think from what the witnesses say, it looks like this!'

Casey bit her tongue so hard she could taste blood.

'Yes, thank you, I know what a fedora looks like. What about the guy *in* the fedora? Did the witnesses in the park give any sort of description? Colour, age, fat, thin, tall, short. Something we can use?'

'Yes, of course, uhm...' Jaitley fumbled around on his desk for papers they both knew didn't exist. 'No. They didn't provide anything.'

'None of them?'

'No.'

The room suddenly felt unbearably hot. Sunlight had been streaming in through the wide sash windows for much of the afternoon, split into thin shafts by the Venetian blinds and visible through the dust. The other detectives and Casey's own team of field agents milled around the room, lost in their own idle activities, doing everything possible to disassociate themselves from the conversation. Casey envied them.

'Detective Jaitley,' she said slowly, 'I'm looking directly at you right now, but in my peripheral vision I can see Agent Martinez resting on the sideboard, watching replays on his phone, while across the room DC Longford is stirring a giant spoonful of sugar into her cup as Agent Cobb figures out the best way to ask her on a date.'

Agent Cobb smirked; Casey had clearly sealed the deal for him, the jackass.

'If I can notice all this, then surely one person – just one single person – in a park full of people would notice some hobo wandering around dressed like a mobster.'

Jaitley raised an optimistic finger. 'Well, yes, they do all confirm he was there, at least. Except for two of them. Two aren't sure. One said he thought he dreamt it.'

Casey sighed. 'Okay fine,' she said, 'forget the park. What about the woman in the apartment? She saw him too, didn't she? Helen...?'

'Minett!' Jaitley said. 'Yes, she did! Her statement's on file, wait one sec...'

Jaitley switched seats to a desk against the far wall, on which sat the kind of computer Casey hadn't seen used since the early nineties; heavy, beige, with a floppy disc drive and a chunky keyboard. Jaitley selected the sound file and fiddled with the volume control until at the last the scratchy recording flowed into the room:

'...out jogging... saw him... looked lovely with that hat, he did, like a matinee idol... colour? Ooh, hazel brown I think... my eyes are hazel, have a look... really suited him though. Mysterious... but exciting. Must have been sweltering, though... looked ever so poorly, like he were about to keel over... his legs were wobbling... couldn't see his face. Thought maybe he had a little drink or two... nearly invited him in for a juice. Just to be friendly, you know... I were a bit sweaty meself... strangest thing though, not ten, fifteen minutes later... I were in the bedroom, just changed, and I looked out the window and there he were again! Right as rain! Walking with a spring in his step... Where'd he go? Ooh, I don't know, love, sorry...'

In the remaining seven seconds of the clip, wherein the first of a hundred more helpful questions might have been posed, the interviewing officer thanked Helen Minett for her time, asked what flavour the juice was and then remembered the tape was still recording.

'Bit suspicious if you ask me,' said Jaitley.

'Suspicious, how? Story's consistent with what we know of the suspect.'

Casey was intrigued; was the young detective about to offer some shrewd insight into the case?

Jaitley shook his head. 'Nah, not him – *her*.'

'Oh.' The hope faded slightly. 'She saw him twice, I guess; what, you think that's too much of a coincidence?'

'Huh?'

There was that screwed up face again, already a common feature of their brief relationship, whenever Jaitley hadn't the first clue what Casey was talking about.

'No, not that,' he said. 'I mean, she said she was out jogging. *During the match?* Doesn't seem right. Argentina against North America, and she wasn't even watching!'

Casey eyed Jaitley disconcertingly. 'Is she *from* North America?'

'No...'

'Argentina?'

'No, Warrington,' Jaitley said, peering at the notes along the bottom of the screen.

Casey opened her mouth and closed it again. She was almost too scared to ask.

'So, what's the problem?'

'It was the semi-final!' cried Jaitley. 'And we were playing the winner! I mean, come on!'

Casey thumped the palm of her hand on the table; there were all sorts of things she could shout right now, but none of them would help. The best thing would be not to look at him – at any of them.

She walked over to the maps on the other side of the room; one of Greater London, one of the British Kingdom, and a third belonging to Casey herself, crumpled, creased and covered with labels, post-it notes, press cuttings and crime-scene photographs. Casey had lifted the continental map of North America from her own desk and brought it on the plane with her. Now it was stuck to a white-board resting against a window-pane.

'What is it with this guy?' she muttered.

The lack of progress could hardly be attributed to the inefficacy of this crumbling suburban outpost and its feckless staff. The Fedora had spent the last few years travelling the globe, leaving in his wake a trail of lives left helplessly short, the life sucked out of them as they cheered and celebrated their teams' victories, their faces contorted into grotesque smiles. No motive, no cause. With each new victim, it felt evermore as though they were mocking her, questioning her suitability to take on their case.

And all there was to go on was him. A character straight out of a film noir, hiding in the shadows. Conspicuous in a crowd yet hidden from sight, the memory of him filtered from the mind of the beholder within seconds of passing by.

There was, however, the occasional picture. Security footage of a hot dog stand outside an Arizona stadium as a young couple sitting in the back row fail to stand and leave at the end of a championship game. A selfie taken by a father and son following the Midlands derby; later, three brothers on a bachelor party were found lying on the men's room floor inside the stadium. Their deaths were attributed to alcohol poisoning, though Casey had read the coroner's report which noted that the youngest was effectively teetotal due to long-term medication. How many other British cases had been misreported like this? Add to these the motion shots and background blurs from across the world piled high on her desk. The images had been sharpened and scrutinised with the best equipment the ACA had to offer, but still it was the same: an upturned collar, a fedora on top and a shadow underneath.

They were chasing a ghost.

'Maybe it's more than one person,' said Jaitley. 'I mean, he's gone all over the world, but never cropped up at customs. Could have accomplices in every country.'

'Great, so it's a whole team, now?'

She was being unfair. It wasn't a bad point; in fact, it was one she routinely considered. An underground network. A conspiracy. But a conspiracy to do what? How would ending all these disparate lives be of any use to anyone? Besides, it didn't matter how many there were; if she could get her hands on just one, it would be start.

Agent Casey sat on the edge of the table once again and let out a deep, weary sigh. She was so tired her eyes ached. Rubbing around them, she remembered the names:

Matthew Blaumann
Eric Carmichael
Miguel Narvaez
Claudia Simmons

'I need to go home,' she whispered.

The memory floated of that last evening before she left, sitting out with Mike in the back yard of their town house off Wisconsin Avenue. The day was sweltering, and the smell of cherry blossom hung in the air, wafting over from the gentle parade of trees along the National Mall. From under the canopy of their swing seat, Casey had watched the boys goofing around in the pool, splashing and laughing without a care for the complexities and trauma of the world.

'Don't forget to take lots of pictures,' Mike had told her.

'I won't have time for sightseeing. Hoping I'll be back by Monday.'

'Whose team are you taking? Jack, stop that!'

Casey remembered the sheepish look on her eldest child's face, silently pleading his innocence on the charge of dunking his brother's head below the surface.

'John Cobb, Tom O'Reilly.'

'Two teams? A little much, isn't it?'

As a public prosecutor, Mike was always well versed on the use of excessive force.

'I can't explain it,' she'd replied. 'but there's something not right. This tournament they got over there; feels to me like this whole thing's gonna come to a head, and I just don't know what to expect. And like I said, I want to be home on Monday.'

Casey felt again the warmth and sweetness of that day, his arm around her. It was comfort like no other. She would call them later tonight; Mike would be getting dinner ready for the boys, so it'd be chaos as usual, but it would be enough to hear their voices.

'Don't worry, you'll figure it out.'

Jaitley's chirpy interruption was like a light being flicked on during a candle-lit dinner.

'How about I make us all a drink? You can borrow one of mine.'

In her periphery Casey saw a chipped earthenware cup being brought towards her against a background of sudden activity. Chairs scraped, feet shuffled, and spoons tinkled, and in the midst of it all Casey made out the heavy click of the kettle being fired up and felt her temper boil instantly. Before she knew what had happened the mug was flying through the air, hitting the wall high up and crumbling to the floor in half a dozen shattered pieces. The scraping, shuffling and tinkling ceased at once.

'*What the hell is wrong with you people?*' she blared, shaking with fury. Slowly she began to walk among them, circling the group like a wild cat. '*Four kids!*' Her voice was deep and resonant when she screamed like this, almost too painful to maintain. 'Do you hear me? Four, lost on *your* watch, and you don't know the first thing about it!'

Jaitley glanced surreptitiously at his wristwatch.

'And yet all you guys wanna do is just...'

Casey broke herself off as she passed the refreshment counter. Stuck on the cupboard beside the whistling kettle was the office's large glossy wall chart for the SyBall World Cup. Within ten minutes of her arrival at the station, Casey had been invited to pick out one of the few remaining teams left in the biscuit tin and join the sweepstake. She'd respectfully declined and urged the field agents to do the same, but at least half their names were now up there. Casey surveyed the group, catching their eyes one by one.

'Joy and Compassion,' she snarled quietly. 'What a croc of shit. Where's the compassion for your victims, huh?'

If that had even the slightest impact, Casey would never know. They all stood, stony-faced, resisting the temptation to stare at the pile of shrapnel on the carpet.

'I'll pay for the cup, Vik.'

Jaitley smiled awkwardly. 'Ah, don't worry, it was an old one. Do you want to borrow another?'

Casey's heart sunk. What was the point of doing anything anymore? She took hold of the door handle.

'No. I... I prefer the machine,' she said.

Back out in reception, the scene had altered. The CCTV was back, the goateed officer was gone and his stocky subordinate had been drawn into doing some actual work; filing papers into pigeonholes under the watchful eye of Margaret Millington, the desk sergeant, who was about the only member of the constabulary Casey had any admiration for.

As matriarch of the foyer for as long as anyone could remember, Margaret was like a wisened old gatekeeper, maintaining strict authority and control over the flow of people in and out of the station. She liked to cut down the young ones with her icy tongue and knowing asides, and shared Casey's own talent for filtering out the nonsense and seeing the single point of truth in a cluster of lies and misdirection. Her uniform was crisp and the tightly bound bun of brown-grey hair complimented her sharp thin eyes to top off the impression of the stern disciplinarian.

Casey liked her for all these reasons and more. Her first words to her on the morning of day one were simply 'So, you're the Yank?' and there had been little else since – including not one single word on the subject of soccer.

There was no acknowledgement today either. Margaret was too busy dealing with the young guy hunched over the desk in front of her, his pen hovering over the sign-out sheet.

'There, please,' she told him impatiently.

The kid scribbled his name, dropped the pen and rose to his full height, revealing the extent of the injuries to his face; the cuts and bruises and red raw skin spreading out from beneath he thick bandage across his nose below a pair of puffy black eyes.

Margaret nodded and pointed to the door.

'Thank you,' he mumbled, but she was no longer interested.

The boy turned and walked across the foyer to the entrance. His hands and wrists were in as bad a state as his face, covered with scrapes and grazes. In the relatively small space, with no other people around, the awkward smile he gave Casey as he passed was inevitable.

The Special Agent responded in kind, raising her cup and even grinning a little. She was impressed – she didn't think kids these days got into fights anymore.

'9

The Outhouse

A police interview room. A uniformed officer with scraggly hair and a dark goatee sits at a desk opposite a young man with a bandaged nose. The officer writes on a notepad throughout the conversation.

PC BAYLEY: What about hair?

JOSH: I don't know… brown, maybe? But it was dark out, so could have been lighter.

PC BAYLEY: Right. But didn't you meet her inside the pub?

JOSH: Honestly, the whole thing, it's made me a little… fuzzy. I can't really remember.

PC BAYLEY: Nothing at all?

JOSH: Well… she didn't want to do it. That much I remember. Seemed to me like she was acting against her will. I didn't think she was a violent person. Not by nature. We were just talking.

PC BAYLEY: What about?

JOSH: Nothing much. I'm a goalkeeper, of sorts. We talked about that.

PC BAYLEY *(impressed)*: Really? Professional?

JOSH: No. Ninth tier.

PC BAYLEY *(unimpressed)*: Oh. Well, good for you. Anything else stolen other than your car and your watch? Phone? Wallet?

JOSH: No.

PC BAYLEY: Did you have them on you?

JOSH: Yes.

PC BAYLEY: Where?

JOSH: In my pocket.

PC BAYLEY: Your pocket? With your keys?

JOSH (*stutters*): Y-yes.

PC BAYLEY: So, let me get this straight: this girl – who you don't remember the look of – assaults you, takes the watch from your wrist and the keys from your pocket... but *leaves* your phone and wallet behind?

JOSH: I guess...

PC BAYLEY: Any reason she might have done that? Was she disturbed?

JOSH: I... I don't know... like I said, it's –

PC BAYLEY: 'Fuzzy'. Got it.

Silence. Josh squirms in his seat. PC Bayley stares at Josh, then leans back and throws his pen on the notepad.

PC BAYLEY: Fine. Go see Margaret at the desk, she'll sign you out.

***

Josh stood at the corner of the field without any real idea about where to go or what to do next. By now it was mid-afternoon, that time on a summer's day when the sun beat down like a furnace from a cloudless sky and bathed everything in a golden hue, the air warm and sticky. A nauseating haze rippled off the far end of the field and the surrounding rooftops of the Belmont Park estate, the series of picturesque cul-de-sacs and large, comfortable homes straddling the border between London and Surrey, where he'd lived all his life.

The western edge of the estate backed onto the park itself, a wide expanse of fields and woodland pristinely landscaped for civilised enjoyment, replete with a children's playground, picnic area and a 5,000-seat football stadium, the home of the Belmont Park Rovers. The place Josh had first seen Lexa staring at him from her seat in the crowd.

No match today though. The park was quiet. Nearby a young mother and her daughter were enjoying an ice cream in the shade of the branches. Behind them a dog barked, one of those scruffy, white-furred things, goading his owner into throwing the ball as far as possible. Along the edge of the green three young men, bare-chested and bronzed, walked along the path leading from the pond and the Bovill Arms on the other side, kicking a ball to one another.

The heat of the day was making his swollen nose hot and tender, as though it were being barbequed by the sun. His night on the ward had reminded him that Belmont Park had once been the site of an old hospital. A black-and-white photograph on a park noticeboard showed the site from above; one main building at the centre of a maze of smaller conservatories where patients could be exposed to the elements in hope of curing their tuberculosis….

Josh shook his head. He was procrastinating. He needed to get to Lexa before the police did. Apathy had replaced efficiency in modern law enforcement, but still at some point today some officers would have gone to the Bovill Arms and conducted a rudimentary survey of the crime scene. They would also, if they were being thorough, have spoken to old Mick, who probably gave them the description of Lexa that Josh hadn't, and told them she'd asked for him specifically. From that, even the current crop of detectives could presume the attack was premeditated.

She had gone to the trouble of seeking him out and Josh needed to know why. He wanted to give her the chance to explain herself, but was rooted to the spot by the knowledge he was probably wasting his time. Lexa was likely to be long gone. She could have driven his car through the night before anyone even started looking for her. She could be halfway across Europe by now, for all he knew.

Lexa stared at Josh from the driver's seat of his car, sheltered by a small canopy of ash trees on the opposite side of the field. She wondered if her attack had affected his vision. The Nissan was covered by the shadows of the leaves and was a similar kind of green to the hedgerow alongside, but still, a car was a car and she couldn't believe he hadn't seen her.

She had spent the past two nights holed up in one of the old hospital outhouses, which had been enveloped over time by the woodland. In the future the building was still there, a decaying relic of a long-forgotten age, somehow standing when everything else had crumbled into dust. Her father had identified it early on as a good hiding place; abandoned, close to the location of their target and big enough to house the Vessel. The rickety French doors were wide enough to drive through, and while she hadn't planned on keeping the car, a hopeful part of her clung to the idea of ditching the Vessel once it was all over and driving as far away as possible from her life.

But for now, the craft provided warmth and shelter and Lexa was nervous every time she was forced to leave it. Hunger and thirst were nothing new, but she had got to a point that morning where she couldn't hold out any longer. With her hood up and her head low, she had strolled across the green and around the pond to the newsagents a little way down from the Bovill Arms. She had seen the police officers inspecting the tarmac outside, stroking their chins and casting cursory glances over the wall and beneath the parked cars. Although they had gone by the time she'd left the shop with some apples, buns and water *in an actual bottle* stuffed inside her hoodie, Lexa had still felt the need to go a long, circuitous route back through the park, getting lost numerous times and needing to consult local area maps at bus stops.

It was on the way back, as she trudged through the grass with her head still covered, sweltering in the heat, that Lexa had first looked across the green expanse and saw the tiny figure with a little white smudge across his nose entering into the park.

After leaving Josh in a crumpled heap on the ground, Lexa had spent a lot of time chastising herself for holding back. The injuries might have been enough to keep him from playing, but she couldn't be sure. The hospital was too exposed and the wait for his discharge had been frustrating, but now her patience had been rewarded as the opportunity to try again suddenly presented itself.

Josh was about a hundred metres away, edging further onto the field. The way he stood, looking purposefully around at nothing in particular, made it obvious he was looking for her. Lexa shifted into gear and crept along the grass, ignoring the gormless smiles of the bystanders who waved as she drove past. The little green Nissan moved like a wild cat on the hunt, slow at first, eyes never shifting; and then, at the precise moment, she sped up, the stealthy pace accelerating quickly into a gallop.

For all his surveyance, Josh still hadn't noticed his own car racing towards him, but he would have to turn around soon. Turn and run. Give himself a chance to go home and dare not leave until after the match and then everything would be fine. He just needed to look...

Yet with half the distance covered, Josh remained where he was, rooted to the spot, gazing out into the oblivion of the London suburbs.

Lexa screamed. 'Turn around, you idiot!'

The car bumped and jerked the faster she drove; her heart thumped; the adrenaline coursed through her. Lexa had been fixing and driving cars since she was twelve. Her knowledge of the combustion engine had saved her life more times than she cared to remember. She could downshift at speed while racing over an uneven terrain scattered with the debris of twisted metal and human bone. But here, in the safest, most peaceful place she had ever been, Lexa was struggling to keep control. Her fingers clasped tightly around the steering wheel until her knuckles turned white.

'Turn around!'

And then, as though he had heard her voice above the roar of the engine, he did. Josh spun on the spot and stretched out his arms. It was too late to run.

'Lexa! No... stop!'

Lexa opened her eyes, her hands still wrapped around the wheel, and saw up close the damage she had done to Josh's face the night before.

It wasn't that bad.

His nose was puffy but the bandage was clean. Dried blood clumped around the edges of his nostrils could easily be wiped away with a tissue. His hands, laying pointlessly on the bonnet, were red raw and bruised, but he stood as well as he had done when they first met.

Josh was fine and he shouldn't have been. She should have slammed both those hands in the door of the car. She should have crushed his legs with its wheels and been halfway down the road before he had a chance to scream. She should have put him in hospital for weeks and put an end to this whole damn thing.

But she hadn't. Twice now the chance had come and twice Lexa had failed to take it. Nothing had changed. The world was still in danger. Maybe it forever would be, and that was the point she was missing. Yet there he was in front of her, staring with his panda eyes, daring her to put it right. One quick slam of the accelerator and surely it would all be over. Her foot hovered over the pedal and she begged it to take control.

But it didn't. It wouldn't. Somehow Josh, with his heavy breathing and comical injuries, was stopping her from making the logical choice. Lexa turned off the engine, stepped out the door and walked towards him. Josh eyed her all the way and when she lifted her hand to the raw, blistered skin, he flinched.

'Don't...'

Lexa sniffed. Where she came from this was a paper cut. Josh followed her hand as it lowered, then looked to his car and then back to her face.

'Are you trying to kill me?'

She shook her head. 'No.'

'But you want to hurt me?'

'I don't *want* –'

'Then why? What have I done?'

'Nothing,' said Lexa. 'Not yet.'

Josh said nothing more, but she could see confusion supplanting the fear in his face. He believed her even though it didn't make sense to. Perhaps that was a good thing; if he were open to ideas outside of reason then maybe Josh could cope with knowing the truth and he'd be courageous enough to make that choice for himself.

Lexa walked around the car and opened the passenger side door.

'Get in,' she said. 'I want to show you something.'

The journey took less than a minute. Stepping into the passenger seat of his car, Josh was unsure if Lexa had been lying about not wanting to kill him. But by the time they arrived, he was certain.

The outhouse was the perfect tribute to every gruesome horror film his sisters forced him to sit through. Old, abandoned, secluded. The trees above were blocking out the sun, shrouding the area in a musty shadow. Inside he imagined scythes and pickaxes hanging from the rafters; a long metal table with wrist and ankle straps; warnings to future victims written in blood across the wall. Goose pimples rose on his forearms.

This is it, he thought. *This is where I die.*

Lexa stopped the car halfway across the threshold of the rotting French doors. He knew what she was doing – blocking his only way out.

'I didn't tell the police a thing,' he said, 'about what you looked like, or anything like that. But the old guy behind the bar, Mick, might have said something.'

Lexa shrugged. 'That's up to him, isn't it? Doesn't make much difference to me, but thank you all the same.'

Josh shivered. The air was cooler inside than in the open field.

'Do you live here?'

'At the moment, yes,' she said, 'I suppose I do. Come on, get out.'

He didn't move. 'Why can't you tell me now?'

She sighed and leant her head on the steering wheel. 'Because if I told you now, you'd never believe me. I'm giving you a chance. This is the most important thing that will ever happen to you.'

Josh studied her face. Her freckled cheeks seemed to bloom beneath the green reflection of the leaves, accentuating her youth while her large, sunken eyes bore the weight of a lifetime's experience.

'And if I don't?'

'Then I'll drag you out myself and, make no mistake, I *will* run you over.'

Josh closed the door behind him and disturbed a pair of collar doves nesting in the rafters. A shaft of light shone through the gap onto a floor laid with ceramic tiles, mostly intact but covered with mud and leaves. The air felt dry and had a musty, earthen smell, the kind of odour that gave you a headache if you stayed in it too long.

Beyond the light, Josh spied something large hiding in the shadows at the rear of the building. It was round, that much he could tell, and as he took his first step closer the temperature inside the building seemed to rise. It seemed like whatever was ahead were reacting to his presence by radiating out waves of heat, accompanied by a gentle trilling which Josh could feel rather than hear.

Behind him, Lexa reached through the car window and turned on the headlights.

Josh stumbled at the sight.

The machine – if indeed, it *was* a machine – was around twenty feet tall, two thirds as wide and with a top-heavy structure in the shape of an inverted cone, and capped by two semi-circular domes which curved down to a sharp point at its base. The smooth surface was a greenish-brown colour with occasional flecks of orange, reminiscent of faded copper, and had no visible joins except for the array of long, gun-metal grey fins bolted onto the hull, custom-made additions that were aesthetically mismatched.

And, it was floating.

Josh tried to speak, but no words would come. He wanted to run, but couldn't turn away. Fear and wonder were pulling him forward like a moth to a flame. The beauty of it was frightening. Shaking, terrified, but deeply curious, Josh stretched out a hand to lay upon the perfectly formed carapace.

The quickening footsteps echoed around the outhouse.

'No, don't...!'

Lexa intercepted in time, grabbing his arm and pulling it back. Josh blinked, as though snapping out of a trance.

'What's wrong?'

'I should have told you,' she said, 'if you touch it, it'll think you're an intruder.'

He stepped back. Was that what the fins were for? They did look pretty sharp.

'What's it going to do? Punch me in the face?'

Lexa smiled. 'No, but you'll wish it had. Instead, an electro-magnetic pulse will shoot up your arm and down your spinal column. You'll be paralysed and your heart will either stop beating altogether or palpitate so fast the blood rushes to your head and you pass out – or die, depending on your constitution.'

'So… how do you get in?'

The smile was now a smirk. 'For the first time? With the severed hand of the previous owner slammed against the side. From then on it requires DNA coding. A drop of blood into the Core plus some special software to manipulate the gene sequencing so it doesn't treat you as a foreign organism.'

'A foreign organism? Like me?'

'For now.'

'Thanks.'

A look of curiosity passed over Lexa's face; of careful consideration and a weighing up of her options. She let out a heavy breath and wiped a few strands of loose hair from her face and tucked them behind her ear.

'Listen to me,' she said. 'Only a few people in human history will ever do what you're about to do. More people have landed on the

Moon. You will never think or feel the same way ever again. Your whole perspective is about to shift in ways that you cannot possibly begin to fathom.'

Josh shrunk; Lexa's voice had taken on that same belittling tone his dad used when delivering one of his lectures on the rights and wrongs of male adulthood.

'So, can I trust you?'

He scoffed. '*You* trust *me*? Really? You remember that's my car you stole, and I still have your boot print on my chest.'

Lexa sneered at him. 'Can I trust you?'

Josh held onto his answer for as long as he dared. 'Yes.'

For a few seconds she stared at him, searching his defiant face for signs of uncertainty. He tried not to flinch.

'Okay. But you'd better hope you're telling the truth.'

Lexa reached up and laid her palm onto the hull, in the same spot where Josh had nearly placed his. At once the colours of the exterior began to move, forming contours in the shape of her hand and radiating outwards. The browns and greens and oranges swirled, merging and separating, like drops of oil floating in a pool of still water. The movement spread quickly and soon the entire outer shell was a rippling mass of colour, like the storms of some great misshapen gas planet, billowing and undulating restlessly around one another.

A moment later and something new caught Josh's eye: a long streak of ocean blue emerging from within the copper patterns and trickling its way down from the crevice between the two upper domes. About a third of the way from reaching the base, the rivulet stopped briefly and then, inexplicably, began to pour itself out from the shell at an impossible angle, caring nothing for gravity as it expanded and moulded and settled into the unmistakable form of a solid set of steps. Above, the long streak had left behind a thin opening, following its vertical path and beginning now to widen, pushing against the surrounding eddies until it formed a loose rectangular shape.

Just big enough for a person to walk though.

Beyond the opening, there was nothing; or, at least, nothing Josh could see behind the blinding wall of light now illuminating the darkest recesses of the outhouse.

Josh couldn't move. He could hardly breathe. His head spun; there was evidently something real in front of him, yet he couldn't believe in it. A numbing contradiction of his senses that only increased when Lexa walked ahead and casually ascended the first two steps. They remained in place, solid and immovable, taking her weight without any support beneath them.

'Let's go,' she said, beckoning him with her hand.

Josh still couldn't move.

'You're safe now,' Lexa reassured him, 'it knows you're my guest.'

'You want me to go in there... with you?'

'Yes. I mean, break your promise to me after less than a minute if you must, but don't forget that means I'll have to...' She held up her fists as though she were turning a steering wheel, and then shrugged. 'Up to you.'

Josh took the humour as a sign they had made the next step in their brief relationship. A twist of fate had bound them together and so long as he went where she went, then everything would be fine.

His calf muscle trembled as Josh lifted his foot onto the first of the Impossible Stairs, still expecting it to collapse beneath him. Lexa turned and disappeared into the light, leaving only a hazy shadow for him to follow up the remaining stairs and inside. As his eyes adjusted and everything became clear, he heard her voice beside him.

'This... is the Vessel.'

'10

The Vessel

'The Vessel?'

'The Vessel. Yes. What do you think?'

Josh scoffed. 'It's...'

He tried to take it in, but the task was beyond him. The interior chamber seemed larger than the outer shell ought to allow, yet the warmth of the heat trapped within made Josh feel unexpectedly cosy, the perfect kind of temperature for an afternoon nap. The circular walls were milky-white and, upon closer inspection, built of a pale, fleshy material; endless lines of muscle-like tissue overlaid by a thin, translucent membrane. Around his feet a thick blanket of fog covered the floor like a disco smoke machine. It parted gently as Josh took a few timid steps forward.

'Pick some up,' said Lexa.

The invitation caught him off guard. Josh had much rather stand in the middle of the chamber with his hands in his pockets than touch anything at all, but the expression on her face suggested this was part of the trust game they were now playing. His knees were bent and his hand was halfway there before she added:

'Just don't breathe it in.'

Pausing for only a second, Josh tried to look untroubled by the words as he scooped a small heap of perfect white mist into his palm. The feeling against his skin was of nothing. It was like holding air. His anxiety seemed to lift at once and his train of thought meandered to unexpected places. He wondered what his family were doing at this precise moment; his dad out in the garden, perhaps, with a glass of beer, wondering how long he could stop people from finding out his son was beaten up by a girl; his sisters upstairs, texting, scheming, giggling; his mum visiting the elderly neighbour down the road, telling her all about how her son was beaten up by a girl.

If only they could see him now. If only they could sense what it was like to be inside the Vessel and breathe in air so light you might float away like a feather caught on the breeze. He wafted his hand gently from side to side and the little clump of cloud flittered away into the atmosphere.

'Its... incredible,' he managed. 'What is it?'

'I'll show you.'

Lexa had been leaning against the edge of a desk, which, much like the sharp fins clamped to the outside, was made of metal and looked horribly out of place. A wooden three-legged stool stood before it, onto which she now turned and sat down on, her back towards him. As he approached, Josh could hear the sound of a computer processor whirring into life.

Lexa's laptop was silver-grey with a black keypad and had been manufactured by a company he knew. The slimline design suggested it was a relatively new model, but judging by its condition, it had been thrown across the room a few times, smeared with mud and then bandaged up with duct tape and stored in a damp cupboard. It was like a brand-new car that had been taken straight from the showroom to a demolition derby. The homemade metal plinth on which it stood allowed room beneath for the various cables and gizmos and springy bits of wire, which fed to a large transistor battery soldered onto the hinge. The whole thing looked as though it had been retrofitted by a crazed scientist in his attic for some wacky invention, which Josh was beginning to suspect wasn't too far from the truth.

Peering in for a closer look, Josh's attention was grabbed by a spot in the centre of the chamber where a soft glow shone from beneath the fog. The gentle undulations of the cloud swirled around the light. He suddenly pictured himself as an astronaut, looking down at a great storm over the ocean, mesmerised by its power.

'That's the Core,' said Lexa, still typing.

'The Core?'

'You like to repeat things, don't you? It's the engine, I suppose. Remember that sharp bit at the bottom? That's that. Made me gawp like an idiot the first time too.'

Josh tried to chuckle, but there was nothing funny about it. He felt hollow inside; a kind of sickness and yearning mixed together.

'What are you typing?' he asked, looking to distract himself.

'I'm communicating,' she said. 'We can't speak to the Core like they do, so we use this instead. Connects through a reconstituted Wi-Fi.'

'Oh.' Josh couldn't tell if Lexa was purposefully inviting questions with every response, or if he was meant to wait to be told.

'Who's "they"?'

Lexa wagged her finger at him. 'One thing at a time. Explanation is nothing without context. Look at this.'

He moved around and stood at the desk next to Lexa and looked at the screen. It was split in two; on the right, an erratic green line, like a sound wave, with a yellow dot holding firm on a specific point. On the left, a map of tightly condensed streets cut through by a river, with a blue triangle flashing in the centre. Straddling the two windows, a dialogue box displayed the words:

UTS Confirmed.

'This software is incredible,' she said. 'Ten years using a bunch of hard drives salvaged from ruins. Built in underground tunnels and bunkers. Programmers running, fighting, *dying*, as they worked to create something you couldn't even begin to conceive as even remotely possible.' She shrugged. 'And yet, it's so simple. I bet even you could use it.'

Josh frowned. Was that a joke or an insult?

'All you have to remember is location on the left, time on the right. And then off we go.'

Lexa pressed the return key and the chamber fell dark. The light of the Core had dimmed to a pale glow, but was now growing again, spreading out through the cloud in luminescent waves. A metallic thrum permeated the air, rising quickly into a pounding beat, *whump, whump, whump*, like a piece of corrugated tubing being swung around in circles, echoing off the double-domed roof.

Thousands of tiny bright beads, like shooting stars, were zipping around the walls, leaving effervescent trails that twinkled before they faded and gaining such speed they merged into a whipping, iridescent blanket wrapping around them.

Nothing was discernible to Josh now; not the vapours around his feet, not the desk in front of him, nor the girl standing next to him. Her face was there, but the definition had been lost amidst the rage of electricity swirling around them. Panic rushed through him, terrified his mind might scramble to the point he would never recognise her again. He reached out his hand, which shook with the fear that his arm might stretch forever and never find anything. Lexa smacked his fingers and said something that sounded distortedly like 'Stop it'.

And then it was over.

With a diminishing whirr, the Vessel powered down; the light drained and retreated back into the Core and the walls lost their shimmer. Everything was as calm as it was moments ago; except for Josh, whose hand, still raised, shook the with intensity of the experience.

Lexa smirked as she walked away and lay her hand on the wall. The entrance slid open as before and the Impossible Steps led out into the darkness.

Josh wasn't an idiot. He knew exactly what had happened. *Time on the right, location on the left.* It wasn't that hard.

'When are we?'

'See for yourself,' Lexa said, offering the door.

144

The air whipping in from the outside was cold and the darkness absolute. As he crept closer, Josh could hear the sloshing of the river down below against the eerie silence of the city.

'It's freezing!'

'It's winter.'

The icy cold bit hard on his injuries. Within a matter of seconds his face had gone numb and his fingers turned blue. It wasn't just winter; it was winter at night, high up in the sky.

'How did it make you feel, Josh?'

'How did what make me feel?'

'The Core,' Lexa said. 'What was it like?'

He was shivering uncontrollably. Lexa must have been feeling the bitterness too, but she didn't show it.

'I don't know,' he said. 'I guess I felt…'

'Happy?'

If he'd been able to think straight, he might have corrected her. It wasn't happiness; more like… serenity.

'Yes. I suppose. W-why…?'

'Because that's what it wanted.' Lexa took in a deep breath of the frozen air as though it were a summer breeze. 'It's a drug, infecting your senses and pulling you in. The Core made you happy because it thrives on the taste. Do you understand? You are past the point of no return. You need to steel yourself against everything that's coming. You need to ready your mind. A warm coat isn't going to be enough to protect you.'

The noise was approaching.

'What does that mean?'

Lexa looked up into the night. The fleet of Heinkel bombers passed overhead with an ear-shattering roar, flying so low the Vessel shuddered and the strength of the backdraft threw Josh off balance. Lexa grabbed him by the sleeve.

All around them the city was lit up by fireballs blossoming in the sky, the air erupting with the whistle of falling bombs and the thunder of the bombardment, the bluster of the aircraft engine and the desperate whine of the air raid sirens. Josh clasped his hands over his ears.

Their position high above the Thames gave them a skyscraper's view of London. Tower Bridge was a little way ahead, and to their left the firelight illuminated the baroque dome of St Paul's Cathedral. There was a famous photograph, Josh recalled, of the cathedral rising above the smoke as everything around it crumbled. Was this the night it was taken?

The wound on his nose burned and itched as he sniffed against the flow of tears. There was a final crash and a pause long enough to hear the screams of the people running to the shelters.

At last it became too much.

Backing away into the chamber, Josh found Lexa's stool and sat at the desk with his face down in his palms. The wind dropped and the noise faded and the only source of light came once again from the Core. He allowed the silence to prevail for a moment and then wiped his eyes with his sleeve. His arm was resting on the edge of an old notebook, dog-eared and well-used, buried amongst the jumble of wires beneath her laptop.

Having closed the entrance, Lexa turned to face him. Outside the muffled rumble of the Blitz could still be heard as she pulled the notebook from under his arm and tucked it beneath a pile of papers.

'I understand this must be tough for you,' she said, 'and I know you have questions –'

She broke off. If the sympathy wasn't sincere, then there was no point saying the words. Her tactic may have been heavy-handed, but she didn't regret it. He would have to cope with much worse. What was regretful, however, were the nagging doubts that returned as she watched him sitting on *her* stool, sniffling and shaking at *her* desk. Another opportunity to stick to the script had gone. One quick push into the freezing water and Josh would never be seen again. Problem solved.

But no.

Here he still was, taking up space in the Vessel because something unfathomable wanted Lexa to let him choose his own destiny; one more luxury to pile onto his privileged life. She was being careless and weak. What would her father say if he saw her now, looking for an easy way out?

'I'm fine,' Josh muttered, 'I just need a minute to process.'

Lexa bit her thumb. She wanted to punch him.

An awkward silence passed between them for an excruciating length of time before eventually Josh turned to her. The feckless twit looked almost angry with her.

'So, correct me if I'm wrong, this...' Josh twirled his finger around in the air, '...is a time machine?'

'It is now, yes.'

'It is *now*?' he repeated. 'What was it before?'

'A warship.'

'Right, of course...' The flippancy in his tone repulsed her. 'But not, like... a *human* warship?'

Lexa quickly surveyed her thoughts before responding. Was humanoid the same as human?

'No,' she decided.

'And... are you?'

'Am I what?'

Josh swallowed his breath. 'Human?'

'Yes, of course I am!'

Insulted by the insinuation, Lexa went to say more, to rage at him a little bit, but managed to hold herself back. It was probably a fair question; and to her surprise, Josh hadn't sulked at her curt response. Instead, he shrugged his shoulders and gestured casually again at the Vessel's interior.

'So, where does this come from?'

Another rumble. Lexa knew the shell was robust enough to hold up against most types of weaponry, but there was no point in taking the risk. Brushing Josh aside, she tapped in some new coordinates and the chamber was consumed once again by the maelstrom of light.

***

The Vessel hovers above the ground, still and silent in the low evening light. The footage is grainy, distorted. Icons in the top corner display the battery power (low) and the date (incorrect).

'Is it on?'

For ten minutes Josh watched the video of Lexa dutifully assisting the man she referred to as the Captain, scratching his chin and shifting uncomfortably on the hard seat of her wooden stool.

Peering through the static, he tried to get a better idea of the aged figure. How old was he? Fifties? Sixties? Difficult to tell, as it was clear the passage of time and circumstance hadn't been kind. His thoughtful manner and earnest tone were let down by a tousled mop of grey hair, unkempt and bedraggled and matted in knots which reached down to his shoulders. On hairstyle alone, the old man could have been the future version of PC Bayley.

There was certainly something familiar about the Captain; but even if Josh could imagine the constable with the same pale skin, the same sunken features and same set of grime-covered overalls ripped at nearly every seam, there was no mistaking those eyes. They weren't Bayley's, they were Lexa's; weary yet determined, ablaze with a fire that kept pushing them on through the wreckage of humanity.

Josh had tried to stay focused on the casual back-and-forth between father and daughter, and the Captain's awkward attempt to sound imperial for the camera, but he couldn't help but notice the state of the land around the Vessel. It was no more than a bog, littered with mangled branches of rotting tree bark and lumps of broken concrete sinking into puddles of murky brown water. In the background a small building poked out from behind an area of fire-ravaged woodland. Even in its advanced state of decay, Josh recognised it as one of the old hospital outhouses scattered around Belmont Park.

The devastating scenery had served to distract him as the conversation went on. Listening in, Josh felt as though he were intruding on some private family moment. He could have guessed that the Captain was the only person Lexa dare show any vulnerability in front of, and when her on-screen counterpart became fearful, she moved away from the desk and out of his sight. Even through the filter of the scratchy video, the act of fatherhood felt monumental; the Captain's words of comfort were tender and sincere when he must have been as scared as she was.

Josh had already noted that the laptop Lexa was holding in the video wasn't the same as the one he was watching on; it had the same eccentric array of gadgets and components, but the casing was black and the design was different.

A prototype, perhaps, only marginally less attractive than its successor. It wasn't in the chamber now, though, as far as Josh could see. Maybe the reason for that was on screen. The Captain had had to prise the laptop from Lexa's hands while she fumbled around telling him he was too weak to run – but for all the care he took with it, resting it unsteadily on his forearm, it wouldn't have surprised Josh to see it fall and sink in the sodden earth.

Instead, the Captain seemed far more concerned with giving Lexa his notebook in return. The slightly overstretched arm, the fingers clasped tightly around the tatty cover as he near-enough jabbed the notebook into her stomach; it was all very... *deliberate*.

Only once he was certain the scrappy old pad was secure in his daughter's hands did the Captain show any real interest in the black laptop. He typed one-handed, his fingers gliding effortlessly over the keyboard, entered his final command and watched as the Vessel started to spin.

Very, *very* fast.

Turning on its central axis, the Vessel's shape was still easily discernible; the sharp point at the base looked as though it were barely moving – yet the oily colours that had been gracefully twirling and intertwining moments before were now an imperceptible blur. Blinding streaks of light were left in their wake as the sharp metal fins tore at the fabric of the world; the atmosphere set aflame as it began to weaken and combust. The air whipped and the currents ripped through the trees, their branches dancing and swaying restlessly. Unseen, the tripod, bullied by the wind, yielded at last and the picture lurched to one side, ending with an undignified squelch as the camera hit the mud.

Only the top half of the Vessel remained in shot, bulging out from the left-side of the frame, and Josh felt tempted, at first, to realign the footage by tilting his head, but the effort was hardly worth it as soon little was visible beyond the gauze of light. In slow, pulsating throbs, the Vessel shone a brilliant white light, flaring off the lens.

Then, in a flash–

'Wait! Stop!'

Her voice was barely audible over the blast of winds that scratched and hissed their way through the laptop's speakers. On screen the light began to fade. Josh turned to the version of Lexa there in the chamber with him.

'Keep watching,' she said.

He blinked and rubbed his eyes, the lingering aftermath of the pure white screen distorting his vision as the picture returned. The dark hues of the sky and the mud resumed their place as the Vessel powered down under the Captain's computerised command. His daughter's shadow fell across the foreground as she lifted the camera back upright and revealed to Josh one final, astonishing twist.

He leaned forward, wondering if his eyes were still struggling to focus, only to discover the illusion was undeniably real. Where moments earlier there had been one Vessel hovering above the dirt and debris, there were now two.

One next to the other.

The new Vessel hissed softly as thin vapours of stream ran up the sides, cooling in the evening air, and its fins were glowing beneath a shimmering haze of heat; but in all other respects the two machines were identical.

The Captain, quivering with shock, turned on the spot as he sensed Lexa's approach. A gasp escaped his mouth. It was her smile which led to the breakdown in composure, freeing him to burst into laughter and fling his arms around her. Josh studied Lexa's face as she lay her head on the Captain's shoulder, looking to see if she were crying or not. After the embrace, the Captain took her hand in his, gripping her fingers.

'Are we really going?'

'Yes.' The Captain beamed. *'Yes, we are. Right now. There is not a moment to lose. Unscrew the camera, take it with you.'*

Lexa threw a look straight into the camera, and for a moment it seemed she was staring directly as Josh.

'With me?'

'Yes! For prosperity, like you said! We're making history today, my darling. And no-one will ever believe us unless we have proof!'

'Yes, but surely –'

'Oh, you know me, I'll only forget to press record. Better you do it.'

The cloud shifted as the real Lexa circled the wall of the Vessel and away from her view of the screen. Her former self was now casting a shadow over the frame, which wobbled as it was unfastened from the tripod and held clumsily in her hand. Beyond the view of her waist Josh could see the Captain gazing up at the sky, his face overcome with horror.

'Lexa, run!'

A distant but ferocious roar blew through the speakers and echoed violently around the chamber. Lexa was running now, the camera in her hand rolling from side to side, moving towards one of the Vessels, the machine and its surroundings tipping and keeling to a backdrop of jumbled sounds: her body rubbing against the microphone, the squelch of her feet through the mud, the piercing shrieks and the bellowed voices.

'We should go together!'

'Stick to the plan! Follow the instructions in my notebook and I'll meet you there!'

The picture settled. She was beside one of the craft now. Her hand reached up to touch the coppery tinctures of the outer shell. There was another roar, closer this time, fierce and guttural, and a sheet of orange light consumed the screen from one side. Screams followed, and a second later the video cut to static, the white noise ringing in Josh's ears.

He stared through the blizzard, expecting something new to burst out of the screen, another experience to chip away at the reality he thought he knew. When nothing came, he lifted his eyes towards Lexa.

'What happened?'

'Firebreather Squadron,' she said, plainly, as she walked around the Core and to the desk.

'I'm sorry… *Firebreather?*'

'Stop repeating things. Imagine a dinosaur, add a pair of wings and some flames coming out its mouth and… well, that's about it.'

'You… you mean like a dragon?'

'No, I mean like a weapon. Genetically engineered to look exactly how people in your time *think* a dragon should be. Psychological warfare. What you thought was fake is actually real, and it's coming to kill you.'

'And that man – your father…'

She looked surprised he would ask.

'It was a scavenger unit. Over the years a lot of their craft crash-landed or were shot down and hoarded by resistance groups. The squadrons could usually seek them out because the Firebreathers were drawn to them – just like you were. So, we'd wait for times when the skies were dark or we could suppress the Core, but as soon as we powered the Vessel and the second one appeared, it would have been easy for them. Should have been more careful, I guess. But we weren't. I got to the Vessel in time, he didn't. End of story.' Lexa reached across him and closed the laptop lid. 'Don't ask for it again.'

Josh felt a heavy lump in his throat. He felt like he should say something, but had no idea what. He'd never lost a family member before. Relatives were like planets orbiting around the sun – even when you couldn't see them you knew they were there, moving along a path so resolute you gave little thought to the idea that one day it would end.

'Lexa, I –'

'No.' She shut him down quickly. 'I don't need your pity. The only reason I showed you is because I never thought I'd ever have to explain this to anyone, and I only want to do it once. So what I need from you is to just shut up and listen to me. Can you do that?'

Josh nodded.

With a tired sigh Lexa stepped forward, pushed Josh off her stool and sat down. For a moment it seemed as if she were alone again in the Vessel, organising her thoughts for her own sake rather than his. She followed the gentle roll of the cloud encircling the chamber and moving slowly inward to the Core, and wondered where she should begin.

'11

The Mountains

The last of the sun dipped below the jagged horizon, the light reflecting off the snow-capped peaks and basking the rocky slopes below in a violet hue, the distant edges of the range crisp and unfiltered against the hazy orange sky.

Lexa sat at the bottom of the Impossible Stairs with her legs dangling over the edge. All around, the crumpled landforms provided plenty of ridges and plateaus, cool and inviting in the shadow of the massif, but instead she had chosen to 'park' the Vessel in the centre of the valley, high above the ground.

The view was undeniably breathtaking; a panoramic vista the like of which Josh had only ever seen in photos which captured the silence but never, he realised, the stillness; the peace and calm, the sense of hidden activity and the harmonious changes in the landscape; how the snow faded beneath the summits and the seemingly lifeless rockface gave way to spruce tree forests, mossy grassland and the crystal clear waters of the lakes. But still, the air was cold and the height was alarming, and every new step on this journey made him increasingly wary.

'Where are we?'

'Tatra Mountains,' Lexa replied, without turning around. 'Slovakia.'

On a different day Josh might have felt embarrassed for never having heard of the place.

'Oh.'

'Won't actually be known as Slovakia for some time, though. Right now this is all part of Hungary.'

'I see.' He winced at the sight of Lexa swinging her legs back and forth. 'Don't you think you should come inside?'

'Why? It's beautiful out here. Feels like you're floating.' She pointed to where the lowest peaks of the range were being consumed by the shadows of its neighbours. 'In about 500 years my great-grandparents will be born somewhere over there in a mining village they'll never leave. Extraordinary, isn't it? Two tiny footnotes in the great story of humanity, and here I am, their descendant, officially the world's first time traveller.'

'Yes, that's...'

Josh tried to think of something befitting to say, but was struck by the realisation of Lexa's lonely situation. He was the world's second time traveller and from her point of view this still left her with no-one.

'I would urge you not to read too much into this,' Lexa said quickly. 'You know what war feels like now. The noise, the heat, the smell. You know what it costs. So I thought it would do us both some good to find somewhere quiet to talk and where I could still throw you out if I had to. And this... this was the first place that came to mind.'

Josh stepped back into the Vessel. Directly below, a faint rustling came from within a thicket of trees as a lone roebuck emerged into the open and ate the berries off a nearby bush.

'The Guiding Principles are a load of crap. Agree?'

'Uh... I...' Josh faltered. Some things in life were simply unquestionable, which made it rather difficult to answer when questioned about them.

'Do you agree?'

'I mean, they're certainly well intentioned, but I suppose it's a little much to expect everyone to feel the same way –'

Lexa cut him off. 'Okay, stop. God, it's like you're scared of your own opinion. They're a lie. But not just a lie, a *manipulation*. The result of being able to see just far enough into the future to know how things *might* turn out, that with a few adjustments here and there, you can control how things ultimately *do* turn out.'

'Why would someone do that?'

She shrugged. 'Same reason those wolves down there are stalking that deer.'

In the last of the light, Josh looked over the edge of the Stairs and scoured the valley until he spotted the two grey wolves moving quickly across a steep, craggy slope, padding gracefully along with their heads low and in absolute silence. Descending gradually, they kept pace with one another until the foliage thickened and they could split, one maintaining its path, the other clambering down, hidden by the bushes. It was clear the plan was to attack the buck from either side and cut him off from re-entering the woodland. Josh studied the scene for a moment, feeling both terrified and oddly privileged.

'Okay then, who are the wolves?'

'Euphorivores,' she said. 'We call them Euphors, for short. *Joy Eaters.* Extrasensory beings who feast on positive emotion. *Our* emotion. Been around as long as we have – longer, probably – living alongside us and influencing society as they wait in hunger to execute their masterplan.'

Josh scratched his forearms. Dragons, time machines and now this? He wondered what else he'd be expected to believe before the day was out.

'What masterplan?'

'One big feast. Emotions are nothing more than chemical reactions; whenever we're happy or sad or scared or angry, there's a release, a scent we leave behind.'

'A scent? Like a hormonal thing?'

Lexa shook her head. 'Hormones are for our benefit. This is something else, something tangible, something only they can perceive. And if those feelings are positive, then they're delicious. Food you'd do anything to have. And like any food source, you have to farm it, cultivate it and then *harvest* it.'

Down below, the wolves had slowed their pace and were creeping along over the mountainside as the clueless prey continued to eat.

'That's what the world is,' she continued, 'an enormous food factory. To make someone laugh, you have to tell a joke; to make them happy, you have to give them something they want; to make *everyone* happy, you first have to make them believe they all want the same thing. Catch!'

Her arm lurched and a small red object flew over her shoulder. In the split second before it hit him, Josh thought it might be a cricket ball and he jumped backwards and dug his elbows into his stomach with his forearms outstretched. But the thump against his chest wasn't as hard as he expected and he fumbled the catch, letting whatever it was fall to the Vessel's cloud-covered floor. He reached down and picked it up.

It was an apple.

'Interesting,' she said. 'Not what I expected but it proves a point. I thought you were either going to catch it, or drop it and plant a new apple tree in the valley.'

'Or, you could have missed me.'

She smiled. 'Where I come from you always back yourself.'

Without a shred of respect for the enormous drop inches from her feet, Lexa stood and walked slowly up the Impossible Stairs towards him.

'But if I were a Euphorivore,' she continued, 'then I wouldn't have that problem. I could look deep into the Core and see beforehand that the chances are you're not going to make the catch. So if my plan to destroy the world relied on you holding that apple, I would know not to take the risk. I'd make you believe, without a shadow of a doubt, that this apple is going to make all your dreams come true; that existence is meaningless without it, so if you let it fall you might as well go with it.'

Her shadow fell across him as she climbed, the chilly mountain air again taking hold of his composure. Lexa was good at this.

'Then, when the moment was right, I'd walk right up to you –'

She reached the top step with precision timing and grabbed hold of his wrist. Her eyes were deadly still as the wind whipped strands of hair across them.

'– and instead of throwing it, I'd place the apple slap down in your palm and squeeze your fingers around it, so there was no possible way you could drop it.'

Lexa took his opposite hand and pressed it down on top on the apple so it was hidden within his grasp. Josh felt the skin break and the juice start to run down between his fingers.

There was a clatter of rocks behind them. The roebuck had seen the wolves. The ambush exposed, Josh expected the animal to run, but it was holding its ground, staring down the hungry predators. A standoff had ensued, the wolves appearing calm, stepping back but holding position on either side of their target. The smallest wolf, the youngest perhaps, the one who had remained further up the slope, was the first to lose its nerve and darted forward like a spring-loaded weapon. The roebuck leapt backwards in a tangle of spindly legs and bolted, skirting the edge of the woodland, almost into the path of the second, stronger wolf, and making off across the valley floor. The wolves pounded behind at a blistering pace, and within seconds the first was close enough to launch itself at a hind leg and sink in its teeth; the buck screamed and kicked its attacker away with a strong hoof and kept running. The chase continued until the roebuck reached the lake, bellyflopping into the water and swimming just as clumsily.

But it was enough.

The wolves prowled the wide bank for a few moments, and after finding no natural means of getting across, they turned and left. As they skulked back across the grass, their pride wounded and their hunger left unsatisfied, the elder stopped and looked briefly up at the Vessel, angry, perhaps, that there had been witnesses to their failure.

Josh twisted his wrist free from Lexa's hand.

'This is crazy,' he said firmly. 'You're crazy. I don't know what goes wrong in the future, but this isn't it. No way. You can't eat an emotion, and you can't just tell everyone what to think and hope that's enough to brainwash them.'

Lexa scoffed. 'Really? You know that for a fact, do you? Because a moment ago I asked you if you thought the Principles were a lie –'

'Crap, actually.'

'– and you could hardly bring yourself to agree with me. This, from the guy who apparently doesn't 'think' the way he's supposed to. The Euphors' hold on humanity includes you too, Josh. Maybe not to the same extent as everyone else, but you're not immune to it. No-one is.'

'Except for you?'

Lexa didn't answer.

The valley was beginning to annoy him. The insinuation his thoughts were not his own was insulting – and yet oddly believable.

'Okay then, how exactly do you harvest an emotion?'

'With a harvester,' she said. 'A big ship – their Flagship – orbiting around the Earth. Launched undercover and hidden by subterfuge and stealth from every telescope and every satellite in the world, and with a Core wider than this valley, built to suck up

162

all the joy from the face of the planet in one hit; bringing enough food to last them for generations.'

The sky had darkened into the evening twilight, the distant mountains a ragged line of shadow against the spectral gloom. The Core of the Vessel, undiminished by the approaching night, lit up their faces like a campfire, reflecting the shiny surface of the apple as Lexa held it in front of his swollen nose.

'They could have chosen anything; equal wealth, perhaps, or an end to all hunger and disease. But it wouldn't have worked. People want to be distracted from the state of humanity, not cured of it. They want to be entertained; but Euphors are smart enough to know that guaranteed thrills get boring after a while. True happiness has to be earned, like the sense of release when you've been worrying for so long and then everything turns out just as you hoped. So, they had an idea...'

Her voice softened as she leant forward and Josh could see the light reflecting in the deep, angry pools of her eyes.

'Football.'

Josh blinked. He had guessed this was coming, but hearing the word, with all its embedded ordinariness, spoken out loud at the peak of her apocalyptic discourse was very strange indeed.

'Football?'

'Football. A game. The world's most popular, I am told, with winners, losers and, most importantly, a sense of the unknown. Millions of people, all nervous with anticipation and wrecked with an excitable fear. And the closer it gets to the end, the more it builds, until –' Lexa mimed an explosion with her fingers. '– a whistle is blown and everyone erupts with a split-second blast of pure, unfiltered joy.'

Josh stroked the meagre stubble around his chin as the realisation entrapped him like a prison cell.

'You're talking about the Final?' he said. 'British Kingdom versus North America.'

'That's the one. With the tools they have, determining a winner is easy.'

'America, I take it? Must be; bigger area, more peo–'

She snapped. 'Do you ever go outside, Josh? Do you even know what's going on?'

Lexa grabbed a scruff of his sleeve and pulled him over to the laptop. After a few commands were thundered into the keyboard with academic speed, a collage of file photographs, newspaper articles, witness statements and police reports filled the screen, like the findings of an off-grid private investigator in some moody thriller.

Josh scanned the headlines. Unexplained deaths at sporting events across the world. Victims with macabre joker smiles. No obvious motive. No definable cause of death. No obvious connection between the victims...

Lexa dragged one particular news clipping to the top of the pile. Neat columns of oriental characters ran down the page. In the photo, against the backdrop of an enormous stadium, officers were blocking the crowd from getting near to the bodies beneath the sheets.

'Look there,' she said, pointing at the throng of onlookers. 'You see that?'

Josh peered closer to where Lexa was singling someone out near the back. Someone quite short. So short, in fact, all that could be seen was the top of the face, which itself was immersed in shadow by the brim of a smart hat. A fedora, or perhaps a trilby – Josh had never been sure of the difference.

'Who's that?'

Lexa didn't answer and instead brought up another clipping belonging to a Californian newspaper and dated two years previously. The headline ran:

WRENS' SHOCK CHAMPIONSHIP WIN OVERSHADOWED BY DISCOVERY OF TWELVE BODIES NEAR STADIUM.

In this picture the victims had already been removed and only their painted outlines remained, while a team of pensive-looking investigators surveyed the scene. Josh's attention was immediately caught by one particular officer in the foreground; her back was half turned, revealing the initials ACA on the rear of her jacket, but there was enough of her face to make Josh think he had seen her somewhere before.

But before he could make the connection, Lexa had zoomed in on the text of the article and a witness statement referring to 'some guy dressed like a gangster' seen lurking around an hour or so before the bodies were discovered.

Similar accounts followed in Canada, Australia and cities around Europe; wherever there was sport, there was death, and what linked them was the man in the hat. A press conference in

Toronto during a major tennis tournament featured a dour-faced detective with the fedora in his hand (definitely a fedora – soft brim, unfixed) pleading for information. Lexa paused the video and reached for her father's notebook.

'Remember what I said about living alongside us?' she said, flicking through the beige, crumpled pages. 'Well, blending in is not as easy as it seems.'

Lexa handed Josh the notebook on an open page with every available scrap of space taken up with small, scribbled scratches of handwritten words. A main block of text sat neatly in the centre, with corrections and addendums squeezed in at various angles in the surrounding margins. Near one corner there was a small circular drawing of a naked figure – a crude facsimile of the Vitruvian Man, but with the addition of a set of glow lines encircling an oval shape in the centre of the chest.

At the top of the page, the title had been underscored with a wobbly, slanting line punctuated by an ink blot:

Anatomy of a Euphorivore

In the first sentence Josh read a repeat of Lexa's description of Euphors as *'extra-sensory beings'*, followed by:

Mouths, therefore, are a misdirection. The skull could be mistaken for human's were it not for the fused jawbone, while an 'unfiltered' view of the face would most likely reveal the vestigial mouth holes of a bygone evolutionary era. Physical feeding was, in all likelihood, once part of their biology, and a small number of specimens have been discovered with tongues possessing active taste buds – but the developmental loss of teeth and an ill-equipped digestive tract indicates these can now only be employed in the rare enjoyment of fluids.

General consumption therefore takes place via the tattoo-like markings which cover the scalp. Each individual's markings are different, like a fingerprint, with a wide variety of patterns and styles which may indicate homogeny with a particular ethnicity or ancestry within their own species.

Josh looked again at the drawing in the corner and the pair of zig-zag lines running across the forehead.

They are the visual aspect of a complex system of highly sensitive neural receptors which draw in waves of raw human emotion. The 'food' is then filtered through a network of axons and nerve fibres down through the neck and to the lifestone: a small organ of semi-translucent muscular tissue, irregularly shaped and harder than bone, in the centre of the chest, that turns emotional resonance into physical nutrient to be dispersed around the body. Equally then, as with our own mouths, the receptors serve a secondary function: communication. A conversation that would take two humans several minutes to say out loud, passes between two Euphorivores in a blink of an eye. Some have described this telepathy as being able to project dialogue through a single thought, but this definition is too grounded. Powered by emotion, they don't think about what they want to say, they feel it.

Extraordinary as these discoveries may be, I am personally more confounded by the receptors' illusory abilities. A Euphorivore can look at any one of us and plant belief in our heads; belief in a creed, or a doctrine, or belief that when they talk to us, the words are being sounded out by the

lips of a fully-formed mouth inside a head with an ordinary scalp. This,
however, requires the exertion of large amounts of mental energy, and
many Euphorivores, we discovered, eased the effort by investing in high-
quality wigs or by wearing a hat.

'So it's not the same guy?' Josh asked.

Lexa shrugged. 'Can't say. A fedora is quite a flamboyant choice; probably why there's so much on record. What's certain is that he, or she, or they, are part of a worldwide network of operatives. Their job is to maintain the chain of command, pass messages between various factions and report back to the Flagship. Snacking as they go along.'

Josh tried to ignore the trembling in his fingertips as he skimmed the remainder of the article. In almost every other regard, Euphorivore physiology was comparable to humans. Respiratory, circulatory and reproductive systems were identical. Height, weight and skin tones varied and no two individuals were the same. Cell deterioration did take far longer and an average lifespan had yet to be determined, but their bodies had proved just as susceptible to fatal injury. Immune systems were, however, much stronger and they could better regulate their temperatures, allowing for greater success in adapting to hostile environments, including the British summertime, when they could comfortably keep their chests covered up through the wearing of thick tops.

Shaking his head and dropping the notebook on the desk, Josh looked again to the screen and, in particular, at the woman in the blue ACA jacket.

'Why don't I remember any of this?'

'Because you were made to forget,' Lexa replied. 'You probably heard about it at the time and the next day –' she clicked her fingers '– it was gone. Their agents are everywhere; business, government, schools, culture, anything you can think of. And why? To delude an entire planet into thinking a former colonial ransacker, the rebranded and repackaged British Kingdom, is now a shining beacon of joy and compassion, and that no matter what country you come from, seeing its team become champions of the world is going to make you happier than you can possibly imagine.'

Her voice lowered to a clear whisper and she took a step closer, as though this were the secret she'd brought Josh all this way to reveal:

'You're going to score a goal, in the very last second of the game. A moment my father said was specifically designed to "combine the thrill of the ball hitting the net with the absolutism of the full-time whistle". Except the goal is questionable, there's an element of doubt whether or not it should count. Everyone is on the edge of their seat, waiting for the decision, and finally the goal is given because the game officials are all Euphorivores anyway and they allow it to stand. That goal is the apple in your hand. You win, the world rejoices and the Harvest is complete.'

Lexa lifted his wrist and took the oozing lump of fruit Josh had forgotten he was still holding.

'Game over,' she said, and took a bite.

Outside the Vessel there was nothing but black. Even the lower half of the Impossible Stairs had been swallowed by the night. In the featureless landscape, sounds had become accentuated; the ripple of the lake, the wind through the trees and the crumble of rock, each connected by the scurry of animal life in the vicious habitat.

Josh searched his thoughts for a light amongst the darkness and a safe passage home. He wanted Lexa to be wrong. Any kind of flaw in her story would do; some thread to unpick.

'So your mission is to prevent the goal.'

'Yes,' she said, eating.

'Are you sure that is even possible? You and your dad were caught. If you've come back to stop them, surely they'll come back to stop you. They must've known where you were going?'

Lexa's cheeks were stuffed with apple chunks, like a squirrel with a mouthful of nuts.

'No chance.' Cream-coloured flecks flew out of her mouth and tiny wet pieces stuck to her chin. 'All Euphorivore craft have the potential for time travel, but our research suggests they never utilise this because they think it's too dangerous.'

Josh wiped his face. 'Why?'

'Because it is. Small mistakes can result in unimaginable consequences. Euphors created the Cores to power their ships and to glimpse into the future. The Captain was the only one to combine the two, for the sole purpose of going back in time and eliminating the necessity to do so. That's a paradox, which, unless you subscribe to quantum mechanics, may lead to the implosion of the universe. But the world's doomed already, so who cares?'

Lexa ripped off the final piece with a crunchy slurp.

'Quantum mechanics?'

'Alternate realities,' she said. 'You might think history is set in stone, and that even time-travel forms part of the pre-ordained

170

events that can't be changed, like those wolves spotting us, or this...' Lexa casually tossed the apple core out of the Vessel and into the darkness. 'None of those things should alter the life of these mountains because they were destined to happen. But *this*...'

She held down two keys on the laptop and the montage of press clippings switched to a single still image of the video's opening frame, the lone Vessel waiting yet again for her father to approach.

'...proves there is another option.'

An empty silence passed between them, as though the explanation for this were so obvious it didn't need saying out loud.'

'Oh...' Josh said. 'Does it?'

'Yes. Because if you can create a universe where there are two Vessels, then presumably you can create a universe where there is no Vessel at all. Every change sets off a new series of events; a parallel timeline that runs alongside all the others. If I succeed in stopping the Harvest, the Vessel will still be converted into a time machine, but in an alternate version of the future that, hopefully, we'll never see. The one I grew up in.'

Josh thought for a moment, his head spinning with the twisty conundrums of time and space.

'So what you're saying is, you shouldn't have thrown out the apple? Because of the ripple effect?'

'World's doomed, remember?'

She flopped down onto the three legged-stool and ran her hand over her face. She looked tired. Josh saw her eyes flick from the notebook to the video. He didn't know what to say. The silence was shaming and he felt relieved when she broke it.

'They must have been desperate.'

'Who? The Euphors?'

'The wolves. Roe are small but to give chase on a buck at this altitude at this time of year?' Her fingers stroked the surface of her father's handwritten words. 'Must've had no choice.'

'You know a lot about wolves.'

She closed the cover. 'I know about killing to survive.'

Suddenly animated by a business-like efficiency, Lexa tucked the notebook back into place beneath the laptop, straightened a few loose papers along the way and set about configuring a new time signature.

The blue triangle zoomed in on the Surrey border, flashing and turning, flashing and turning. Was there something he'd missed? Because if they were charting a course for home, then there was still one thing Josh really needed to know.

'So where do I come in?' he asked.

The roof of the outhouse was now visible on the Map, poking out from beneath the line of trees. Behind them, the entrance to the Vessel sealed shut and a heavy warmth filled the chamber.

'What do you mean?'

'I mean, how do I factor in all this? I assume it's one of those chance encounter things. Something like... the referees break down on the way to the stadium and I give them a lift?'

The new signature appeared in the centre of the screen. Her fingers hovered over the keypad.

'Give them a...? Haven't you been listening. I told you – you score a goal in the last minute and win the game.'

'*Me?*'

'Yes, you!' Her face was turning red. 'Who else would I have been talking about?'

A cold tremor ran down Josh's spine. His hands shook and black spots blotted his vision. He had to speak or else he might faint.

'I-I thought you meant "you" as in "we", like the Royal We – we, us, the whole country...'

Lexa batted away his words as though they were flies swarming around her head.

'Shut up, just shut... it's definitely you. It *has* to be you. You're Joshua Pittman... my father looked you up...'

'Well then, he got it wrong.'

The stool tumbled violently across the floor, breaking apart the cloud.

'Don't you dare!' she screamed. 'You're a footballer, aren't you?'

She was truly frightening. His legs threatened to give way and his nose throbbed in time with the thump of his heart. His conviction was all he had to keep him going.

'I'm a goalkeeper! An *amateur* goalkeeper! I can't just walk up to George Castle and say "hi, can I be your number nine on Sunday?" I'm not the guy you think I am, I'm not...'

The realisation dawned. Josh pressed his fingers into the nape of his neck, his arms hanging down over his chest, and walked around the edge of the chamber, rising to a nervous pace as he tried to absorb the enormity of her mistake.

Lexa had attacked him outside the Bovill Arms to prevent him from being match-fit. That was the reason. Then she'd tried to kill him, but instead invited him into the Vessel, shown him horror and wonder and told him a story to convince him of his destiny. She was asking him to take responsibility, and in doing so had given him a sense of purpose missing from his life.

And all because she came from a future where people had absolutely no idea how national football teams picked their players.

'It's PJ you're after,' he said. 'PJ Pitman.'

'Who?'

'Nathan Pitman Junior. Pit-man the Hit-man.' He paused for the recognition he knew wasn't coming. 'His first name, his real name, is Joshua – but no-one calls him that. He's the British Kingdom's star player, more of an attacking midfielder than an out-and-out striker, but he's the one you want, not me.'

Back behind the desk, Lexa had already run the search and could now only stare at the screen, pulling a nail with her teeth.

'Lexa, I'm sorry...'

'Where is he?'

Josh sidled back towards her, moving slowly, as though he were creeping up on a wild animal.

'You won't get near him, and you shouldn't, not like this.' He gestured to his injuries. 'There has to be a better way, I'll help you –'

Lexa grabbed Josh by the throat and slammed him against the wall.

'Where is he? Tell me or I'll kill you!'

Struggling for breath, Josh believed her. He was collateral now; he had let her down by being a nobody. And yet, for the good of humanity, he would have to trade his life for that of the biggest *somebody* on Earth.

Joshua Nathaniel Ayodelé-Pitman.

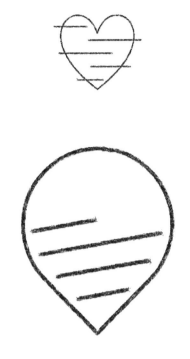

The False Nine

'12

Hitman, Pittman & Bayley

Joshua Nathaniel Ayodelé-Pitman – known to the world as Nathan Pitman Jnr – bounced the ball off his left knee for the 223rd time in the space of around four minutes

There was contentment to be found in commanding the flight of the ball with the repetitive accuracy of a ticking clock; the unthinking control as natural as breathing, his conscious mind set free to wander and ruminate on his own brilliance. It was the mark of true talent – to know what you're doing without knowing how you're doing it.

He could keep going for up to thirty minutes or more, the leg barely flexing beyond a twitch of his muscles, dictating how far he wanted the ball to rise with each turn. Show-boating had never helped a player on the pitch and so the steady rhythm of the knee was always his preferred choice, but if he chose to risk it all by throwing in a trick or two – straightening his leg and letting the ball fall into the crook of his foot, then spinning his foot around as it lifted through the air and landed on the back of his neck – then it came only from an adolescent need to mix things up occasionally and try something new.

He was only nineteen after all.

Five minutes and the rhythm showed no signs of abeyance. He didn't even flinch when Troy Simpson, the captain, called from the other side of the training pitch in his thick West Country brogue.

'Oi, PJ! Over 'ere!'

The knee still in position, the ball still bouncing, PJ glanced over to where Troy stood with three others, all wearing the same red, white and blue training kits, all mugging around him like playground goons hanging off the popular kid. Troy self-identified as the handsome jock of the national team, passionate and athletic with a square jaw, sparkling teeth and a new haircut every week. PJ could imagine him fitting in at an American high school, prowling the corridors in a Letterman jacket and taking the head cheerleader to the prom. As a player, however, Troy was raw and unpolished, prone to heavy tackles and persistent bookings, and who held onto the captaincy only by virtue of his enthusiasm, looks and a knack for goal poaching.

With a minor adjustment of the quadriceps, the ball flicked off PJ's thigh and sailed down to his feet from where it was volleyed in a perfect arc towards its mark. Troy readied himself with a little shuffle, but he misjudged the trajectory entirely and the ball skimmed off his calf and rolled away into a nearby bush.

'Little off target there, Hitman?' Troy cried as he reached beneath the thorns.

Hitman.

The nickname PJ hated only slightly more than PJ. Pseudonyms were, he'd learnt, an unavoidable trapping of fame, given how much a celebrity's image was shaped by the conversations and printed words of others. They were easy to say and suffused with mockery and endearment, which, PJ thought, pretty much summed up his relationship with the public.

The chief curse of his various monikers, however, was having to listen to his mother constantly chastise him about them.

'Why don't you go on television and tell people to call you by your real name, Ayo?' she would bark, using her pet name for him without a shred of irony.

He knew full well that by 'real name', she meant anything as long as it didn't have 'Junior' tacked on the end. That was the bit which really upset her. It was a false suffix, added on by his agent two years earlier once PJ had progressed out of club football and into the Regional League, from where it seemed obvious his future lay with the national team.

But for his mother, her lonely heart still aching years after the divorce, the generational title did nothing but offer Nathan Senior (as his dad now liked to call himself) another victory in their ongoing war of attrition. The guilt was there somewhere, bubbling beneath the surface in the hope of being noticed, but nevertheless PJ couldn't help but smile whenever he pictured his father, ever plumper as the years passed, in an ill-fitting shirt, sliding into a leather recliner in the BK Stadium's hospitality suite and helping himself to canapes and champagne brought over by the waitress.

'That's my boy down there,' he would probably say with a mischievous wink, beaming as she nodded dutifully back.

And therein lay the thinking. The elite twenty-three-man squad chosen to roll out and perform at the SyBall World Cup, on home soil no less, were meant to understand their role as conduits for the nation. Every victory was the people's victory, every failure their failure. Players had to tread the line between idol and everyman. And so, as his star rose, there was concern that PJ's hyphenated surname had something of a lopsided quality, a sense that it was neither here nor there, his cultural groundings therefore undefined as a result. Plus, it had far too many letters for the millions of replica shirts that were manufactured before the tournament.

'Pitman Jnr' was short and had a warm, homely feel – it suggested tradition, continuity, family. Kinship at the heart of the Guiding Principles. With the decision rubber-stamped by the Department for Footballing Activities, Nathan Pitman Junior was introduced to the world on his debut for Greater London, a 2-1 victory over Northumbria in which PJ scored the winner.

He was now a government employee, but there were times when he felt more like property; a plasticine model out on display for people to press and mould and shape however they saw fit. Politicians, agents, family, friends, teammates – he was never anything more than what others wanted him to be.

Ayo.
PJ.
Nathan Junior.
The Hitman.

Somehow, *Joshua* – the name he'd been given at birth – never made the list.

He sat on the grass and rested his wrists on his knees. At the end of a full day's practice, the sky had turned ashen blue and a mild breeze billowed through the trees which bordered the training ground's southern extremity. With all the scheduled exercises now complete, the squad had been given an hour's free time out on the pitch to work privately on aspects of their game they felt needed improvement. For PJ, this was the opportunity to break his keepie-uppie record; for others, it meant a cool sixty-minute period of showboating, joke-telling and all-round chest-puffing. Troy's request for PJ's ball had itself been a coda to a long speech on the power of perseverance and grinding a person down until eventually they agreed to go out on a date with you.

'What you have to do,' Troy's theory had begun, 'is reiterate the logic. She is the most powerful woman in football. I am captain of the world's best team. Right? We are both *fit*. Therefore, it is nothing less than a gift to the sport that we go out together.'

Of the assorted whoops and grunts that followed, the most audible had belonged to Jake Terrier, a dreadlocked winger – and Troy's wingman – who looked more like he should play guitar for a band than football for his country. Maybe he was terrible at music too. PJ strongly suspected he'd only made the team because his surname reminded people of the Prime Minister's dog. Appropriate for the man who hung off Troy's leg like an excitable puppy.

It was probably too far to admit that PJ was *annoyed* by Troy's date with Temperance Newhart. Irked, maybe. Baffled, certainly.

Until now, Troy's 'logic' had always failed to account for Newhart's sophistication, intelligence and poise, in contrast to, well, *him*. But in finally saying yes, the Secretary of State for Footballing Activities had gone and thrown all logic out the window. Maybe the end of the tournament was the end for her too – a chance to let her perm down and enjoy herself.

Newhart wasn't that old either, at least not by looking, so the victory wasn't legitimate. The Secretary could only have been a school age older than Troy, so he could brag all he wanted, but he didn't have what PJ had – a text from Evie Longford.

PJ took his phone from his kitbag on the nearby grass and read it again. Once famous, twice-divorced, and the wrong side of – what? Fifty? Sixty? Plus, she had a pop-star daughter. A gateway to a younger model; he'd get bonus points for that. The girl was no Mary-Jane Castle, of course, but then who was?

Evie's message had been languishing inside his phone for a few days now, the most recent in a long thread which had begun – to PJ's immense satisfaction – just a few hours after filming on the advert had wrapped. From that moment on it had been a forgone conclusion – he'd sealed the deal without trying, and all he needed to do was choose where and when. After the Final, perhaps, on some secluded beach on the other side of the world. That was his first thought, but ever since that old bint with the red hair – who'd encouraged him to do the advert in the first place – had made it abundantly clear how upset the Department were about it, the temptation to pull the trigger on Evie Longford sooner rather than later increased with every passing hour.

Screw 'em.

If he couldn't control his own name, what could he control? Were there any perks to being famous? His first season with Greater London had been gruelling enough – three games a week for nine months, and seemingly endless travel in between. How was he supposed to uphold his reputation for rolling out of nightclubs at two in the morning with a girl on his arm, if he never, *ever* got the chance to go?

The intense schedule and the pressure heaped on players by wild-eyed fans and the relentless media made him wonder if his mind was simply too young to deal with it. His team had won the Regional League with time to spare, and with PJ himself emerging as the season's top scorer; but then as soon as he lifted the trophy above his head, the focus shifted to the SyBall World Cup and suddenly he found himself the poster boy for the national team.

Photographers camped outside his home for weeks. Nice enough, but blood thirsty in their hunt for the best shot. Newspapers printed double-page articles scrutinising – but never criticising – his form, his style, his strengths and weaknesses. He posed for innumerable selfies, signed a bound volume's worth of autographs and answered the same stupid questions about upcoming matches which more or less asked him to predict the future. In the street people yelled at him, the drunker the louder, either to wish him luck or offer him some keen tactical advice, all in the hope he might turn their way and acknowledge their existence.

The wave of adoration felt crushing at times, and it had come as something of a relief when the Department told him he had been assigned his own personal bodyguard. Though he'd never dare to admit it, Ernie Strong's first day on the job was followed by the best night's sleep PJ had had in a long while.

Strong was over there now, in fact, on the edge of the touchline, staring like he always did at PJ, perfectly still and with his hands buried deep in his pockets. His eyes were narrow and weirdly unblinking, always on the lookout. Dark bags hung beneath them either side of a long, crooked nose. His loose skin hung beneath his chin and sagged in folds around his neck. All in all, he looked permanently unwell, but if he were suffering with something, he didn't let it affect his duties. If anything, he was a little over-zealous, quite happy to manhandle anyone who got too near, including certain friends and family PJ hadn't yet told him about. But for the most part Strong kept his distance. He didn't speak much; in fact, he barely spoke at all, and that appeared to suit the pair of them just fine. A professional working relationship.

Still, there was one thing PJ was dying to ask him: why, in the middle of a blazing hot summer, did he always wear such thick jumpers?

A little game of five-a-side had broken out on the training pitch. A positional running game – no dribbling and only two touches before a pass. Others were drawn in and before long PJ was being beckoned. He rose a dismissive hand into the air.

'Nah, you boys go ahead. Wouldn't be fair to the other team.'

Troy scoffed and shook his head

Whatever. A good player knew when to train and when to rest.

PJ's mind wafted back to the job in hand. The semi-final against Brazil has been a relatively quiet one for him. Defensively they were all over the place and he and Troy had found it easier than normal to get in behind their lines. From short range Troy was the target man, leaving PJ isolated on occasion, but still he'd bagged his obligatory goal, a rare header to guide in Danny Holt's wicked cross.

The match summed up the tournament as a whole, with each game exhibiting a strange, shifting tempo, at times unbearably slow and then suddenly wild and frenetic. Opponents appeared uneasy to be playing the hosts and unable to decide whether to roll over and die or come out baying for blood. The result was an odd mix of both. Challenges were rash and clumsy, and even when they weren't, the referee's decisions still went the home team's way.

Nothing George Castle had taught the players about their opponents seemed to matter on-field, and for whatever reason that unpredictability was playing to their advantage, with even the most speculative attempts on goal finding their way into the back of the net. While PJ thought it too much to say they were coasting through the tournament, he did wonder if it had been held in a different country, whether their route to the Final would have felt quite so… *charmed.*

But if the British Kingdom were benefiting from the best teams in the world buckling under the pressure, then they would find North America a different proposition altogether. The ultimate underdogs had ripped up the rule book. Defied the odds. They had nothing to prove and nothing to lose. They would play their hearts out no matter what, which made them potentially dangerous opponents. There was no room for complacency.

In spite of all the baggage that came with it, PJ wanted to win. More than anything in the world, he wanted to win.

Decision made. PJ tossed the phone back into his kitbag. Evie Longford would have to wait.

***

Josh landed on the hard ceramic floor of the outhouse with a heavy thump. The impact sent a shock wave up from his pelvis through to the top of his head. His nose throbbed and he cried out in pain, but at once he scrambled to his feet and was up on the first step of the Vessel before Lexa had a chance to turn back inside.

'Lexa, stop! Don't do this! If you hurt him, you'll –'

'I'll kill him if I have to!'

Her scream echoed in the rafters and silenced Josh long enough for her to give him another unchallenged push off the Impossible Stairs.

He hit the ground on his side, grazing his elbow. After the night spent in hospital, he was getting pretty fed up with all these injuries she kept inflicting on him.

Josh stood again, but this time couldn't stop her disappearing into the light, and he only made it to the second step before the immovable block turned into its viscous gloop and swept out from under him, sending him crashing for a third and final time.

The Vessel accelerated into a furious spin and the wind inside the outhouse blew him clean across the tiles, the electric streaks of light burning the skin on his palm as he lifted his hand to cover his eyes.

Then in a flash, it was gone.

And so was she.

PC Harry Bayley – known to his mates as Hay Bales – drummed his fingers on the desk for the 223rd time in the space of around four minutes.

The station foyer was empty, as it was most days, with no one except his colleagues or the odd American agent passing through. There had been that kid this morning with the broken nose, whose date had mugged him, or something. He ought to remember; being asked to take the witness statement had been the professional highlight of Harry's week.

Aside from that thrilling diversion, the day threatened to be another long and uneventful one. At least it was Saturday, and the Final was tomorrow, which meant there'd be all manner of build-up and analysis, match repeats and general atmosphere of excitement to while away the tedious hours on duty.

But then Harry's hope for the day had crumbled when, on returning from the interview room, he'd found *all four corners* of the security monitor showing CCTV footage and DS Jaitley standing behind the counter with the remote in his hand.

'Sorry, Bales,' Jaitley had said with a sheepish shrug. 'It's Agent Casey. She says it's unprofessional.'

Harry's fellow desk jockey that day, Special Constable Nicky Barnes – short, stocky, not long out of senior school – sneered as he scurried out of the foyer, muttering some decidedly un-Principled words about where Agent Casey could stuff her professionalism, and the vivid manner in which she could return to where she came from.

'You're alright, Vik.'

Harry had done his best not to sound like a child who'd just been refused an ice cream.

'Third Place Play-Off tonight, though,' said Jaitley. 'Unless something major turns up I don't think we'll stay late, so how about watching it around my place? See who else wants to come; I'll order some pizza and we'll make a night of it.'

In the wake his half-hearted nod of acceptance, Harry had been left to stare at the lightly falling dust through the shafts of sunlight from the windows for the remainder of the afternoon.

Vik Jaitley wasn't really the sort of bloke he liked to watch football with – his basic knowledge of the game was poor – but Harry never passed up the opportunity to hang out with the detectives. He envied them, especially now they were working with Jen Casey, a proper, bona fide agent actually up for a fight. The slam of the CID office door, the raised voices and the sound of crockery hitting the walls were welcome notes of music to interrupt the daily drone of white noise. And all in service of an actual, real murder investigation! What Harry would have given to be a part of it. It was how he imagined life in the force to be: blood, sweat and tears. Up 'til late and awake at dawn, connecting the dots, bending the rules and playing the system until the bastards were caught.

He leant on the counter and let out a loud sigh, the kind of slightly false noise one might make when trying to attract the sympathy of someone nearby.

Except he was all alone.

224, 225...

Time to mix things up. Harry slowed the speed of the drumming and focused on the difference in tone between finger taps on the wooden counter – hard and hollow – and the open page of the sign-in book – soft and dense. He noted the subtle changes in pitch and composed a playful pitter-patter before his eyes were drawn to the last name on the page.

Joshua Pittman.

His own interviewee. It hadn't struck him before, mainly because the lad had referred to himself only as 'Josh'. But seeing the name written out in full, there was a flicker of recognition.

Joshua...

Wasn't that the Hitman's real name? PJ Pitman. Was the J for Junior or Joshua? He couldn't remember. It didn't matter. A split-second rush of giddy excitement followed as Harry cheered the moment, only to be quickly undone by the infectious malaise of the day, and he slipped into deep thought about whether or not having the same name as someone extremely famous would be classed as being a coincidence.

Probably not.

A second later, the entrance doors burst open and Josh Pittman marched in past the vending machine and up to the desk. His face was red, and he breathed heavily though his swollen nose. The sweat on his skin glistened in the overhead light as he leant on the counter and bent his head low to catch his breath.

He'd been running, clearly.

Harry stood up straight and gulped like a fish.

'W-wow, Mr Pittman. I was just thinking about you.' He'd hoped it were possible to say that without sounding weird, but apparently it was not. 'How can I help you?'

Josh raised his head and said in a gravelly voice: 'I need to speak to the American.'

'I'm sorry... who?'

Josh snapped. 'The woman who was here. I don't know her name, but I saw her earlier on my way out. She works for the ACA. I need to speak to her right now.'

'Oh, you mean Agent Casey,' Harry said. 'Right. Okay. I'll see if she's about. Take a seat.'

Bemused, Harry hopped off his stool and trundled down the corridor to the hallowed realm of the detectives. He knocked on the door's frosted glass pane a few times, daring himself to go louder, until at last Jaitley opened the door wide enough to allow a deep, mid-flow roar of anger to escape into the hallway; something along the lines of *'long enough to catch this asshole'*, but Harry couldn't say for sure.

'What's up?' asked Jaitley in his usual cheery manner.

'There's a guy out front asking for Casey.'

Another booming chastisement resounded off the walls:

'...stay in this goddamn country another minute!'

Jaitley screwed up his face. 'Now isn't a good time.'

'Oh,' said Harry. 'No worries, I'll tell him to come back.'

As Jaitley nodded, there was the sound of footsteps slapping against the linoleum floor behind them.

190

'Tell her it's urgent!'

'Mr Pittman, please…',

It had been a while since Harry had used his authoritative voice, and he had to say he rather enjoyed it.

'No!' Josh shouted, dodging Harry's outstretched hands and looking impatiently for a way pass Vikram Jaitley. 'You don't understand, I –'

'What's all the fuss here, sir?'

A cold chill blew down the corridor. Serjeant Millington had appeared out of nowhere, like a spectre through the walls, as she often did whenever voices were raised in her station.

'You shouldn't be down here,' she said, calm but utterly terrifying. 'If you'll kindly return to the waiting area.'

'Tell her I know about the deaths in San Francisco,' Josh went on, reaching onto his tiptoes and calling over Jaitley's shoulder into the room beyond.

Margaret's hand landed softly on his shoulder and he lowered his arm back down. His restless verve turned to a childish whine, but still he persisted.

'Toronto, Sydney…'

'Sir, calm down…'

'I know about the man in the hat! The Fedora, that's what you call him, right? Please!'

The bellowing stopped. A moment of eerie silence passed, and a shadow fell across the open door as Agent Casey emerged from within. She looked Josh up and down with a mangled grimace.

'You were here earlier, weren't you?'

Josh nodded. All except Margaret Millington stood back as Casey came into the corridor. Harry gulped; he expected Josh to retreat, but instead the lad held his ground.

'Alright kid, you got my attention. What else do you know?'

'Everything,' Josh said. 'But you're not going to believe any of it. I'm still not really sure I do.'

Casey scoffed. 'Well, that's a great start. Come with me. Jaitley, you too. Bring a pen.'

Harry watched with astonishment as Agent Casey led Josh to her favoured interview room at the far end of the hall. In just three days the Americans had declared full ownership of the room, mostly because of the extra degree of privacy offered by the sealed-off set of faulty toilets next door.

'What do you make of that, then, Margaret?'

He looked across to Sergeant Millington, who was following the trio's path with an expression of stony indifference. At the sound of his words, she turned on her heel and walked off towards reception.

'Back to your post, please, PC Bayley.'

Her slow-moving visage disappeared back into the shadows. Harry was left alone in the corridor, the noise from the CID office already beckoning him. Jaitley had rushed back in to collect his notepad and hadn't shut the door behind on his way out.

There it was; the scared ground Harry had coveted for so long. Everything was in reach; the evidence pinned to the walls; the tea, the coffee, the plain clothes; the casual chat now that Casey had left the room. He could finally be a part of it. An outcast at first, for sure, but even just the faintest acknowledgement of his existence could be the first step on his journey to a fulfilling future. One where he could pick out his own shirt and tie in the morning, maybe a leather jacket and some sunglasses too.

But then Harry couldn't help noticing the remote control sitting on Jaitley's desk. The possibilities of the afternoon abound; Casey was busy, Margaret was lenient as long as it was quiet. Maybe there was something to be salvaged from the day.

Without being spotted by the roomful of investigators, Harry darted into the office, swiped the remote and a moment later was back at reception, switching the security monitor over to *SyBall Daily*.

Joshua Pittman, he thought to himself. *What are the chances?*

'13

Heart of Stone

P J threw his phone into his kitbag and, as he looked across the length of the training field, noticed the sway of the trees along the southern border. A breeze had whipped up, almost instantly, from the hazy static of the warm afternoon, and the atmospheric pressure had risen, the expanding air pressing against his chest.

Others had noticed it too. The games and the banter had stopped as the sudden change in weather caught their attention. A few looked to the sky – it wouldn't be the first time some high-ranking Department official had dropped in unannounced by helicopter. Troy Simpson grinned; perhaps his new date was paying him an unexpected visit.

But there was no sound of approaching rotor blades; all they could hear was the rustle of the leaves, followed then by a gut-wrenching shriek, as though the air itself were crying out in pain. Machete-like blades suddenly appeared out of nowhere; scorch marks spun like shooting stars, chasing each other's tails around an empty space, wobbling and creasing as the structure of reality faltered and the large object behind the collision of light and noise pushed itself into existence.

Sparks flickered off the fins; the fizz and the hiss and the metallic thrum became louder as the heart-shaped object wound down and came to a stop. It looked oily, damp even, as steam evaporated off the surface and the tempest of browns, oranges and greens settled into a calm undertow.

The radiating heat was immense, but there were still goosebumps on PJ's forearms. His state of shock was such that he barely noticed when George Castle brushed him aside as he made his way through the crowd to investigate. An assortment of coaching staff and other training ground employees had all stepped outside to join the players as they heard the commotion.

The manager stood a few feet in front of the others, took a deep breath and grimaced. He went to speak but a voice behind beat him to the punch.

'Do you know what it reminds me of?'

PJ picked up on the attempt at a hushed, reverent tone; but Troy being Troy, it came out as more of an inconspicuous blurt.

George scowled at him. 'Shut it, Simpson, you prat!'

The craft was glowing now, or at least the air around it was; an ethereal shimmer reflecting off the leaves of the trees behind it.

Troy persevered. 'No, no, hear me out. Look at those colours. A bit like the outside of the BK, don't you think?'

Jacob Terrier nodded vigorously. PJ could imagine him as a toy dog stuck to the dashboard of Troy's car, bobbing his head in perpetual agreement with his captain's every word.

'The stadium's blue,' a voice droned. Alex Shoreham, centre back.

PJ snorted. Out of the corner of his eye, he could see Danny Holt – Jacob's opposite number on the wing (and in most other ways, too) – smirking back at him.

'Yeah, I know that,' said Troy, 'but there's something about them, the way they mix together.' He clicked his fingers and pointed. 'I bet you anything it's for the Final. The closing ceremony. Or the winner's ceremony, definitely. Reckon that thing's gonna crack open any minute and someone'll walk out holding the cup.'

A ripple of agreement reverberated around the group.

'Waste of bloody money,' George muttered.

As the idea of the most elaborate prize-giving ceremony in the history of the world took form, a silky ooze slid out of the shell and solidified into a set of floating steps (the supports were hidden by mirrors, presumably). Then, against the glaring light from the opening left behind, a shadow appeared.

Troy beamed. 'See, I told you!'

The silhouetted figure stepped forward, surveying the group. A few winced as a foot landed on the first step, expecting it to give way. But the stairs held firm, and as the visitor descended, the light of the evening sun fell across her face.

Three instant observations registered in PJ's mind: the girl was young, she was pretty (a little dowdy, perhaps, and not dressed to her strengths, but still attractive) and if she were meant to be holding a trophy, she had forgotten it.

Similar thoughts must have been running throughout the group, because again he felt the mood change. Elbows were nudged, eyebrows were raised and there were shuffles of animated swagger. A couple of smooth greetings were called out and someone near the back had the balls to wolf whistle.

Amateurs, thought PJ.

The girl took no notice as she looked reticently from man to man, disappointing each one in turn as she denied them the merest hint of a smile.

'Which one of you is Nathan Pitman?'

Every head turned to PJ.

At first, a small swell of discomfort churned in his stomach. It had been a long time since he'd been anywhere without being recognised at first glance, and the stern manner in which the girl had called his name convinced him that she wasn't here for a selfie.

Nonetheless, a girl asking for the Hitman was still a girl asking for the Hitman, and he wasn't about to let these losers notice he'd been caught off guard. With a grin as wide as his face would allow, PJ spun on his heels and walked backwards away from the group, wagging his fingers in smug satisfaction.

'Better luck next time, yeah, boys?'

It had never felt so forced. The thrill of making a move in some other setting – a nightclub, an after-party – was always laced with a motivational terror as the adrenaline pumped through his body, especially when people were looking. This was different – he was genuinely afraid.

He'd have to be particularly charming.

Spinning back, he made the conscious decision to stop when he was still within touching distance of George Castle. He could see her more clearly now – deep wrinkles in her forehead had been formed by her persistent frown. Her cheeks were freckled, her eyes were dark and if PJ had to guess, he'd say she'd been in a few fights recently. But overall, worth a second look.

'A very good evening to you, miss,' he began. 'I'm Nathan, but you can call me PJ. In fact, you can call me anything you like.'

There were a handful of cheers; as an opening gambit it was tried and tested. But the girl, hearing it for the first time, offered no reaction as she stepped onto ground level and approached him. He rubbed his hands together and nodded towards her craft.

'That was quite an entrance you made there. I like it, I like it. How may I be of service to you today?

George Castle mumbled, 'Watch yourself, Pitman.'

But PJ was past the point of no return. Whoever the girl was, the game had started. Again, she said nothing.

'What's your name? C'mon, tell me.' This was another tactic, the illusion of bringing someone shy out of their shell. 'Because now you know me, don't I deserve the pleasure of knowing you?'

Lexa took a deep breath and tried to draw in the boy's remarks, hoping the excruciating attempts at charm and refinement would resolve her into doing the right thing.

No mistakes this time.

Nathan Pitman opened up his hands and shrugged. 'Well? I ain't got all day. Got a pretty big match tomorrow, I need my beauty sleep.'

Repulsive chuckles echoed around him. It was all the encouragement she required. Her fist clenched beside her and into it she focused everything; the time she had wasted with Josh, the anger and the stupidity, the frustration and the tiredness. The glove was in her pocket still, but she didn't need it – not only would it give the boy time to run and cower, but there was something about the finality of her journey that made her crave the rawness of her skin against his. Her knuckles squeezed, her fingernails dug into her palm; she stepped forward and rose her fist…

Thwomp!

The hit was so powerful that Lexa was lifted off her feet and thrown across the grass, the pain spreading quickly across her chest from the point of origin. She landed in a heap. Her arm took the brunt of the fall and her cry was more of anguish than anything else.

As the initial shock subsided, the commotion surrounding Lexa came into focus, the exclamations and trampling of feet; but she barely had time to raise her head before her attacker was back at her side. He clambered across her, driving his knees into her thighs and pinning her into the mud. The stench of his breath and grotesque determination of his face, inches from hers, was horrifyingly familiar.

Lexa struggled against him; she could hear the shouts and protests and saw the arms pulling at him, but the Euphorivore kept on pushing. He bore down on her shoulders, kneading into the nerve endings of her bad arm and sending sharp pulses into the ends of her fingers.

'Ernie! Mate, what you doing? Get off, you're hurting her!'

The pain ravaged through her, but she held in the screams. Even if this were it – the end of her mission, of her life, and of the world – she would deny the filthy bastard the satisfaction. He leaned forward until their noses were almost touching. Sweat beads on his greasy forehead traversed across the thin dark lines beneath his skin that were the avenues to the larger markings hidden beneath his hair.

He snarled, 'Where did you come from?'

Lexa saw his lips move, but his voice was detached from the words they formed, as though they were already a memory inside her head. She felt sick with the sensation.

'Go to hell,' she whispered.

The Euphorivore growled, a wave of mutual contempt flowing between them. He shifted his position, laying one arm across her chest and taking hold of her neck with his free hand. The scramble of coaches and players clamouring to lift him off her intensified. There were hands on her legs and arms now too, desperately trying to slide her out from beneath him, but Lexa knew better how futile their efforts were. He might have looked old and wrecked, but he could crush her windpipe in an instant, and she could only assume he was hesitating to prolong the agony.

'Fight back,' he said. 'Go on.'

Lexa gasped for air. He eased his grip around her throat and the relief of feeling his body lift off hers was like swimming up from the seabed and breaking through the surface of the ocean. It seemed the incessant jostling by the squad and the staff had finally broken his concentration, or else just got on his nerves, for then he stood, hunched like a wrestler in the ring.

Out of the crowd one of the players ran forward, his dreadlocks trailing behind him, and punched the Euphor square in the face. His head jerked to the side and he teetered off balance for brief moment, but then in one swift movement retaliated with a rising left-handed slap across the player's cheek.

'Ernie, stop!' PJ pleaded, from a safe distance. 'It ain't worth it!'

'My name is not Ernie!'

The group backed off. The dreadlocked player had writhed around on the ground with all the theatricality the Captain told Lexa to expect from footballers, but now his teammates had to hold him back from having another go.

Coughing and wheezing as she went, Lexa rolled onto her side and pushed herself up from the turf. As soon as she was upright, she reached into her pocket.

'Ernie' was at full height now, looking with narrow eyes along the faces formed in a semi-circle around him. He was panting and his shoulders rose and fell with every heave of his chest. But anyone who took this as a sign of exhaustion was wrong. He wasn't tired, he was exposed. His cover was blown, but his kind weren't the type to panic.

The clip of the button across her wrist brought his attention back to her. Sunlight reflected off the blades, shimmering as she drew her fingers in and out. Inside the leather was cool against her skin and she could feel the blunt ends of the blades where she had sewn them between the layers of material at the fingertips. She ought to lunge for PJ. If she took him out first, then whatever happened next was immaterial. The world would be safe. But she had never killed a Euphor before, and this guy was right there...

A smug, salacious smile drew across Ernie's lips. He knew what she was thinking. Their eyes met. He was bigger, but she was faster.

Together they flinched –

'Don't move, asshole.'

The woman was standing just a few feet away from Ernie, but with their focus squarely on one another, neither he nor Lexa had seen her approach across the soft grass. She stood with two firm hands on the dart gun pointing directly at the Euphorivore's head. Her steely expression was immediately recognisable from the files on Lexa's laptop, but only now could she see the depth of emotion behind the glare – the weariness, the bitterness, the fire struggling to keep itself alight.

Lexa recognised it all.

Behind Casey stood her team of agents, uniformly distanced in heroic poses and staring down their sights at their target.

The training ground had gone deadly silent. The players were even further away than before, trapped in an imaginary bull pen with their coaches and service staff, each face wrecked with fear. In the middle was PJ, terrified but healthy and unhurt.

Silently, Ernie obeyed Casey's command, doing his best to match her ice-cool stillness, but coming off like a dormant volcano about to blow.

'Are you alright, miss?' said Casey, her eyes still fixed on her suspect.

The question gave Lexa pause to quickly check herself over. The pain in her chest was easing, and while her right arm still throbbed, it was no worse than she had experienced before. Her throat was sore, though.

'I'm fine,' she croaked. 'But you need to go. You don't understand, I'm –'

Too late.

Lexa couldn't say for certain what happened, but most likely Casey had caught a glint of light off one of the blades, and for the tiniest of moments her attention shifted away onto Lexa's glove – giving Ernie the opening he needed. Casey yelled as his wrist collided with hers, her arm jerking awkwardly as the dart gun flew out of her hand and landed somewhere in the lengthening shadows of the trees. The Euphor ran – not at Lexa, but towards the other agents.

'Fire, goddamn it!'

Casey's order resonated, but before the agents could react, they were taken out by a thunderous blur of kicks, punches, shoulder slams and body blows. His speed and movement were phenomenal. Yet as the first batch of tough, athletic men fell to the ground, those bringing up the rear were able to get their shots off. Ernie dodged the flight of the darts as best he could, but couldn't stop one grazing his thigh, and he buckled at the knees and let out a roar of pain.

Blue lights flashed as a convoy of police cars arrived and stopped outside the main entrance. The noise of the sirens filled the air and chaos reigned. Physios and team doctors were attending to fallen agents, while players were rushed back inside and stood watching through windows.

Lexa's only option now was to get back inside the Vessel and try again; come back later tonight, perhaps even arrive in one of the adjacent fields and sneak in under the cover of darkness and attack PJ in his bed. Or maybe she should wait until the morning; with less time for recovery the injury wouldn't have to be quite as severe.

But Ernie was hobbling now, making his way to the trees along the border. He had lost all interest in her and his battle now was for escape.

Escape to tell the others.

Fight back, he'd said.

A second later, Casey's voice rose into the sky: 'No! Don't!'

Too late.

The *click-zip* sound of the shots punctured the air in quick succession. All three darts entered through his back, tearing through the skin and muscle of his upper body; the first two became lodged somewhere inside him, while the third ripped a path back out again through his abdomen.

The ferocity and immediacy of the pain had struck Ernie Strong like a firework going off inside his head. He could no more see, nor hear, nor think, than summon the effort to disguise his screams. Around him hands were cupped over ears as the excruciating noise shattered the limits of human endurance and nestled itself into the deepest recesses of long-term memory.

The feeling was of being burnt alive from within; his arms and legs twitched and faltered with every movement, and his vision alternated between shadowy darkness and blinding white light. He fell to his knees and wretched, hoping his redundant gag reflex would quickly awaken to expel the toxins building up in his gut. It was an undignified end, but he expected little else.

Steel yourself, you're almost free.

Lexa lowered Casey's dart gun, her hand still shaking from the recoil, and dropped it to the grass in the same place she found it. Then, before anyone could stop her, she was running up behind Ernie. She could pin the bastard down where he lay and with her glove claim the spoils of victory.

Except before she could get there, Ernie lifted himself, agonisingly, to his feet and stumbled in the direction of a small pavilion on the edge of the pitch. He took only a few steps before losing stability again, and saw that Lexa was behind him.

Throwing her full weight into it, she slammed shoulder-first into his body. The wooden slats of the pavilion splintered as the heavy Euphorivore crashed into its wall.

She heaved herself against him, and though his arms went limp at his sides, Ernie remained on his feet. His clothes were sopping with blood and a grotesque squelch rose from between them as Lexa pressed closer. Again, they were inches from each other, but this time her hand was free. Hooking the blade through the dart hole in his jumper, she ripped up towards his neck and then slid her hand through the opening. Her fingers found the centre of his chest, and he winced as the tips penetrated his skin.

It was in there; Lexa could feel it already.

She wanted to say something meaningful, like 'This is for my father,' but she couldn't speak. Instead they stared at one another. The commotion and interference around them had faded and slowed to a misty haze. There was pressure behind her hand, sinking the blades deeper into his flesh.

Ernie let out one final blood-curdling shriek, which sliced like a knife across the backs of her eyeballs.

And then, silence.

Lexa took a step back and watched his body slide down the wall and slump into the mud. Her heart was pounding, and she drew in the warm evening air to suppress the conflict of relief and despair coursing through her.

The distorted shapes and hollow cries of people moving towards her came into focus. Along the front face of the pavilion Lexa saw two men standing at the edge of the grass. The first, a scruffy-haired man in an ill-fitting suit, was handing out orders to uniformed police to assist the Americans in surrounding her, his face straining too hard to look serious.

The other was Josh Pittman.

Lexa couldn't decide if she hated him more or less than the dead Euphorivore. Maybe she should rip *his* heart out. Discreetly, she began to work through the oozy lump of flesh in her hand, tearing through the tissue with the thumb-blade as quickly as she could without being noticed.

'Ma'am, turn around, slowly.'

The last of the muscle fell from the stone.

How far away was Josh from her? Ten metres? Fifteen perhaps? The agents were out of darts, but still they could catch her before she got there.

Reading her intent, the scruffy man took half a step in front of Josh and held up his arm to shield him, but Josh pushed him away and stepped forward.

'Lexa, I –'

She flew at him.

All she needed was to get close, just for a second, and without encouragement Josh had moved to within a bound's distance. He recoiled, but Lexa grabbed a tuft of his shirt, and in the shadow of the space between them, took his hand in hers and then squeezed his fist tight around the stone. Somehow she had avoided scratching him with the blades.

Pity.

Lexa held her grasp for as long as she could and bore deep into his eyes with disgust, until at last her arms were wrenched behind her back, the glove whipped off, and her wrists locked into a set of handcuffs.

She snarled at Josh. 'You have no idea what you've done.'

Casey led Lexa away along a huddled line of traumatised footballers. Some jeered, others cowered, and another, a tall one with perfect teeth, fainted at the sight of her blood-covered hoodie. At the head of the group was Nathan Pitman Junior, his arms folded tight to his chest. She tried to stop in front of him, but was hustled along by Casey.

'No, wait,' PJ called after them.

An older man beside him sneered. 'Pitman, what the bloody hell do you think you're doing?'

'I just gotta know something,' he said to Lexa. 'Why did you come here? Was it for him...' PJ pointed over to where a group of officers and agents were clustered around the remains of Ernie Strong. '...or was it for me?'

Lexa sighed. The mission was unravelling fast, and so too was her will to carry on with it. Her arm ached, her throat was sore, and the handcuffs chafed. She had lost the Vessel, the glove and her best chance of success all because some undercover Euphorivore came out of nowhere and goaded her into battle.

Her second big mistake.

The first was standing on his own now, resisting the urge to look more closely at the object in his pocket. There was no reason for Josh to be here and certainly no reason to trust him; but the narrowness of PJ's question and the look of fear on his face forced Lexa into believing that, instinctively, she had done the right thing.

'Lose the game,' she replied. 'Lose the game, or everybody dies.'

'14

Nutmeg

No matter the weather, nor the season, the belfry was always windy. Fifty-two metres above ground and exposed to the continual whip off the Thames, the campanile was a continuously dark, cold, iron-grey space of metal walkways and low hanging girders. The door from the freestanding hatch at the top of the stairwell was lashed to the bannisters with a piece of string tied to the handle. The brickwork either side was covered in graffiti; names and messages scratched out with screwdrivers and Swiss army knives, laying claim to some small piece of history. A toolbox lay next to some warm high-visibility jackets and a pile of hard hats dumped unceremoniously in the corner overlooking Westminster Abbey.

Apple Blossom sniffed the jackets, momentarily considering their worth as a new bed.

Access to the other side meant climbing over a small bridge which skirted the edge of the Great Hour Bell hanging in the centre; thirteen tonnes of dusty-looking copper and tin surrounded by cage fencing and suspended above a crash-mat built of seven old railway sleepers. The four smaller bells hung further up, lurking in the darkness.

Ray Albright side-stepped the vertical cable which ran through a hole in the floor to the hammer on the quarter bell above him. Everything inside the square perimeter of archways was drab and dirty and entirely functional. If he could get pass the wire mesh onto the balcony, then he could look over and admire the gold leaf on the heraldic shields, the turrets and the large stone sceptres on each corner.

During his exile, Albright had had plenty of time to do his research on the tower and consider its suitability as a private communications hub. Its shape, exclusivity and close proximity to the seat of power had made it the only option, but still it had felt prudent to get some understanding of the place so he could begin his plans for retrofitting the spire. The internet had, of course, proved useful, but he would later curse his own naivety for thinking that fictional depictions would help too. Every film or television programme he could find each had its own wildly different interpretation of the interior. Where they seemed to inaccurately match, however, was in showing the bells and the dials within one large, cavernous space with rickety wooden walkways and giant cogwheels turning inches from your face.

As his plans for the invasion grew, so did Albright's frustration with the general ignorance of pop culture. Clearly no-one *ever* thought about these things; production companies raked in millions by offering two-hour packages of absurd concepts and glaring inconsistences. And why? Because the audience favoured the ridiculous over the sublime. Magic was real, but only when it furthered the plot; people had superpowers, except when they didn't; serpents had wings and could breathe fire, but never burnt their mouths.

And the hero always won.

In his opinion the only form of mass entertainment that wasn't a prefabricated fantasy had been sport. But Albright had turned that into fiction too – because deep down, wasn't that what these mindless apes really wanted?

He stood at the wrought iron steps which led to the gantries above the belfry. Steep and narrow, with a low banister, which in high winds might as well have not been there, it took Albright longer to negotiate than the entire main stairwell he'd just climbed. His cane often became stuck in the footplates and he had to take short pauses to swear, catch his breath and wait for Apple Blossom to nervously jump each step in turn. A younger, less cautious version of himself used to bundle her up in his cardigan, leaving one less hand to grab hold of something. But priorities prevailed, and as much as it pained Albright to think about, it was better now, on this final excursion, to let her fall rather than risk not making it to the top.

The tragedy was one that neither had to endure as the stairs led onto the upper section of the spire. This area was much like the belfry, only smaller, with clear plastic panels now blocking access through the arches, and instead of a huge bell at its centre, there stood a large glass dome.

The Ayrton Light had been one of the few benchmarks of the tower that Albright hadn't dwelled much on the name of, primarily because very few people knew it was there or what it was called.

The beacon was traditionally illuminated, like a lighthouse, whenever Parliament was in session, as a democratic invitation to the horde outside to come in and watch. But with democracy as much an illusion as everything these days, the array of tungsten bulbs had since been removed and the Ayrton Light was made strictly out of bounds to everybody except one man and his dog.

Albright opened the access pane and stepped inside, the heat of the greenhouse enveloping him. A beer fridge under the control panel contained bottles of ice-cold water, and after Apple Blossom had been served a replenishing drink she curled up into her basket and watched her master settle into his chair and begin the start-up sequence.

The collection of images slid over one another as they roamed across the panel, the moist colours around their edges merging and breaking apart, leaving behind irregular web-shaped patterns. His fingers traversed the surface with the skill and confidence of an artist, bringing the pictures together into a collage. He could see them waiting for him, drunk with eagerness and excitement. He could see the generations of hunger; a celebration fuelled by the ache of their want.

The control panel was circular but for a gap through which he and Apple Blossom had passed into the centre, but now Albright turned and pushed the two ends together with his hands, like a deity joining two seas to create an ocean. Once the circle was complete, the beads of light began to shoot around the surface, faster and faster until he was encased by a series of electric-white rings, the tiny vignettes of his brethren sinking further out of sight

Ray Albright felt his spirit soar. He held a hand to his chest as the dizziness threatened to overcome him, caught out by the leap of exhilaration that might tear the very life out of him. The sun had lowered but the day was far from over. The whole of London was laid out in front of him, basking in the haze of the summer heat.

His empire. His dominion.

The skyscrapers sparkled and the river glistened as millions of encounters came and went without ever knowing he was there. Over to the north-west Albright could make out the BK Stadium's brilliant blue antenna rising like a spike out of the ground, towering over the bowl and the seemingly endless rows of little brown homes.

Settling into the moment, Albright took his phone from his pocket and checked the time. 5:36pm. Nearly full-time in Manchester. Middle of the day in Brazil.

He laid the phone squarely on the control panel, where it sunk part-way into the oily fluid; the autumnal colours seeping over the edges like a symbiote merging with a host. The streaks of light grew in speed and brightness. His finger hovered above the screen and his eyes flicked towards Apple Blossom, who was quivering by his feet.

'I know you don't like this, sweetheart – but last time, I promise.'

Albright tapped the SyBall App and said:

– *Home.*

***

Caroline Pitman stroked her son's head as he ate his dinner. To celebrate his return, she had made his favourite – sausage, chips, peas and lots of tomato ketchup – certain it would make him feel better. But instead the plate was greeted with a mumbly 'thank you', and the food consumed slowly and mechanically as Josh sat staring out into the middle distance.

Running her fingers through his hair, a part of Caroline hoped he might try to shake her off, in the usual manner, with a flick of his head. It had been a staple of their relationship since his early teens. Once a sign of his pubescent march towards adulthood, tonight it would be the mark of normality she yearned for. Yet minutes had passed and still Josh allowed his mother to feel his thin strands brush against her palm as though she wasn't really there.

But at least his self-absorption meant Caroline could study his injuries without being reprimanded for undue staring. Josh's nose was still twice the size and twice the redness it ought to have been, and the bandage she had offered to replace before made it look larger still. Puffy, black bruising had formed beneath his eyes, and every time he opened his mouth, his skin wrinkled, and he winced in pain.

He looked so different – nothing like her own little Joshie. She would have to shake herself off soon and do something else, otherwise she might burst into tears.

'So, what did the police say, sweetheart?' she asked casually, as though it were a common dinnertime question.

Josh swallowed another mouthful with an overloud gulp.

'Not much,' he said, directing his answer into his food.

'Really?' She picked up her husband's empty plate and tried not to let the shake of her hand rattle the cutlery on top. 'They must have said something. You were with them most of the day.'

'I went for a bit of a drive afterwards.' He caught her eye quickly and then turned away. 'To clear my head.'

Caroline watched as he forked the last piece of sausage and pushed it around the plate like a tiny mop, scooping up as much of the ketchup as he could along the way.

'They don't think they'll find her,' he added.

'Oh? Well, they found your car at least.'

With the fork held halfway to his mouth, Josh followed his mother all the way as she leant forward, kissed him on the head and walked off into the kitchen. A rush of panic raced through him. He hadn't mentioned anything about Lock Niss before now. So much had happened since Lexa had tried to run him over with it that he'd almost forgotten the car was stolen in the first place. His mind had been consumed with heavy thoughts of war-torn London, medieval wolf hunts and gloves with sharp spikes.

At first it had all seemed too expansive to comprehend; too many impossible things flying around at once, but soon after being thrown from the Vessel in the old hospital outhouse, they had compressed into a singular point, knotted together by the decision to go back to the police station and intervene on her plan.

And now someone was dead.

When stacked up against these other events, the theft of his faithful four-wheeled chuggy-buggy of sanctuary had fallen low on his list of considerations. Now it was parked outside the house in

215

its usual spot next to the family Volvo, unassuming of the adventure it had been on.

But the hint of suspicion in Caroline's voice was undeniable. Josh had hoped the trauma of his experience would spare him from any detailed conversation, but what little he had said was already too much. He was holding back, and she knew it. A mother always knows, she would probably say.

His leg shook under the table. Josh hated lying to her, but what was there to gain from telling the truth? He knew what millions didn't; that it was probably too late. A girl from the future had been moments away from saving the world, but now thanks to him she was in a police cell. Thanks to him, and his act of illogical conscience, his own family were in danger. Josh could beg and plead with them all he wanted not to put the Final on tomorrow, but without a convincing reason, it was unlikely to work. The temptation would be too much. He could smash the TV. Board up the doors and windows. Crush some sleeping pills into their morning tea.

But what then? He'd seen the Captain's video. The sludge beneath his feet. The landscape burning in the background. Was surviving the weekend really the better option?

That was a point: was Josh still alive somewhere in Lexa's world? Or had he snuffed it five minutes into the first battle with the piss still dribbling down his leg?

In his cosy home, at the end of a nice meal, the guilt and stress hit Josh like a wrecking ball. Spots appeared before his eyes as blood rushed to his head; his heart raced, and that last bit of sausage felt like a jagged rock scratching his throat.

'Yes,' he managed to say with a hard, painful swallow. 'She'd dumped it in the park.'

Caroline was in the kitchen, her hands submerged beneath the soapy water in the sink.

'With the keys?'

Josh screwed up his face. *Please. Please just drop this.*

'Yes.'

'But not your watch?'

Damn.

The watch was probably in the Vessel somewhere, buried under all the junk strewn across her desk. He had never even thought to look for it.

'No.'

As he ran his finger along the neck of his fork, Josh stared out of the window into the back garden, with its fresh cut lawn, neat rows of potted plants and long-forgotten action figures buried in the soil, and considered the virtue of following the path of least resistance. Of sitting in front of the TV tomorrow and letting fate decide. At least if it did all come to end, he'd no longer have to suffer the recrimination coming at him from all sides.

Preferably though, he'd like to see the air above the patio rip open like a sheet slashed across the middle with a fiery blade, and for the Vessel to arrive with Lexa inside, here to tell him the world was saved, all was forgiven and he should pack a bag and come with her on an adventure through space and time.

He wished so hard he didn't even notice the arms sliding slowly around his neck and across his chest. By the time he felt the pressure on his collar bone, Josh was already being lifted out of his chair, which landed with a crack on the laminate flooring. The fork flew out of his hand, the silence of its flight followed by the *tinkle-thud* of its collision with the sideboard. A second set of arms wrapped around his abdomen, giving leverage and speed to his abduction, and before he could call out, he was already on the ground, being poked and jabbed by two giggling blurs of long black hair.

'Give us all your money!' one squealed with delight. Jessica, the youngest by all of seventeen minutes. High-pitched. Excitable.

'Yeah! Pay up or we'll smash your face in!' Sophie, the mastermind. Cunning, ruthless, with a teeny-bopper's voice laced with genuine menace.

Experience had taught Josh that as a pair they had little time for playful sibling rough-housing. This was an assault, a masterclass in humiliation. Josh struggled against them but it was no use; his legs were pinned by theirs, pushing down like heavy dumbbells across his thighs, and within seconds the attack was redirected onto the known fault line just below his ribs, the relentless pinching and prodding of which would render all movement into an involuntary and uncontrollable series of body spasms.

The giggling reached fever pitch. In the pockets of breath between the convulsions, Josh resisted the urge to cry out for his mother, but the sound of the commotion had already travelled easily into the kitchen.

'What on earth is going on in here?' Caroline barked, adopting the lower register used exclusively for the beratement of her daughters.

The chuckles developed into barrel rolls as the twins fell away either side of Josh, too overcome with joy to even try and get up.

'For goodness sake, he's only just come out of hospital! What is wrong with you?'

Sophie and Jessica locked eyes for a moment, each expecting the other to provide an answer, but this resulted only in renewed fits of laughter.

'Get out of my sight this instant!' Caroline was closer now, flicking her tea towel at them as though she were shooing away a pair of stray animals from her flower beds. 'Go on, get out! I mean it! I don't want you in the house.'

The girls took their cue and scurried off, out of the dining room and down the hall towards the front door, passing their father as they went. The racket had finally been enough to rouse Frank from his armchair, where until now he'd been happily sat ignoring his family and listening to the post-match analysis on the third-place play-off.

Brazil had won.

The door slammed and the house fell silent. Josh was still on the floor. There were no new injuries, expect for a sharp twinge in his thigh from when Sophie's knee had leant on the keys in his trouser pocket.

Except his keys were on the hook. Then he remembered:

The lifestone.

Caroline leant over him, her head blocking out the glare from the overhead bulb.

'Josh, sweetheart, are you alright?' she asked, adopting the higher register used exclusively for fussing over her son.

'I'm fine, mum.'

'Let me help you up.'

Josh flinched at the first touch of her hand on his forearm, as though the skin beneath his sleeve were as hot and swollen as his nose. A tingle shot up his arm from the point of contact.

'I said I'm fine!'

The dejection in his mother's eyes as she pulled away was unbearable. Yet more guilt for him to burden. Josh rolled onto his side and pushed himself up into a sitting position, each movement an aching reminder of the various injuries Lexa had inflicted. He paused before lifting to his feet, fearful of the head-rush that would make his nose burn even more.

Out in the hall he found his father lingering by the door to the living room. Josh could feel the shame and embarrassment radiating off him like an electric heater.

'What?'

Frank shook his head. 'Nothing, son. I'm just glad you're okay.'

The pitying slap on Josh's shoulder was like being hit with a slab of rock.

'Wanna watch the highlights with me?'

Josh smiled. The forced sincerity of the gesture was almost sweet.

'No, thanks. I'm pretty tired. Think I'll head up now, if that's alright?'

'Of course it is, my darling.'

Caroline watched from the end of the hall as Josh ascended the stairs, and considered offering to bring him up a cup of tea in half an hour or so.

Best not, on second thoughts.

Instead she returned to the kitchen, with the tears glossing the edges of her vision, and wondered if a jury would convict her if that night she chose to smother her daughters in their sleep.

Even beneath the unremarkable light of Josh's desk lamp, the lifestone glistened and sparkled like a cut diamond; which was odd, given that its surface was smooth and its shape irregular, like a marble that had warped under exposure to extreme heat, and then cooled and solidified again. Holding the stone close to his eye, Josh saw that the glittering array came from miniscule flecks, barely visible through the translucent amethyst hue, which reflected the light like tiny pieces of tin foil. It occurred to him that the strangeness of its inorganic quality (the walls of the Vessel looked like living tissue, this didn't) was matched by the notion that the sparkle was only visible once the stone had been removed from the body it had grown in.

Perhaps that was the point. Whatever material gave Euphorivores their ability to feed on emotion was resting in the palm of his hand. It was outside of nature, or what he had assumed nature to be. A beautiful little rock whose talent and scope were so beyond comprehension that maybe it was best to stay hidden and out of human hands. Mankind wouldn't be able to cope with how it felt.

How Josh had felt.

After the lifestone had been pressed into his hand at the training ground, he had watched helplessly as Lexa was led away by the police. Everyone around him was still reeling from her violent encounter with PJ's bodyguard, locked in a state of bewilderment and revulsion, but Josh followed the car with her inside until it had disappeared through the gate and beneath the trees.

The look she had given him in that final moment was devastating; a torrent of anger, betrayal, and disappointment combined into a single hard stare. Josh had wanted to run after her; to tell Casey and Jaitley it had all been a mistake, but his shame had rooted him to the spot. In hatred of himself, Josh had clenched his fists, one hand squeezing tightly around the lifestone...

And that's when it happened.

That feeling.

It had risen up though his arm, navigating its way through the network of nerve endings and the thread-like sinews of his muscles and electrifying the surface of his skin until every hair was on end. His arm felt light, with the other by comparison becoming like a dead weight pulling him down, only for the sensation to then spread evenly throughout his body, restoring the balance. The rush to his head was an intoxicating hit; luxurious and dangerous, enlivening his soul, as though he were finally awakening from the restrictive dream he'd been sleep-walking through his entire life. His nerves tingled and itched with newfound verve; his senses sharpened, the smell of dew drops on the leaves and the freshly trimmed grass infiltrating his nasal passages and lessening his wound, the light of the sun shining brighter as it sunk towards the horizon, the conversations around him sharp and acute. A rejuvenation he didn't deserve, but rich and warm and affirming, nonetheless.

At its peak the energy growing inside him had tried to push its way out of every pore and escape into the world beyond. Unable to cope with the intensity, Josh had unthinkingly opened his hand and let the lifestone drop to the grass.

By then Lexa was gone, and no residual euphoria remained within to make him feel any better about it. Using only the tips of his fingers, he'd gingerly picked the stone up again and placed it in his pocket, where it had remained until now.

There was a strong temptation, in the relative privacy of his bedroom, to clasp his fist around it once more and see where it would take him. If he could withstand the possessive power long enough, then perhaps he might catch some glimpse into the world of the Euphorivores and be witness to something – *anything* – that might alter the situation for which he felt largely responsible.

But he didn't.

Josh feared the seduction would lead him down a rabbit hole from which any attempt to return could cost him his life.

Like PJ Pitman's bodyguard.

Instead, he placed the lifestone in the middle of his desk, and leant back in his chair, stretching out the toll of the day and taking in the familiar, ordinary environment of his room. Only it was less ordinary now, given that Josh had just met most of the people staring out at him from the glossy posters on his wall:

Ben Castle, with the ball between his gloves, his image fading thanks to the sun streaming through the adjacent sash window.

Troy Simpson, tugging at the badge on his shirt, roaring with pride.

PJ Pitman, mid-sprint, his jaw slightly sagging as he dribbled past a blurred-out opponent.

There were others; some he'd seen tonight but couldn't remember their names, plus a few uncapped players of the two Regional League teams – South East and Greater London – which both fell under the fandom of the Surrey border where he lived. In this house, support for either team would alternate, depending on which one Frank decided was in better form that season.

It was his father who had demanded the posters be hung, part of the plan to instil some verve for the sport in Josh, alongside persuading/ordering him to join Belmont Park Rovers. It was decorative propaganda; the pictures replaced the old film posters – the sci-fi sagas and action comedies, with their plucky heroes depicted beneath the looming face of the antagonists – that had been there since Josh was small. As if the message weren't clear enough, Frank hadn't even bothered to take these down, and instead left corners of the contraband imagery visible beneath the portraits of the 'true' heroes.

'Football is real life,' he'd said.

Well, you got that wrong, didn't you, Dad?

It was all as much a fantasy as anything else you could pay to watch.

If anything were true, it was that there were times when Josh was quite happy just to sit and stare at the new posters, and ponder just how ridiculous the Department's spiral crest was; and in his mind's eye the picture would change and be replaced with his own design, each one unique, each one dripping with symmetry and symbolism. Like a flag they would be complex in their simplicity; colours, words and shapes put plainly together to connect the touchstones that one group of people honoured, but that others didn't. Though he cared nothing for football, Josh at least knew this was its point.

The government – who turned out to be a bunch of murderous, lying bastards after all – argued that the old ways were divisive, and continuing them would only seed disharmony. But the way Josh saw it, Albright and co. were confusing division with diversity. Differences mattered. Agreement was boring.

His life was boring, before today.

Looking up at the wall behind his desk stacked with his sketchpads and folders, Josh's eyes scanned over what had been his only act of insubordination: a cartoon, his own drawing, of a squirrel, dressed as a superhero and holding a football, with his name scribbled underneath: *Nutmeg*.

'A play on words to denote when a player passes the ball between the legs of an opponent'.

It was more or less the only picture Josh had ever drawn that wasn't for himself, and yet was the only one he kept on show. Dressed in his super-suit, hand on his hip, his smile warm and innocent, the squirrel spoke to Josh in ways he couldn't fully describe. The cheery little creature's eyes were wide and bright, with hard little pencil dots right in the centre, burgeoning with hope and positivity, unafraid to show the world what made him special. A manifestation in graphite lines of everything his creator wished he could be, gentle yet persistent, bold, brave and impossible to ignore. The super squirrel was always there, always encouraging, ready to listen and waiting patiently for Josh to set himself free.

You must be pretty disgusted with me today, right, Nutmeg? Well, join the club.

Josh dropped his head, too ashamed to look at the chubby-cheeked doodle in the face, and his attention was again drawn to the lifestone. Why exactly had Lexa given it to him? To stop the police getting hold of it? She must have believed her plan was still salvageable if he could somehow get it back to her. But he had arrived *with* the police, and so if that were case, it was one hell of a risk. And she was in their custody, too; so Lexa wasn't reliant on him just for the lifestone – but as a means of escape.

Did that mean then, she still... trusted him?

He could hear Nutmeg chirping away at him.

Take it to her! Find a way!

Josh leant forward to pick the lifestone up again, but stopped himself halfway, leaving his outstretched arm hanging in the air. There was something he hadn't noticed before; the way the stone refracted the light of his lamp in every direction, projecting a violet flower onto the sheet of paper beneath. He looked at his own hand and observed how the thin rays spread further out, a delicate coating masking his olive-coloured skin. It was the same everywhere he looked – the base of the lamp on the right, the coffee mug full of pencils on the left, and directly ahead onto the row of disordered sketchpads.

He stared at where the light shone brightest along the tattered spines of his collection. His mouth widened, his throat became dry and his breathing quickened. He reached out again, slower this time, not so close as to cast a shadow with his hand, but close enough.

Close enough.

'It can't be…' he said, so quietly he barely heard himself.

Frank opened his eyes. It wasn't the clamour of heavy footsteps on the stairs that had woken him, nor the frantic scrambling for keys out in the hallway, but the slam of the front door. He could only have been asleep ten minutes or so, but it was long enough for his neck to feel stiff from the awkward position of his head in the armchair.

Wincing from the discomfort, Frank lifted himself up and peered out the window in time to see the little green Nissan reversing out of the driveway.

Where's he off to now?

In the semi-darkness he saw Josh slamming the car into forward gear and tearing off down the street. The fluidity and urgency of the manoeuvre flickered a memory in Frank's mind; of Josh passing his driving test, of shaking his hand but wanting to hug, the sense of pride made larger by the added feeling of shameful surprise. He had expected him to fail.

As the noise of the engine faded so did the memory, and he turned his attention back to the television. Geoff Sterling was in the middle of his closing remarks, beaming intensely from his seat on the virtual pitch as he talked up tomorrow's Final with lavish hyperbole, and then letting it all drop as a woman with a headset came into shot and handed him a sheet of paper.

'Breaking news now from the homeland of our honoured bronze medallists', Sterling purred, his composure instantly regained. 'It seems that...'

The host stopped, squinted at the pages and then looked off-screen.

'Is... is this true?'

'15

Enemy at the Gate

Pulling up to the fortified entrance of the British Kingdom national team training ground, Josh realised he had underestimated just quite how busy it would be outside the main gate. It was the second time that day he'd passed down the narrow road, which snaked its way through a thick wooded area and up to the vast, modern complex; but on the first occasion he had been in the back of a police car, and the tinted windows had disguised the true scale of the obstructions, which were quickly parted anyway by the blue lights on the roof.

No such allowances for Lock Niss.

He knew the news outlets would have been there since the beginning of the tournament. White vans with antennas and satellite dishes attached to the roofs were parked up along both sides of the road, while further up a huge press pen marked out with Tensa barriers was set up beside the gate, packed full of camera crews and well-dressed reporters. But the arrival of the police on the day before the final had not gone unnoticed, and a second enclosure had been hastily erected on the opposite side to make room for an increased media presence.

The polite, patient manner in which news crews waited for their hourly reports on the team's status was gone. Instead the press pens had become more like bear pits, with rabid journalists clamouring over each other to be the first to feast on any scraps of new information from nearby officers.

And it wasn't just the media who were hungry. Josh could hear the noise from the far end of the road, more like an angry mob than a crowd of worried fans. Deeper voices of enforcement and pleas for calm pocketed their calls.

By now the sun was dipping beyond the tree line and in the distance he could see the single storey reception building up-lit from the ground. But he was still some distance away and the crowd were beginning to swallow up his car, slowing him to a crawl. Directly in front were three men all wearing shirts with 'Pitman Jnr' printed on the back.

There was no point continuing on like this. Josh stopped the car and squeezed out of the door and into the throng, taking one last look at his prized possession. The poor thing had been through so much already, what kind of state would it be in when he got back?

Would he get back?

He checked the lifestone was still in the pocket of his jeans. There was no real plan to any of this. He'd had the entire journey to figure something out, but all he had was the hazy belief that going back to the training ground was a better idea than going straight to the police station. He didn't really know what he would do once he was there, and he certainly hadn't factored any difficulty getting in.

Josh allowed himself to be swept along with the horde, dealing with the tussle of bodies and outstretched arms as they came. He even joined in with the odd cry of 'Why won't they tell us anything?' The mood was unsettling – it had been a long time since most of these people had worried about *anything*. One man in a green goalkeeper's shirt had a booming voice that drowned out those around him.

'What about Ben Castle? Is he okay?'

Searching for anyone who would listen, the man turned to Josh.

'All these people are so concerned with PJ,' he said. 'But Castle, he's... well, he's the greatest living goalkeeper. If anything's happened to him...'

'I'm sure he's okay,' Josh said.

In fact, Josh *knew* he was okay. If anyone in the national squad could handle themselves, it was Ben Castle; a stocky, hard-as-nails monster of a man, with razor-sharp reflexes and the agility of a gazelle, whom Frank Pittman encouraged his son to watch footage of at every available opportunity.

Plus, Josh had seen him just a few hours earlier and he was absolutely fine.

'Just believe. Union JAC.'

The loud man smiled. 'Union JAC,' he repeated with a calming breath.

Leaving his new friend behind, Josh moved on, squeezing his way through to the front and up close to a long wall of police constables, their faces weary from the subjection to the constant verbal barrage.

'Stay where you are, sir, no-one's allowed through,' said the nearest.

'You don't understand, I was here earlier. I came with the police. I'm Josh Pittman.'

'Sure you are, sir.'

'No, not...' Josh grunted with frustration. He'd been stopped by the only policeman in the world who knew PJ's real name. 'What about Agent Casey? Or Detective Jaitley, is he still here?'

The officer sniffed. 'Never heard of him.'

The moment was slipping away. He needed to think. Lexa was depending on him. He looked up and down the line of peaked caps and luminous jackets in search of a familiar face. Even PC Bayley would do.

'Mr Pittman?'

Josh lifted onto his tiptoes at the sound of his name and waved his arm in the air.

'Yes, it's me, over here!'

'Sir, please!'

The officer was not ready to give in, but then a pair of hands broke through the human barrier and with the strength of authority split the line as though they were clothes hanging in a wardrobe.

'Let him through, for God's sake,' Vikram Jaitley barked as he grabbed Josh's arm and pulled him in.

The officer glared at him with a *what makes you so special?* scowl.

The line closed back up behind them, leaving the police blockade to answer similar questions from an increasingly belligerent crowd.

'I was beginning to think you weren't coming,' said Jaitley. 'It's been a bloody nightmare, Mr Pittman, if you'll excuse my language. It was quiet enough when I left, but then news broke about Rio and all hell broke loose. We've managed to keep the press from finding out what happened in here, but it's only a matter of time, I guess. Only reason Casey let me come back was to arrest you, but now –'

Josh stopped in his tracks. 'Sorry, just a minute – arrest me? What for?'

'For destroying the –' Jaitley paused. 'Of course, you don't know, do you? How stupid of me.'

Jaitley surveyed the scene and nodded in the direction of a narrow footpath, guarded by two of Casey's agents, that ran along the edge of the reception building.

'Come with me, don't say anything.'

They walked through a small gap between the building and the field of reporters, who became louder and more animated at the sight of a non-uniformed officer.

'Detective, can you give us any updates?'

'Witnesses heard screaming; can you explain?'

'Are any of the team injured?'

'Will the Final still go ahead?'

'Who is that with you?'

That last question caught Josh off guard, and in his mind's eye every camera had turned and zoomed in close on his face. He remembered what Lexa had told him high above the mountains: politics, media, industry – these were the levels of power the Euphorivores operated in. But if that were the case, then what was their reaction to all this? They must have noticed something was happening.

The lack of 'government' intervention led Josh to two assumptions:

First, the Euphorivores were not aware of any commotion involving one of their own stolen ships, and second, they might not consider it a bad thing to have the frenzy around the national team whipped up further by the injection of a little panic.

Pushing it all aside, Josh looked straight on as he and Jaitley passed the agents with a nod of heads and onto the path, which was enclosed by the building on one side and a canopy of trees on the other. Now shielded from view, Jaitley stopped and threw a cautious glance in each direction. The demands of journalists were distant but still audible.

'This is really happening, isn't it?' he asked.

Josh nodded. 'Everything she told you is true.'

'Wow, I mean... everything?'

'Everything.'

'Wow.'

Josh gave him a moment as the pooling of a thousand odd thoughts tormented Jaitley's mind; the puzzle of whether he should follow orders and drag Josh back up the path, or push him further down in hope he can repair the damage.

The young detective hesitated.

In recent years Vikram Jaitley had found it all too easy to avoid sitting down and having a good hard think about all the niggles in his professional life, which, like an itchy rash, he had assumed would go away if he ignored them long enough.

There was too much football on TV.

But occasionally, dispiriting flashes of negative thought would emerge, in which he feared the drive and ambition that had seen him rise through the ranks so speedily had been lost. Such moments passed as quickly as they arrived; most mornings the drive from his flat to the station was enough to satisfy himself that he was a talented investigator. Yet once he was sat behind his desk, he found himself struggling to live up to that same lion-hearted impression of himself.

Standing with Josh on the shadowy pathway, Jaitley pictured the craft hovering in the next field and the body long since removed. He thought about Brazil, and the horror of what had happened there; he remembered Matthew Blaumann and his friends with their silent, shrieking faces – and yet even now his focus was drifting, gathering wool on the idea that both these events were tied to two games that Argentina really should have won given the depth and talent of their squad. Then he thought about the thunder on Casey's face if he returned without Josh Pittman.

The day was darkening fast. The air felt cool and sweet. Finally, he said:

'I've got this cousin in India. About six months ago he told me that football is now more popular there than cricket. Can you believe that?'

'Yes, I can,' said Josh.

'Me too. So you know what I did? I booked two weeks off and flew out there for the first weekend of the season. Who played? Who won? No idea. But it was amazing, I'll tell you that.' He chuckled at the memory. 'People think I'm an idiot. And they're right. But I never used to be, I know that much. It's not like I cut tokens out of cereal boxes and became a detective. I worked hard; I was good. My job was my life. I took case notes home every night – I even went through a stage of pinning them up on my wall and linking them up with bits of string, like they do on TV, with suspect photos and a map circled in red, newspaper cuttings... you get the idea. It's actually not as effective as you might think, you lose track after a while. But I gave it a shot. Try harder, do better – if it doesn't work, try something else. That was me, Mr Pittman, that was who I was. But then, one day, I just got bored of it. I wanted to watch football instead. Why? Why would I fly thousands of miles just to see one match? I haven't solved a case in two years. I haven't spoken to...' He looked down to the ground and shook his head. 'Never mind. Listen, the manager told the squad to go to bed. There's still a match to play tomorrow, for the time being at least. But PJ refused; he's still out on the pitch – seems like the perfect opportunity, to me.'

Josh looked down towards the far end of the pathway. 'To do what?'

'I don't know... talk to him. She told him he was going to die if he didn't throw the match. You're the only one who really knows what's going on, maybe he'll listen to you.'

'Maybe...'

'Oh, and the broken toilet's at the very back of the station, and the offices above it are empty.'

Josh blinked. 'I'm sorry?'

Jaitley cocked his head with a wry smile. 'That *is* why you came here, isn't it? I've seen enough films to know how this works. When I saw you last it had just gone six o'clock.' He nodded towards the training pitches. 'You'll have to get past the agents first – I'm afraid I can't help you with that.'

Josh absorbed the information with a slow nod, as though cautiously weighing up how useful it might be.

'My car is still outside,' he said.

'I'll take care of it.'

In the semi-darkness, Jaitley could see Josh moving his hand towards his pocket. He stopped him.

'Keep them on you for now,' said Jaitley. 'Just in case.'

'Right. Okay, thank you.'

Josh turned to leave, but quickly looked back. 'One last thing...'

'She's fine, Mr Pittman. Uncooperative, but fine.' Jaitley smiled. 'And she bloody hates you, excuse my language.'

'Just back off, man! Back off!'

As he emerged from the pathway, Josh saw PJ up ahead, perfectly framed by the shape of the Vessel behind him; the terrified face of the nation's hero set against a twisted metallic heart like the photo on some macabre Valentine's Day card.

The Vessel was floating, inches above the ground in the precise spot Lexa had left it; but now the Impossible Stairs had receded back into the closed shell and the craft was surrounded by a circle of ACA Agents, armed with long range dart guns and all with their backs towards it. Josh wondered if they were trying to ward off the temptation to stare and be drawn in just as he had.

It was into the agents that PJ Pitman now ran, backwards, screaming at Josh to keep his distance, and inviting each man to point their weapons towards the trespasser. He stumbled over a ball on the ground behind him, but recovered nimbly and kicked it straight at Josh – a thunderbolt of a shot, straight as an arrow and rising from the ground at the perfect angle to hit him clear in the chest. It was lightning fast too, and it was only because of the distance it had to travel that Josh had time to raise his hands and push the ball away before it struck. The sharp slap stung his palms, still tender from the cuts in his skin and the bruising around his fingers, and he grimaced with a hissing intake of breath.

PJ pulled a face too, his surprise turning fear into suspicion. He probably wasn't used to having shots like that saved, not by someone like Josh, at least.

Having done himself no favours with the first reaction save of his entire life, Josh held up his hands once more, this time in front of his face, to shield himself from the glut of weaponry on display.

'Please... please, don't shoot!'

One of the agents, a bulky man with a shaved head who looked like he was in charge, took a half-step towards him.

'Freeze! Don't move!'

'I won't, I promise... just please, don't shoot.' His knees bent involuntarily, half-expecting to be told to lie down. 'I was here earlier. Don't you remember?'

'Yeah, I remember!' PJ said. 'Don't mean nothing. How do I know you ain't one of them things?'

Taking care not move too quickly, Josh ran his hands back through his hair and across the top of his scalp, flattening his quiff and showing the full extent of his pale forehead.

'Look... no markings, see?'

Nothing.

No reaction. Josh realised to truly prove his ordinariness he would have to lift his shirt and show his chest; but these guys would probably think he was reaching for a weapon; they might fire before he had the chance.

Then, in complete unison, each man lowered their dart guns and stepped back to their sentry posts around the edge of the Vessel. Their eyes had all seemed to shift at once, from looking straight at Josh to looking past him. He turned in time to see Jaitley lowering his thumbs-up and heading off back up the pathway.

PJ seemed to relax too, for when Josh turned back, he had already taken a few swaggering steps towards him.

'What's your name?' PJ demanded, his chest puffed.

'It's Josh.' He dreaded the next bit, but it had to be said. '...Pittman.'

PJ's stoic resolve broke immediately, and he burst into laughter, an animated, high-pitched titter just the right side of condescending, and he swung his hand firmly into Josh's and shook. The same sharp sting shot through Josh's palm and up his arm.

'For real? Look, it's nice to meet a fan, but seriously, changing your name? C'mon…'

'It's my real name, I promise.'

'Oh.' PJ looked almost disappointed. 'Well, maybe you should change it. People could get confused, you know?'

Now Josh laughed. 'I do know. In fact, it's sort of why I'm here. Do you mind if we talk?' He looked over to the agents. 'In private?'

PJ considered the request with an indignant frown.

'Yeah, sure,' he said, eventually. 'Let's go for a walk.'

'16

One-on-One

In the time it took them to circle the training pitch, Josh had told PJ everything he knew: from his first meeting with Lexa outside the Bovill Arms to his second in Belmont Park, the wolves, the Blitz, the Euphorivores' plans, the tournament and the future war to come, and then finally to the decisions he'd made after she left him, which he could neither explain nor excuse.

Whenever his story strayed too far into the ridiculous, there was always the twenty-foot reminder floating above the grass at one end of the field, and a pavilion wall marked off with blue-and-white police tape and stained with dark splatters at the other.

All mentions of Ernie Strong left a sour taste in PJ's mouth, screwing up his face at the thought of the man in whose hands he'd placed his whole life. But for the rest of the time, he just looked down, nodding his head as Josh spoke. When the tale was over, PJ took a moment to absorb the overload of information and weigh up the decisions now facing him. Eventually he looked up, nodding his head in agreement with something spoken only to himself, and said:

'So – she thought *you* were *me*?'

'Yes.'

'So really, you ain't got nothing to do with this?'

Josh frowned. 'Not as such.'

'Sheesh, as if she really… do you play?'

'Amateur.'

'Striker?'

'Goalkeeper.'

PJ chuckled. 'You see, I knew it,' he said, wagging a finger in Josh's face. 'The way you blocked that ball, ain't no normal lad saving that. You got some skills.'

'No, I really don't –'

'When all this is over, I'll introduce you to Ben Castle. I've played with him and against him, and I am telling you, he is one scary dude. He can give you some proper tips.'

'There's no need,' Josh said, determined to kill off the thread of conversation. 'If you must know, I don't really like goalkeeping, so if we could just focus on tomorrow–'

'Wait, wait...' PJ interrupted. 'You don't like it? Why not?'

Josh let out an affected sigh. 'Because… I'm not very good at it. And I'm the reserve, which is even worse. It's like being picked last in the playground – as long as one other person is better than you, you may as well not be there. So why bother?'

PJ was shaking his head. 'Dude, serious, I ought to get Ben out here to slap some sense into you! He'd be the first to say that everything you do out there is about your own state of mind.' PJ tapped his temple to illustrate his point. 'You gotta believe in yourself! *Especially* if you're the reserve! You've gotta sit there, match after match, and all the time be ready to come on and *bam!* Change that game!'

PJ Pitman was beginning to sound like a younger, more streetwise version of Frank Pittman during one of his regular pep talks.

But Josh also knew PJ was talking for the sake of it, filling time to avoid the bigger issues, much like his hours spent staring up at a picture of a squirrel in a superhero's outfit.

'It's not that simple,' Josh said. 'If I play a match, it's not because the manager believes in me, or anything, it's because the first choice went and vaulted the handlebars of his motorbike. The only expectation people have of me is that I'll mess it up. Have you ever been a goalkeeper?'

PJ balked at the very idea. 'Pfft, no!'

'Well then, even someone as good as you can't know what it's like. You play in the outfield, where the odd scuffed shot or mislaid pass might not come to anything; but if I make a mistake then the ball's in the net. It's the difference between winning and losing. When you win, no one remembers you; when you lose, no one forgets.' Josh paused. 'Not least myself.'

It was an admission to himself more than anything; an admission that sometimes it did matter, that indifference was just a comfort blanket to crawl underneath and shut out the world. To *really* not care about the result actually required a resolve far stronger than he'd ever had. Not with that ever-present look in his father's eyes; the blame, the failure, the disappointment.

Who wouldn't be hurt?

PJ scoffed. 'You think Ben's never made a mistake? Never felt crap about it?'

'I'm sure he has, but he's naturally talented, I'm not. Easier for him to bounce back.'

'Jeez, man…' PJ planted his face in his hands and ran them down his cheeks. 'And you say I don't know nothing? I know better than you. Your shirt ain't a different colour just 'cos you can pick the ball up. Keepers are *meant* to stand out. They gotta make their presence felt – sometimes the game's going so fast, you see a bunch of your guys all together and you can't tell who's who. Except your keeper. They're big, they're noisy, they're angry… and that penalty area, that's their territory, yeah? When the ball gets whipped in, you work for him – he don't care who you are, if you don't do your job, he'll get you for it.' He moved closer to Josh and prodded him in the chest. '*That's* the difference between winning and losing.'

Josh opened his mouth to respond, but nothing came. He'd been stunned into a momentary silence, giving PJ the chance to jump back and perform a little dance on the grass. It was an odd routine, his legs apart and his knees bent as he shifted quickly from one foot to the other. He stuck out his arms and wiggled the tips of his fingers in nervous anticipation, then looked down to the space between his feet and started dribbling an imaginary ball.

'And for me, it's like… when I'm getting ready to shoot…' PJ tapped the ball past one unreal defender and avoided the tackle of another. 'I can see the keeper getting ready to stop me… he's watching everything I do… never takes his eyes off the ball, but still I can feel him squaring up to me. He's trying to intimidate me, put me off my game – it's a test. How much do I believe?'

His chest was heaving, his expression one of piercing, focused determination. He tapped the top of the ball with one foot to take out some of the pace, and with a pendulum-like swing of the leg, powered through, twisting his whole body and lifting himself off the ground.

If the ball had hit the back of an illusory net somewhere behind him, Josh would never know. PJ gave nothing away. Instead he just stared.

'Fear makes you a better player. The meaner the keeper, the better it is. There ain't no feeling in the world like it.' He sighed and shook his head. 'So don't talk to me like I ain't got nothing to lose. She said people were gonna die, them things are gonna get us, but that don't make it any easier... I can't just *miss*.' PJ looked at Josh like a little boy lost in the park. 'So, what do I do?'

For the second time that day, Josh felt so ashamed of himself he could hardly breathe. The guilt he felt for betraying Lexa had been an instant, crushing body-blow, but this – this was actually worse; it had risen up through the length of their conversation and was eating him from the inside out. Asking PJ to throw the game for the sake of the world was like telling him to cut his own leg off.

It was quiet now on the training ground. The summer evening was bright still, but without the stifling haze of the day. Casey's agents maintained their circular vigil, unmoved since their encounter with Josh. The ball PJ had kicked at him lay near the touchline on the opposite side.

'Let's have a kickabout.'

PJ cocked his head, like a confused puppy.

'Fancy it? Would be quite a thing to tell the manager I trained with the Hitman. Might get me some games.'

'Alright.' PJ grinned. 'You're on.'

Before Josh even reached the penalty area, PJ had effortlessly jogged to collect the ball and dribbled it back into play. The nearest set of goalposts weren't as close to the Vessel as he might have liked (the ones on the rear side were closer), but not wanting to arouse suspicion, Josh chose them anyway and went and stood beneath the crossbar, ready to play.

The goal seemed bigger than those at the Belmont Park Rovers Stadium. The posts were metal, probably steel, coated in gleaming white without a single chip in the paint, nor a patch of mud or stain of grass. The net was cut exactly to size, with no excess heap at the bottom, and pulled tightly along the top edge to produce a perfect string-woven cuboid, and it was this, Josh realised, that had the effect of widening the goalmouth beyond the stretch of the average human being.

PJ's first shot, softly hit from just outside the penalty area, did little to disturb the clean shape as it flew past his opponent and into the bottom corner.

This was going to be embarrassing. But Josh expected nothing less. Pitman versus Pittman was a David and Goliath affair, and while Josh didn't quite believe he could slay the giant, he did hope he might be able to at least put a chink in PJ's armour big enough to dent his confidence ahead of tomorrow. It wouldn't be easy – earlier PJ had actually been aiming for him, and even then, he could only manage a cack-handed slap rather than a catch.

What followed next was a fluidity of movement that was sometimes hard to follow. PJ showed no mercy, shooting, striking, tapping and volleying between the posts in quick succession; angles ranged indiscriminately from the acute to the obtuse, distances varied and trash-talk meandered between the inviting – 'Check out this bad boy!' – and the graphic – 'I'm gonna rip a hole right through your stomach!'

Again, and again, Josh picked the ball out of the back of the net, each time a little slower than the last. Most had sailed past, way out of his reach; two had gone between his legs and one had bounced off the inside of the post, hit his hand – which jerked awkwardly – and spun away behind him. The fruitless exertion was exhausting; his nose was killing him, his head ached, and his panic grew over PJ's impressive display – the goal he was set to score the next day was meant to be a close call. The Euphorivore referees would make sure it was given, but North America would still have to fight like lions to force PJ even slightly off target.

After each defeat, Josh did his best to look the part as he volleyed the ball back into play. He was no better with his feet than with his hands, and it wasn't until the fourteenth attempt that the ball finally travelled far enough to land near one of his targets – a tall, goofy-looking ACA Agent with a goatee beard, who looked down at the ball rolling to a stop as if it were a bomb about to explode.

'Oi, mate, give us our ball back!' Josh said with a laugh, affecting his best 'lad' voice.

PJ tittered. 'Yeah, on me head, son!'

The agent turned his head gingerly to find every single one of his compatriots staring back at him, willing him with their eyes.

'Kowalski,' said one, 'dude, this is your chance! Kick it!'

Agent Kowalski gurned a self-satisfied grin and nodded. This was his moment. He set his dart gun on the ground and took a few steps back. Eyeing his target to the sounds of deep-voiced encouragement, Kowalski galloped forwards and, on his final step, slipped in the mud, landing with a flump on his backside. His foot, however, still made contact with the ball, which, as encouragement turned to ironic cheering, flew at a skewered angle away from PJ, who was athletic enough to traverse the waylaid distance with Olympian speed, rise with a strong push off the ground and thud the ball with the top of his forehead.

Another agent read the trajectory and, with lightening quick reactions, dropped his own gun with decidedly less care, nestled his elbows into this ribs and cupped his outstretched hands to perfectly collect the ball and bury it safely into his chest. The first time PJ had been beaten that night. Agent Hicks' dimpled face lit up like a child on Christmas morning.

Perfect, thought Josh, jogging forward.

'Well caught! How about you go in goal for a little bit? You're wearing gloves and my hands are red raw!'

Christmas had just become Hicks' birthday too.

'Really? Aw, man, that would be… really?' His voice squeaked with excitement.

Josh waited for the protest from a burly superior, particularly that guy with the shaved head who'd been watching with narrow, suspicious eyes, but none came. Instead, the circle began to lose its shape; the agents relaxed, shuffled on their feet, and chatted to one another, all about Hicks' lucky catch and Kowalski falling on his ass.

'Sure,' said Josh. 'Let's do teams. PJ and I can be captains.'

The agents beamed as they ran onto the pitch, leaving the Vessel at last unguarded. By now, Josh knew exactly what Lexa's craft was capable of; it had been designed to predict the future and had been adapted to travel through time. A single, entwined mass of nerve and muscle tissue, grown rather than built, and even with the diminishing beauty of the metal fins graunched onto the side, it had an alluring, seductive quality that made it near impossible to resist.

Euphorivores were agents of bliss; it was both their food and their means of cultivating it. Everything they did was infused with that state of exaltation, and whatever power had gone into the making of the Vessel, and the thousands like it, they had put a hundredfold into the Guiding Principles of Joy and Compassion that were enslaving the human race, fuelled by an emotive connection to the Great Unifier.

It was little wonder then, that a group of armed officers, entrusted to guard the single most important object in the world, would abandon their posts for the chance of a kick-around with the world's most famous footballer.

Josh was the anomaly; he felt the bond far less than most, but it was there nonetheless, burning within him. Though ashamed to admit it, he couldn't deny the thrill of being the one picking the teams for a change. There was a certain rush in selecting the stronger ones first and leaving the weaker to kick the can for a bit longer. He thought his team might show some grumbling displeasure at being captained by the nobody, but the agents were just as happy to tackle PJ as they were to receive a pass from him. Once they were ready to play, Josh positioned himself in the goal at the far end and waited.

Good-humoured and pressure free, it was without a doubt the best game of football Josh had ever played – though his team lost horribly. He knew it wouldn't be long until the game caught the attention of Detective Jaitley or the rest of the squad inside, so he'd have to take his chance sooner rather than later. It was a big risk, but then again, so what?

He was a *goalkeeper*.

Apparently, that made him a renegade; nobody's pushover; a non-conformist who wouldn't be told what to do.

The moment came after the game's seventh goal – and the first scored *against* PJ's team. By then, all the dart guns and jackets had been shed completely and the goal scorer, an agent named Martinez, pulled his shirt up and over his head and ran around the pitch, arms out like wings of an aeroplane. Josh was by his penalty area, aware that the only man between him and the Vessel was Kowalski, who hadn't involved himself much since falling over. But he was tall, and so probably fast.

Josh would simply have to outrun him.

He turned and bolted for the side-line, instantly panicking that he was too slow, like an old nightmare in which the harder his legs pumped, the more he sank into the mud. But before Kowalski even registered his flight, Josh was past him.

'Hey! Hey kid, stop!'

The call brought the attention of his colleagues away from their game and to events further up-field. Some were quicker on the uptake than others, but their weapons were scattered, so by the time an organised squad came to bolster Kowalski's charge, Josh was already standing next to the Vessel, his hand hovering inches away from its surface. It gave off a comforting warmth, which wafted like silk between his fingers. His other hand was down by his pocket, clenched into a fist around the lifestone.

'Don't do it, sir!' cried another. 'That thing will hurt you.'

Josh tightened his clasp around the lifestone and that same euphoric energy pulsed up his arm, a shrill of electricity awakening every nerve in his body, his sensory functions amplifying the sounds of screaming officers, the blinding glare of the floodlights, the smell of mud and grass and sweat, the cool breeze on his skin and the inexorable pull of the Vessel. He spurred his mind to break through the noise and chaos, to ignore the distractions and find a clear, focused passageway.

He closed his eyes and allowed everything to slip away; there was a serenity to the emptiness, the gentle feeling of an enormous weight being lifted from his shoulders.

Then, as a new light flooded around him, he was amazed to find himself suddenly no longer in the training ground, but *back in his own room, standing on the bed and looking out of the window...*

He rests his hands on the windowsill and sees that it's a beautiful day; the sun is bright, and the butterflies are out. There is a silky feel to the air. A bird whistles in the tree and he follows its flight as it swoops down towards the sundial. He spots his toys all still out on the lawn.

To one side there is the low but constant whir of a miniaturised motor. Josh looks and finds his little model of the Solar System on the shelf above his headboard. He's shocked. The model had broken years ago, Jupiter having snapped off its thin plastic stem, and yet here it was, good as new, each and every planet present and correct and orbiting around the sun in perfect synchronicity.

There's a noise coming from downstairs, but before he can move, he notices a sheet of paper has appeared on the windowsill. Josh looks back to the wall above and sure enough, the picture isn't there anymore. It's in front of him.

The drawing is of Nutmeg, the squirrel, dressed as a superhero, holding a football.

Josh opened his eyes.

'Sir, on the ground, now! Do it or we will shoot!'

But it was too late – his palm was on the surface of the Vessel, the warm wetness of the outer shell oozing around the contours of his hand.

The agents took a collective step back as the entrance widened like some metallic curtain, bathing them in the pure, ethereal light that escaped from the chamber. The residue of the liquefied hull slid down at an angle to solidify into the self-sufficient stepping stones that led down to the ground.

Agent Cobb, the one with the shaved head, had had enough. He blinked, snapping himself out of the trance; yet before he could make even half a step forward, Josh, bursting with energy and confidence, swiped his hand off the Vessel and directed it straight at the agents – arm straight, fingers splayed, the tips bent forward; a death grip.

Every set of eyes on the pitch focused on his palm, flinching at the slightest movement, too scared to shoot, just in case it unleashed some kind of supernatural fury. He began climbing the

Impossible Stairs, backwards, eliciting more astonished faces as the blocks failed to fall away, never stopping to check his footing or correct his balance, just grinning a wide, satisfied smile.

At the back of the field, Josh could see Vikram Jaitley and the rest of the national squad gathering outside the building.

It didn't matter.

Once he was on the top step, Josh stopped and searched for PJ, who he found hovering, isolated and alone, by the edge of the pitch.

'PJ! Listen to me!'

PJ looked terrified. The last person he'd seen standing on the Impossible Stairs had caused a bloodbath.

'What? Get down from there, you're scaring me, man.'

Josh shook his head. 'Nothing to be scared of. Just do what you feel is right, okay? That's all anyone can ask of you.'

Pitman and Pittman, two young men bound by a wild case of mistaken identity, smiled at each other for less than a second before Josh turned on the spot, lowered his arm and dived inside the Vessel. A brief clamour ensued as the agents fought to be the first to grab a leg, a foot, anything, but were left unsatisfied as he slammed his hand quickly against the inside wall.

Alone in the chamber, Josh could hear nothing except the thump of his heartbeat.

'17

Out of Order

I am born.
I grow up fighting a war against an unbeatable enemy.
I go back in time to stop it.
I get captured.
The war begins.

A police interview room. Lexa is sat behind a small desk, wearing an oversized man's jumper. On the desk sits an old tape recorder. The chair on the opposite side is empty. ACA Special Agent Jen Casey enters the room holding a file folder and a takeaway coffee cup.

CASEY: Want some?

LEXA: No.

CASEY: You don't like coffee?

LEXA: I've never had it.

CASEY: Never? Well, this is your chance, kid! This is from a nice place a few blocks away. Kinda wish I'd found it when I first got here – none of these guys said anything. Sure I can't tempt you?

Lexa says nothing.

CASEY: Okay. If you change your mind just ask, Miss...

LEXA: Lexa.

CASEY: Oh, that's right... *(opens the folder and checks the document inside).* No last name. What, they don't have those in the future? Y'all like Madonna or something?

LEXA: Who?

CASEY: Alright, fine, forget your name...

Agent Casey tosses the file onto the table, then sits in the empty chair and presses a button on the tape recorder.

CASEY: Interview commenced at...

Agent Casey reaches into her jacket pocket and pulls out a clear zip-lock evidence bag with a wristwatch inside. She checks the time from its dial.

CASEY: ...5:56pm. Officer in charge, Special Agent Casey of the American Crime Agency. Suspect is... who the hell knows, some kind of time-travelling avenger, I guess. So, Miss Lexa... *(drinks a large mouthful of coffee)* Josh Pittman –

Lexa looks away in disgust.

CASEY: – he tells us you went to the training field with the expressed intention of harming, or at least by some method incapacitating, Nathan Pitman Junior. That correct?

LEXA: This is such a waste of time.

CASEY: Hell yeah, it is! Five years I've been working this case and you're my first arrest, you know that? I've got a guy on the slab with half his chest missing and all kinds of weird gunk oozing out of him, and a suspect who's acting like she's been pulled in for a parking ticket. What about this, huh?

Agent Casey reaches into her opposite pocket and pulls out another clear evidence bag containing a razor-tipped glove.

CASEY: Where does this come from? Did you make it? Buy it? Steal it from Freddy Kreuger?

LEXA: Who?

CASEY *(angry)*: Don't screw with me, kid! You're in a lot of trouble as it is, so make it easier for yourself and start talking.

Lexa looks at the glove.

LEXA: Have you told your superiors at the Agency about Nathan Pitman's bodyguard yet?

CASEY: The guy you killed? Ernie Strong.

LEXA: If that was his name.

CASEY: Why would I tell you something like that?

LEXA: Good, that means you haven't. Let me go and we might still get out of this alive.

CASEY *(laughs)*: Ha! Sure, I'll get right on that. You ain't going nowhere, missy.

LEXA: Fine, then the moment you file your report we are as good as dead.

CASEY: What in the hell are you talking about?

LEXA: You work for the enemy. The higher up you go, the more there are. Subjugation of law enforcement is a key factor in the successful promotion of the Guiding Principles. You say five years without an arrest? *(shrugs)* Doesn't surprise me. Your assignments are a misdirection; a brief public charade to give the impression that the crimes committed by those you answer to are actually being investigated.

A pause. Lexa leans forward.

LEXA: Vampires exist, but it's not blood they're after. Euphorivores have been around as long as we have, probably longer. Hunting us, picking us off whenever they were hungry. And then, what? One hundred, two hundred years ago, science and society catch up and death becomes less mysterious. People like you start asking questions. Euphors found themselves at risk of exposure, so they went into hiding, built themselves a big ship and blasted themselves off into space under the cover of some nuclear weapon test in the South Pacific. And while they waited, we proved to them what they already knew: that happiness is a construct of pain. They watched as your country used Nazi technology to give Russia the middle finger by putting a man on the Moon. Suddenly the whole world felt smaller. People felt connected. For one moment rivalry turned to unity. And that is all they need – one moment. That moment is very soon, Agent Casey, so please, let me get back to the Vessel so I can save everyone's life.

Lexa and Agent Casey hold each other's stare until Casey scoffs and gets out of her chair. She paces the room, thinking. Lexa waits. Eventually:

CASEY: Vessel, huh? Is that what you call your flying saucer?

LEXA (*sighs*): You are not listening to me –

CASEY: Oh, I'm listening alright. And it's okay, you know... it's okay.

Agent Casey switches off the tape recorder.

CASEY: Because I believe you. Things ain't what they used to be; I've seen that. You know what it takes for someone like me to get to this position? *Balls.* Ever since the Academy I've had to act like one of the guys. Nights after work, grabbing a couple of beers, watching a football game – I'm talking real football, here – just to keep on the inside track, when all I wanted was to be at home. And then suddenly it all changed. Instead of punching each other on the arm, they wanna hug and cry and flip the channel to, you guessed it, *soccer.*

Agent Casey walks around the table and crouches beside Lexa.

CASEY (*whispers*): And then there's you. I look at you, Miss Lexa, and I see that darkness. There's a rage behind those pretty little eyes and I can tell that you don't belong here. So as an investigator, I have to ask myself – is she here to save us, or is she one of them?

Lexa is sickened by the suggestion.

LEXA: Why would I kill one of my own people?

CASEY: That's a dumb question from someone who wants me to believe she beat the crap outta Josh Pittman just to save the planet. Perhaps the truth is you guys were planning to replace Pitman Junior with a clone or something; some lean, mean soccer-playing machine who'll guarantee the Brits don't lose. And maybe Strong didn't get the memo, tried to protect his player and had to be taken out. Collateral damage.

LEXA: I... *(bites her finger)* nothing you're saying makes any sense. You're twisting everything to suit yourself. You are just like Josh – you think you're immune, but you're not. It's there, believe me. The suppression of your will has stopped you from going home, Agent Casey, and if that weren't true, I would be out the door.

There is a knock at the door.

CASEY *(shouting)*: What?

Detective Sergeant Vikram Jaitley enters the room with a small pile of papers. He is visibly shaken.

CASEY: Yes?

JAITLEY: Sorry, I... these just came in, and...

CASEY: Damn it, Jaitley, get on with it.

DS Jaitley composes himself.

JAITLEY: Rio de Janeiro. There was a big screen event on Copacabana Beach, about a quarter of a million in total. They were watching the third-place play-off between Brazil and Argentina. The game finished, and...

Jaitley skims through the papers and shakes his head. Lexa rises from her seat.

LEXA: It's a test. Has to be.

CASEY: What, you think it's them? Showing their hand a little early, don't you think?

LEXA: Discretion isn't necessary when you have control of absolutely everything. By tomorrow morning everyone will have forgotten.

CASEY *(to Jaitley)*: How many?

A pause.

CASEY: How many, Detective Sergeant?

JAITLEY: All of them.

Suddenly the ground beneath them starts to shake and the walls begin to crumble.

***

Josh was in the Vessel.

Alone.

For the most part, everything was as he remembered it. The soft glow of the Core lit the chamber and gleamed off the translucent membrane covering the walls. Opening and closing the entrance with his hand, the surface had been smooth and oily on the outside, sticky and congealed on the inside. He rubbed his fingers together to feel for the residue of either, but found only the mud and dirt of the training ground turf.

The temperature was cool, like the inside of a fridge, and the thick cloud around his feet appeared dormant. No puffs of vapour trailed into the air, even as he waded through it towards the desk. In the centre, he noticed the Core's pulsations were much slower, the light dimmer perhaps, as though this too were sound asleep.

The table had been a mess of papers the first time he saw it, but nothing appeared out of place. More importantly, the laptop was still there – surely the first thing to go into an evidence bag if the police had managed to find their way in.

Josh pressed the power button and listened to the ancient processor. As he waited for the start-up screen to load, he reached under the plinth and pulled out the notebook. The old, ring-bound journal belonging to Lexa's father was familiar to him now, but on those first occasions Josh had been blindsided by how poorly it had aged and how well it was used. He read the first page, twice, and then turned to the last. There he saw the truth he feared – the black, hardboard cover, scuffed and dented beyond recognition; the post-it notes and extra bits of scrappy paper sticking out the sides; the crinkled, yellowing pages with seemingly endless notes on enemy positions, timescales, diagrams and indecipherable equations; the personal reflections on the decades-long battle and his fight to protect Lexa the way he'd not been able to with her mother. The dense, musty smell.

It was all a disguise.

The weight of his whole life crashed down on top of him. All of his decisions; every move he had ever made had led him to this point, and now Josh had to find the will to carry on down a dangerous path. He had to because he owed it to Lexa, and because the Captain had just sent him a message through the eons of time that he was more, much more, than a victim of mistaken identity.

He checked his watch, and then realised he didn't have it.

It was probably in the chamber somewhere, buried under some papers. Never mind. He took out his phone and checked the time: 8.24pm. It had been just after six, Jaitley had told him. Not too far to travel for a solo flight. If Josh could follow the instructions, then he could make amends for his stupidity and get Lexa's mission back on track.

He could, possibly, tell her the truth about himself too.

Perhaps.

But maybe not.

He found the page:

Temporal Displacement

The most important thing to remember before attempting to fuse the Core's dual directives for the purpose of time travel is the importance of where over when. Though our objective is a second chance at time, time itself must always remain secondary to your physical environment. Why? Because we are, all of us, guilty of the lazy assumption that locations are static. They are not. The Earth orbits around the sun at approximately 67,000 miles per hour, while the Solar System itself hurtles through the cosmos at around eight times that speed. Therefore, if you travel through time without anchoring yourself to a fixed position, then you will find yourself floating in the vast nothingness of space, with only a few seconds to contemplate the enormity of your mistake.

There are two applications on the computer – repurposed software once used for navigational and administrative purposes: the Map, a two-dimensional layout of the Earth through which you can vector your coordinates by dropping a pin onto your desired location, and the Calendar, a basic interface with dropdowns to select your time and date (configured by default to British Summer Time).

These two programmes, once set, will then link their commands and provide you with a Unique Time Signature; a line of code that assimilates the Vessel's power drives with the Core's precognitive functions and forces them to act as one, thus transporting you from the 'Here & Now' to the 'There & Then'.

And that was it.

He checked the following page.

Nope, that was it.

No detail on the complexities of the programme; no description of the applications' interfaces or aesthetic peculiarities; no trouble-shooting guide. Josh wasn't *too* worried – he'd ordered tickets online and zoomed in on towns and cities out of nothing but curiosity on many occasions. Whilst he'd been reading, the laptop screen had faded to a still photograph of a coral reef, its underwater splendour of colour and activity blemished only by the scuba diver in the background and the sentence in the middle:

Please enter your password.

Josh stared back in horror.
Password? What password?
His eyes darted around the screen, thinking maybe he'd missed something, an icon he could click on to bypass the login. But there was nothing, not even a *'Forgot your password?'* button. He looked back into the notebook. His mouth went dry. The space beneath the last sentence was so overgrown with little pencil drawn diagrams and schematics relating to some other experiment, that the additional line at the bottom of the page seemed, at first glance, unrelated.

But before you do any of this, you'll need the password. If you don't know what it is, you shouldn't be reading this.

Caught between urgency and panic, Josh went searching for the answer in places it couldn't possibly be. He scanned the walls, hoping the veins and sinews beneath the membrane would form together to produce a word; he checked the papers cluttering the desk, lifting them up in crumpled bundles, making sure he hadn't missed any waylaid post-it notes. He looked beneath the laptop, on the underside of the plinth, and then under the table.

Nothing.

He sunk his hands into the cloud, lowering himself until his chest and stomach brushed the surface. The floor had a clammy texture, and before long his palm slipped and he rocked sideways, his head falling momentarily beneath the vapours.

Josh choked and sputtered the bitter taste out of his mouth. His whole body jerked upwards and he whacked his head on the underside of the table. He swore, loudly, reached out for Lexa's three-legged stool and lifted himself up, rubbing the newly-formed lump at the back of his head.

After a few deep breaths and a calming stroll around the chamber, Josh resumed his search with a hopeful glance at the laptop. But the reef was still there and so was the request; the gateway to salvation blocked by a triviality. As a human being living in the early twenty-first century, it was Josh's default position to be eternally frustrated by the endless need for online passwords – but this one was a real sucker-punch. For his own accounts, he'd developed a nifty little system to make each one unique but easy to remember. A system he'd shared with people if ever he thought they might be interested.

People like...

He stopped pacing and flipped the notebook back to the first page. It was there that the Captain had written his final words. Why were they at the start and not the end? Was it so Lexa wouldn't see them, or to make sure Josh did? If so, how would the Captain have known that? Looking again at the name scribbled at the bottom, Josh realised he had more power to control events than he'd first thought.

As his finger hit the first key, a message cautioned him that an incorrect password would shut down the system. The Captain was putting an awful lot of faith in him. He ignored the warning and finished typing:

49g9yqhe

Josh squeezed one eye shut and hit *Enter*.

***

All three lost their balance.

Stumbling backwards like a clown slipping on a banana skin, Jaitley landed on his backside beneath a shower of cascading police reports. Casey reacted quickly, grabbing hold of the door frame to keep herself upright. Lexa too managed to stop herself from falling by catching the edge of the table. A rumbling sound rose up around them.

'What is that, an earthquake?' Casey shouted.

Jaitley was struggling to get back on his feet. 'We don't... t-tend to get...' he began, but then immediately gave up.

Only Lexa recognised the sound.

Casey stepped back into the middle of the room as a large crack appeared down the entire length of the wall. The plaster crumbled, fell and smashed into a cloud of thick grey dust which billowed into the air, the plumes visible through the blinding streaks of light which ripped through the wall from the other side.

Then, as quickly as it came, the disturbance subsided. The ground no longer shook, and the dust began to settle. Two evacuee mice climbed their way out of the rubble and scurried off in search of a new home. On the other side of the great gaping hole in the interview room, a toilet bowl lay in pieces amongst the broken tile and glass from the windows. A fountain of murky water spraying upwards from an exposed pipe was slowly flooding the floor. Bigger, bulkier blocks of masonry fell from the ceiling, allowing in the cool breeze of the evening air and the twitter of clueless birds coming into roost. A damaged strip light fizzed and crackled as it lay awkwardly on the topside of the Vessel.

Josh stood at the top of the Impossible Stairs, surveying the damaged he had caused.

'Pittman?' Casey spluttered.

'I'm sorry,' said Josh 'I've made a mess, I know, but – Lexa! Lexa, come on.'

The agent protested. 'Uh-uh, no way! Don't even think about it.'

But it was too late; Lexa had swiped the evidence bag from the table and skipped up the Stairs, which were already receding back into the shell. As the entrance sealed, Josh turned and called out of the steadily shrinking gap.

'Vikram Jaitley!'

The stunned detective leapt to his feet at the unexpected sound of his name.

'Y-yes?'

'The training ground – one hour from now. Make sure you let me in! And bring my car back!'

Josh threw his keys, aiming for Jaitley's feet, but missed; instead they flew past him and landed in the corner amongst the rubble. Jaitley's mouth wobbled a little, yet before he could articulate any sort of response a micro-storm of wind and light and thunder had left nothing for him to answer to except the wreckage of a perfectly ordinary out-of-order toilet.

***

The slap was sharp and quick, catching him full-palm across the cheek. Her rough nails scraped the tender red skin around his nose and tore the stitches across the bridge. His head jerked to the side and he let out a yelp which echoed off the walls of the chamber. Warm blood trickled out of his nostril and over his top lip.

Lexa recoiled with her hand still shaking.

It hadn't been as satisfying as she'd hoped; the sight of him fumbling for a tissue in his pocket made her anger boil again and she had to resist the urge to step forward and have a crack at the other cheek.

Instead, she watched in scorn as he worked to stem the flow, her eyes scanning his body and taking stock of his physique. Josh was tall and lanky, but by no means thin. His muscles were healthy and modestly defined. His skin had an olive tint from the past few weeks' exposure to the summer sun, while a childhood spent in near continual darkness had turned hers from its natural peach – her mother's inheritance – to a pale, off-pink hue, specked with pastel red marks, trails of light blue veins, the brownish remains of bruises that would never heal, burns, cuts, grazes and other assorted reminders of her dangerous existence.

Josh's hands were sleek, and the injuries she'd inflicted gave them an unearned impression of manliness. He had a comfortable house to go home to and a loving family to moan about. Lexa had nothing except the Vessel and her mission – and thanks to Josh, she had them both back.

Damn it.

'Thank you,' she said.

Josh dabbed the last drop of drying blood from his lip. 'You're welcome.'

She ignored the sanctimony and turned to the laptop. The aerial view on the Map was immediately familiar.

'The Tatras?'

'It was in your search history,' said Josh. 'Seemed easier. I thought maybe we should go back for that apple.'

He tried to chuckle, but it came out as a nervous snort.

Lexa scoffed. A new window appeared, into which she thunderstroked a long stream of indecipherable code. A vast star map extended across the screen – millions of tiny white lights on a deep blue background. Flickering in unison, three small circles isolated different areas of the map and then linked together to form the flashing blue triangle. She could feel him glancing over her shoulder.

'Where are we going?'

'Nowhere yet,' said Lexa. 'Did you hear about Rio?'

'Jaitley mentioned something at the training ground, but I didn't... is it bad?'

'Pretty bad. Hundreds of thousands of people and they just... drank them up. All of them, in one go.'

Her fingers lifted off the keypad and a still silence settled in the chamber. She clenched her hands into fists and squeezed them tight, for fear that if she didn't, her nerve would falter and those same fingers would go back and delete everything she had just written. The triangle settled on a point in the centre of the screen and a small box appeared, asking her if she wished to proceed.

'The Captain...' Lexa paused to correct herself. '*My dad* told me everything. Every little detail about what the Euphors were like and what they did to get what they wanted. But he never once mentioned Brazil. Never said anything, never wrote anything down.' She wedged her pinkie nail between her front teeth. 'And then that bodyguard, there was something really strange about him. He should have overpowered me, but when we were fighting, it was like he was... giving up.'

Her head slumped forward, the laptop waiting for its answer while she searched for some of her own. In the silence of the chamber, Josh went to place a hand on her shoulder but pulled out at the last moment.

'You can't save everyone,' he said.

'What is that supposed to mean?'

He shrugged. 'Perhaps the Captain wanted you to see it. So you'd know what a Harvest looked like, how it felt, and he didn't tell you because he knew you'd probably try to prevent it

270

happening, you know? He didn't want you to lose sight of the bigger picture.'

Josh might as well have given her a mud sandwich to eat.

'No. That's too cold,' she said, 'he wouldn't have done that. It's something else. Maybe it's me being here, or him not being here – maybe it's you, I don't know, but something is making ripples and they've noticed. The plan has changed.'

Lexa shook her head, staggered by the possibility. Maybe this was the consequence of the discarded apple; a 700-year-old anachronism rotting into the ground and spreading its influence through time.

'I think he never told me about Brazil because in the world he knew –'

'– it never actually happened.' Josh's voice rose barely above a whisper. 'You could travel back in time and take out the entire team, poison all their dinners the night before the match, but they'd see it coming and find a way around it.'

'They adapt. It's what they do best. Ugh, I can't move in this bloody thing.'

Lexa took off the baggy jumper given to her by the police, revealing a filthy camisole underneath, covered with mud and grime and recent blood stains. She threw the jumper into the cloud beneath the desk and rooted around in the same spot for a new hoodie; smooth, clean, and recently stolen.

'But we can adapt too, right?' said Josh, looking back to the screen as she zipped up the hoodie.

The star map, the blue triangle and the question box were still there, waiting.

'I'm sorry, we?'

'Yes,' he said. 'I'm sorry for what I did – it was stupid and put everyone in danger, and you were right; I'm not immune. I thought too much about PJ, and the Final, and my brain got frazzled, and...'

Josh paused and turned to face her. He seemed brighter than before, less hesitant, as though his path ahead had suddenly become clear.

'It's simple for me, now. We either sort this thing or I'm dead tomorrow anyway. You have a plan, I'm guessing; but whatever it is, I can't let you do it on your own.'

Lexa's eyes rolled as she pondered the absurdity of his offer. It had been less than a day since she had threatened to run him down with his own car if he didn't commit to helping her. Only now, when she knew he was the wrong guy completely, was he actually willing to help her, being all chivalrous and ridiculous like some low-grade knight who got picked last for the Crusades.

'Oh, Josh...' she said with a sigh, and ran her finger across the mousepad.

The cursor hovered over the question box.

Do you wish to proceed?

'You have no idea how much –'

She clicked *Yes*.

'– you are going to regret that decision.'

'18

The Flagship

The Core burst into life, inflating like a balloon beneath the surface of the cloud; huge puffs of wet vapour shot into the air and flooded the chamber with a pure, white nothingness.

Then, in a fierce, jolting reversal, the Core sucked all the energy back in; every particle of bright luminance was swallowed whole by a hungry monster in the bowels of the Vessel, leaving behind only the familiar backlit display of the laptop and the collective radiance of millions of electric pulses zooming through the sinews of the walls around them.

How many trips had Josh taken in the Vessel now? Four? Five? None had been like this. The pulses sped round at a velocity at least a hundred times faster than before, like thin neon strips whizzing past him. The after-effect was dizzying. The Core heaved, its musty light rising and falling in irregular rhythm. Even the sound was different, the centripetal *whumps* displaced by an uneven, high-pitched whirr, as though some caged beast beneath were screaming and protesting its torture.

Josh lifted his hand to cover his ears, only to find his arms were too heavy. His whole body felt like a dead weight, and as the lights spun faster, so it seemed he was being pulled to the floor, his singular mass collapsing under its own density. His knees buckled and the tendons in his neck stretched as his shoulders sunk further. He couldn't remember eating a solid ball of lead before the trip, but there was one inside him now, making its way out of his stomach and down through his intestinal tract.

He tried to scream, but the muscles around his mouth were tightly gripped by the iron vice squeezing his head. He could turn just enough to see Lexa in as much discomfort; standing in front of her desk, bow-legged with an uncomfortably arched back, her fingers digging deep into the wood of the tabletop. The grimace on her face tightened as she let out a low groan that helped her suck up the claustrophobic assault on her body.

The laptop, too, was rattling away, but the metal plinth kept it in position, and it was still possible to make out the screen. Josh watched as the little triangle repeated the same action, again and again:

Flash three times. Spin. Zoom in.

He recited the words to himself in a steady, light rhythm, hoping it would distract his mind from the crushing sensation of skin and bone turning into heavy rock.

Flash three times. Spin. Zoom in.

Flash three times. Spin. Zoom in.

Josh kept up with his chant for as long as possible, focusing his thoughts until suddenly something new appeared on the screen. A star, in the centre of the triangle, its large size marking it out from the million tiny dots around it.

Flash three times. Spin. Zoom in.

With each pass it grew larger and larger, until Josh could see that it wasn't a star at all, but an actual object floating out beyond the stratosphere, defined in space by glittering light on one side and shadow on the other. He wanted to call out to Lexa, who was crouched with her forehead on the table and her fingers grasping at the strands of her hair, but he was by now completely incapacitated and could do no more but observe as the object grew bigger, gaining texture and body and shape.

A shape that drew instant comparison with the Vessel itself. The upper section was a great, bulbous dome of enormous girth, across the surface of which Josh saw a series of huge hexagonal plates sliding slowly over and around one another, coated on the darkest side by a kind of shimmering luminescence like the reflection of the moon on a rippling sea, only to become near-invisible as they moved out of the shadows and into the direct sunlight.

Beneath the dome, the sides funnelled down with a smooth, inward curve to a long, needle-thin point at the base, completing the picture of a giant inverted teardrop floating in space.

The Vessel suddenly calmed; the tremors receded, and the Core mellowed and dimmed to a hazy glow. The tiny pulses of light slowed and faded away, like a million shooting stars burning out and darkening the sky.

His body was feeling light now, but was so absorbed by the picture on screen, that he failed to notice when both he and Lexa rose into the air, as though gravity were trying to atone by turning them into feathers, floating effortlessly on a mild breeze.

They spread themselves wide, their fingers wriggling and rippling in their newfound freedom. Lexa spun herself to face him, twisting herself into a natural sitting pose. Josh couldn't imagine ever forgetting the smile she gave him, as she hung there in the centre of the chamber, like a floating Buddha. He would always remember it as the first genuine moment of shared experience between them a smile that wasn't hiding a persistent hardship or a reluctant duty, but instead beamed with an innocence and beauty that for just the briefest of seconds set her free of everything.

And she was sharing it with him.

He swam through the air towards her, the unencumbered movement lifting his soul; he could feel the warmth of a vibrant blood-flow through his body and every cut, scratch and bruise he had lost their desire to cause him pain.

He smiled back. But then a thumping sound from deep within the Core jolted them out of the moment, and they came crashing down, along with the various objects and loose bits of paper which landed back onto the desk in an even worse mess than before. Both ended up on their backsides, choking on the fumes.

Lexa was first to her feet. The Vessel had shut down and an eerie, cold silence had descended around them. Josh placed a hand on the desk and lifted himself back up; the laptop screen had turned a harsh metallic blue with a small text box in the middle:

System Offline.
UTS/BEARING assimilation could not be resolved.

276

He looked around him. The Core had dimmed to a hazy half-light, and Lexa had to peer closely as she rummaged through the papers until she found what she was looking for; a clear zip-lock bag with something inside. The chrome casing reflected the Core's glow.

'Is that my watch?'

'Yes,' she replied, removing it from the bag.

Josh stared in horror. 'Look what you've done to it! That was a birthday present.'

Lexa scoffed.

Birthday present.

She'd never had a birthday present in her life.

'It's just the strap,' she said, 'the clock still works. I'm sure you can get it fixed.'

He lingered near her, inspecting the damage. The dial was cracked and the metal strap hung off the lug pins on either side. Lexa secured it around her wrist with a length of duct tape and some spare copper wire she found under the plinth, then bent down in front of the laptop and set the watch to the time in the corner of the screen.

'What are you doing?' Josh asked.

'I'm taking it with us.'

'Why?'

'Because I took the wrong bloody bag, that's why!' She threw the empty zip-lock into the cloud. 'In the police station; I wanted the glove, but I couldn't see properly under all that rubble, and so instead I ended up with this thing. Still, I thought, make the best of it, right? Even if we can't protect ourselves, at least we'll know our time of death.'

Lexa stormed past him and over to the creamy white walls of the chamber. The stress was like a knot in her chest. All around her was baggage; useless adornments that did nothing but weigh her down.

'I've brought us back a few hours,' she said, trying to calm herself. 'It's a stupid risk, but I don't know how long it'll take us to get there. Hopefully it's enough.'

Her hand rested against the wall and the entrance opened like a black hole tearing the shell apart.

Josh looked out into the open. 'Get where?'

But Lexa was already outside, grateful that the Vessel had landed them somewhere dark. As she crept down the Stairs an unpleasant odour began to drift up through her nasal passages; an odd stench, but one with which she was vaguely familiar.

For three years she had worked with the Captain on the Vessel; before that she was too young, and had to stay below ground, reading and learning whenever and however she could. As she grew older, she noticed the seasons becoming more extreme; the permanently blackened skies that shrouded the Earth had acted as a mass pollutant and shut down the Gulf Stream; winters became brutally cold, temperatures dropping so low that even stepping outside for too long was potentially suicidal. Summers were the opposite; those long, hazardous days spent uncovering the Vessel's mysteries in the thick humidity and soaring heat that could blister skin even through the dense black fog. It was on these days that her father remarked on how the air smelt the same as the Vessel had when it was first opened by that severed Euphorivore hand; a boggy, sweaty stench; a mix of ammonia, stagnant water and other elements that had no human comparison.

Reminded of that smell, Lexa resisted the urge to pinch her nose – she wanted both hands free for whatever might be lurking in the shadows.

'God, I think I'm going to be sick.'

Josh had emerged from the Vessel and stood on the Stairs behind her.

'Ssh! No talking!' Lexa put a finger to her lips. 'And no puking,' she added, wincing in discomfort.

There was a sudden pain in her sinuses, catching her across the bridge of her nose and beneath her eyes. The air didn't just smell different, it felt different too. She tried to ignore it as she stepped off the bottom Stair and her foot disappeared beneath the fog.

Looking ahead, the only source of light was a hazy green shroud with no obvious point of origin. Along with the light of the Core spilling out of the entrance, it was enough to see the same puffs of cloud which covered the floor of the Vessel, rolling quickly and purposefully; soft, undulating waves rising and crashing down on one another, heading off in a single direction away to some imperceptible point in the far distance. With no alternative signposts, Lexa saw no other choice but to follow it.

'Hurry up,' she whispered.

Josh stepped nervously down and followed. As the Vessel closed behind him, the shadow ran up what Lexa now realised was a wall rising above them, the fog breaking at its base. They looked to each other in the murky darkness. The warmth and familiarity of the

Core's glow now gone, they were left abandoned amongst the gloomy emerald shadows. It was like a witch's dungeon. The dank smell and clammy heat seemed to intensify instantly.

'Lexa,' said Josh.

'Ssh.'

He wiped his brow and squinted. 'What happened with the Vessel? Is it damaged?'

'I don't think so.' Lexa reached out for the wall and recognised its texture even in the dim light; the uneven structure of fleshy tissue, the intricate weaves of skin and muscle connected by long sinews of cartilage.

Josh pressed. 'Then why did it act like that?'

She ran her fingertips across the oily membrane. 'It was torn, I think. The Core. Caught between what it was and what we've turned it into. It would explain the bumpy ride.'

'Bumpy ride? It nearly killed us.'

'You wanted to come,' she said. 'The Vessel isn't a machine. It has a connection, like a homing signal, only more organic. We could suppress it, but it's still there. It remembers. Deep down all it wants to do is go home. So I let it.'

'You *let* it?'

His tone angered her. 'I used an encryption key to reverse the coding and remove the lock.'

'Should you even be able to do that?'

Lexa looked along the path of the cloud. Further ahead the light was brighter; the semi-darkness would only disguise them for so long.

'How long do you think you can hold your breath for?'

Josh shrugged. 'I don't know, two minutes maybe. Why?'

'This cloud's about a foot high, should be enough to hide in if we lay down.'

Lexa turned and waded on through the field of white, following its course but sticking close to the wall. She glanced quickly back to the Vessel, but it had already faded from view, lost in the darkness.

Josh followed quietly behind her.

The silence scared him, although he knew breaking it probably wouldn't end well. He wanted to reach out and grab her; feel the warmth of her skin in contrast with the cold sliminess of the wall and the growing horror that with every touch a ghost in the darkness was touching him back.

But then he stopped.

The surface had, until now, felt seamless. There were ripples and bumps, and his stomach turned at times he thought he was running his hand over a few strands of varicose vein; but the outer skin itself had been undisturbed.

Now there was something new; a break in the surface – a thin, shallow groove, which, as he ran his index finger along it, he found to be quite long and crooked. Josh turned to face towards the wall; it was hard to see, but he could just make out its trail, stretching diagonally upwards beyond his reach. The skin along the edges felt different too; moist still, but less so, the texture much rougher, bobbling along and, to his disgust, flaking in some places. At first, he thought it could be some kind of laceration, a long wound still in the process of healing. But as Josh explored further, inspecting the areas of wall either side, he found those same thin veins he had felt earlier were running towards the line. The muscle too weaved its way towards it, giving a definite mass to its edges. This was no injury; it was meant to be there; it was part of the fabric of the wall, not an interruption to it. It was tense too, as if the two sides were squeezing themselves together on purpose – like a giant set of pursed lips. The revulsion was overwhelming.

This time he really should be calling out to Lexa. She might not have stopped once to check he was still behind her, but she had a right to know if they were about to be eaten alive by the place. Yet the intention failed him as, in that moment, his curiosity took hold and he found himself pushing his middle three fingers into the crevice. He felt the lips instantly tighten up to repel him. Against his better judgement he persevered, pressing harder and bringing in his other hand to help. There was a secret beyond, and despite the voice in his head telling him to stop, he couldn't. He wouldn't. His fingers sunk in, and from there it was easier, the oily surface acting as a handy lubricant to slide his palms through. But still it resisted, the aggravated muscle pulsing and throbbing as it fought to deny him.

And then, breakthrough.

The first Josh knew of it was when he could see his thumbs again, caught in a small chink of light that escaped through his hands. The initial breach was enough; his fingers suddenly became free as the entire length of the crevice opened with a sticky sound like two rashers of bacon being peeled apart. As the fissure grew, so did the amount of light it allowed in, and in a moment a huge shaft was flooding inside. The brightness pierced into his eyes, and when finally he felt brave enough to uncover them again, he let out

282

a whispered gasp of amazement and stumbled backwards, his legs weakening as he looked upon the source of the light.

It was the sun, pure and unfiltered in the vacuum of space, reflecting off the wide surface of the Earth below him.

'It's a window.'

A window with no glass, but still it was protecting him from being sucked out into the void. He took a few slow, cautious steps towards the edge and dared himself to peer closer. From this distance the planet appeared to him as though on a wide, flat canvas; too close to appreciate the curvature of the globe or the thin corona of the atmosphere.

The blood rushed to his head. He felt wobbly; it was like looking over the edge of a cliff, only this time he was struggling with how far 'down' actually was. His senses were so confused it seemed entirely plausible that if he were to fall, he might land across Italy's boot-shaped peninsula and break his back.

To his left, Josh could see a large cloud system hanging over the north Atlantic, itself a perfect flat sheen of royal blue with nothing to suggest the continual rolling of its waves. The system drifted over much of the ocean's eastern half, a long white brushstroke in the shape of a banana. The lower half clipped the north-west corner of Spain and swept up and over the Bay of Biscay, while at its northern extreme, the cloud masked most of Iceland, the Faroe Islands and the Shetlands, before becoming caught the snow-capped peaks of Norway and breaking off into smaller storm cycles. Josh was no expert; he couldn't say how many satellite photos of the Earth he might have seen in posters or school textbooks over the years, but there was something about this picture that was a little off – the way the great crescent of cloud curved around the British Kingdom without actually encroaching upon its airspace. Smaller flecks drifted here and there over mainland Europe and towards Asia, but there was not a single whisp he could see anywhere above his home country.

Was it possible? Were the Euphorivores controlling the weather too? He tried to remember the last time it rained back home, or even the last time he saw a cloud. Nothing came to mind. Why would they need such a clear view? Looking to his right, Josh noticed the large, menacing shadow laying across the flanks of Eastern Europe. Russian and Middle Eastern cities glowed in the distance. He thought of the toy Solar System, still on the shelf in his bedroom; the little plastic Earth on its delicate spindle, passing through shadow and light as it spun on its axis and whirred around the lightbulb sun in the centre.

Now it was all playing out for real in front of him. Dusk in the former Soviet bloc meant late afternoon in the British Kingdom and with it the dizzying realisation that as he looked down on his mottled green island, he was in fact looking down on *himself.* An earlier version, in the police station, perhaps, demanding to see Agent Casey; or at the training ground, at the moment Lexa pressed the lifestone into his hand; or maybe it was even later, and he was at home, eating sausage and chips and being harassed by his sisters. A miniscule clone re-enacting the events of his betrayal.

There were millions of people down there, billions, and he couldn't see a single one. The land and seas were teeming with life, in all its chaotic forms, yet from this height they were so perfectly still and peaceful it barely seemed real. To see with his own eyes was a privilege beyond compare; the unexpected advantage of 'mistaken identity'. Maybe PJ Pitman ought to be the one up here, not him.

Except now Josh knew the truth; it was there in the Captain's notebook, as clear as the sky below him. His insignificance was his advantage, and no-one – not Lexa, not even the Euphorivores with all their technological clairvoyance – could have predicted the role he would play.

A cold hand reached from behind and clamped over his mouth. 'Get down!'

Lexa wrapped her other arm around his waist and pulled him down into the fog. Josh tried to muffle words of protest but gave up when he realised his head had disappeared beneath the surface. The view of the Earth had gone, and he could see nothing but the cloud, rolling over him as though he were standing upright inside a chimney stack as the thick smoke billowed past.

Lexa released her hand and placed a finger to her lips. It was already becoming too much to hold his breath; he clasped his nostrils between his fingers, aggravating his wounds. The heat and humidity felt worse beneath the cloud, the wetness sticking to him like a damp cloth. He could see the beads of sweat on Lexa's forehead and wondered how she would know when it was safe to emerge.

Not yet.

A set of heavy thuds, three, maybe four, pounded the ground somewhere nearby. Josh felt the tremors running through the floor and rippling through the fog. Their bodies tensed and their eyes fixed on one another. For the first time he was aware of how close they were, lying on their sides towards each other. Their stomachs were touching and her knee was digging into his thigh.

Another crash.

And then another; the long, hollow sounds echoing off the walls. His swollen nose raged with the lack of air and a tight, piercing pain caught him behind his eyes. He puffed out his chest slowly. Lexa must have assumed he was going to get up, because at that moment she pinched his arm. Her eyebrows furrowed and she was shaking so hard he could see her windpipe straining helplessly to swallow the last of the air in her throat. He took the risk and heaved again, ignoring the protest in her eyes, imploring her with his own. At last she responded, pushing out against him and as he relaxed, their chests lifting and falling in a gentle see-saw rhythm. All the while, the stomps were becoming louder and the vibrations stronger, each sound now more like a sonic boom than a shuddering crash. Closer and closer they came...

And then, silence.

A large shadow passed over the cloud, blocking out much of the sunlight still pouring in through the window. Her eyes glinted as they widened, most likely they had registered his horror. He'd been forced to arch his back, pushing his stomach further into hers, because there was something poking him between his shoulder blades. Something smooth and sharp that Josh couldn't imagine as anything else but a claw.

It was a sign of the inevitable; either the fumes would get them, or the shadow would. He resisted the temptation to put his arm around her. He was weakening anyway; consciousness slipped as his eyelids grew heavier...

But then a new sound found its way through the cloud, quiet and deep; a low-level growl like a guard dog snarling at a stranger, with an inflection that suggested the early stages of a hunt. Then in a flash it rose up to a deafening roar, in parts as thunderous as a lion and in others like the erratic screech of a howler monkey. Josh moved to shift his hands to his ears but couldn't find the strength.

Lexa didn't react at all – her eyes were closed.

The ferocious noise waned and silence fell. The shadow swung away quickly, and the crashing footsteps thundered off at a speed faster than they had approached.

The shock and relief overcame him, jolting his senses to the point he even thought the air had returned to his lungs. But the respite was fleeting, and panic surged swiftly in its place. Lexa hadn't moved. His leaden arm lay close to her head and he was able to grab a tuft of her hood. He tried to pull her up, but his body was having none of it. The loss of air had drained the energy from every part of his being, it felt easier now to submit and in his foggy state considered how peaceful it would be to fall asleep next to her...

The thought was broken.

Lexa was staring at him.

'What the hell did you think you were doing?' Lexa gasped as she drew in as much of the warm air as possible.

'I'm... I'm sorry,' Josh replied between short, deep breaths. 'I don't know what happened. I couldn't... I couldn't help myself.'

'Try harder.'

The pair were leaning against the wall, their chests heaving, coughing out the excess gas that had found its way into their lungs.

The rush of pure air coursing through her body made Lexa light-headed.

Josh mopped his brow with his sleeve. 'I take it that was one of those dragon patrols?'

'Firebreather Squadron,' she corrected. 'No, it was just one. But I think there are others nearby. No Euphor on its back either, we were lucky.'

'Lucky?' Josh wheezed, bringing on another coughing fit.

Lexa lowered her voice. 'They have no sense of smell – neither would you if you shot fire out of your nostrils. But a rider would have sniffed us out.'

Josh said nothing, taking a moment to allow his faculties to return and, with it, his grip on the situation.

'So, this is really it?' he said. 'This is their… *space station?*'

'Their Flagship, yes.'

'And they're all in here somewhere?'

'Most of them.' A pinch of irritation slipped into her voice.

'Are you crazy? The two of us can't take on their whole army – you didn't even bring the glove!'

'We're not here to start a fight, this is just reconnaissance, nothing more.' Lexa checked her surroundings and looked at the time on Josh's watch. 'We haven't got long until that match finishes, we need to go.'

'What match?'

'The one with Brazil.'

'The third-place play-off? Against Argentina?' Josh nodded. 'Of course, Rio – that's why we're here.'

Lexa's focus was returning, her senses unscrambled, and again she looked down the trail of cloud to where the murky light grew brighter.

'No-one's ever seen them eat,' she said. 'Not on that scale. The more I can find out about them, the more I can... figure out a new plan, I guess.' She turned back and shoved a finger in his face. 'So, until then, we just need to stay hidden, *stop touching things* and get out as soon as we can. Do you understand?'

'Yes,' said Josh. 'I'm sorry.'

Next to them, the window in the wall had begun to close itself up, the sticky edges resealing with an unpleasant squelch. The Earth disappeared quickly from view and Lexa was surprised by her disappointment that she hadn't taken the chance to really look at it.

She stuck out a hand. 'The lifestone, have you still got it?'

Josh patted his trouser pockets long enough for it to become irritating. 'Yes, I do. Let me just...'

The light was fading fast.

'Give to me.'

Finally, he dug into one pocket, fumbling for eternity until at last he took out the translucent little rock. Even as shadow converged around them, the lifestone still managed to find a sliver of light to sparkle off its smooth surface.

'Quickly,' she said. 'Don't drop it.'

Josh placed the stone in her palm just as everything turned to black. They stood in silence for a moment, and with her eyes struggling to penetrate the darkness, Josh could have just as easily been a thousand miles away than right in front of her.

Walking on, Josh thought about the shadow of the night racing across the surface of the Earth. He'd never been scared of the dark; his home had always been so safe and secure there was no need to be afraid. But the image of the light being swallowed up with unrelenting menace shook him to his core. If the Euphorivores got their way, and Lexa's 'reconnaissance' came to nothing, then there would be no dawn breaking on the other side; no respite from the dark.

'19

Euphors

It was almost an hour before they heard another sound.

Josh was grateful for the silence, a sign that he and Lexa were still alone. After their escape from the Firebreather, capture seemed inevitable. More than once Josh thought he'd seen movement in the shadows, of figures hidden in the darkness ready to leap out at them; but as time passed and their journey continued uninterrupted, he told himself it was nothing more than a trick of the light, caused by the untempered flow of the cloud through the swampy green sheen. It wasn't until Josh saw a spot of white light in the distance that he also picked up on the low rumbling sound coming from the same direction. Lexa must have noticed too, for her pace slowed considerably.

'Stay behind me,' she whispered.

Josh was already behind her. He had been the entire time. The patch of light grew larger and brighter as they neared, until eventually it permeated the gloom and lit their path ahead. Above and around them, the architecture of the enormous space they'd been walking through was revealed; to Josh it seemed like the

Euphorivore equivalent of a great banqueting hall, held aloft by a long stretch of vaulted arches. Reaching the nearest by edging his way around the wall, he gazed up to the apex high above him. Again, the smooth, uneven structures were similar to the Vessel's interior wall – sinews and tendons covered by a slimy membrane.

'Do you think it came through here?' he said, craning his neck as far back as it would go.

When Lexa didn't respond, he turned and found her looking down, studying the cloud rushing past their feet. It was moving much faster than before – so fast the field of thick white fog had flattened out, the momentum leaving no time for plumes and tendrils to billow up into the air. Their legs did little to interrupt the flow as the cloud streamed beneath the archway, and with no thick puffs here and there to break up the panorama, the ripples rolling along its surface revealed a more defined pattern: the cloud wasn't drifting forward under its own power – it was being dragged, as though a giant vacuum cleaner beyond the arches were sucking it in.

'Doesn't make sense,' he said.

Lexa turned. 'What doesn't?'

'You'd expect to feel a breeze. But there's nothing. Like it's not even there.'

Passing beneath the archway took longer than expected. Single file, and on a relatively straight path, the distance between each arch appeared short, but Josh estimated they had walked the length of three football pitches before reaching the end. The light grew stronger, casting long shadows in their wake. They kept close to the wall, hiding behind each upright and peeking around to check their path was still clear. With every pass the rumbling became louder and soon revealed itself to be not a single sound, but a collection; a disordered overlap of rustling, stomping and shuffling without any sort of uniform pattern, never registering beyond a low undercurrent – a backdrop to the main event.

As they reached the final arch, and could go no further, Josh expected to be confronted with the source of the light, only to find that it was still some way off; a smoky canvas hanging in the distance, spreading its lustre up the path behind them.

But the faraway light was no longer of interest; their attention had been drawn instead by what lay between.

Josh stood close to Lexa, using her to anchor himself to reality. He felt breathless. Nothing in their journey – not the length of the walk, nor the size of the arches, nor even the sight of the Earth – had been enough to prepare him for the enormity of the space now in front of them. If there existed a limit to which a great bulk of nothingness could be enclosed by a built structure, then this, surely, had to be it.

The circumference of the vast circular rim upon which they stood could only be easily measured in miles, the diameter so great that from Josh and Lexa's perspective it seemed more like a bottom-heavy oblong; an egg shape with the two of them positioned at the flattened base. Lining the perimeter were yet more archways, the same height as those they had just passed beneath. They must have led to thousands of similar pathways, for out of each poured the same thick sheets of cloud, rolling out of the darkness and cascading over the rim like puffy white waterfalls, drawing their eyes down to where it fell. The relentless mass descended from the level of their feet for what looked around 200 metres before landing on another, much larger horizontal ridge. Josh and Lexa's own perch offered only a metre or so of standing space between the archway and the edge, while this second platform comfortably offered twenty times that distance – yet in comparison to the vastness of the void it surrounded, this still seemed perilously narrow.

After hitting the level ground, the cloud continued its march towards the centre and made its final plunge into the abyss; a great chasm with central nucleus so immense a whole town could have fitted inside it. There the streams converged and blended, swirling and pooling together in a giant cauldron of thick, white haze. Tendrils as large as buildings rose into the air, and Josh realized it was one of these misty pylons that had been illuminating their path through the archways, because far beneath an expansive blaze of light was permeating through the swathe, like sunrays cutting hazily through the smog over a polluted city. Billions of particles that could neither be seen nor touched burning together, bigger than any single object that existed on Earth, yet Josh knew at once exactly what it was.

The Core.

The Vessel had one, and so did this. The heart of the Flagship was glowing and breathing serenely in an ocean of dense vapour, shrouding everything in a pure, unfiltered sheen. Josh took in the sight in an instant, his eyes absorbing every extraordinary detail at a speed quicker than his thoughts could process. Yet the most alarming feature of all, the one which had compelled Lexa to grab his arm and pull him back, was neither the Core nor the cloud above it. It was the partial restriction of the cloud from their view, between the points where the streams landed on the ledge below and where they tipped over into the Core itself.

'Oh crap...' Josh whispered.

The cloud couldn't be seen because it was passing through the legs of a great swarm of Euphorivores, who were covering every inch of the ledge that encircled the void. Josh looked across to its opposite side, where the gathering merged into a single, indiscernible mass.

'There must be millions of them,' he said.

'It's okay. I was expecting this.' Lexa peered over the edge. 'Maybe not quite this many.'

Josh thought back to the Captain's anatomical sketches; the description of the vestigial mouth holes and the decorative markings across their bare scalps. Without the psychic disguises used by Ernie Strong, the Fedora and untold others back on Earth, each one exhibited these unique features, yet still he was taken back by just how *human* they looked. They were male and female, dark-skinned and fair; some were short, others tall, but all were noticeably thin, with long, gaunt faces that made it difficult to tell how old they might be, though Josh could sense the slow passage of time. Even those head markings were not enough to shatter the illusion, looking more like tribal tattoos than extrasensory organs. Perhaps it was the clothes, too. Josh had half-expected them to be naked, or at least wearing some kind of retro-futuristic spacesuits; but instead, he saw them dressed mostly in rags, unkempt and unwashed, stitched together from clothes of a bygone era – presumably from the last time they were on Earth.

Although they were cramped together on the ledge, the entire swarm was moving; it was clear that the rumbling sound Josh and Lexa had been hearing was the Euphorivores shuffling around, brushing past one another and jostling for the best position. They pushed each other as they came too close, fought as they pushed too hard and pulled each other apart as fighting turned to embracing, and in some places, dancing. They weren't an army; they were a rabble. Yet despite this, there was not a single word spoken, nor a scream, nor a shout, nor a song to sing along to.

Lexa was tugging him on his sleeve.

'Are you ready?' she said.

'For what?'

In one swift move Lexa grabbed hold of his hand, interlocking their fingers, and squeezed as hard as she could. As she tightened her grip Josh felt a hard lump digging into him, which he quickly realised was Ernie Strong's lifestone wedged between their palms. A thunderbolt shot up his arm with a force so great it almost knocked his head back. Every muscle in his body tensed as though they were about to rip through his skin. Every strand of hair took on a life of its own, squirming and wriggling and pulling at his scalp. His teeth gritted, but his mouth widened; his ribs tightened, but his chest heaved; his toes curled but his feet stretched. The energy tore through him in a flash, taking hostage of his insides and pushing them outwards so he felt twice the size he should have been. His eyes sharpened and he could absorb a million tiny details at once, trapping them in his mind like insects in a jar. Yet something about the alignment of his vision made him wobble, as though he had taken two sidesteps to the right without noticing.

Not only that, but the lifestone was now in his opposite hand and Lexa's palm felt completely different, like they were melting into one another, making it impossible to tell who was who.

The light of the Core rose up, swallowing everything in its path, and then, as it retreated, the light turned to gold, illuminating the far end of the *long corridor he is suddenly standing in. The floor is covered with grease, and he slips and falls against the steel wall to stop himself going to ground.*

Where am I?

Josh hears heavy footsteps and turns to see a woman running towards him, dressed in a blue jumpsuit.

'Excuse me,' he says. But the woman ignores him and runs past. He begins to cough, and only now does he notice that the corridor is full of smoke and the temperature is unbearably hot. Ash floats in the air and falls like black snowflakes, disintegrating upon contact with the grease. He realises the light in the distance is coming from a fire, and his first reaction is to turn and look for Lexa.

But she isn't there.

The lifestone isn't in his hand either. His palms are clammy and covered in soot.

'Lexa! Lexa, where are you?' His panic swells, bringing a hollow sickness to his stomach, and this only intensifies with the sound of the alarm above his head. A screeching, wailing siren with a red light that can be seen spinning through the smoke. It's thicker now, but there are no windows to let it escape. The bunker is deep underground.

'Lexa!'

There are more people in the hallway now. Some are running away from the fire, but more are running towards it. All are wearing the blue jumpsuits, and none, it seems, can hear him.

Out of the crowd, Josh spots a man. His face is familiar; a recognition Josh can't quite place his finger on. The man stops across the other side of the corridor and searches the faces of the others as they pass by. He looks up and down the hallway and when he moves, Josh feels compelled to follow him, turning the corner at the far end into another long corridor. Then another. Then another. Each one more crowded than the last. It becomes difficult to see through the smoke stinging his eyes and he struggles to keep up.

At last, the smoke clears and, in the corner, Josh can see three people huddled together on the floor. They see the man and stand up to greet him. One of the three steps forward: it's the Captain, his face covered in those ancient scars, his hair withering but not yet as grey. Josh assumes then the frightened little girl holding the Captain's hand is Lexa, maybe eight or nine years old, and the small slender woman next to them is her mother. The resemblance is striking.

'Everyone okay?' the first man asks.

The Captain nods his head. 'We're fine. Squadron?'

'Three units. We're outflanked.'

'And the Vessel?'

'Found it.'

'Damn.'

The first man smiles. 'This one's not meant to be. We'll get there.'

The man leads the Captain and his family through another warren of corridors, and again Josh follows. The little girl looks over her shoulder at him and stares him in the eye.

298

Can she see me?

Finally, at the end of a narrow passage, they reach a door with the words 'NO ENTRY' written in thick red letters. The group go inside. The first man locks the door behind them, and they are plunged into near darkness. The large room is full of pipes and electrical wires running the length of the floors and ceiling. They follow the metal gangway and go down a large flight of stairs. At the bottom, the man opens a heavy trap door in the floor, which squeaks on its hinges, echoing off the walls.

'Get in!' he tells them. The Captain, Lexa and her mother clamber into the space below, and without thinking Josh goes too. Although they are cramped inside the tiny shelter, they still do not acknowledge him. Lexa buries her face in her father's chest.

'Aren't you coming?' the Captain asks.

The man shakes his head. 'I'll distract them.' His voice becomes lighter. 'I'm feeling particularly happy right now, so I'm sure I'll be enough for them.'

Suddenly, there is a loud crash from above and an orange light floods into the room. The man shuts the trap door, but as he does, the light catches his face and Josh notices his scar – a thin one above his eye, long since healed, and thinks perhaps he doesn't know him after all.

The trap door closes, and the man is gone. Josh expects the darkness to envelop him, but instead everything turns white.

The Euphorivores were a loud, raucous bunch.

Fighting to be heard, every individual voice was lost in the cacophony of millions more joining together to form an impenetrable wall of sound. In the foreground, pockets of laughter could be made out; great bellowing guffaws, like drunken pirates in a tavern. Screams of delight, a thousand strong, broke through on occasion. There was goading of brawlers, cheering of victors, whoops of joy and good-natured sing-a-longs, all cut through with a palpable sense of anticipation.

And thanks to the lifestone squashed between their hands, Josh could hear every part of it, pure and unfiltered, his brain hearing what his ears couldn't, the words passing clear as crystal through his heads. He was still reeling from his experience in the bunker, and for a moment was caught between the two places, thinking the roar of the crowd was the rumble of the fire come to swallow him whole. But then he turned and saw Lexa once again as he knew her, not as a little girl running for her life. He tried to catch her gaze, but she refused to match it. Little beads of perspiration were running down her face.

Had she seen what he'd seen? Or had she seen something different, something from his own life? He might have asked her, but the noise was so loud she probably wouldn't have heard him anyway.

It was a relief, then, when every Euphorivore suddenly became silent and the entire assembly stopped and looked straight up. Josh and Lexa followed their gaze to where the domed roof of the Flagship rose so high above them that the very top appeared through a kind of unreal haze, like a desert mirage. There was something about such a substantial volume of air inside a structure big enough to fit a mountain that made it feel incredibly dense, as if it were a solid lump bearing down on top of them. Josh felt his knees bend and his back arch, buckling under the weight of a heavy nothingness.

The two tiny humans hand-in-hand, shared a brief memory of being back in the Vessel, looking at the little triangle on the laptop, flashing and zooming in on the Flagship and those great hexagonal plates sliding over and around one another – for here they there were again, on the inside as well as the outside, hundreds of metres wide and shimmering as though covered in reflective glitter.

But, as Josh craned his neck back to the nearest part of the dome just above the archway, he saw it wasn't glitter at all, but tiny little screens; electronic ones, like small flat panel televisions, numbering into the billions, amassed together in groups to form the roving plates, which were beginning to slow and settle into position. Smaller, darker plates emerged from the gaps in between, which Josh noted were actually pentagons, designed to act as conduits between the larger shapes as they fixed themselves into place like a great geometric patchwork, then merged into a single metallic sheet covering the entirety of the dome.

Josh had turned at just the right moment to see all the screens cut to a dark, motionless background, but the memory of what each one had been playing lingered as a set of afterimages floating across his eyes: a woman holding a microphone, a brightly-coloured animated cartoon, two children chasing each other around a field, and the perhiperary of dozens more individual transmissions. Now they were all gone, and the displays were turning in colour to form a single picture: a sky-blue background, a dark-green cardigan with a subtle silver pinstripe, a white bushy beard and the unmistakable, ruddy-cheeked face of Ray Albright.

– *As if things weren't strange enough,* Josh thought.

– *I've known stranger,* thought Lexa, in reply.

His heart skipped a beat.

– *You can hear me?*

– *Sort of.*

– *Me too. Except it's more like... I can feel you.*

– *Stop talking.*

Neither had ever seen a person's head strewn over such a wide area before, and for Josh it was remarkable how different someone looked once you got a really good look at them. That sincere smile, which had enamoured so many with its distinctive blend of sincerity and mirth, was reshaped as a dangerous and mischievous grin of self-satisfaction. His pupils, once revered for their generous and inviting nature, were jet black pools surveying the scene for anything they might want to devour. Over his shoulders the two Gothic towers of Westminster Abbey rose into the sky.

– *So, what, he's the king of the Euphors?*

– *More like a god. They worship him. They'll die for him, as long as he feeds them first.*

Across the scores of little screens, and above the baying throng, the Prime Minister beamed, exposing the rank little hole in place of his mouth.

– *Good evening, everyone!*

The effect was disorientating; the booming voice and the crowd's roar of approval ought to have been reverberating off the wide curved walls, but instead they sat as unfiltered nuggets of sound inside his head.

– *Yes, yes; alright, calm yourselves down. I know you haven't gathered here tonight to listen to me drivel on, but please, if you'll allow me a few words.*

Albright spoke in a poised but triumphant manner, reminiscent of the kind of bombastic campaign speeches he'd given over the years, declaring victory before the war was won. He stroked his beard thoughtfully.

– *They're a bothersome lot, aren't they? Always have been. Fussing around like they own the bloody place. Growing their society, developing their technology, striving always to make themselves happier. Happier! And Lord knows we helped the buggers! Drove ourselves out of our own home!*

Albright waved away the thought.

– *What's done is done. No more looking back. Today we stand on the edge of salvation, ready to reap the rewards of our labour!*

He was pumping his fists now. He paused for a moment to let the words sink in, then continued in a lower, more reverent tone, an accomplished orator in complete control of his audience.

– *Never shall we go hungry again. Our integration back into their precious sodding society has provided us with the tools to bring together a disparate, selfish race in one decisive moment of joy and celebration. The pieces are finally in place. Observe, my friends; witness our revival…*

As the last sentence resounded, Albright's image faded away, the peachy tones of his skin, the white-grey of his beard and the dark of his cardigan pixelating and merging into one another and reforming as an entirely new picture, one which made the Euphorivores gasp and squeal with expectation. It wasn't as sharp as Albright's visage had been; it was patchy and out of focus, with round black shapes and thin white scratches across the screen. The image flickered, cutting ahead and jumping back again, and the

303

colours became saturated until at last they settled to reveal a wide field of green.

Down below, the light of the Core was beginning to brighten.

The crowd inside the BK Stadium were in full voice, chanting anthems and waving flags as the two teams filed out of the tunnel from the dressing rooms and lined up neatly on the grass beneath the towering presence of the enormous ice-blue antenna, which rose organically into the sky and glistened in the perfect summer's sun.

– *That's the Final… that's tomorrow?*

– *It's a prediction. Nothing else.*

The world's media jostled for position in their cattle pen for the best shot of the twenty-two most famous men in the world. North America in red, and the beaming heroes of the British Kingdom in a traditional royal blue affair, clashing with the green of the BKDFA spiral crest over their hearts. At the far end of the line, PJ Pitman stood staring into the middle distance; to the unknowing eye it might seem as though he were trying to filter out the occasion and focus on the game, but Josh could see the fear and panic written all over his face.

The fans ruffled and roared again as a small delegation appeared on the pitch. A dozen well-groomed men and women strode up towards the row of players. At the head of the pack, Ray Albright was acknowledging the crowd by raising his cane above his head, its round glass handle twinkling and reflecting its hues like a multi-coloured disco ball. The Prime Minister walked along the line, chatting and joking with the players, but spent the most time with PJ, resting one hand on his shoulder and shaking it firmly, just as an advertisement popped up along the bottom of the screen. Sunny, the tournament's mascot, was skipping along to reveal the SyBall App's latest betting odds:

**BRITISH KINGDOM TO WIN 3-0 AND PITMAN TO SCORE FIRST:
WAS 3/2 – NOW 4/1**

Laughter rose up across the Flagship. The Euphorivores, the master forecasters, knew something the world did not. After a final thumbs up to the home team, Albright smoothed down his sleeves and headed over to the four referees standing between the two teams in their black-and-white striped shirts and baseball caps, taking their hands and gripping them tight. They nodded sincerely at everything he had to say, as Temperance Newhart stepped ahead of the delegation and handed the match ball to the first official, then hugged him for a long time. A few feet away, Troy Simpson's face dropped with jealous dismay.

The picture changed again to a wider shot of the pitch, jumping forward in time to the match in full flow. North America were in possession, passing cautiously back and forth between the central midfielders and the wingers. In the top corner the score-line read:

BKM 0 – 1 NAM | 74:47

A small, sprightly North America player trickled past two British defenders as a distorted collection of watery sounds

305

calibrated into the clear, expositional voice of a seasoned commentator.

'Simon Fuentes has found some space on the edge of the penalty area… North America looking for a second to add to Lamoureux's headed opener… nervy times for the British Kingdom… out to Glover, back to Fuentes… Baines has made a run into the six-yard box… Fuentes… Baines… Oh! Emmett Baines sweeps it into the bottom corner! I can't believe it, they've got another! The British Kingdom are now two down with less than a quarter of an hour to go! But wait! No… the linesman's raised his flag for offside! The goal won't stand!'

A handheld camera trundled forward for a close-up of the official holding out his orange-and-yellow checkered flag.

'What drama! From the replays it looks as if Baines is a good yard or so onside. But we are not the ones who have to make these difficult decisions, and we applaud those who do. Here's Baines now, he's gone over to shake the hands of the linesman and thank him for the judgement.'

The Canadian striker jogged away merrily as the referee blew his whistle and Ben Castle placed the ball for a goal kick.

– They're manipulating the match.

– Small changes; divert the course, set a new path. It's what they do.

The match clock jumped forward again: 85:39. North America were still leading by a single goal, but the action was now on the other side of the pitch.

'That's better from the home team… Simpson shoots! Wide! Did that come off a defender? Yes, it's a corner to the British Kingdom. Lyons runs over to take it… there's a lot of shoving going on in that penalty area. Here comes the cross… looks good… oh my word! Lykke gets two hands to it, but he fumbles – was that a push by Danny Holt? Referee got a good look *at it. Both teams are scrambling for the ball, North America can't clear lines... Simpson... it's in! GOOAAALLL! Troy Simpson has levelled things up with less than four minutes of normal time to play! What a Final we have on our hands now! Come on, lads!'*

Again, the picture altered, skipping ahead to the eighty-ninth minute.

'Lamoureux again! The shot is tame. The referee's assistant steps forward... my word! Just a single minute of added time! Half an hour extra looms unless one of these teams can produce something in these last seconds. British Kingdom playing out from the back... Lockard, but Glover is there... across to Alex Shoreham... Daynes now, looking for support. Here's Danny Holt... Pitman is making the run. Out to Terrier... the home side need to do something here... Simpson wants it... Still Terrier... Oh! What a pass that is! Pitman's run onto it, the fans are roaring him on... fifteen seconds... 'Shoot', they're crying, 'shoot!' He's gone for the volley... over it goes... oh my God! Would you believe it! Has it been given...?'

Every spectator – in the Flagship and in the stadium – watched the replay in amazement as PJ's strike flew over the head of Jesper Lykke, hit the crossbar and ricocheted down onto the white goal line, by which time the goalkeeper had adjusted his position and pushed the ball away from the net. Further back, the referee pretended to take consultation from the linesmen through his earpiece, before turning and pointing to the centre spot.

'The referee says yes! He's done it! He's done it! PJ has won it for the British Kingdom! The crowd are delirious! I'm delirious! I can barely breathe! You will never see anything like this ever again! Pitman is being held aloft by his teammates! There's barely time for the restart, the British

Kingdom are about to be crowned the SyBall World Cup champions... the referee checks his watch, the whistle's in his mouth, this is it, this is the moment that will be remembered for all –'

The picture cut to black and silence descended. Josh could feel Lexa's heartbeat thumping through her hand.

– Are you ok?

– Yes.

The tiny screens lit up across the dome and the face of Albright returned once more to finish his address. Wild cheers greeted his reappearance.

– Thank you, thank you. No, please... thank you. Enjoy this moment. Savour it. Never...

Albright paused again, as if unsure of how he should continue. Josh could sense Lexa having none of it – it was all part of the game.

– Never be ashamed of who you are. Some people talk of 'alternatives'. Pah! What good would that do? They have risen above their natural order; forgotten their place in the food chain, time and again turning violently in on themselves. Instead of a slow, meaningless path to self-destruction, we'll prove just how bloody merciful we can be. We'll show them a glimpse of a world they could have created, followed by a nice, quick death to rid them of it.

Lexa tightened her grip around Josh's hand.

– It won't be quick for everybody

Josh felt the pain behind that thought course through him like a cold breeze. The sensation was so strong, it accentuated the warm feeling on the outside of his thigh, which until now he had failed to notice. Lexa caught him as he reached into his pocket.

– What are you doing?

Josh pulled out his phone. It had survived Lexa's attack outside the Bovill Arms far better than him, sustaining just a few scratches on the back of the casing. A few hours earlier, he had taken it with him when he'd left for the training ground and not looked at it since. It was a wonder he still had it, considering all the thrills and spills he had gone through. But there it was, the heat of the battery permeating through his palm. The screen was on and he found himself staring again at the face of Ray Albright. It was the same feed as the one playing above him, only shrunk to a more manageable size. In the top right corner of his screen, he could see a watermark of the SyBall App's spiral logo.

He caught eyes with Lexa and thought for a moment she'd said something, but the message was jumbled, as though her thoughts were too confused to communicate clearly – it matched completely the look of dread on her face.

– *We have shown them joy without reservation. We have shown them compassion without boundary. We have shown them their humanity…*

Albright leant forward, his giant head growing with encroaching menace across both the huge expanse of the dome and the small screen of Josh's smartphone.

– *And now they will repay us.*

'20

How to Name Your Dragon

On Copacabana Beach the festivities were in full swing, the revellers unperturbed by the late afternoon sun blazing over Rio de Janeiro. In front of the long row of nightclubs and high rise hotels, overlooked from on high by Christ the Redeemer, large outdoor screens had been set up at regular stages along the length of the beach, elevated on scaffold structures to allow passage beneath, while others had been placed at ground level along the promenade of the Avenida Atlântica next to the cafes and juice bars.

The largest of these screens had been erected near the southern tip of the bay, stretching widthways across the beach down to the water's edge. It had been there since the tournament began, showing every match live and drawing huge crowds, even if neither a South American team nor the British Kingdom were playing that day. A stage jutted out in front of the screen, flanked on each side by giant speakers and concert lights, and from dawn to dusk musicians, singers and dancers from all over the world performed in front of the thousands who swarmed the two and a half miles of soft white sand. It was billed as a cultural carnival, celebrating the diversity of nations and people, separated only by sea and brought together by the *Grande Uniformador*.

This morning the party had begun just as the first light broke over the ocean's thin horizon, and the crowd had grown so large it had spread into the sea, with hundreds standing waist-deep in the water. Though the Final was still to come the following afternoon, today's third-place play-off match against their favourite rivals would be the home team's last game before they flew home. Samba dancers in sequinned outfits with bright feathers had paraded up and down for hours on end, bare-footed kick-abouts dotted the length of the beach, and in the evening, whatever the result, a fantastic firework display was scheduled to take the festival long into the night.

Above the main stage, two enormous Brazilian and Argentinian flags fluttered side-by-side on the coastal breeze, matching countless more being waved in the hands of the excitable crowd in a kaleidoscopic field of rippling colours, the locals more than happy to laugh and dance with their southern neighbours. But for the past ninety minutes, there had been no music to dance to, and pockets of nervous tension had risen throughout the crowd, as in Manchester the Brazilians frantically defended their narrow lead with just a few minutes of the match left to go.

Josh scanned their faces, so young and tanned and beautiful, spread across the dome of the Flagship.

   – This is live, then? Like a test run?

   – More like a foretaste.

There was a tremor beneath their feet. The Euphorivores felt it too. Below them, the thick curtains of frothy cloud that poured out of the archways began to twist and turn, creating little storm pockets; bolts of lightning shot across the surface and the Core brightened as the vapours started to swirl, like a witch's brew being stirred inside a giant cauldron.

There was a reaction on the beach; the home fans held their breath as, unseen by those in the Flagship, Argentina's Adriano Flores sent a finely struck shot just wide of the goalpost.

A thick nausea settled deep in the pit of Josh's stomach.

– *I don't think I can do this.*

Suddenly, there was painful rip of his senses; in one quick movement, he felt as though all the fluids in his body had drained out of him, his bones had turned to jelly and he was about to collapse in a deformed heap on the ground.

'We don't have to,' said Lexa, turning to face him.

It was strange to hear her voice again, with all the inflections and imperfections of soundwaves moving through the air, and there was a moment of adjustment before he looked down at his hand and realised that Lexa had let it go. His palm ached and disliked the feeling of being empty.

Lexa checked his watch. 'Come on, before we get caught.'

'What about Rio?' Josh whispered, pointing up at the Copacabana. 'You wanted to see it.'

'There's no need. We have to go back.'

'But – all those people?'

Lexa bit her lip. 'There's nothing we can do. Better them than all of us.'

'*Lexa…*'

'No!' she snapped. 'I know what I have to do now, and it doesn't involve staying up here and getting ourselves killed. What are you doing?'

Josh had squeezed his eyes shut. His body was frozen, his voice quivered with fear.

'*Lexa… please be quiet,*' he whispered. '*Behind you*'.

Lexa spun slowly around, aware now of the new sound, like that of a ship's sail beating against the wind. She clasped her hand to her mouth and stumbled back, reaching for Josh's hand but finding only his wrist.

They had waited too long. On the ledge below, every single one of the million or so Euphorivores were staring straight at them, still and silent, peering at them with eyes that were more fascinated than angry. There was no need to attack; all they had to do was wait and let the Firebreather who had found the intruders take care of business.

The creature hovered in the air, only a few metres away from the edge of the rim. It looked exactly how Josh imagined it would. Its bat-like wings were outstretched, flapping steadily and precisely to keep itself in one fixed spot, like a hummingbird, only thousands of times bigger and slower. Its reptilian body was covered in glassy scales in varying shades of red, from burgundy hues to a scarlet underbelly and rose-coloured pigmentation around the muscle joints. It was broad and heavy set, with a large heaving chest leading to a long, slender tail which flicked from side to side. Four stumpy legs the size of tree trunks hung down from the torso and razor-sharp claws stuck out with a menacing curve from its paws.

Josh squirmed at the memory of the pincer jabbing between his shoulders as he hid beneath the fog.

The Firebreather hovered closer, stretching its neck and cocking its head to one side. The eyes were yellow with dark green pupils and sat close together above a long, bony snout. The skin around its cheeks was rough and haggard, bearing ancient scars of old battles. A thin crevice ran from the back of the skull and down the forehead, drawing all the features inwards and setting its face into a permanent sneer. Set within the crease and glinting in the light of the Core like a third eye in the centre of its head, was a large ruby lifestone. It flared its nostrils and sniffed the air.

'I thought you said they had no sense of smell.'

Lexa's mouth gaped open. 'I... I've never seen one like this before.' She tried to step away, but Josh held her back.

'Don't move,' he whispered. 'Its vision is probably based on movement. Birds of prey see their targets better when they're running away from them.'

'What are you talking about? Let me go!'

Lexa tried to break free of his grip, but he dug his fingers further into her wrist. The dragon's eyes narrowed and fixated on them as a forked tongue slid out of the mouth with a serpentine hiss. The lips curled, revealing a row of enormous teeth, all crooked fangs except for a set of silvery molars on one side of its mouth.

Josh lost all feeling in his legs and thought for a moment he might wet himself.

'Oh God... I was wrong... Lexa, I'm sorry, I'm so sorry...'

'Stop babbling, you idiot, and run!'

They spun quickly around and made off back through the archway. Lexa was quicker and better qualified to know how fast to go to outrun a Firebreather, but as they headed for the boggy green fug in the distance where the Vessel was hidden, Josh could sense she was holding back, checking her run and slowing herself so she could keep alongside him. He felt like he should push her on, to force her to leave him behind if she had to, but his courage abandoned him.

Four familiar crashes hit the ground behind them, followed by an ear-shattering roar, which sent a shockwave through the air that nearly toppled them both. The thunderous footsteps rose into a gallop, gaining ground at a fearsome pace. The entire passage shook as if struck by an earthquake and only Josh and Lexa's own momentum kept them from losing their feet.

Josh could already feel his muscles burning as he powered through to keep pace with Lexa, running with his head down as he heard a second, different roar echo off the high walls. A throatier, more gargled bellow that came from up ahead. The Firebreather behind them stopped, as did they, then cocked its head and let out a quizzical grunt.

The second creature emerged from the darkness, ducking its head beneath the apex of the arch and blocking the path entirely. It strode slowly forwards, each footstep pounding the ground with an air of angry authority. Its gaze shifted between all three of the newcomers, considering each one with equal disdain and transfixing them by its unhurried approach. This was a far bulkier beast than its crimson cousin. The cheeks were fuller and thick rolls of fat hung beneath its chin. The wings were smaller and unlikely to support its weight in the air. The tail was shorter, its legs were squat and, as it walked, a flabby belly brushed along the ground. Skin tones were more naturally defined, an autumnal mix of oranges, browns and dark greens, similar to the outer shell of the Vessel.

The new Firebreather stopped in front of them, panting noisily. A horrid odour wafted out of its mouth, a putrid blend of what smelt like petrol and out-of-date chicken. The two creatures craned their necks forward over Josh and Lexa; snarling, sneering, sizing one another up. It seemed both had forgotten about the tiny humans caught between their standoff, until Josh realised the dragons were most likely arguing *about them*.

'What do you think?' Josh said. 'Seen one like this before?'

Lexa shook her head. 'Not that size. He must be a defective clone, or just very old. Either way I think we can outrun him.'

'And the other one?'

'Shouldn't need to. If we can get the other side of Fatso –'

'*Fatso?*'

'– he'll block Red's path long enough to get a head start. Normally you'd go through their legs, stab a spear through the heart, then get out before it collapsed on top of you, but this one...'

'Won't get past his stomach.'

'Haven't got a spear, either.' Lexa looked from one side of the archway to the other. 'We'll have to split up and go round the outside of his legs. It'll confuse them both. I'll go left, you go right.'

'Right... my right or his right?'

'Your right.'

'As I'm facing him?'

'Yes.'

'Right…'

Josh looked at the narrow gap between Fatso's leg and the wall. The intensity of the growls were building up; one Firebreather had speed and agility on its side, the other strength and mass – and neither were prepared to make the first move. Teeth bared and claws clenched, scraping along the ground with an unbearable screech. Lexa laid a hand on Josh's chest.

'Wait for it… wait for it…'

Finally, the tension snapped as Red barked at his opponent and darted forward, startling Fatso into a retreating jolt.

'Go!'

Josh felt the shove of Lexa's hand before they separated, and he ran at full speed towards the wall. A cacophony of bellowing howls filled the air. Fatso's body wobbled and jerked, and Josh had to swerve to avoid being hit by the scaly sheets of skin. Nearing the leg, he estimated the position of Fatso's foot below the cloud, leapt over and then disappeared into shadow as he squeezed himself along the giant midriff.

On the other side of the archway, Lexa screamed. Josh shot round in a panic and looked up in time to see Red's tail sail over him and slam into Fatso's face with enough force to push him off balance. With his left legs flailing in the air, Fatso's right legs buckled under his full weight and he fell to the ground with a shriek. The reverberations spread across the floor and up the arches, which shook unsteadily.

Josh scanned the area. Red was stomping away, back towards the rim. He could hear Lexa's cries fade away over the pounding footsteps, and as Red flicked his head to one side Josh could see an animated shadow dancing around the beast's neck.

'Lexa!' Josh cried, as he pieced together what had happened:

At the moment they had parted, Red had made a decision and chosen Lexa. But it was the wrong option for a quick bite: Lexa was too quick, too experienced, and he succeeded only in snatching the hood of her zip-up jumper. The long fangs had pierced the material and now she was dangling below his chin, squirming and struggling with all her might to set herself free.

Josh chased after them, ignoring Fatso as the heavy lizard thrashed his legs around in vain to pull himself up.

'Lexa! Your zip…!' he screamed. 'Undo your zip!'.

She called back 'It's stuck!' but Josh could barely hear her. Fuelled by fear and adrenaline, he made a futile but full-hearted attempt to jump and grab hold of Red's tail, missing by some distance and landing on his feet just as Lexa was carried back out into the light.

By the time Josh ran back out, Red had already launched himself off the platform and was circling around the open space of the Flagship, much to the delight of the Euphorivores, who were cheering in telepathic silence. Red was playing to the crowd – he could just as easily flicked Lexa up in the air like a rag doll and caught her in his mouth, but instead spread his wings and soared down over his audience then swooped up over the cloud, dodging the tall tendrils with aerobatic ease.

Lexa swung from side to side, fearful with every turn that her hood would rip or Red would just get bored and let go. To make matters worse, her zip had finally loosened, and every bump of the erratic flight pulled the hoodie apart a little further. She clasped her fist around the tab, but could feel it dragging down against her skin.

Below her, the Core was opening up. The swirls of cloud had formed into an enormous whirlwind; a tornado within the shaft of the funnel, picking up speed, churning, twisting and expanding, until slowly a wide chimney spread open from the centre and down into the indeterminable depths of light below.

Red lifted his nose, adjusted his wings and snapped his tail, rocketing himself through the air. Lexa took in the pictures as they flew close to the dome. Time in Manchester was almost up and the beach atmosphere had loosened in anticipation of victory. The same feeling ran through the Flagship; the colossal engine was running smoothly, the Harvest's final test run was about to commence, and the Euphors were ready to eat.

The situation seemed entirely hopeless – but hopeless situations were a normal part of Lexa's daily life, and while she was alive and hanging beneath Red's mouth, rather than dead and inside it, there was still a chance. Red was swerving and looping in no particular pattern, but she had managed to keep a vague sense of her bearings by the occasional glimpses of Josh perched back out on the rim above the cloudfall.

Fatso hadn't gotten to him – not yet at least. It was encouraging, at least, and if he could find a way to help her instead of just standing there, even better. But as Red circled around yet again, ready to dive bomb the excitable mob, she could see Josh's back was now turned and his heels were moving dangerously close towards the edge.

Fatso lowered his head and stared angrily at Josh. If the old Firebreather hadn't been agitated before, he certainly was now. One half of his meal was already gone, and he seemed fiercely determined not to be denied yet again. His ragged, ageing lips parted to reveal two rotten rows of teeth – nothing like the pearly white fangs Josh had seen in Red's mouth before. There was one similarity, however, which Josh both expected and feared – the same strange cluster of flat metallic molars at the back. Each tooth was the size of Josh's fist, smooth and rounded at the edges, but if he'd looked closer, he would have seen the tiny scratches on the surface. He didn't need to look. He already knew what they were.

Fatso clenched his teeth, squeezing the giant molars and holding the position tightly for a moment before jerking the lower part of his jaw to one side. Josh braced himself for the end, but nothing happened except the sharp, quick sound of the molars scraping against one another. The creature tried again: this time a bright, electric flash flickered out from between the teeth.

Josh shook as the pages of the Captain's notebook passed fearfully through his mind:

If there's one thing we know from human experience is that with genetic engineering comes genetic weakness. Large-scale autopsies have revealed Firebreathers to be something of a physiological mishmash: their skin is reptilian, yet their blood is warm. The claws are long like a hawk's, but retract like a lion's. The wings are threaded with thin bones which aid

320

manoeuvrability, but the membranes are as thick as rubber, which prevents tearing but means flapping for too long wastes energy.

If nothing else, their capacity to breathe fire should be evidence enough that their anatomy is not naturally evolving, but rather a product of careful design. A gland in their lungs emits an extremely volatile chemical compound with properties similar to hydrogen and methane, which rises up their windpipe and fills their mouths and nasal passages. Then they grind their back teeth together, like two pieces of flint, creating a spark and igniting the gas.

Some studies of their cell structure have indicated Firebreathers may be susceptible to early ageing and decay as a result of their genetic mutation, but their lives are long enough to present a formidable threat.

Another flash.

Josh winced – still no fire.

Fatso's glands must have seen better days, but the old beast persevered. A shadow ran across the wall and Josh felt the whoosh of air sweep past him as Lexa called out his name. His heels were at the edge. He turned and peered over his shoulder, desperately hoping his legs would hold out and stop him from falling.

Below, the Euphors were still fixated on Red's aerial display, watching as he dived headfirst into the whirlwind and began racing alongside the speeding cloud, showboating his youth and agility. Lexa swallowed her breath as the world turned white. Her legs sailed behind her and she struggled to keep hold of the zip as Red accelerated forwards and her hoodie billowed in the wind. She could feel the light radiate through her body, the luxurious warmth urging her to let go and be free.

Her hand tightened.

Josh watched as Red and Lexa swept down and were dwarfed by the immense spiral churning relentlessly. Then, at the moment they were swallowed whole by a great flurry of bright mist, he saw Lexa call for him again; but this time the sound would not travel. They were gone.

She was gone.

The world faded around him, every sound, every movement, the chaos of it all slipping away and focusing his mind onto a single clear objective. His fists clenched so tight he could feel the thump of his heartbeat in his fingertips.

There was no other choice. He turned and ran towards Fatso, his arm swinging upwards as he neared; and as Red had slammed his tail into one side of Fatso's face, so Josh struck the other side with his forearm, catching a few jagged teeth, tearing his sleeves and grazing his skin. Fatso barely moved but let out a surprised hiss followed by a fierce guttural growl.

Josh spun on his heels and ran back the way he'd come, pounding the ground and hitting the edge of the rim as hard as possible to launch himself into the air. Behind him, the Firebreather finally got the spark he needed, and a fireball exploded out of his mouth with a furious roar. The colossal heat seared across Josh's back and he cried out in pain as the force of the blast hurtled him forward at an inhuman speed, taking his trajectory way over the heads of the mesmerised audience and down into the Core. His arms and legs flailed uncontrollably as he tumbled through the air, the blood rushing to his head as he struggled to reposition his body against the strength of the updraft. Even the smallest movement required a huge effort and each attempt to right himself was hampered by the invisible ropes pulling his limbs out of their sockets.

Then everything settled as he plummeted past the Euphorivores and became caught in the slipstream rotation of the cloud, allowing him to float on its path. The swirling vortex somehow seemed less expansive as it rushed past, the sense of width indiscernible at such speed, but Josh took comfort from the knowledge his airways were free of the choking mist, and the moment of calm provided him with an opportunity to fix himself into the torpedo shape he'd been aiming for, like a skydiver before the parachute opens, and he could dive forward with a degree of self-control.

He scoured the blaze of churning light below him. Up on the rim Red and Lexa had been tiny specks in the distance and he had lost sight of them as soon as he became caught in the torrent. There was a chance they were already out of reach, if Red had chosen to fly miles off to the opposite side, but to Josh's relief he saw them directly below as they swooped past a giant tendril, already making the flight back to the surface. He could see Lexa struggling with one arm already fallen out of her sleeve and the other resisting the same fate.

'Lexa! I'm coming!' he shouted, his voice lost within the whistles of the wind.

Perhaps sensing Josh's interference, Red began some close quarter circling to helter-skelter his ascent to the top. There would be no way Josh could keep his body like an arrow and make the small adjustments necessary to keep above the Firebreather's path. To make things worse, the creature then arched to the left and changed direction by dipping one wing, then the other, and gliding from side-to-side in a perfect S-shape.

But at least he was closer now.

'Lexa, hold on!'

The bulging mass of crimson scales rushed beneath him – if Josh were lucky, he might just be able to grab a hold of…

Thwump!

The end of Red's tail pummelled into his chest, knocking the air out of his lungs. He wrapped his arms around and tried to grab hold of the skin underneath – it felt rough and dry, the scales packed tightly together. Josh clenched his fingers and dug in.

Red let out a fearsome shriek and lurched upwards, the graceful rhythm of his wings becoming erratic as he tried to rebalance the weight of his new passenger, and in the tumult Lexa's hoodie tore free from the jaws and she was tossed into air. She sailed back over Red's body in a perfect curve, catching the rear edge of his wing and locking eyes with Josh as she fell.

He dived after her. Her hoodie was now completely inside out, snapping and rippling like a flag in a gale, and attached only by one stubborn cuff turned backwards over her hand, pulling her arm upwards and mercifully slowing her down.

'Josh!'

'Keep hold of the…'

He swallowed a large mouthful of air, stifling the end of his sentence.

Like those same invisible ropes around his joints, the pain in her shoulder must have been too much and she started flicking her wrist, working the sleeve little-by-little over her hand. The hoodie slipped over her fingers and shot off into the air at tremendous speed, missing Josh's head by mere inches.

His focus narrowed once more in the quiet calm that followed and he could see nothing but Lexa below him. The features of her face had disappeared beneath a silhouette's shadow as the light etched an iridescent line around the shape of her body and shrouded each strand of her hair in an ethereal glow. Even as she called out his name, her arms outstretched, the sound of her voice felt drowsy as it travelled up to him.

The mission was over. They had failed. None of it mattered now.

He just had to get to her.

Something twinkled. A tiny reflection of light caught in the shadow of her chest. Something on her camisole, Josh thought, a sequin or diamante sewn into the fabric. Only it wasn't moving with Lexa as she drifted from side to side. The ornament grew in size as it lifted out of the shade.

It was the lifestone.

Lexa had had it last – Josh guessed it had fallen out of her pocket before the hoodie had flown away. It seemed unnaturally stable as it hung in the air, as though the Core's supernatural atmosphere were keeping it balanced, floating in the space between himself and Lexa. He was falling faster now and, as the gap shrunk, he came so close he might just be able to reach out and grab it.

Around them, the world began to lose its sharpness, the relentless waves of cloud passing up and over each other as they spiralled down into nothing more than an indistinct white haze. Josh watched the definition of Lexa's body fade and merge with the light as it grew brighter, leaving only the tips of her fingers in focus as she reached for him.

But Josh's attention had, for the first time, pulled away from Lexa. He was inches from the tiny rock and began again to feel its warmth entering his body through his palm and up his arm. His fingers arched, ready to grab; Lexa was calling out, but her cries were languid, like the wail of a ghost, and the commanding power of the lifestone was too much for him to ignore.

I can get both...

It was beginning to hurt; the rush of wind inflaming the scars on his face, the weight of his legs pushing down into his torso, the light of the Core glaring into his eyes. His teeth clenched. His senses faltered. The gap between him and Lexa may have been opening up again for all he knew, but he couldn't be certain. It didn't matter. Josh needed nothing except to know exactly who and what he was. He was an amateur footballer. A failed artist. He had no natural talent and no-one had ever heard of him.

Just... a little... farther...

His anonymity made him special. He was a lone warrior – a silent hero known only to himself simply as...

Got it!

Josh slammed into Lexa, colliding painfully like a heavy rock falling out of the sky and landing flat across her body, knocking them both sideways and into a disorienting tumble.

Their arms grappled around for one another, and for a long handful of seconds they barrel-rolled through the air with awkwardly entangled limbs, until finally Josh lost his grip and peeled away from her.

He was holding the lifestone tight in one hand, but his mind was so scrambled that instead of enlivening his whole body as it had done before, he could only perceive a burning sensation from his arm up to his shoulder. His other hand was clinging to Lexa's forearm but slipping slowly down to her wrist. With a grimace, Lexa swung her free arm around and grabbed his elbow, sinking her nails into him and pulling herself closer.

'Josh! What are you doing?'

'I don't know! I don't know! I...'

The vortex started to shake; gently at first, then rising up into a series of volatile convulsions, as though reality itself were beginning to crumble around them. The swirls of cloud were everywhere and nowhere. They had fallen for miles and were close now to the Core; they could feel the particles of light crawl across their skin as it breathed in and out.

Yet Josh found this all too easy to ignore. He could only look into Lexa's eyes, knowing he was right where he needed to be.

'I just couldn't leave you.'

Lexa looked to say something back but the words never came. Instead, she drew her arms around him and they held each other tight as the light turned to dust, and from dust to nothing.

In Manchester, the referee blew his whistle and the game was over.

Brazil had won.

'21

Rare Visits to the Tea Cupboard

The President of the United States leant back in his seat, high above the Gulf of Mexico aboard Air Force One, fast approaching the airspace of northern Cuba. In ten minutes or so, Havana would be visible out of the right side.

Except today he didn't look as the thin strip of coast emerged from the haze. Instead, the commander-in-chief was watching TV in his private office, breathing a long, slow breath, and feeling that if he didn't pull himself together, he might cry. A minute earlier, the plane had dipped and every light on-board had flickered, but this was not the reason his hands were shaking. In fact, he had barely noticed the turbulence at all. He had been too invested in the recorded highlights of North America's semi-final win over Argentina, while the SyBall App pinged him real-time updates of the third-place play-off (which he barely looked at – it was a loser's showcase, in his opinion).

The President had watched the semi-final live, earlier that week at Chapultepec Castle, splitting a bottle of Mezcal with President Reyes and getting ashamedly tipsy. He had a lot of time for the

Mexicans; after all, the Hispanic preference for soccer had aided the growth of the sport in his own country, and the friendship between the two nations had anchored the mandate on which he was elected: an open-arms manifesto that stood firmly against xenophobia and isolationism, and made the old notion of American Exceptionalism seem exceptionally vulgar.

For the SyBall World Cup, both their national teams had qualified individually and both had been knocked out in the early stages. By the laws of the tournament, no American or Mexican players would line up to represent their continent in tomorrow's Final, and the British had made it clear they shouldn't encourage their citizens to root for North America; but come on, why the hell not? You had to support *someone.*

The semi-final had also provided the perfect excuse for the two to continue discussions for greater cooperation. The United States hadn't embraced de-militarisation in the same way other nations had over the past decade, on the grounds that its armed forces accounted for one of the world's biggest employers, had world class education programmes and fielded soccer teams which were highly competitive in the collegiate sports leagues.

But the Anti-Ballistic Treaty, championed by the British Kingdom to eradicate every bullet, missile and nuclear warhead from the face of the planet, had meant the munitions industry was forced to reinvent itself and, under his initiative, had begun developing long and short-range arrow weaponry on a monumental scale. While this had not been against the terms of the Treaty, it was certainly against its spirit. But these were economical decisions, completely necessary, and so despite them he was still able to convince the world – and himself – of his idealistic agenda.

Reyes agreed whole-heartedly; if anything, he was much less optimistic about the intrinsic goodness of outsiders. There was no trust without suspicion, and it made sense for the wealthy nations to protect themselves; Mexico was now part of the great American estate, taking an equal share of the land, the riches, and the golf courses.

The deal was done. The model of the American Crime Agency's cross-border operations would be expanded into a unified military; a shining global example of peace and goodwill, armed to the teeth with an endless supply of little fibreglass darts.

But, as the sky-blue airliner settled back onto its smooth course *en route* to London, his thoughts moved away from political triumphs and turned to the many and varied indiscretions of his past. What an unforgiveable man he used to be; womanising, ill-tempered and unspeakably cruel, obsessed with money and power. Both were tools which allowed him to do good in the world, yet he could feel nothing but condemnation for himself.

He left his office and headed off down the corridor, receiving at least a dozen salutes before he reached his private rooms nestled in the tail of the plane. He opened the door to find his wife, impeccably presented, even with her shoes off and feet up on the couch, reading a novel in a classic white Hepburn. The sight of her lifted him and again he had to resist the urge to weep. The First Lady closed her book and glided across the room.

'What's wrong? It was just a little turbulence,' she said, stroking his sleeve. 'You're normally such a good flyer.'

'I just wanted…'

He was shaking again, a nervous exhilaration he hadn't felt since their wedding day. He held onto her shoulders and looked deep into her eyes.

'I just want to tell you that… I'm sorry. For everything. It's been too long coming. From now on I promise I am going to be the husband you deserve.'

'Oh, Donald,' she said. 'You're so silly.'

Even so, she too couldn't stop the tears from streaming down her cheeks.

As the plane continued its path across the Caribbean Sea towards a seemingly endless ocean, Mike Casey and his two young boys, Evan and Jack, watched the Brazilian team congratulating one another from their comfortable Virginia living room, less than five miles from the White House.

Of all the matches they had watched together, Mike had enjoyed this the most, as it reminded him of the six months he and Jen had spent in South America, travelling up the Pacific Coast and hiking the Inca Trail. The wild landscape of mountains, forests and deserts had taken their breath away, as had the contagious zest for life shown by the people they met along the way. At the time, neither could quite understand the local passion for *fútbol*, but this was where opinion had begun to split over their seventeen years of marriage. He saw it as a great stroke of luck her current case had taken her to the British Kingdom in time for the Final, and hopefully she'd return home with a fuller appreciation of the game.

In the meantime, live footage of events from across the pond had acted like a stepping-stone, drawing Mike and the boys closer to her as the days passed and the house felt emptier. It hadn't taken long for the three to settle into a cozy routine for their afternoon soccer games. While Mike prepared the snacks, Evan and Jack would spend the morning deciding which of the two teams they were going to support. The winner received one of Dad's special congratulatory hugs and today it was Jack's turn to feel the arms wrap around him and a warm victor's kiss on the top of his head.

'Well done, Jack! That was close – I thought for sure Argentina were going to snatch one at the end there!'

Usually this was followed by a victory dance around the room, but today Jack slumped back onto the sofa with his head down. Mike glanced to Evan to check he'd painted the correct flags on each of their faces. There was no mistake – Evan was sporting Argentina's sky-blue triband, while Jack had spent the afternoon with a yellow diamond across his face, smudged now from the stream of tears.

Mike knelt beside his son. 'Hey, what's the matter?'

Jack lifted his head with a phlegmy snort and wiped his nostrils with his cuff, dirtying the sleeve with streaks of snot and paint.

'I miss Mommy,' he said.

Mike smiled as he reached for a tissue and began to mop up the mess under Jack's eyes.

'I know, buddy,' he said. 'We all do. But she'll be home very soon, okay? You can tell her about all the fun we've been having. You think you can do that?'

Jack nodded bravely.

'Good boy.'

'Hey Jackie, let's play outside!' Evan's shrill voice was overflowing with enthusiasm. 'You can be in goal.'

Mike watched the boys outside in the yard and realised a two-week vacation at the end of the summer would not be enough. They ought to be spending quality time together as a family; Jen should cut down her hours at the Agency and he'd do the same. Even better – they should quit work altogether! They could downsize and still have enough money left over to buy an RV and take the kids on a road trip across the country. Jen would love that.

The brothers' giggles filled the air, rising into raucous laughter as Jack slipped in wet mud and landed harmlessly on his backside. Mike's heart burst with excitement – he couldn't wait to talk to Jen about his idea the moment she walked through the door.

On the opposite side of the world, a similar thought passed through Rajesh Jaitley's mind as he shut down his tablet and put it safely away in his rucksack. It was nearly midnight in Goa, hours since he'd watched the sun disappear behind the ocean's thin horizon, and he marvelled at the moonlight glittering across the surface of the water. The temperature had dropped considerably but the air was warmed by the line of small campfires dotted along the beach, lit by holidaymakers who danced around them, singing, laughing, and pairing off for romantic strolls down by the shore. Still, it was cool enough for the beautiful South African girl sitting beside him to accept his offer of a jumper over the shoulders. At the far end of the beach, an array of Chinese lanterns had been released from the tip of Sinquerim Fort, which caught the breeze and floated up and back over the headland.

Rajesh filled his lungs with the sea air and smiled as he realised at last just how lucky he was. Life felt exquisite. He turned and looked back at the hotel buildings beyond the beach. Born in a village just outside Panaji, he'd worked in coastal resorts since he was fourteen, welcoming the world in all its complexity and diversity – but now it was time for a change.

'I think it's time to leave our jobs,' he announced.

The girl raised an eyebrow. 'Oh. Really?'

'Yes, I do.'

Rajesh expected some kind of counter in that broad Afrikaner accent he loved so much, but when none came, he assumed he was free to lay out his idea.

'We should go on a trip. Japan, America, Europe. We could stay with my cousin Vikram in London – he's a cop. And then after that I'll take you back to Cape Town and you can introduce me to your family.'

His friend laughed. 'And why would you want to meet them?'

Rajesh dug his toes into the sand as the fires crackled and flickered either side of him.

'So I can marry you.'

The girl with the chestnut-coloured hair covered her face with her hands.

'You want to marry me?'

Her bald boyfriend shrugged. 'Yeah, why not?'

His face winced; the gravel was digging into his knee. He teetered off balance and had to steady himself on the low brick wall, but with his tight t-shirt and bulging muscles, even the clumsiest of moves made him look good. The Bovill Arms car park may not have been the most romantic location in the world, but choosing the place they met and where they seemed to spend half their lives, was just charming enough to work. He didn't even have a ring; but then, he'd only made the decision to propose about thirty seconds before.

A huge roar of approval rose from within the Bovill Arms. The girl turned, using the distraction to think about her answer.

It had been a day for unexpected proposals – an engagement outside the pub, and inside an unexpected offer to buy everyone a drink. But then, Tony was feeling generous. The way the manager of Brazil was weeping and embracing his players on live TV, tighter than a drunk father whose kid had just married his best friend's daughter, brought on a wave of affection for his own team, all of whom – minus his goalkeepers – were celebrating with him now. What they were celebrating exactly was unclear, but the buoyancy of the mood permeated through each of them like a warm breeze sweeping in off the coast; it was almost transcendental, the feeling of being inside a moment they were sharing together.

Around the corner of the bar, Mick clicked his fingers impatiently in Callum Owen's face.

'What you 'aving?'

Callum stared into his glass. 'Not for me.'

'Not for…? Come on, your gaffer's paying.'

'I said, piss off Mick!'

Callum downed the last of his beer and walked across to the blonde-haired girl sitting by the window. Fiona's shift couldn't have long finished – her nurses' uniform was still visible beneath her shawl – and this was probably the last thing she wanted in front of all her snotty-nosed mates from the hospital, but he wasn't prepared to squander his moment of courage. Spontaneity was charming; you never knew what might work unless you took the chance.

'Can I speak to you, please?'

Fiona's friend snorted into her glass.

'Alone.'

It ought to be easier than this – the girl he had known for years; the longest relationship of their lives; the only person he had ever been intimate with. Conversation ought to flow, fueled by the connection they once had. They ought, at least, to be friends.

Outside, the car park was empty except for that couple who were always there, once more inspecting the deepest recesses of each other's throats with their tongues. Callum planned to lead her across the road to the pond, but Fiona had already stopped a few feet from the door, facing him with her arms folded.

He took a breath. 'Fiona, I…'

'That's a nasty cut above your eye,' she said.

She was interrupting him on purpose.

'It's nothing. Accident in the gym'

'You should get that looked at.'

He shook his head. 'It's fine, really. Listen, I... I wanted to ask if you'd...' Callum winced with embarrassment. 'If you'd be interested in –'

'Fifi? Is everything okay?'

The glossy tone dripped like oil. Even the footsteps on the gravel sounded posh. Fiona's new boyfriend hadn't been sitting at the table when Callum walked over; probably he'd been in the toilet, congratulating his reflection on being the most handsome man alive.

Dr Grayson slipped an arm across Fiona's shoulders. For a moment Callum hoped she would shrug him off, but there it stayed.

'Owens, isn't it?' he said.

'Callum.'

'Ah yes, of course; you turn out for Belmont Rovers, don't you? I've seen you play. Fifi, this guy's got a left foot like you wouldn't believe. Shame about the other one, eh? Might have had a career ahead of you.'

Callum read the expression on Fiona's face; she wanted a large hole to appear in the tarmac and swallow her up.

'Listen, I don't know what you two little birds were twittering about out here, but why don't you come in and have a drink with us, hmm? What's your poison – lager, is it?'

A moment of unspoken conversation passed between Callum and Fiona, a reminder of the half-glances and the knowing smiles that marked the heyday of their time together.

– *So, this is it? He's what you want?*

– *Yes, thank you. He is.*

337

Callum smiled at Dr Grayson. He didn't know his first name – Bertram or Tristan or something like that.

'Nah, you're alright, mate. Think I've had enough.'

The branch recoiled with a snap as Callum ripped the leaves from the hedge at the corner of the car park. He yomped along the pavement, heading in no direction in particular, the little pieces of torn leaf fluttering behind him like a paper trail.

Catie switched the vacuum cleaner off just as Callum passed along the front of her building. She might have seen him outside the window, but she was too consumed by her chores to look. The past couple of days had been spent in a fastidious cycle of tidying and crying, tidying and crying; but now the flat was spotless, and she felt too wrecked to start the process over again. Instead, she lay on her bed, gazing up at the swirling textures of the sponged ceiling until spots appeared before her eyes.

The phone was ringing.

She didn't move; she already knew who it was.

Mum and Dad.

Catie let the call go to voicemail, and in the resulting silence thought again about calling *his* parents. It was the middle of the day in Wisconsin. But what would she say to them? She'd never met them. What would be the benefit of a stranger phoning up to jump in on their grief? They might press her for details, too. She'd been there when it happened, while they were half a world away.

The grainy lines of the ceiling formed yet again into their faces: those uniform expressions, frozen in the act of grotesque laughter.

Was it the food – had they eaten something she hadn't? The tortilla dip, maybe?

No.

No, it couldn't have been an accident. Maybe it was a suicide pact she hadn't been party to. An agreement to pop something in their months and bite down as soon as she'd left the room.

What was it he said?

You're right, we're gonna get our butts kicked on Sunday, so please let us enjoy this!

Were they really *that* excited North America had won, they couldn't bear the thought of carrying on with nothing in the future to match that feeling? Unlikely as it seemed, still a surge of bitterness and anger so strong swelled within her that she felt sickened by it. She reached for the phone and sat up. A SyBall App notification was flashing in the centre of the screen: a Brazilian flag and a bronze medal emoticon. Catie swiped it away and searched the names on her list of contacts.

The call went to voicemail.

'Hi David, it's... it's Cate.' She paused and thought about hanging up. 'How are you? I know it's been a while, and... I know you still blame me for what happened between you and...' The tears were coming again. She squeezed her eyes. '...Miguel, but... I'm going to come and see you play next season. I promise. I don't know if Mum told you or anything, but I really need someone to talk to, so... you're probably in the pub right now, so call me back when you get this message. Please.'

Catie McCrea ended the call, wiped her eyes, and went into the kitchen to find the marigolds draped over the tap. The fridge could probably do with cleaning again.

The door slid open and two men, one swinging confidently on his crutches, the other hobbling unaided with his foot in a brace, came out of the hospital's main entrance. They stood at the top of the stone stairs leading down to the pavement and drew fresh gulps of air for the first time in days. It was late in the day, but the sun was still shining, and a gentle breeze took the edge off an otherwise strong summer heat. A smile passed between them. Brian looked at his watch while Scott stared down at his feet. Neither spoke and neither moved.

Nearby, a young woman, sitting on a bench in a dressing gown, finished her phone conversation with the words 'I miss you so much' and then made her way back indoors. Brian and Scott stepped aside to let her past and watched as she passed through the reception towards the lifts and up to the wards.

'Fancy a pint?' asked Scott.

'I thought you'd never ask,' said Brian.

Three floors up in the High Dependency Unit, Gillian Bannick squeezed her husband's hand and searched yet again for any sign of movement. Nothing much had changed in the last three days – which was good apparently – but she could no longer bear the tubes running in and out of him like some twisted science experiment and the relentless sound of the monitor above his head.

Beep. Beep. Beep.

She let go of his hand and studied his surgery scars; the old ones, from the first accident. If she pulled his skin and rubbed the surface, she would feel the tips of the pins threaded throughout his finger bones. They were reminders; warnings he had chosen to ignore.

Gillian squeezed her eyes and tried to block it all out. For the past few minutes, she had been tormented by a vision of the accident – not as a witness, but first-hand through Martin's own eyes. She could feel herself slamming into the car and suffering the onslaught of pain in a sickening slow-motion replay.

Outside in the corridor someone cheered and snapped her out of her violent daydream. She rested her head on the bedsheets and sighed.

Beep. Beep. Beep.

'I've got something to tell you,' she whispered. 'I'm afraid we might not be going scuba diving again next year.'

She held the sheet tightly in her fist and pulled it close.

'We're going to have a baby'.

A couple of miles away, Frank Pittman woke up. It was a strange sensation, considering he hadn't been asleep. He was in his favourite chair in the living room, warm, comfortable, and well-fed; but with the match on television keeping him sufficiently alert, there had been no chance of drifting off for an afternoon snooze. Why then did he feel as if he'd just come round from a long and peaceful sleep? The kind of sleep a person had when they'd been allowed to rest for as long as they needed, then woken with a clear head and feeling as light as a feather.

Frank tried to stand but his legs were a little shaky. He leant on the armrests and lifted himself slowly, an action the girls would no doubt interpret as a sign he was becoming old and decrepit, when in fact, he felt quite the opposite. The weight of the years seemed to lift off his shoulders and his eyes took in the surroundings of the home he'd lived in for half his life as though he were seeing it for the first time. His body felt healthier too, the air flowing cleanly in and out of his lungs, to the point he felt strong enough to go outside and run a mile.

He didn't. Instead, Frank looked around and wondered where Josh was. He had a vague recollection of him running out the door not long ago, but the memory was fuzzy. He glanced out the window. The Nissan was still in the driveway.

Josh was up in the bath, that was it. Nursing his wounds while Caroline made his dinner.

Frank thought about going up to linger casually on the landing and catch him on the way out of the bathroom. But instead, he turned and looked down at the wooden TV cabinet. Inside were stacks of old DVDs they hadn't watched in years.

Whatever happened to those lazy Sunday afternoons when he and his son would settle down together after a roast lunch and put a film on? Every week Josh would sit there, as still and silent as a rock, staring in wide-eyed wonder, his mind lost, swept away on epic adventures of wild derring-do led by ragtag groups of square-jawed heroes and misfit underdogs, plucky teenagers and daredevil archaeologists.

It was all nonsense as far as Frank was concerned – but he'd spend all week looking forward to that moment when the credits rolled and Josh would start chewing his ear off about how amazing it had been. Frank would take it all in, but often as he listened, he imagined the day, when Josh was old enough, he could stop him in his tracks and say:

'It might seem amazing now, but let me tell you something, there's nothing quite like missing the whole film because you're in the back row with the girl of your dreams.'

That was what those afternoons meant to Frank; a chance to remember a time when the optimism of youth and the onset of adulthood merged together to make a young man feel he could take on the world. Those days were gone, but he had made a vow to himself long ago to help his own son navigate those tricky rites of passage.

But instead, all Frank did was watch football.

Over and over again.

Why? Without Josh there football was boring. In fact, Frank *hated* football. Only on reflection did it feel like an unpleasant addiction; a habit he couldn't kick.

Sophie and Jessica were looking up at him from the couch, plotting his downfall as always. But he didn't care. His mind cleared and his legs regained their strength, and he wanted nothing more than to go to the kitchen and put his arms around that girl from the cinema while she waited for the oven to preheat.

Once their dad had left the room, the twins turned their attention back to the TV. The Brazilian players were climbing up through the stands towards a large podium where a member of the Royal Family was waiting to present them with their medals.

Hands shook with nerves and hearts thumped as one sister had a sudden urge to finally tell the other, the person she trusted most in the world, that there were times – lots of times – when she didn't feel like being a girl anymore.

At the same moment, the other sister had a sudden urge to reveal she already knew, and that she cared more deeply for her now than ever before.

Caroline watched her daughters scurrying up the stairs as her husband led her into the dining room and sat her down. Alone in the chair, she could hear the kettle being switched on and the element roaring into life. The fridge door opened and each of the cupboards were slammed shut one-by-one.

Top left, above the sink, she said to herself.

She took off her apron and placed it neatly on her lap. It was a pity really. At any other time, this would have been a welcome surprise. But right now, Caroline didn't want Frank to make her a cup of tea. She didn't even want to make her son's favourite meal.

No, what she wanted was for her husband to come back in from the kitchen, kick the kids out of the house and ravish her right there and then on the table.

In another kitchen, a short while later, Asher Bloom put down his slice of pizza, rejected his girlfriend's offer of a lift home and walked out of her life forever.

The Final Third

.

'22

Back to Earth

R ed stretched out his wings and glided down through the vortex in a perfect spiral. Like all Firebreathers born with his crimson colourings, he was a pedigree, and the leader of his pack. His physical strength was matched only by his mental sharpness and he understood that flying too close to the Core was dangerous; no matter how tough your skin, particles of sentient light could seep through the pores and take apart the victim from the inside out. It wouldn't hurt and it wouldn't take long – one moment the unlucky soul existed, the next they didn't.

Red's instincts were guided by flickering memories of adventurous elders – the mutants bred in vast Euphorivore laboratories in the bowels of the Flagship – who flew off to explore the depths and never came back. Left to fend for himself, the eager young pup may have been destined for a similar fate, but as the first of an advanced generation conceived through natural reproduction, he was born with the intuition to quickly analyse a situation and decide whether a course of action were either brave or stupid.

It was only today that Red's sense of survival evolved to cope with the notion that some deeds were both brave *and* stupid.

Josh had never ridden on the wing of a dragon before (and a *dragon* it was, whether Lexa liked it or not) and was surprised by how rough it felt. The thick sheets of skin pulled tight between three bony appendages had looked smooth from a distance, but up close were ravaged with creases and wrinkles from a lifetime of opening and closing. Sharp, prickly hairs covered the surface of the membrane and irritated his palms.

The greatest surprise, however, was finding himself on the wing in the first place. He could remember falling, but had no memory of landing; the light had been so strong he'd closed his eyes, and on opening them again had simply found himself there, clinging on for dear life as the Core rumbled below, threatening to reach out and pull him down.

From out of the gentle glide, Red suddenly banked to the right, catching a slipstream, and soared upwards away from the light. Josh tightened his grip and grimaced as the air drove against him like a gale-force wind. He could feel his grasp slipping, and only then began to notice the small reflexive twitches that pushed against him from different parts of the wing; subtle little movements that kept Josh in place as Red adjusted the pace and direction of his flight.

'Josh!'

Lexa's voice struggled to carry through the rush of air, and it came to him like a muffled cry in the distance. He forced his head around to the only place it could have come from. Of all the surprises in the last few minutes, this was by far the best: there she was, holding on to the opposite wing and peeking over the row of spikes which ran the length of Red's back and down to his tail.

'Josh, thank God! Are you okay?'

Josh shouted his response, accentuating the movement of his lips. 'I'm fine! Are you?'

'Yes! Isn't this amazing!'

Amazing?

A wide beaming smile drew across her face – it was the most beautiful smile he had ever seen on another person. Their time together had been brief, but it was enough for Josh to know that Lexa was angry. Angry at the life she had led, angry at the mission she had been handed – angry at him, even. She had lost everything and everyone she loved – it had made her hard and untrusting and sceptical. Yet here she was in the most dangerous place imaginable, risking her life to ensure no one else would face the horrors she had – and it seemed as though she were *enjoying* herself.

They rose higher, the cloud zipping past in a hazy smear as above them the wide opening at the top of the funnel became visible for the first time. Red beat his wings, turning Josh's stomach like a sharp dip on a rollercoaster, and accelerated his body upwards until he caught a new stream.

Settling again, Lexa stretched out her arms like wings of her own, closed her eyes and let the air wash over her. She was finally free, if only for a moment, of the pain she had carried for too long.

Passing the white waterfalls near the top, Josh saw that the enormous swirl had begun to slow and the light of the Core was dimming down to its dormant glow. He became more nervous the higher they flew. Once they reached the top he and Lexa would be exposed, and if the thousands of punch-drunk Euphorivores didn't get to them, then surely one of Red's own kind would be waiting beneath the arches to show far less mercy than he had.

With a final flourish, Red swooped in close to the edge of the opening, skimming through the cloud with the tip of Lexa's wing-carriage, then circled and shot upwards like a rocket, the Euphors passing quickly by in an indiscernible blur. As they neared the bottom edge of the giant dome where Albright's broadcast had been displayed, Red arched his tail over his back, causing his whole body to flip forward and dive straight back down again. The hairpin motion had turned them upside down; their legs flopped, and their arms buckled under the weight of their own bodies. This time falling would have been inevitable if Red had not judged the correct moment to decelerate and curve forwards by raising his head, levelling himself out and settling into a gentle glide a short distance above the crowd.

Josh rolled over and leant back against the side of Red's torso, pulling up his legs and tucking his knees under his chin, in the hope of shielding himself from view. It was a token defensive gesture – Red was sure to land anyway and the Euphors would tear him limb from limb, or try to make him laugh and then eat his soul.

'That's impossible…'

Josh reopened his eyes and looked across Red's back to see that Lexa had crept forward and was peering over the edge of the wing. He turned and gingerly leant over on his side.

One thing was for certain: whatever had happened had affected all of them. The Euphors were motionless – completely and entirely still. Not a flinch passed between them. Not one eyeball rolled up to follow the path of the Firebreather passing overhead. Some were sitting, others were kneeling – some were even laid flat out on the ground. Many were still huddled together in their little groups as they had been during the Rio celebrations, their arms wrapped tightly around one another. The majority, though, were standing, lost and alone in their own little worlds. It was like an eerie art installation on an industrial scale – millions of life-like statues, all painstakingly sculpted into individual poses, with one common element:

Each of them had placed a hand on their chest, covering the spot where under the skin their lifestone lay nestled between their ribs.

Josh found it an oddly moving sight, as though every Euphorivore had stopped for a moment of reflection. But for what? He raised his voice to ask Lexa what she thought, but before the words could come out, he felt a crush of pain across the back of one hand, arching his fingers and forcing them together in a fist. The voices suddenly rose up in unison, filling the void of the Flagship. He expected screams or wails or pleas for absolution, but it was nothing of the sort.

They were singing.

A tender, soulful chorus, more like a harmony of sounds rather than a recital of lyrics. A sweet and unforgettable melody. Beautiful, uplifting and pitch perfect.

His hand relaxed and the Euphors fell silent once again.

Red darted forwards, adjusting his trajectory here and there, lining himself up with one of the arches, and dived straight in without touching the sides. Once through, he landed immediately with four heavy thumps. They were back in the arched hallway and the Firebreather could go no further; his path was still blocked by Fatso's heaving bulk asleep on the ground, the snoring loud but content. Red flapped his wings like a bird ruffling its feathers, then tilted to allow Josh and Lexa to slide off the back and drop safely to the ground.

As his two passengers squeezed past Fatso and scurried off into the darkness, Red couldn't help but feel a twinge of sadness. He had grown fond of the tiny intruders and there was a flicker of memory of the day his own children had flown off to make their own way in life. Once again, his job was done, the adventure was over and there was nothing left to do but settle down next to his old adversary and take a well-earned nap.

'That was intense.'

Lexa didn't reply. She couldn't even look at him.

Intense?

Idiotic was a better word. Reckless. Shameful. Disgusted with herself. She had always been so careful. Her mission was her life – she didn't expect to go home, she didn't expect to survive, but she did expect to do her duty.

Instead, she had gone to the most dangerous place imaginable and let her guard down and allowed herself to feel… *nothing*. A blissful emptiness she had never thought possible. Then, as she flew, the emptiness had turned to a childish glee coursing through her body; light and pleasant and liberating, but too unfamiliar to feel truly comfortable. There'd been a naughtiness about it too, a suggestion she was doing something wrong. It hadn't worried her, it was exciting, it was the audacity of allowing herself to smile as an act of rebellion or an outburst of repressed rage.

Oh God, Lexa, what have you done?

Her father's voice rang in her head, telling her to forget and move forward. But the moment Lexa returned to the Vessel it had all come flooding back and for the first time she found herself questioning her motivation. Time was running out, there was so much to do, but she was rooted to the spot, staring at the cloud around her feet and digging her teeth into her thumbnail, bending it at the tip. The idea flickered through her mind that it might be best if she just lay down amongst the vapour, close her eyes and never wake up. The world would still end, but it wouldn't be her problem anymore.

But then Josh was still here; if she went ahead with it, he'd only do something stupid like try to save her.

Again.

Lexa could tell he wanted her to say something. He wanted to talk about what had happened in the Core and ask questions she didn't want to know the answer to. In her world emotional complexity was an unaffordable luxury; life was hard but simple, if you spent too much time thinking about your feelings, you were as good as dead. Except now her mind was in a whirlwind, spinning a confused cocktail of fear, anger and something else harder to describe – an awakening she felt she needed to suppress.

'Lexa?'

The nail snapped.

'We have to go,' she said, storming across the floor of the chamber and over to the desk.

She opened the laptop and the screen flickered into life. Her hands hovered over the keypad but went no further. The simple act of typing felt like a gargantuan effort for which she no longer possessed the will. Every keystroke was another step forward into battle, another step closer to death. Her hands clenched into fists and her head lowered.

'I'm sorry,' she whispered. 'I'm so sorry.'

Josh came closer and spoke over her shoulder. 'You don't need to apologise.'

'I'm not talking to you!'

Josh recoiled, his back straightening and his eyes blinking. One of his hands twisted at the wrist and his fingers arched involuntarily into hooked claws.

'You shouldn't even be here!' She jabbed a finger at him, her rage seething. 'You're a mistake! I should have fucking killed you when I had the chance! I should have beaten you to death and then you wouldn't be here interfering and messing things up and putting everything at risk! Give me your handset!'

Josh's mouth opened and closed like a fish gulping for breath. He looked panicked.

'There! In your pocket!'

'You mean this?'

Josh pulled his phone from his jeans and held it in front of him. Lexa snatched it from his hand and stepped back.

'Don't come near me.'

Josh nodded in obedience as she began scouring the small black tablet for its power button. She turned away, unable to bear the broken expression on his face. He was clearly hurt, but then what did he expect? A 'thank you' every time he swept in to rescue her?

Live my life then see how fucking grateful you feel.

Lexa found the button on the side and the screen lit up. A keypad popped up below a blank text box.

'How does this work?'

'You need my password,' Josh said. 'H-seven-five-J-three-T. If it locks you out again just remember it's the word 'Nutmeg' with each letter replaced with the key to the top left. It's a good technique – I'd recommend it to anyone.'

Lexa punched in the password and found herself looking at a picture of a cartoon squirrel overlaid by a digital clock across the middle of the screen. She looked down at the four symbols along the bottom: a globe, an envelope, an old-style telephone receiver and a camera. Her frustration grew; the phone was close to being flung across the chamber and it was almost by accident that she swiped the clock away and discovered a second screen littered with icons, including an inverted green teardrop just below the squirrel's elbow.

'This!' she barked, holding the phone up and pointing at the tiny graphic. 'This was in the corner when Albright's broadcast came up on your screen, what is it?'

Josh peered forward, squinting his eyes to exaggerate his usefulness.

'That's the SyBall App.'

Lexa stared blankly. 'An *app?*'

'It's run by the government,' Josh said. 'You can stream live games, make bets, it's all free –'

'Wait, wait...', she interrupted. 'Make bets?'

'For money, yes.'

Lexa shook her head in disbelief and threw the phone back at Josh, who fumbled his catch. Then she sat on her stool and looked down into the Core. In its restful state it emitted a low static light which barely broke the surface of the cloud. Her fingers drummed along the top of the desk. To Josh it probably looked like she was deep in thought, but in truth Lexa was merely taking a moment to strengthen her resolve. Everything was obvious, her instincts had been right, and her fate was sealed – might as well get on with it. The only consideration was whether she could believe the Euphors would really be that mischievous.

Lexa turned back to the laptop and began typing, this time without the reluctance. A small black window appeared into which she began writing long lines of code from memory. It was a frustrating process, but one the Captain had considered completely necessary. If the enemy ever got their hands on the laptop, the Calendar and Globe applications would be useless to them; time travel was simply not worth the risk. But there was a third programme, far more valuable, hidden within the Core's synthetic conscience; an Aladdin's cave accessed only through a backdoor route designed to preserve the only treasure humanity had left.

As she worked, Lexa could feel Josh's lingering presence. The first shreds of guilt – another unwanted emotion – were entering her mind, and while she was unmoved to do much about it, the silence between them was becoming uncomfortable.

'I assume you're familiar with the internet?' she asked.

'Yes...' Josh said, confused. 'Are you?'

Lexa shrugged. 'A little. Resistance groups in different parts of the world used it to send messages to each other. They were encrypted in social media posts. Sounds clever, right? Except the Euphors knew they whole time – they were stringing us along, using the messages to smoke us out, until eventually they got bored and shut the whole thing down.'

A smile drew across Lexa's face as she thundered away at the keyboard.

'But what they didn't know was my father managed to salvage this one single databank – a repository of everything that has ever been said, written, photographed, learnt; every story, every chronicle, every archive and record of everything that has ever been done – and began storing it all on different remote access servers – 'clouds', he called them – passing from one to another, always a step ahead, until finally we had the Vessel and it was all downloaded into the Core.'

'From one cloud to another!' Josh joked.

It was a feeble attempt at humour, but even she agreed anything to take the edge off the moment seemed worthy enough for an airing.

'He said it was apt.' Lexa hit the return key. 'The Core designed for our extinction used to preserve our history.'

The laptop's display flashed erratically as the Core's light grew brighter and then quickly dimmed again. The picture on screen settled and revealed a webpage full of small boxes surrounded by photographs and a row of quick-link tabs across the top.

Josh recognised it instantly.

'Is that... *Digipedia?* My God, I use that all the time! Everyone says it's unreliable.'

'Well, after tomorrow it's all there is.'

Josh watched Lexa type a single word into the search bar and scour the first few lines of the resultant article. Deep down he was still shaken from the outburst. But if he were meant to feel aggrieved at the way she had spoken to him, then it had failed to materialise. Instead, he felt embarrassed. Lexa was a warrior and so it was inevitable, if naive, that he had come to see her as invincible. It was a mindless presumption. The long fall into the Core of the Flagship showed him Lexa was just as vulnerable as anybody else; she was barely an adult, no older than him, who by the misfortune of time and place had had her entire life stolen from her.

But I'm here now. You can push me away, but I won't leave you. Not again.

Lexa muttered as she skimmed the lines of text. 'Developed by Winsome Free... beehive... doesn't surprise me. Name, name, name...' She scrolled down. 'Name. Entered into the register... discussion in the House of Commons... Society Football... light-hearted exchange on the application's betting function, Prime Minister Ray Albright denied the name also alluded to the legend of...'

Lexa clicked on a link to a new article, and after seeing its title placed her hands behind her head and let out a long sigh.

'Maybe you do all deserve to die,' she said.

Josh looked down at the screen. The article Lexa had found was on *Sybils* – women in Ancient Greek mythology believed to be oracles who spoke the words of the Gods. The exact nature of their legend differed by region and by era, but the link had shortcut to a subheading on the kingdom of Phrygia. There the Sybils were synonymous with the story of Cassandra, daughter of the Princess of Troy, who was cursed by Apollo to utter prophesies no-one believed. Underneath, a quote from the philosopher Heraclitus:

'The Sibyl, with frenzied mouth uttering things not to be laughed at, unadorned and unperfumed, yet reaches to a thousand years with her voice by aid of the god.'

Josh had got the point: prophesies, predictions, betting – it was all one big joke. SyBall was a glimpse into the future for a population too lost in the fug of their devotion to the Guiding Principles to notice just how wrong everything was. He had a vision of the Prime Minister, with his long, white beard, sitting on a throne atop a cloud, surrounded by marble pillars; instead of a woolly cardigan he wore a flowing, gilt-edged toga, and instead of a cane, he held a bolt of lightning.

The image seemed to fit.

What if the legends of ancient civilisation weren't legends at all, just misunderstandings of the truth? What if Sybils, heavenly mouthpieces searching for a meal in a world where football and digital communications did not yet exist, were telling people to go out and paint the town red, to live life in one long hedonistic riot of wild abandon? This would have boosted their disregard for

Cassandra, who spoke not of decadence and debauchery, but of death and destruction.

'They've been laughing at us this whole time,' Josh said.

'It's worse than that.' Lexa gestured towards Josh's phone. 'If you had to guess, how many people would you say – around the world – use SyBall to watch football?'

That was an easy one.

'All of them, I'd say. The Department bought up all the leagues' broadcast rights and made the app free to download.'

'On those?'

'On anything. Phones, tablets, televisions –'

'Large outdoor screens?'

Josh nodded. There was no need to say anymore – the extent of the Euphorivores' master plan was clear. SyBall was not just an abstract code, it was a weapon. In the final minute of the match, the referee would rule PJ's goal in favour of a victorious home team, causing millions around the world to cheer into their screens and sending a massive ball of positive energy straight up to the Flagship to be stockpiled within its Core like a celestial larder. If the Euphors had been around since human life began, then their progressive outlook had to be admired. Still, there wasn't a Wi-Fi signal in the world powerful enough to connect a smartphone to a space station.

'They're using a transmitter,' said Lexa, as though reading his mind. 'Something that can receive and collate all the signals from all the different data networks and then blast the whole lot up in one go.'

There was an element of doubt in her voice and Josh thought he knew why: if this were all true, then surely someone in the future would have realised and argued that intercepting the signal was a far more logical plan than going after PJ Pitman. Her father had known so much about the Harvest; he had known about the Flagship – yet this, clearly, had never been mentioned.

Josh knew the truth, of course. The Captain had been forced to play a careful game with his own daughter, picking and choosing what she needed to know about his past and her future, with the fate of the world resting on those decisions. How heavy it must have weighed on the poor man's shoulders to never know if he had found the right balance. Now Josh was the one withholding information, and while it felt deceitful, his instinct was to keep playing dumb for now.

'So where is it?' he asked as Lexa stepped back towards the laptop. 'The transmitter?'

She turned to him and raised an eyebrow.

'Where do you think?'

'23

Heroes

D S Jaitley put the phone on loudspeaker and set it in the gulley next to the gear stick.

'Hello?'

'Hi, Charlotte, it's me.'

'Vik?'

'Yes. Heh, I guess that means you don't have my number saved on your phone anymore.' He regretted the comment instantly. 'How are you doing?'

The gears crunched angrily as he shifted into third and the car jolted forward.

'Are you driving?'

'Yes, but don't worry, it's not mine.'

'Huh?'

'Belongs to a witness. I'm just taking it back to the station. Bit of a crazy story actually, you wouldn't believe me if I told you. Well, I mean I could tell you, if you'd like...'

'What do you want, Vik?'

'I, um...' He took a deep breath. 'I just wondered if you and the boys would like to come round to my place tomorrow to watch the match? I'll get some snacks, maybe some pizza, make a party of it. For old times' sake. Your mum could come too.'

And his parents, and whoever else wanted to come. The more the merrier. They could all watch the Final together, laughing and joking, rekindling relationships, making up for lost time... and then, at the last moment, there might be a 'power cut' – a total blackout that silly old Vik wouldn't be able to fix until after the final whistle.

'This is a joke, right? I haven't spoken to you in, what is it, two years?'

It was three years.

'And then suddenly you... argh! God, it's like you know...'

'Know what?'

There was a long pause.

'There's not a day goes by that I don't think about her. But we're happy now, we've moved on...' She took a deep breath. *'Except tonight, I don't know, I can't get it together; the kids are acting weird, and then out of the blue you ring, and...'*

'But that's what I mean! Tonight! I feel it too...'

'Goodbye Vik.'

'No, Charlotte, please...'

'I said goodbye.'

The call ended.

'Goodbye.'

He'd blown it. Or rather, he'd blown it *again*.

The first time was that day three years earlier when he'd taken down everything from his wall; the police reports, the newspaper

363

cuttings, the maps, the CCTV stills and the lengths of string that linked them together. Last of all, he'd taken down Aimee Mitchell's school photograph.

Bundling it all up, he'd berated himself with profanities which grew more colourful with each new adhesive mark left exposed on his wall. There was a match on TV, two teams he had never heard of. It wasn't Vikram's usual way of letting off steam, but something inside him had said it was worth giving it a try, even if it meant forgoing his usual Sunday evening ritual: dinner with Aimee's family; a ritual more of comfort than of hope.

The strain of events had caused Aimee's parents' marriage to break down, and while her father moved as far north as his work would allow, her mother had stayed with Charlotte and her children – three raucous boys who would never know their long-lost aunt. Rarely did they talk about the case; it would only dampen the mood. It was enough simply to feel connected; to believe that someone outside the family still cared, that Aimee's life still had meaning.

So, what had changed? Vikram had become irritated by his lack of progress, for sure, but that had never stopped him before.

As he drove Josh Pittman's little green Nissan back from the training ground, he tried to remember why he hadn't gone for dinner the next week, or the week after. Why he had accepted a transfer to a station on the opposite side of the city. Why he'd made those decisions just as he was becoming close to Charlotte. Though they'd agreed to take things slowly, he had laid awake on more than occasion wondering whether he could see himself as a step-father to those little monsters.

These days Vikram lay awake thinking about what formation George Castle should play. Cases didn't bother him the way they used to. He plodded through his assignments with pedestrian ease, ticking the boxes so he could tell the victim 'we're doing everything we can.' All the while, Aimee's folder was buried under a dozen more in the bottom drawer of his desk, untouched and unread for too long.

What was the point? She wasn't coming back, not now. Better instead to enjoy life; put the football on and spend his hard-earned cash flying halfway across the world just to experience the match-day atmosphere. He'd spent his entire life on a lost causes – he deserved the break.

He stopped at a red light and rested his forehead on the steering wheel. Everything was backward. His mind felt foggy, caught somewhere between dreamlike compression and devastating realism. Clearly, he hadn't been himself, and there was a sense that he, and others like him, were not to blame for their nonchalant attitudes. But as the light turned to green, Vikram thought more about the idea that had entered his mind the moment Josh had thrown him the keys and disappeared with Lexa in a blaze of light.

The golden opportunity to put everything right.

The plan was still in its early stages, but it more or less involved waiting until the world had been saved, signing a dart gun out of the weapons unit and using it to force Josh or Lexa to take him where he wanted to go. Once he was back in that bitter January, he would find the kidnapper lurking by the canal path and put an arrow in his head before Aimee even got there.

Yes.

Vikram smiled as he pulled into the station and parked in one of the visitor bays. He felt for the bag in his inside pocket and checked in the wing mirror that the lump wasn't too obvious. He walked across the tarmac and saw that a high wire fence, covered in white canvas, had been erected around the rear courtyard and down the side of the building wall, masking everything except the grey-slate roof and the bright exterior lights which craned over the closed-off area. Some of the rubble from the demolished toilet walls had spilled beneath the last of the fence panels, away from the glare of the lights.

He stopped in his tracks as the shadows of two broad, swaggering figures passed behind the canvas. Casey's agents. They too had been called back from the training ground, travelling together in a police van. Manly banter passed between them. Vikram turned and decided to go in through the front.

There would be consequences, he was aware of that. He might trigger a paradox, or an alternative reality. That was Lexa's plan, and it was fine if the future was the hellscape she described, but Vikram couldn't take that risk. If he killed the kidnapper and Aimee returned home from school as normal, then he'd never have a reason to travel back and kill the kidnapper. Vikram would be imprisoned for murder in the past and would still be there now.

It was as he thought. He'd have to leave his old life behind and start a new one; a lone warrior, always on the move, jumping through time on a quest to solve crimes moments before they occur. Maybe take a punt at these other-worldly bastards, too. Rip them apart. Spread the joy running through their blood all over the floor…

Vikram pushed the idea to the back of his mind for now and kept walking. He rounded the station building towards the main entrance. As he approached, he saw Margaret Millington, the desk sergeant, standing with her arms behind her back on the front step. There was an A-frame next to her with a sign that read:

All visitors and staff subject to enhanced security checks. Your co-operation is appreciated.

His blood ran cold. The bag seemed to grow inside his jacket. He pulled his ID card from his pocket and held it up in front of her.

'Evening, Mags. How are we?' he said coolly.

Margaret looked down at the card, then up at his face, and back at the card again. They had known each other for years.

'Good evening, DS Jaitley,' she said. 'I am well, thank you.'

Vikram nodded and took a step towards the door. Margaret raised her hand to stop him – she was holding a comb.

'Really?'

'Agent Casey's orders.' Margaret slipped into a robotically delivered pre-agreed line. 'If you wish for this inspection to take place in a private room and/or by a male officer, please say now and these arrangements will be made. If you wish to make a complaint against me and/or the nature of these inspections, then I am happy to give you my officer number and/or elevate your complaint to my superiors on your behalf.'

Vikram smiled – he liked Margaret. And the last thing he wanted was to arouse suspicion. He lowered his head and let Margaret run the comb gently through his short black hair. The inspection was brief and perfunctory.

'Your chest, too,' Margaret said afterwards.

'Excuse me?'

He cursed himself; he should have expected this. He had seen Ernie Strong at the training ground and observed his true form, the markings across his scalp, the lifestone below his neck.

The desk serjeant sighed. 'If you wish for this inspection –'

'No, no, it's okay,' Vikram said, unbuttoning his shirt as naturally as he could without his arm touching against his jacket.

He pinched the layers of clothing together and a bead of sweat trickled down his spine.

As Margaret peered down to take a look at the dark forest of hair on his chest, Vikram tried out a casual deflection and looked across the street to the neat row of houses on the other side.

'What have you been telling people happened here?'

He could feel her warm breath on his skin. Margaret straightened back up with a smile, pleased with what she had seen.

'Maintenance error. While making refurbishments to the washroom facilities, workmen struck both a power line and a gas pipe. The electrical sparks ignited the gas and *whoof!* The room exploded. No-one was hurt.'

'Lucky.'

His concentration slipped; reaching again for his buttons, his hand brushed across the breast of his jacket and inside the bag crinkled. Margaret might not have noticed if he hadn't reacted with a wince, screwing up his face and baring his teeth. She lowered his arm slowly down with two fingers, opened the jacket and removed the clear plastic evidence bag from his pocket.

The little razor-sharp blades, sewn into the fingertips of the old leather glove, glinted in the porchlight above Margaret's head. Her eyes caught his. There might have been recrimination behind the glare, but Vikram couldn't be sure. An eternity passed. Margaret Millington placed the bag back inside the pocket.

'Thank you for your co-operation, Detective Serjeant Jaitley.' She smiled. 'Bloody Yanks, eh? Think they own the place.'

Relief flushed through him so quickly Vikram thought he might wet himself. Heading inside, he put one hand on Margaret's shoulder as he walked past.

'Stay safe, Mags.'

Inside the station, most of the staff had piled into rear offices and were crowded around the windows overlooking the courtyard, ignoring the young constables ordered to prevent them taking pictures on their phones. Access to the courtyard had been restricted to only a short list of authorised personnel, including Vikram, but thankfully he only had to show his ID again to pass through.

The courtyard was a large area of patchy grass and broken concrete, with no official purpose but for lunch-hour kickabouts, private conversations and sunbathing. This evening, however, it was a base of operations. Various functionaries from the forensic unit were pacing around with clipboards, comparing notes and shaking their heads in disbelief. Over to one side the American agents were huddled together in front of the canvas fencing, near to where a large table had been brought out from the briefing room with a flat screen television set on top it, its cables trailing back inside the building through a window. A single lead connected the television to an open laptop with a thick black box fixed untidily onto its back. Stood in front of it was the girl, Lexa, typing quickly. Josh Pittman, Agent Casey, and two other agents were next to her.

Vikram observed this activity through his peripheral vision, seeing it all without really looking. His attention was focused on the Vessel, standing impossibly on its downward point in the centre of the courtyard, soaking up the limelight as it basked beneath the harsh glare of the lights. It looked more impressive than it had before.

Majestic.

Vikram was transfixed; drawn in by what he knew to be real but struggled to believe, his breath feeling cold on this warm evening, his hands shaking. He listened. He could hear the Vessel calling to him, telling him that all things happen for a reason; they had been brought together to do something noble, something so perfect the world would not, and could not, understand.

The decision was made.

He was going to save Aimee Mitchell's life.

'Jaitley!' Agent Casey barked.

DS Jaitley snapped out of the trance the Vessel had put him in and looked over.

'Quit gawping and get your ass in gear.'

Josh noticed something different about Jaitley as he sauntered over. At the training ground there had been a naive innocence about him, which was gone now and replaced by a thoughtfulness that made him look much older.

'Alright people, fall in!'

Jen Casey's impatient accent travelled easily across the courtyard. The forensic team took this as their cue to disappear back inside while the agents strode confidently towards her.

Josh had felt a little unusual himself ever since Lexa had landed the Vessel in the police station following their escape from the Flagship. Scanning the faces of the burly agents – the very ones he had blindsided at the training ground – it was like being back on the pitch with Belmont Park Rovers. Only they were the home team now, out for revenge after losing face the first time. Casey was still pissed off at them for letting him go and, as they approached, each one caught his eye, lording their masculinity and hurt pride over him. And just like on the pitch, Josh wasn't sure he could rely on his own team for back-up – Lexa had hardly said a word to him since they got back.

DS Jaitley reached into his pocket and picked out the keys to Lock Niss.

'These are yours, I believe,' he said as he threw them over.

Josh fumbled the catch and they dropped to the ground. He reached down and let out a yelp as he smacked his elbow on the side of the table. The laptop rattled.

'Josh!' said Lexa, in a tone that reminded him a little of his father; a combination of embarrassment, irritation and disbelief all rolled into a single utterance of his name.

He stood back up. Some of the agents were laughing. It seemed no matter how many dragons you outran, you could always rely on the older boys to make you feel small.

Agent Casey stood with her hands on her hips. It had taken a very long and shouty conversation – during which Josh and Lexa were ordered to be handcuffed three times – to convince Casey that the Harvest was the real threat and couldn't be prevented without her help. Since then, a plan had been devised and a little while later Casey had gone inside to change out of her trouser suit and into a set of dark blue combats, heavy boots and a dark blue jacket with 'ACA' printed on the back in big, chunky letters. It was the same jacket Josh had seen in photographs of Casey inspecting bodies outside American football stadiums. Her gold badge hung on a chain around her neck. One hand was pulling back the jacket, exposing the dart gun holstered onto her belt.

He felt queasy.

'Okay,' Casey began, 'let's go through this one last time.'

She nodded at Lexa, who, without looking back, hit a key on her laptop. An image of the BK Stadium appeared on the television screen; a well-framed photograph taken at an angle looking up at the arena's enormous steel-blue antenna.

'This is our target location. According to these two felons, this tower you can see is no ordinary transmitter; it's connected to a ship, orbiting around the Earth, ready to eat the happy right out of your ass the moment the Brits win the game.'

Casey waited for a reaction – impressively, no one flinched. No one tittered. The events of the day and the formidable presence of the Vessel had converted them all to a belief in the fantastical.

'Miss Lexa?'

Josh noticed Lexa's grimace at the sound of her name. She tapped the key again. The image changed to a schematic diagram of the stadium's lower levels, downloaded from Digipedia.

'This service road,' Casey said, pointing to a circular line around the outside, 'runs beneath the seating bowl. Vehicles enter from the north-east corner, turning right for maintenance and deliveries, left for team coaches. You'll note that, according to the plan, the road comes to a dead end just beyond the entrance to the main locker rooms. However...'

Lexa didn't wait for a prompt this time. It was another photograph: a selfie, posted by @TroySimpsonOfficial, showing the striker standing in front of his coach beneath a dimly lit underpass, grinning inanely. Behind him, his teammates were picking their luggage out of the hold. The message below read:

Just arrived at the @BKStadium for #RegionalLeagueSemiFinal! So excited!! Big shout out 2 all our fans – wud not b here w/o you!! #UnionJAC #ComeOnYouWyverns

Agent Casey let out an exasperated sigh, as though she were unable to decide which aspect of all this was the most ridiculous.

'Now, we can presume from the sunlight coming in through the vent in the upper corner that the interior wall is *behind* the camera. That would make the supposed dead end over here, to the right. But as you can see, the road continues.'

The group leaned forward in unison. Only a little of the road was visible behind Troy Simpson's shoulder, but it was enough to see that the road did indeed continue, sloping downwards. A wooden sign stood in front of the Tensa-barrier which cut off the road, the words too blurry to read.

'This road, we now believe, leads to a restricted area directly below the antenna. Once we have arrived, this will be our exit route *away* from the basement levels and out onto the perimeter walkway.' Casey clicked her tongue. 'We're not coming in through the front door, people.'

She raised her eyebrows, somehow using them to point over the group and at the Vessel behind them. The other agents grinned, relishing the opportunity to take a unique ride. Lexa sunk her teeth into her thumbnail.

The briefing went on:

'Two teams! The first, led by Detective Serjeant Jaitley and myself – call sign Team Alpha – will proceed directly to the field where our focus will be to be apprehend the *linesman...*' Casey turned to Josh. 'That right?'

Josh nodded. 'Mm-hmm.'

'The *linesman*,' she repeated, twisting her tongue incredulously around the word, 'operating along the southern boundary of the playing area. Miss Lexa needs the antenna to be operating at maximum capacity, so it is imperative we take him into custody in the *very last minute* of the game, quietly and discreetly. We will outnumber him. Nonetheless – this is an alien son-of-a-bitch and so may possess abnormal strength. You are therefore permitted to use as much force as you deem necessary to contain the situation. Prepare yourselves for a fight, gentlemen.'

Josh raised his hand, like the quiet pupil at the back of the classroom, suddenly compelled to ask a question.

'I'm sorry, excuse me…'

'You got something to add, kid?' said Casey, looking both amused and outraged.

'It's just that, firstly, Euphors aren't aliens and secondly… the whole place is going to be crawling with them. They're not going to let you walk right up. Shouldn't you at least be undercover or something?'

'What, you mean soccer shirts and warm woollen scarves in the middle of July?'

Josh shrugged. 'Maybe.'

Casey smiled and gave her answer to the whole group, rather than directly to him.

'Negative. Police units will already be in position around the venue – not because they expect fan trouble, but just to give the cops in this pixie-land of yours something to do.'

The other agents chuckled.

'So, Mr Pittman, our presence will not seem conspicuous. However, we do not hold tickets for the game and we may need to use our authority to gain access to the public areas.'

'You probably wouldn't need tickets if –'

'Josh… don't.' Lexa had cut him off with a whisper and a shake of the head.

Josh was irritated, but decided to protest no further. Lexa had cajoled Casey into providing her with her own armed guard to protect her while she worked to sabotage the antenna. He hated the guns, and he hated Casey's assumption of authority, but Lexa was smart, she knew what she was doing.

He hoped.

'Team Bravo, led by Agents Nash and O'Reilly –'

Two square-jawed Americans stood to attention at the sound of their names.

'– will remain behind with Miss Lexa and the alien craft while she does... whatever it is she needs to do.' Casey pointed again to the barrier behind Troy Simpson. 'Consider this your front line. No-one gets past.'

One of the agents stepped forward. 'Excuse me, ma'am?'

Josh recognised him immediately; stocky, shaven-haired, the one who'd been the most difficult to coerce into the game with PJ, and who'd nearly caught him before he disappeared inside the Vessel.

'What is it, Cobb?'

Agent Cobb rose to his full height, jutting his chin. 'With all due respect, but as a Senior Field Agent, surely I should be taking command –'

'You?' Casey snorted. 'After the job you pulled at the soccer camp? Letting your whole team get suckered in by *this* guy?' She jabbed a derisive thumb in Josh's direction. 'I don't think so. You're under Nash until I say otherwise.'

Defeated, Agent Cobb stepped back into formation, scowling at Josh, as Casey perched on the edge of the table. Grins widened. Chests puffed with pride, the adrenaline already flowing. She looked back solemnly.

'Ya'll know my boys, Jack and Evan, right?' she said.

The agents glanced at each other.

'They're into comic books. Sure, these days all they talk about is sports, but still there's this big pile of magazines on the shelf between their beds.' Casey sniffed and scratched the length of her nose. 'And sometimes, when I've had a crappy day and the boys are asleep by the time I'm home, I like to tip-toe in and pick one up. It's comforting; listening to them breathe while I flick through the pages of some crazy space story. Takes me away from the real world – helps me cope with all the darkness out there.'

The group stood in withdrawn silence. Smiles dropped. Heads that had been nodding in anticipation of the adventure held still.

'Or it used to. Now I don't think it'll work. Lines are blurred. 'Cos we're all about to be part of some crazy space story. We're going to *travel through time*. That's big, right? Big enough to change your perceptions, maybe leave you wondering what the limits really are. If the sun rises tomorrow, then that's on you, and you will forever live your lives knowing just how close we came. So, before we get going, I have just one last thing to say to you all.' Casey stood and took a step forward. 'Get. Over. It.'

Josh had never wondered what a bunch of tough guys looked like when trying to supress bewilderment in front of a superior officer, but now he knew.

'You have a job to do. There won't be a world in which to ponder the mysteries of life if you don't get your head in the game, right here, right now. Do I make myself clear?'

An emphatic chorus of 'Yes ma'am!' rose into the encroaching night sky.

'Alright then, assemble your teams and check your weapons. We roll out in two minutes.' She clapped her hands together with a sharp crack, piercing the air. 'Let's move!'

Two and a half minutes later, Josh strode up to the Impossible Steps of the Vessel, bringing up the rear as Lexa remorsefully led the group inside. He was doing his best to move with courage and confidence, but in truth he was terrified. He thought by now he'd be flying high on the adrenaline of his mission; he was possessed of knowledge which no-one else had and was bolstered by a belief he simply needed to follow the path and see where it led him. Both those things provided Josh with a sort of temporary immortality, which made him, as he saw it, an important asset. Lexa was the captain of the ship, of course, her father's natural successor; Casey and her men were the muscle, the back-up; but Josh, standing behind them all, was the playmaker. The one who had brought them together and endured all manner of earlier trials to bring them to this point.

It would be nice if the group could think of him as having an aura; an indescribable something they couldn't quite put their finger on. But instead, it was clear – perhaps necessarily so – that they considered him just an add-on, there by accident or default to incite condescending scoffs among the collective. If he was allowed to remain, it was only to boost the primacy of everybody else, so long as he didn't mess anything up.

He was, in short, a substitute goalkeeper.

And it was about to get worse.

'Not you, Josh,' Lexa said to him as he reached the penultimate step.

'What?' Josh retorted, though he knew what was happening.

He met Lexa's stare, mustering as best he could a steely look of determination to be allowed on board. But her face was steelier, more determined.

'It's too dangerous.'

'Dangerous?' Josh pointed to the sky. 'We were up in the... thing, you know? We escaped the... the... *too dangerous?'*

'Yes!' she barked.

'No!' he barked back, surprised he had done so.

His heartbeat rose, his hand ached once more. Adrenaline pumped through him, fuelling a hollow rage so uncharacteristic he was a little scared by it.

'You're not dumping me again! Casey needs me in the stadium. I've seen the predictions; I know what happens!'

On hearing her name, Casey reappeared at the entrance, backlit by the ethereal glow of the Core. She spoke with an icy cockiness, as though this were just a normal day in the office.

'What else is there to know?' she said. 'We let the game play out, then we take out the guy –'

'The *linesman...'*

'– as soon as Pitman – not you, the other one – receives the ball in the ninetieth...'

'...but *before* he shoots. That's a tight margin. I can help!'

Casey sighed. 'Go home, Mr Pittman. We got this.'

Josh flicked his gaze between Casey and Lexa long enough for the first to tire of the argument and disappear back inside. He felt the air sticking inside his throat. Lexa stood in front of him, perfectly framed by the shaft of light pouring out between the

379

smooth sides of the entrance. Loose strands of hair were blowing across her face – she looked like an angel in jeans and a hoodie, arriving from on high to herald the end of his journey.

'Lexa –'

'Casey's right,' she said. 'You should go home and tell your family you're not watching the match. Take them somewhere safe. If they get angry with you, good, it'll help keep them alive.'

'This isn't fair, Lexa,' he said bitterly. 'It doesn't make sense. I should be with you; I should always be –'

'Josh,' she whispered, squeezing his hand.

The ache in his palm lessened. Dusk had turned to night. She leaned close to him. Her wide eyes stared deep into his soul.

'Thank you.'

Lexa let go and stepped up into the Vessel. In that moment Josh knew. This wasn't just a mission – it was a sacrifice. Casey, Jaitley, the agents, it was all an act. A cloak and daggers performance to buy her some extra time to carry out her plan, but not enough to bring her back again. His natural instinct was to leap forward and force his way in, but instead he found himself retreating. He stepped off and before he could look again Lexa had disappeared inside and the Impossible Stairs were retreating up into the shell. The light shrank from the courtyard until the Vessel begun to spin, the metal fins ripping through the air and leaving behind streaks of lightning in their wake.

Suddenly Josh was alone. As the leaves on the trees settled from being blown in all directions by the backdraft, Lexa's final instruction repeated like an echo in his mind.

Keep them alive.

The words were a reminder that the world was not a singular place. It was comprised of lots of smaller worlds, private worlds, each one as important to those who inhabited them, each one in need of saving.

There was more than one way to be a hero.

'24

A Midsummer Night's Dream

The empty train pulled away, leaving Asher Bloom alone on the platform. At this late hour the station was unmanned; the ticket office and the news stand both had their shutters down and the electronic barriers were open. He took a deep breath. The night was warm, but it was good to breathe fresh air once again after so long on the stuffy carriage. It helped to calm his nerves.

He looked at his watch: 11:45pm.

Should be enough time.

Throwing his ticket into the bin as he passed, Asher left the concourse and headed up the main road towards the town centre. On the other side of a roundabout, a large glass-fronted shopping centre marked the entrance to the High Street. Traffic passed infrequently and, in the pockets of quiet, the sound of his footsteps on the paving slabs made him feel very noticeable, for although the restaurants and bars had all closed for the evening, there were still plenty of people about.

Most were too happily caught up in their own lives to look up at him, but as his eyes became fixed on a young couple holding hands and smiling coyly at one another, he was startled by a group of drunken revellers who bounded up to him chanting some unintelligible verse. One of the group, the tallest and the widest, shook Asher's shoulders.

'Cheer up, mate!' he shouted, before exposing his bum crack as he tried – and failed – to leapfrog a bollard.

His friends helped him to his feet and Asher watched for too long as they headed down the street, their raucous laughter disturbing the otherwise peaceful night. How easy would it have been to just give in – to follow them into a dark alley and treat himself to just a taste. The leapfrogger alone would have been enough to satisfy the hunger burning in his stomach. One fat drunkard and he could be free of the guilt and the stress and willing denial of who and what he was.

But no.

Asher had made this journey to escape the dungeon of self-recrimination by atoning for his desires, not surrendering to them. Besides, he was less than seven miles from the national team training ground, well within the government's designated 'no-feed' zone. Now that he thought about it, holding the meeting this close to London seemed a pretty bad idea.

What if someone recognised him?

Asher walked on and took in his surroundings, hoping it would push the concern from his mind. The old High Street was short, narrow, and lined on both sides by tall, thin buildings that were much older than the array of food and retail outlets which occupied their ground levels.

Further along, past the attractive pub with hanging baskets above the front windows, a wrought iron fence marked the edge of the churchyard. Next to the gate stood a stone war memorial and a parish noticeboard, which displayed service times and a flyer for a children's playgroup, inviting parents to sign up by contacting the organiser through her MySy page.

He passed the church, its medieval spire lit up by four large halogen lamps around the base, feeling oddly justified. This place was a warm, untroubled fusion of the old and the new; typical, so he believed, of the kind of England – *England*, not the British Kingdom – that existed before he and the others arrived. A place that once looked to the future by embracing its past but, thanks to the Great Unifier, was now stuck in the quicksand of its present and slowly disappearing beneath the surface.

With the town centre now behind him, he followed the route given to him through a maze of residential streets, the houses decreasing in number and growing in size the further he walked. Lights were on and cars were parked, but still he was struck by the eerie emptiness which lingered all around him; the silence was confirmation that despite best efforts, little had changed here. Wealth was meant to be immaterial in this new world, but its power had clearly been underestimated, and those with the money were still choosing to cocoon themselves in the safe, comfortable worlds of their own making.

That, and it was midnight.

Turning the final corner onto a long, crescent-shaped road, he could hear the gentle lapping of the waves on the river and the boats moored along the bank, creaking and bumping into one another. He reached the house and stood for a moment at the end of the garden path, considering it a point of no return; his last chance to turn and head back to the station without anyone knowing he was there. He could go back to Mary-Jane and excuse his absence (and the text) with some affecting story about 'needing to be alone', accentuating the tortured genius persona she seemed to have a thing for. Maybe he could even persuade her to avoid the match...

But what then?

There was nothing he could do for the rest of her family, so how could he possibly stay with her, knowing his part in the grief she was soon to suffer?

It dawned on him that his reasons for being there might not be as altruistic as he thought. He wanted Mary-Jane there to see him throw himself into a noble cause, instead of thinking he'd abandoned her. Opening the gate, Asher made a promise to himself: he would try to live. If Mary-Jane was missing him, if she cared for him as much as she claimed, then she would have a chance and afterwards he'd find her. It was a gamble, a flip of a coin on her life – but then this world was all about playing the odds.

He walked forward. There were no flowers in the garden. The path bisected a neatly cut lawn, unadorned except for a bronze sundial on a marble plinth; outdoor lights embedded into the garden hedge were casting shadows across the dial plate in every direction.

The house itself was large but welcoming and Asher felt immediately elevated by the building's easy charm. He wasn't usually impressed by big houses – the Castles had an enormous house, a gaudy modern mansion with eight bedrooms and an underground swimming pool. But this house had character. Double-fronted with modern sash windows, it was built of red-brick, covered in ivy, within a thick timber frame. Smoke rose from the top of a central chimney and into the warm July night. The fire would be for effect only.

Asher rang the bell and a minute later a woman stood in front him, holding the oak door halfway open and blocking the entrance into the house with her body. She was short but gave the impression of height with a straight back, raised head and an imperious gaze that surveyed him from top to bottom. He was no good with ages, but he guessed she was meant to be around the mid-fifties – about right for someone dressed in a royal blue naval uniform with gold lines around the cuffs. The blouse under her jacket was buttoned up to the top and all but a few wisps of blonde hair were hidden beneath a white peaked cap.

'Can I help you?' she asked, her voice clipped and direct.

And cautious.

Asher looked quickly around to check no one was watching and then lifted his hat. The expression on the woman's face instantly changed, as though he were no longer a stranger to her, but instead someone she had been expecting but wasn't sure would turn up.

– *Oh, I see. Right. Aren't you a little young?*

Asher shrugged.

– *To them, maybe.*

– *True enough, I suppose. What do they call you?*

– *Asher Bloom.*

The woman considered the name, repeating it back to herself in the silence of their connection, as though it were a riddle.

– Asher? I'm not sure I –

– It means 'fortunate'. 'Blessed'.

– Does it, indeed? A subtle choice, I like it.

She smiled at him like a mother would – pride tinged with sadness – and then extended her hand, which he shook, confused at both the formality and cultural appropriation.

– Faith Goodwill. Admiral of the Fleet and First Sea Lord.

Asher put his hat back on.

– My girlfriend is George Castle's daughter.

– Ah. Well, in that case you'd better come in.

Goodwill opened the door fully and Asher passed into the hallway, taking off his shoes and placing them at the end of a long row of footwear in front of the skirting board. Even at this dark hour the Admiral was clearly very house-proud.

– Everyone's in the conservatory.

He followed her through into a spacious lounge with cream-coloured walls, punctuated with carefully chosen areas of exposed brick and wooden beams running across the ceiling. A luxurious three-piece sofa set surrounded the fire, which snapped and crackled in the hearth. Sideboards and cabinets were propped against the wall, their tops littered with ornaments and collectibles from across the globe.

As Goodwill led the way towards a set of French doors, a framed photograph on the wall caught Asher's eye and he stopped for a closer look. It was a wedding picture. Goodwill was there, but this wasn't her marriage. She was standing to the side, her bright medals with colourful ribbons reflecting the sunlight, with a group of others spread either side of the happy couple. Asher recognised the groom, looking smart in a bespoke morning suit, but not the bride, who, like the Admiral, wore full-dress uniform rather than the traditional white gown.

– *I introduced them.*

Goodwill had joined Asher at his side.

– *So, I suppose you could say this is all my fault. I thought about having her deployed at the last minute to some dark corner of the Earth, but it would have aroused too much suspicion.*

She paused.

– *I think he understands that.*

Asher stared at the happy scene, saddened by the true celebrations of togetherness and companionship the world could offer.

– *They take risks they're never aware of.*

Goodwill smiled again and carried on into the conservatory, which ran the length of the house and overlooked a narrow garden leading down to the riverbank. The room was full of people – far more than he'd been expecting – milling about like guests at an elite dinner party. Many were uniformed, of varying service and rank, but the majority were suited, with a few sporting either a mayoral chain around their necks or a presidential sash across their chests. Others were less formal, dressed in work overalls or tracksuits with the name of some Regional League team on the back, or decked out in the kind of deliberate high fashion usually reserved for movie stars and musicians. In the corner a chief executive of a stadium construction company and an award-winning film director, whom

Asher knew to be brother and sister, were locked in a consoling hug.

The mood was too sombre, even for him, and so he passed around the edge of the crowd to the windows on the far side. A small boardwalk led off the grass to where Goodwill's rowboat was moored, bobbing up and down on the water. Downstream, on the opposite side of the river, Asher could see a young boy playing keepie-uppie with his bare feet. He was around his age (*supposed* age) and showing off some impressive skills. On the pitch this type of show-boating would be considered arrogant and disrespectful to both your teammates and your opponents, but in the context of one boy's late-night moment of privacy, it felt blissfully innocent. A joyful act that existed for its own sake.

– Asher? Is that you?

He turned and recognised at once the florid-faced woman striding across the room towards him. Back home – *up there* – she had been a family friend whose intelligence and zeal had seen her rise quickly through the Euphorivore hierarchy, and who would later make the arrangements for Asher's commission. On Earth, however, she was known as Baroness Winsome Free, a former communications executive who had been offered a peerage and a place in the Cabinet to head up the Department for Culture and the Online Society and the development the SyBall App. She was dressed in her trademark trouser suit – salmon pink today – and her dark red hair was twirled up in the gravity-defying style known the world over as the Burgundy Beehive.

The Baroness grabbed Asher by the arm and pushed him back towards the house.

– What do you think you're doing?

Officially she was still his superior officer – superior, in fact, to everyone in the room – but he was younger, stronger and under the assumption her authority was irrelevant now, and so stood his ground and squirmed his arm out of her grip.

– Same thing you are.

– No, Asher, you mustn't do this – I can't be responsible for you too, you've got to go.

– I can look after myself. I may look like a child, but I'm not.

Winsome changed tack and stroked his cheek. Another appropriated gesture.

– Yes, you are, you're just a baby. Don't throw it away like this. Go home.

Asher stared at her for what felt like a long time. Winsome wasn't particularly old herself, not really, but for as long as he had known her, she acted as though she could summon the wisdom of advanced years through her knowledge, energy and ambition. Now Asher had those things too and wasn't there to be pushed around – especially not by this hypocrite.

– Go home? You're the one that brought me here! You gave me this jacket, this hat. So too late, Baroness, you already threw my life away. What about you? Why are you here?

Winsome took a step back, smoothed out the sleeve that had become crumpled in the tussle and passed her words back to him in a single, instant, fragile thought:

– When you've been watching them as long as I have, on the other side of those screens, you start to rationalise. To question the necessity of a race so completely unaware of the beauty and improbability of their existence,

beyond what they can give you. Albright calls it 'showing them their humanity'. And he's right, you know, because time and again we observe them looking beyond themselves into the stars and delving into the mysteries of the universe, when the answers are so close you wonder how they can be so blind. I see it when a family sit down together to cheer a team, or a couple get distracted from the screen by the sight of each other's faces – I see it when I look at that photograph in the living room. And it tortures me, because you realise that there is an alternative – I know it, you know it, and what's more, they know it – Albright, Newhart, that greasy bastard Fortuna. But they would rather see the world destroyed than stomach the idea of sharing it. How long do you think our Harvest will last once human existence becomes nothing but a continuum of misery and despair? Might be enough for me, but for you? I'm not so sure. Power is an illusion, Asher Bloom, a mask, and in this house all it means is I was the first to be lied to, and my suffering is such that I could feast tomorrow on this whole rotten planet and it still wouldn't be enough. That, sweetheart, is why I am here. Good enough for you?

Winsome released Asher from the extrasensory grip that had been stronger than the fingers around his arm.

Behind them, Faith Goodwill walked back into the conservatory. The group all turned and shuffled between each other for the best view of the man following her. The sense of anticipation hung in the air, their muttered observations passing between them like a cerebral chatroom. The man stopped and looked around and over their heads until he could see Winsome Free moving around the edge of the conservatory to join him.

Asher stayed near the back, hoping to avoid any further conversation, and peered forward between the shoulders of a

391

police chief inspector and a talent scout for the East Midlands. The man at the front looked more awkward than nervous, with the ill-fitting suit, skew-whiff tie and odd socks a far cry from the morning suit had worn on his wedding day. In his hand was a large metal suitcase, which he lifted on to a small table already set in place for him. Unlocking the catches, Felix Gently then turned to address the group.

– *It's a pleasure to see you all. I'm sure you'll join me in expressing our gratitude to Faith for having us here tonight, and to Winsome for bringing us all together. If there's anything more frightening than joining a rebellion, it's organising one. The extent of their risk should be matched by the weight of our thanks.*

A silent smattering of agreement thread between each of them like a psychic web, and while Goodwill countered with a reserved smile, Winsome caught Asher's eye once again. He knew what she must have been thinking – where had *his* invite come from?

– *This afternoon, we… sorry… we, uh…*

The Minister of Defence stuttered and shook his head.

– *I give briefings all day long in this blasted job, you'd think I'd be able to get through this one.*

Gently smirked.

– *Maybe I am a spineless wretch after all.*

Sympathetic laughter ran through the room.

– *You already know what you're doing. I don't need to lecture you. Instead, it is with sincere regret I remind you that none of it will make any difference. We are too late. If we are to accomplish this, then we do so for ourselves, and for those we are leaving behind.*

From somewhere in the middle of the group, a lone voice landed softly inside each of their heads. It said:

– *In that case, it'll make all the difference.*

A swell of pride rose visibly in Felix Gently, and Asher witnessed in him something he had never seen a Euphorivore do before – he wept.

– *Thank you. Thank you for being here.*

With nothing more left to say, Gently lifted the lid of the metal case. Asher shuffled forward and joined the queue, as one-by-one the Conservatory Group helped themselves in a polite and orderly fashion.

***

Josh rests his hands on the windowsill and sees that it's a beautiful day; the sun shines brightly and there are butterflies, some red, some white, fluttering around one another. One butterfly hovers above the rose bush, unsure whether to land. A pair of birds are whistling in the tree and Josh follows their flight as they swoop down together and perch on the sundial. He sees his toys all out on the lawn; what fun it might be to go out and play for old time's sake.

It is a balmy July day and his mind is full of action and adventure and hidden dangers lurking in the shadows. By his hand on the sill is a little motorised model of the Solar System; he presses the button and the tiny planets begin their orbit around the sun in perfect synchronicity. He looks at the Earth and sees the moon on its own little axis, but when he looks closer, he sees it's not the moon at all, but the Flagship – a tiny plastic teardrop no bigger than a pea. He leaps off the bed and barrel rolls onto the floor – he dodges the swing of Red's tail, twisting and flipping like an action hero.

'Josh!' His dad is calling up the stairs to him. 'It's on, get down here.'

Josh knows what's expected. He gets to his feet and runs out the door and down the stairs. The living room is bright, the sun glaring in through the open window and washing out the picture on the television screen. The room is uncomfortably hot; an intense heat coming from the kitchen singes his skin. There is no-one to be seen. He spots Sophie and Jessica's mobile phones – one on the sofa, one on the floor. The match has already started, but if no-one else is watching then it must be okay for him to go outside.

He runs through the kitchen, expecting to see his mother, but it seems she is missing too, though she could just be hidden somewhere behind the thick smoke. The temperature is unbearable and ash floats in the air and falls like black snowflakes, disintegrating upon contact with the grease. There is a light in the distance. He looks around for Lexa, but she isn't there. His hands are clammy and covered in soot – he thinks he can see something in his palm, beneath the skin, but he cannot tell for sure.

'Lexa! Lexa, where are you?' The panic rises as he turns back to the living room, but all he can see is the long stretch of hallway. The alarm wails and screeches above his head, the red light spinning through the smoke. It's thicker now, but there are no windows in the kitchen to let it escape.

'Lexa!' There are people in the hallway. He thinks they might be his family. He calls their names, the heat burning his throat. They are all running away from the light; they are wearing blue jump suits and none, it seems, can hear him. There's another figure, further ahead, darting forwards. Josh feels compelled to follow him – there is something familiar about him; a recognition Josh can't quite put his finger on.

'Wait! Stop!'

But the man keeps going, turning a corner into another long corridor. Then another, and another. It becomes difficult to see through the smoke stinging his eyes and he struggles to keep up. Another turn and again he can see the light. The smoke clears a little, and over the man's shoulders he can see the edge of the lawn. The man stops in the doorframe and for a second Josh thinks it is the Captain. He shortens the distance between them and reaches out with his hand – he is about to touch the man's back, but Josh just runs straight through the shadow and finds himself alone again, out in the bright sunshine.

He enjoys the feeling of the cool, clean air filling his lungs and the sweet smell of the willow tree from his parents' garden. But the sensations fade as Josh realises he is standing at the edge of a football pitch. There are goalposts at either end and the training ground buildings are on the other side. His toy action figures are nestled in the grass at his feet. He looks up and there is a boy in front of him, wearing a leather trilby with a matching jacket. His face is anguished. He speaks without talking.

– What do I do, Ernie?

Ernie?

Josh looks down again and sees he is wearing a thick sweatshirt and jogging bottoms. The clothes are blue, but a lighter shade than the jumpsuits worn by those trapped in the smoke-filled hallway, and they are adorned with the BKDFA spiral crest. They are the same clothes PJ's bodyguard had been wearing the night he fought with Lexa.

The night he died.

Josh responds involuntarily, his mind thinking the words rather than saying them.

– I shouldn't be telling you this, but… there's going to be a meeting. The night before the Final. Here's the address.

There is a piece of paper in his hands. Josh looks at it before he passes it to the boy. It is a picture of a squirrel, dressed as a superhero, holding a football.

– What about you?

At the far end of the pitch, someone is watching them. One of the players, Josh thinks, with long hair down past his shoulders.

– I'm too old for a mutiny. When you spend as long as I have in the service of others you start to realise the only side you should pick is your own. I've had my chances; do the right thing, do the wrong thing – even try to find peace with it all. But now here I am at the end of my life and I feel precisely nothing. So be a traitor, don't be a traitor. I really don't care.

The boy's face changes and suddenly it is PJ Pitman standing in front of him, his kit muddy from the game of one-on-one.

– Do what you think is right.

There is an ear-piercing shriek and the heavy sound of feet pounding the earth. Josh turns and finds he is running towards Lexa. Her eyes are full of rage, aggression and hate; her arms are raised, and the glove is over one hand, the tiny blades coming closer and closer towards him.

They collide. The world tumbles and spins as they fight. He is stronger than she is; he could throw her off easily, but chooses not to and instead allows himself to be pinned to the ground. A grasping pain sears through his body, blinding his vision: the tips of the blades are piercing his chest.

'Push,' he tells her. 'Push.'

But Lexa is losing her nerve. She doesn't want to do it. Instead, he does it for her, grabbing her hand and digging her fingers in. The blades sink deeper, the pain is unbearable, but the release is pure bliss. Time slows, and Josh feels a wave of calm wash over him. It is just as he imagined it would be, and it is a relief to know his predictions were right. He will not fight this. This is what he wants, and he is grateful to her. The only regret is the voice calling out to him in the distance as his life slips away:

– Got what you deserve, traitor.

He tries to push the words away and in his last breath focuses only on Lexa. They are so close they are almost embracing, falling again, tumbling down through the vortex towards the light. The flap of Red's wings are behind them. Maybe he will not catch them this time.

Doesn't matter.

Josh looks at Lexa's eyes again and the hate is gone. The pain is gone, replaced with something else that electrifies his soul, and for the first time in his life he is not afraid. He is right where he needs to be.

The light takes them, but it is impossible to let go.

'25

Josh, You Are

Josh woke in a sweat. His room was warm and stuffy from the morning sun pouring in through his window and aggravating the raw skin across his nose.

He checked the time on his phone: 10:30am. It was past midnight when he'd arrived home from the police station and flopped down on top of his bedsheets. Sleep had seemed an impossibility, his mind too overrun by the events of the previous day. He had travelled through time and space and flown on the back of a dragon.

I ought to be famous.

But, when he'd finally succumbed to the exhaustion, all he could see was Lexa. The way the light from inside the Vessel illuminated the freckles on her cheeks as she told him to stay away.

Go home.

Be safe.

He rolled out of bed and forced himself into the shower and a new set of clothes, the normality of the daily routine crushing his spirit. The house was empty. Heading downstairs, he found a note on the kitchen counter:

Morning sleepy head!
Gone for breakfast at the garden centre to prepare ourselves for the big day! Drive down and join us once you're up – call first and we'll order your breakfast.
Love, Mum xx

Josh stuffed the note into his pocket and picked an apple from the bowl. Without knowing it his family had presented him with a conundrum. They were together in one place, where he could easily round them up, but they had also left him alone in the house, where he was free to slip away unnoticed.

His fingers drummed on the counter and a tingle shot up his arm, every tap reverberating back at him like an echo off the wall – a metaphysical connection to all the mundane objects resting on the counter: the toaster, the kettle, the egg basket in the shape of a chicken. Their reality was accompanied by an acute surreality Josh felt he could hold in his hand.

A minute later, Josh passed Lock Niss in the driveway and set off along the path. He walked quickly with an impatient spring-step, desperate to be further down the road to where his instincts were leading him – Belmont Park.

It was an admittedly odd choice of destination, but he chose not to think about it. He didn't want to start questioning his decisions and corner himself into making the wrong one; better to follow the subconscious voice deep within – the voice that had told him to drive to the training ground, to put his hand on the Vessel, to fly with Lexa up to the Flagship and leap into the Core to catch her.

The world this morning was a little like how the Flagship had been when they'd first arrived – unsettlingly quiet. There was no pedestrian traffic; no dog-walkers, no hand-holders, no ball kickers. Josh had never seen the park so deserted, even in the freezing depths of winter. The desolation peeled back the layers of the landscape; the mournful ruins of the hospital, the tranquil fields backed by the trees, and the monstrous eyesore of the Belmont Park Rovers Stadium, a steel-grey testament to the hidden ugliness of the Guiding Principles.

Only a few years before, his mother's remonstrations at the project had been heard by anyone who would listen (and just as many who wouldn't). People tended to agree, only for opinion to shift the day concept drawings were posted through the estate's letterboxes, detailing a stadium which would merge seamlessly with its surroundings via a large canvas wrapped around the exterior and decorated with sweeping, watercolour-style swirls of blue and green. From a distance, it had been promised, the stadium would be invisible. It wasn't. But by the time it had been built, everyone was so excited about the prospects of their local team, few cared about the bulldozers ripping up the turf, or the trees cut down to make room for the car park, or the supporting mesh of girders left visible beneath the stands. Not if it meant the first match could start sooner.

As he stepped out of the stadium's shadow, Josh wondered if the Euphorivores had bred naivety in humans at the dawn of

400

civilisation, or whether it was just a helpful weakness they could prey upon.

He checked his phone again: 11:45am.

Just over an hour until kick-off. His parents and sisters were probably back home now, settling in with the pre-match build up. Josh hadn't completely abandoned the idea of following Lexa's instructions, although he wasn't quite sure how to go about it. He could say he'd skipped the garden centre to meet with someone who offered him tickets for a fan park down on the coast. They'd had a last-minute emergency and couldn't go. Martin Bannick's family, perhaps, as a thank you for stepping in goal while he was still in hospital...

Leave now and we'll make it down there just in time. I'll drive.

And drive, around and around, 'lost' for hours on end, the wrath of his family raining down on him until it was too late...

Either that, or Josh could go home, stamp on the girl's phones, and then carry the TV upstairs and throw it out of the window.

Simple.

He walked across the field with his hands in his pockets, and up onto a tall mound of grass from where it was possible to see the turrets of an otherwise obscured wing of the old hospital. In the distance, the cloudless sky painted a postcard image of the quaint rooftops and bushy trees of the Surrey suburbs which bridged the border into London. A cool, perfect breeze swept past. He sat, cross-legged on the grass, and around the edge of the trees he could see the first of the outhouses where Lexa had been hiding.

Half a day had passed since Josh had seen the Vessel vanish into nothing, leaving him marooned among the gawking officers. To minimise the risk of exposure, Lexa was planning to arrive in the underbelly of the BK Stadium mid-way through the second half, well over two hours from now. Their journey would be instantaneous, skipping over those hours Josh spent either asleep or aimlessly wandering about the park.

So where was the Vessel right now?

Did a place with physical dimensions exist at the point between two time periods? Or, until their return, were Lexa and her passengers little more than a memory? They couldn't be thought of as dead, because even the deceased left their bodies behind. It was like they had returned to a point before they were born, their existence yet to be proven.

The concept was too much to deal with. He shut his eyes to block out the world and suddenly she was there again. This time it was the evening they had first met, sitting on the wall outside the Bovill Arms. Lexa was looking at him through the warm, still air, the glow of the lantern above the hanging sign bringing out the subtle tones of hazel in her hair. The last thing she told him rang lucid in his ears:

'I wasn't expecting it to be like this. You're not the kind of person I thought you'd be.'

The clarity of this moment heightened the details of her face – the little red mark on her lower lip where she perpetually dug in her thumbnail; those bright, brown eyes, tinged with remorse. The way Lexa looked at him that night was the same as the night before, when she held his hand and then left him behind.

He didn't want to go home. But he didn't want to stay here either and have to forever fend off the emptiness he felt whenever the

Rovers triumphed on the pitch and he had nothing to do with it. Was this the path he was meant to follow? Were there really no other options?

He stood quickly, and the unspoilt view re-emerged out of the temporary darkness, unchanged in its stillness and beauty. There was a noise somewhere; a voice, but not the one inside him.

Someone was calling his name.

Josh looked around and saw he wasn't alone in the park. Two figures were sat on a bench on the far side of the field. As he turned to face them, the one who had been calling stood up and waved his arm in the air.

'Joshua!'

Nobody – not even Lexa – called him Joshua. In fact, the last people to use his full name were the doctors and nurses in the hospital.

'Josh-You-Are!'

Of course. The 'clever' wordplay triggered the memory: it was Scott Baker, the daredevil firefighter with the crushed artery who'd occupied the next bed on the hospital ward. Alongside Scott, the broad-shouldered frame of Brian Kelly remained seated on the bench with his foot locked inside a heavy brace. Presumably they both lived on the estate, though Josh only remembered Brian mentioning his flat was in Belmont Park.

He headed over towards them, traversing the ground quickly in a semi-jog and arriving at the bench just as Scott used his crutch to ease himself back into his seat. Brian looked up from the tablet resting on his lap.

'Hey there, mate, how's it going?' he beamed. 'I forgot you lived around here.'

There was something irritating about the tone of Brian's admission. Like talking to the kid in school who'd been in your class for years and asking: *'so, are you new here?'*

'Yes,' Josh said, feeling there was nothing else to add.

Brian nodded in the direction of the stadium. 'Ever watch the Rovers play?'

Josh bit his lip.

Only when they put me in goal.

'Occasionally.'

'Have to look out for you next time.'

'Wow, your nose is looking so much better,' said Scott, who was studying Josh's face as though he'd been asked to examine a painting to check it wasn't a fake.

'Thanks. Still hurts.'

As Scott leant back, Josh noticed he was wearing the same clothes that had been draped over the chair beside his hospital bed. The top was torn, dirty and spotted with blood from his accident on the cliffs. Brian, meanwhile, had changed out of his paramedic's uniform.

He had been home, Scott hadn't, and now here they were, together.

The realisation reset the balance of the conversation in Josh's mind, as though they had unwittingly exposed a sweet vulnerability which made him equal to them.

'That Owens is good, isn't he?' Brian continued, smashing the illusion. The night in hospital had done nothing to diminish his

404

appetite for conversation. 'Scrappy little bugger. Eye for a goal, though. Big threat for us next season, big threat. Shore up the leaky defence and get Bannick back between the sticks and we might challenge for promotion, what do you think?'

Josh shrugged. 'Couldn't agree more.' He gestured to Brian's tablet. 'Is that the live feed?'

'Will be in a minute, but nah, we're just watching these videos from Brazil. You seen 'em?'

At first the words failed to resonate, such was the casual tone, catching Josh off guard before they stunned him into silence.

Brazil.

Suddenly he was back inside the Flagship, hand-in-hand with Lexa, watching the live footage of Copacabana Beach across the silvery surface of the dome, ninety minutes played and the whistle soon to blow. The Core churning below him. The Euphors in rapture.

It couldn't be.

'B-Brazil? Where?'

'Rio! Mate, it is so funny. Take a look.'

Funny?

The possibilities raced through his head as he circled around the bench and looked at the tablet over their shoulders. It had to be a coincidence. Some other event at some other time, the connections forming in his head just a tired overreaction.

Brian tapped the play button and the still frame image blurred into life. The picture was pixelated and the tinny background noise pierced the tranquillity of the empty park. The hand-held camera, most likely a phone, shook and bobbed and rotated between landscape and portrait modes, but not enough to obscure the scene it was capturing. It was, undoubtedly, a beach. Still, there were lots of beaches in Rio de Janeiro and there was nothing yet to assume this was the Copacabana. But then the camera tiltled up, over the heads of the crowd and the swirls of national flags, and settled on the large outdoor screen that stretched across the sand.

Josh could see the Brazilian team in Manchester, dancing and embracing one another on the grass. Coaching staff and substitutes in fluorescent bibs streamed onto the pitch to join them. It was maybe ten, fifteen seconds after the final whistle. Not long, but if he and Lexa understood the Euphorivore's plans correctly, then the Flagship should have engaged the instant the whistle touched the referee's lips. So why the delay?

The seconds ticked by on the video's progress bar and still nothing. Josh thought the phone would fall as its owner yielded to the pre-Harvest snack, but still it remained. The picture lowered and, with more composure in handling, panned slowly across the crowd.

There was hugging.

Lots of hugging.

Families hugging. Friends hugging. Couples hugging. A thousand private moments on public display. There was kissing too, from coy pecks with soft strokes on the cheeks to wild, full-on, hair-grabbing snogs. Clothes were sparse to begin with on the sun-soaked beach and Josh was sure they would begin littering the sand as the fever grew, but somehow events managed to remain family-friendly. He could even see a few marriage proposals, as a clutch of bare-chested men dropped down unexpectedly down onto one knee.

The camera dipped again and focused in on a happy young girl in shorts and sandals coming towards the screen, skipping and waving her hands. A man's voice came from behind the frame, inviting her to speak.

'Diga algo à mamãe!'

The little girl beamed. *'Olá mamãe! Eu te amo!'*

The scale of the scene and the breadth of the devotion blended together into a bizarre sense of peace that Josh felt deep in the pit of his stomach. Physical connections and victory celebrations were swept away into the sea and replaced with something higher, an emotional purity beyond anything he had ever seen. The test run had failed; the revellers of Copacabana Beach were more alive than ever.

The screen cut to black and began loading the next video: the same scene again from a different angle. But Josh had seen enough. He staggered away from the bench, his legs shaking, his breathing heavy. He tried to piece together the fragments spinning through his mind. Somewhere within the whirlwind was a logical interpretation, a reasoning he tried desperately to grab onto.

He forced himself back to when he'd broken Lexa out of the police station. It wasn't long after Rio had been Harvested, triggering her decision to sneak aboard the Flagship. Evidently, that world no longer existed. Or it did, but he was no longer living in it. Lexa's theory of alternate realities and parallel timelines was true, and somehow, they had passed from one to another. So, did that make Lexa's past (the future) an extension of this timeline, or a variant of it? In the Vessel, she'd said the Captain had never told her about Rio because, she assumed, it had never been attempted. But those people embracing on Brian's screen had clearly reacted to *something*.

Focus... first thing's first.

If the test run had failed, then what was the cause? Did the two of them tumbling through the Core damage it somehow? Were they like bugs in the system, alien bodies that upset the fragile balance of operation? Or were the Euphors simply forced to abandon the test as soon as they saw them?

Wait...

They *saw* them.

That was the anomaly. Josh and Lexa had been less than conspicuous during their brief excursion to the Flagship. Every single Euphorivore up there had watched Lexa dangling with her hoodie caught between Red's teeth, and then every single one had watched as Josh leapt over their heads and dived into the Core. The mere presence of trespassers was proof enough that their cover was blown. Why then, had there been no reprisal? With kick-off now so close, surely there would have been some kind of attempt to tie up loose ends? Should Josh not have expected a man in a fedora waiting for him outside the house this morning?

Yes, the Euphorivores had seen them; but while Red had carried Josh and Lexa out of the Core to safety, each one had become frozen in time, their hands on their chests. Their eyes had been open, wide enough to take in the full oddity of the Firebreather and his two dumbstruck passengers passing overhead, but their bodies did not move.

Escape had been a gift.

Josh looked down at his hand – the one that been aching ever since he felt the rough sinews of Red's skin beneath his fingers – and in one glorious moment everything fell into place. The pieces were laid out before him like stepping stones on a predetermined route; a violent case of mistaken identity guiding the way through everything that had happened, including a chance meeting with Scott Baker and Brian Kelly in the park on a pleasant Sunday afternoon.

Caught in the warm, bright rays of the sun, Josh could at last see the lifestone that had once belonged to Ernie Strong shimmering and gleaming beneath the surface of his palm. He closed his fist around it, as he had done inside the Core, and felt the comfort of its smooth surface nestled within his muscles and between the tendons, rubbing gently against his long thin bones. The pain slipped away; it was natural now – a foreign element with a familiar feel, as if he had reclaimed a long-lost part of himself he didn't know was missing.

A gift.

A gift of –

'You alright, mate?'

Scott had broken his train of thought but couldn't stop the wide smile stretching across Josh's face. He felt giddy and refreshed, a cool sense of ease washing over him, as though he had emerged from a dark, stuffy room and was walking barefoot through wet morning grass. Instinctively, he reached into his pocket and pulled out the note from his mother. He reread the simple message, laced with good humour, a lightness of touch and the infinite realm of maternal love.

There's still time.

'Yes,' he said, 'I'm good.'

'Glad to hear it. Fancy settling in with us for the afternoon? Or have you already got plans?'

Oh, Josh *most definitely* had plans.

'Thanks, but I need to be somewhere.' He turned to face them. 'Listen, would you guys do me a favour?'

Their curiosity piqued, Scott and Brian threw a quick glance at each other and then turned back to Josh.

'Name it.'

'Don't watch the match.'

'You *what*?'

'Just don't watch it – promise me, okay? I can't explain, and I think… *I think* it won't matter now, but in case I'm wrong, in case I miss my chance, I can't take that risk. We'll meet up for a drink later, and if you do this for me, I'll pay. All night. For a year. For two years!'

Scott and Brian laughed. 'You're off your rocker, mate!'

'I know.' Josh beamed. 'It feels *amazing*.'

Left alone, Scott and Brian considered Josh's request until the strange lad was almost out of sight. Which wasn't long, given how quickly he was running to get out of the park. Free drinks for the foreseeable future was a tantalising proposition, but was it enough to miss the biggest match of all time; the single most talked about event between now and the end of their lives?

Absolutely not.

The videos from Copacabana continued on a little while more, the pair mesmerised by the repeat viewings, until the SyBall App cut in automatically to the live coverage. It wouldn't do to miss a second of the action. As the day wore on, the breeze picked up a little and felt sharp against their bare calves and forearms. Brian shuffled up the bench and savoured the warmth of Scott's shoulder, who in return, held the near side of the tablet with one hand and rested the other on top of Brian's thigh.

Although there was still over an hour to go, there was plenty for the pundits – Christine Crawford, Lorraine Browne and three high-ranking Euphorivores – to talk to Geoff Sterling about. Today they had left behind the comfort of their sofa in the centre of a virtual BK Stadium, and were instead broadcasting live from a studio high up in the place itself, overlooking an elaborate closing ceremony down on the pitch, while in the corner of the screen a small clock counted down the minutes until kick-off.

Around the world people gathered, brought together in distant unity through screens of all sizes in every corner of the planet, feverish with anticipation as the moment drew near. They huddled in living rooms, serving tea and singing the national anthem of their new favourite country. They stood shoulder-to-shoulder in over-capacity bars and pubs, supping beers and placing outlandish wagers on the App. They danced in Times Square, roared in Red Square, and sang in Leicester Square all the way up to Piccadilly Circus, where they clambered over the Eros Statue for the best view of the electronic billboards. They packed themselves into school halls, concert halls, stadiums and cinemas. Homes were open to those with none; hospital staff sat around beds of patients with no one to visit them; old rivalries were set aside to make way for new brotherhood.

Even in North America, there was a deeply felt sense of divided loyalty and an unspoken awareness that the trophy wouldn't – *shouldn't* – make the journey across the Atlantic. In ninety minutes, a single game of football would teach the world what it was to truly believe in something.

Union JAC.

Then, at last, anticipation turned to rapture as two teams filed neatly out of the tunnel and lined up on the perfectly manicured surface of the BK Stadium. A thunderous roar greeted their arrival, and in one fluid move the App's broadcast feed panned upwards to absorb the immense seating bowl, which swept away to such heights that from ground level it gave the illusion of the upper tiers bending forward and closing in on themselves, leaving only a small oval opening for the sun to bestow its blessing upon the game.

The crowd bounced and throbbed in a sea of colour and spectacle. Streamers flew, flags fluttered, confetti rained and balloons rose against a colossal wall of noise.

The picture swept back down and, with the camera attached to the underside of a drone, flew off around the pitch, focusing in on a troupe of cheerleaders who performed their routine from the centre circle as a university marching band began their final exit off the grass. The drone followed the path of the band for a moment, then veered and swept over the eastern goalmouth and back into the crowd, drawing up higher and higher until it cleared the roof, and the full structure of the venue's luscious, silky design filled the frame from below.

The surrounding area of coach parks, hotels, fan pitches and the residential rows of suburban north-west London came into view from all sides. The outside of the stadium was as busy as the inside, a horde of tiny moving dots swarming around the exterior like bees trying to find their way into the hive. From this height it was a sun-drenched scene of mass perfection, cut through only by the imposing shadow of the great towering antenna, which stood like a rocket waiting for blast off, its smooth lines soaring past the drone and seemingly touching the sky above.

But the Pittman family are not watching...

Instead, Josh rests the television on the windowsill and sees that it is still a beautiful day; the sun shines brightly and there are butterflies, some red, some white, fluttering around one and another. One butterfly hovers above the rose bush, unsure whether to land.

It is a balmy July day and Josh's mind is full of action and adventure and hidden dangers lurking in the shadows. Behind him there is screaming and hands latching onto his shoulders, trying to pull him back; but he can still hear the birds as they swoop down together and perch on the sundial.

This last bit will be the hardest.

Stealing the house keys, and even his sisters' phones, had been quick and easy, but the television's cumbersome shape is proving tricky. Josh angles the monitor to fit through the window frame, but his father has hold of it now, and as he wrenches it free a corner of the screen knocks his motorised model of the Solar System onto his bed, and he sees that Earth's spindle has been damaged.

No matter – Josh is stronger than all of this now.

He blocks out the commotion and throws. His aim is perfect; the birds scatter as the television lands face down on the sundial, the tip of the gnomon piercing the screen. His family are so shocked they cannot move.

Escape is a gift.

He swipes the sketchpad from his bookshelf, runs downstairs and locks them inside the house.

The roads are empty. As he drives, Josh wonders where they all are; the survivors, the ones who are missing the action and so will live beyond the Harvest. He checks the time on his phone. No chance now of getting to the stadium before kick-off, but this does not matter, as long as he is there for the final whistle. As he speeds along the carriageway, Josh switches on the radio and listens to the commentary.

Time, at long last, for the greatest show on Earth to begin.

'26

The Wrong Guy(s)

L exa stared at Josh until the last of his dejected face disappeared
behind the closing entrance.

Inside, gasps of amazement echoed off the double-domed
ceiling. She tried to ignore them. The Vessel was captivating, but it
wasn't like they'd gone to Mars or anything. They hadn't gone
anywhere yet – they were still at the police station. If they shouted
loud enough, Josh might even be able to hear them.

'You've probably saved his life, you know,' said Agent Casey,
suddenly at Lexa's side, her tone impatient rather than consoling.
'Wrong guy in the wrong place at the wrong time. He should be
grateful he came this far.'

Lexa didn't respond. Instead, she turned away, walked over to
the desk and sat on the stool in front of her laptop.

Even with its battered casing and the jumble of wires and
graunched gizmos sticking out of it, Jen Casey still recognised the
laptop's design from television commercials she could only have

seen in the past year or so. Housed within the sleek, cornerless interior of the Vessel, it looked utterly out of place.

But then, so did the girl.

As a Federal Agent, Casey was used to feeling unwanted on other people's turf; but considering Lexa had turned up asking for help in what was *technically* stolen property, which she could turn over to the US Government with a single phone call, Casey and her team were being given a particularly cold shoulder.

Not that the team were noticing. Vikram Jaitley and the other agents were too busy milling around in stunned silence. Casey had warned them to stay focused, but while Josh Pittman had been trying to negotiate his way on board, she too had taken the chance to absorb her new surroundings and couldn't help being momentarily overcome by its alien charm. In an instant she had felt years younger, lifting the ache that had been pushing against the back of her eyes ever since the plane touched down on this tiny island. There had even been an unexpected part of her that wished Mike and the boys were there to see it too.

But much like the game of soccer itself, the Vessel wasn't able cast its spell over her for very long and she quickly shook herself out of it. This was the last place she wanted her family to be. Never before had Casey felt the need to call home before heading out into the field; it wasn't the high stakes that made her nervous, it was the uncertainty; not knowing what the other side looked like.

What the endgame would be.

'Call your mom, tell her to come over,' she had ordered her husband from a private office in the station. 'I can't explain right now. Get the kids and the dog and head down into the storm shelter. Do *not* turn on the TV, do *not* watch the game… what? *What?* Damn it, Mike, this is not the time to talk about our vacation! Just do as I say! Oh, and take that book you got me for my birthday and read it out loud, over and over, until I call you back. *Why?* 'Cos it's the biggest pile of garbage ever written and I want you to be as miserable as I was reading it. I lo-'

The line cut off.

It could have been the shonkiness of the long distance connection, or the boys messing with the phone, but it had made her uneasy. The idea had crossed her mind of airwaves being freed up to make space for one large signal to spread cleanly across the globe.

Her agents were slipping further, succumbing trance-like to the lure of the craft as the pure-white mist clambered up past their knees and their eyes sunk longingly down into the effervescent light.

'Can you just *back off*, please?'

Lexa's arms were spread wide, blocking two agents, Hicks and Taylor, from encroaching further around into her workspace. The curious pair, who'd spent the first few minutes studying the walls and stroking their fingers along the milky-white membrane, had wandered over to the desk for a better look at the screen and gotten too close.

'Gentlemen!' Casey barked.

The entire unit snapped to quick and apologetic attention – except for Jaitley, who returned a second later, eyes blinking and looking around like a lost passenger who'd fallen asleep on the train. Casey sneered at him as she stepped up to the desk.

'So, tell me then, Miss. Is this going to work?'

Lexa scoffed. 'Are you asking me to predict the future?'

'No, I'm asking if you know what you're doing.'

'Well, I used to. But now my mission's completely screwed and my new plan is about a thousand times more difficult than the first.' She hit *Enter* and looked at Casey with a sickly sweet smile. 'But is it going to work? Yes. Absolutely! Of course it's going to work – if that's what you want to hear.'

Casey stared back at the waspish young brunette with a time machine and an attitude problem, no more a kid herself, and truly wondered if she were ever going to see her family again.

The Vessel shook and the agents stumbled comically as a low *whump-whump-whump* rose up from the Core. Casey looked in all directions as little beads of light zipped past like tiny shooting stars racing one another, twinkling brightly then fading with every pulse. The laptop rattled in its plinth and the notebook next to it shimmied towards the edge of the desk. Lexa dropped down to her stool to steady herself and studied the lines of code rippling across the screen.

'Is this normal?' Casey asked, leaning one arm against the desk.

'This is only a short journey, but –'

'But what?'

'The last trip was a bit turbulent; I think it's still recovering. I need to check the Signature, make sure we're not veering off course. We – we should be fine.'

'*Should?*'

'It's never carried this many people before. You're heavy and you take up too much air.'

'You want us to hold our breaths!?' Casey had to shout over the deafening beat.

'That would be helpful, yes.'

Casey's eyes grew wide. She looked around at her agents, who, on Lexa's last word, were tightening their chests and puffing out their cheeks. Jaitley cupped his hand over his mouth and pinched his nose.

This was it. This was how it all ended. They were going to crash land in the wrong place at the wrong time and there would be no way back. With a picture of her family snuggled up safely reading a crappy book fixed firmly in her mind, Casey braced herself with a long intake of breath, squeezed her eyes shut and then…

…nothing.

The shaking had stopped. The noise lowered with a disgruntled whirr, and daring to look again, Casey saw the lights flitter away into nothing as an unnerving quiet filled the now gloomy chamber.

Lexa stood with a sigh of relief.

'Perfect,' she said.

An expression of pure glee spread across Jaitley's face. 'Is that it? Are we there? Did we just… *travel through time?*'

Lexa glanced down at the laptop. 'Sunday, 12:58pm. Two minutes off target.'

'One o'clock! It was half ten at night a minute ago!' The detective squealed with delight and shook the nearest agent by the arms. 'The Final starts in an hour!'

'Little early, aren't we?' Casey said. 'I thought we weren't due until the second period?'

'Second *half.*'

'Be quiet, Detective Jaitley!' The ache behind her eyes was fast returning. 'So?'

Lexa closed the laptop, tucked it under her arm and went and stood by the edge of the chamber. 'I needed time to synchronise the Core's signal with the antenna's. This is their Vessel, and that should help with the initial connection, but it's our software. I can't just log in. I need to upload the assembly code using a series of ciphers and I can only imagine the kind of anti-virus systems the Euphors have in place –'

Casey held up a hand. 'Okay, okay, I got it.'

'I thought, too,' Lexa continued, 'you might appreciate the time to enter the stadium early, take the time to assess your surroundings, or whatever it is you do. But if I've made a mistake, I'll be more than happy to put the Vessel under even more strain and jump forward an hour –'

'I said I got it!' Casey's voiced echoed off the ceiling and then faded to leave behind a chilly silence. 'Further travel will not be necessary. Thank you.'

A second later the entrance opened and the Impossible Stairs descended into whatever lay beyond. Lexa removed her hand from the wall, smiled at Casey and stepped outside.

This was no longer just a cold shoulder. There was a twitchiness to Lexa's manner, a sort of angry anxiety, which was completely different to the calm presence Casey had encountered in the police interview room. Her agents had probably expected a more explosive response to the way Lexa had spoken to her, but instinct was telling Casey not to push too hard and see how close the plan was to the truth. She wiped the bewildered looks off their faces with a single raise of her eyebrows and then led them down the steps after Lexa.

Jaitley was the last to leave, unable to tear himself away. She ordered him out and watched his feckless face change as he gasped at the sight of their new location: an enormous, brightly-lit atrium, shaped like a cauldron, with the tail end of a tarmac road sloping down from a dark tunnel set into the wall on one side.

This, Casey presumed, was the furthest extent of the service road missing from the BK Stadium schematics, but seen in Troy Simpson's photograph. It was the only 'human' element to the room – everything else matched the same alien aesthetic as the craft that had brought them there. The huge walls had the same milky-white streaks which decked the inside of the Vessel, only markedly bigger, and the twisted undulations of the long, rippling stretches were far more complex and intricate than anything Casey had seen so far. Gnarled branches grew out of the sides and spread like overgrown roots of ancient trees down through the uneven floor and up again, then disappeared into the walls on the opposite side. Small, sinewy weeds sprawled their way in amongst the crevices and across the outer surfaces, connecting together in a colossal network of tendon and tissue.

Casey lowered to her haunches and studied the floor up close. What appeared at first to be a pure-white mass was in fact flecked with subtle streaks of colour – autumnal browns, grass greens and a rich, textured assortment of oceanic blues, which swirled gently to form contour lines around the shape of her boots. With greater caution than she'd care to admit, she reached with two trembling fingers and touched the ground. The surface, as its appearance suggested, felt oily, and the colours followed the trail as she drew a figure of eight with her fingertips.

She chuckled, and a small puff of condensation rose from her mouth and filtered away into the air. The summer had been so glorious Casey wondered how she hadn't noticed it until now.

It was *cold*.

The emptiness too made no sense. Where were all the guys in fedoras and thick sweaters? On the biggest day of their lives, shouldn't a couple have held back to defend their property? She at least expected to hear the muffled roar of a hundred thousand people on the other side of the wall.

But there was nothing, except the sound of Jaitley mumbling away behind her. Had the girl got her calculations wrong? She'd said the trip had been 'turbulent'; what if the Vessel had landed in the middle of winter, six months too late to sweep in and save the world?

Looking around, she saw the others all with gaping mouths, their outbreaths visibly escaping and their bodies frozen into the same contorted pose...

One of Casey's assets as an investigator, so she believed, was the unconscious ability to walk into the scene of a crime and zero in on what couldn't be seen at first glance. The key to unlocking the secrets of any space was always in those tiny details; while others looked for the weapon, the body, Casey instead would note the chipped paint on a skirting board, the broken power socket, the dusted windowsill in an otherwise filthy room.

And so, true to form, when the group had exited the Vessel and begun peering around, Casey's instincts had drawn her focus to the ground. But now they had come together and were all looking in the same direction, craning their necks back as far as they would go and staring straight up.

Casey followed their gaze and couldn't believe she had missed it.

'Well, I'll be goddamned...'

The Core churned in thunderous silence, the thick rolls of cloud spinning like a slow-motion tornado, parting through the middle to allow the light to come through.

It was what Lexa had been expecting; a smaller replica of the Flagship's gargantuan vortex. Only this one wouldn't be as easy to fall through, being as it was *directly above them*, running up through the inside of the antenna that towered over the stadium. The Flagship itself would be positioned directly over the tip, miles above the atmosphere, as though they were two tin cans connected by one very long piece of string.

Only that wasn't the end of it. Just as invisible were the millions more lines of string, spreading out like a spider's web across the globe to every single device logged onto the SyBall App.

An agent with beads of sweat twinkling on his bald head took some deep, edgy breaths, then unholstered his dart gun and pointed it directly at the Core. Casey clocked him immediately and took out her own.

'Lower your weapon!'

'We need to stop pussy-footing around here,' the agent snarled. 'We should get DC on point. Scramble a unit, target some ICBMs and blow this thing sky high.'

'Damn it, Cobb, shut your mouth!'

'Ain't no time for state secrets, ma'am, we need to end this thing.'

Two more of Casey's minions nodded in agreement and raised their guns above them, though Lexa wasn't quite sure why – the Euphorivores weren't going to suddenly emerge out of the Core.

'Have you all lost your minds?' Casey screamed. 'There's a hundred thousand people in this stadium, you want to kill them all? I repeat – lower your weapons, that's an order!'

Cobb was smouldering with the tension. 'With all due respect, but what's the point of having this time vehicle if we can't use it? We need to take control of this situation – we should go back further, put a tactical plan together and strike when those unholy assholes are the only *people* in this place.'

Agent Taylor pumped his fist. 'Hell, yeah!'

'But that might cause a paradox!'

The rising voice had echoed off the walls. Jaitley took a few cautious steps forward, his palms raised as both a plea for calm and a measure of self-defence. No-one was looking at the Core anymore; even Lexa's eyes widened in surprise.

Casey grimaced. 'Excuse me?'

'A paradox,' Jaitley repeated, 'a time loop which contradicts itself. Don't you watch films? You can't change the past without screwing up the present.' He turned to Lexa. 'That's the risk you're taking, isn't it? To change your future – your whole reason for being here?'

Jaitley was looking at her with an odd expression she couldn't quite place – a kind of hopeful concern, as though he were trying to draw the stakes out of her on purpose.

Around them, the dart guns remained as steady as the bodies of their owners, locked in a bizarre Mexican stand-off that hinged on her response. Lexa bit her thumb – this was getting ridiculous. Time was being lost. Her fingers squeezed into her tired eyes and then ran down her face. She regretted deeply letting Jaitley, Casey and the agents come along – all she wanted, really, was a little bit of cover, a wall of protection to let her carry out her plan. Now she felt like ordering them all back inside the Vessel so she could dump them in the Middle Ages in the middle of nowhere and be free of them forever.

'Nothing is set in stone, detective,' she said. 'Things can change, anywhere, anytime, and it won't cause the universe to collapse in on itself, or anything like that. Sacrifices tend to be a little more personal.'

Lexa jabbed a finger at the bald agent, the one who had been demoted in front of all his peers and then scowled at Josh like an angry dog.

'I'm sorry, what was your name, again?'

(She already knew).

He gritted his teeth. 'Agent John Cobb.'

'Right. Let's just say, Agent John Cobb, that your senior authority figures in Washington aren't, for the most part, Euphorivores – because believe me, they are – and that the British Government, who are also, for the most part, Euphorivores, won't retaliate – because, believe me, they will. Let's assume all that and go back, what, a month?'

Lexa took a couple of steps towards Cobb and enjoyed watching him twitch. She scared him – that was good.

'Whatever you were doing a month ago,' she continued coolly, throwing a quick look to the other agents, '– and I'm guessing for most of you that's back home, with your families – that version of you will still exist. And when you come back to today, there will be a new version of you, one who'll never know we were even here. And *that's* the version, not you, who gets to stay at home and be with your family. You wouldn't be you – you'd be an imposter, and you'd have to watch from a distance as someone else with your face lives out your life.' She shrugged. 'Now you look to me like the type of guys who'd rather die than see that happen, so the only risk I'm taking here, Detective Jaitley, is having this conversation with some puffed-up peacock waving his *gun* around; but seeing as another version of me hasn't appeared out of nowhere to help me out, I guess I'll have to work twice as bloody fast to make up for it!'

The final word resounded in the air, like a bullet shot across an empty desert, and one-by-one, with Cobb taking the lead, the agents' guns lowered.

Lexa held the command of the room for a few moments, a hopeful sign she had regained control of the situation. The agents were locked in their positions by a sense of embarrassment and wounded pride.

Casey reholstered her weapon and clapped so loudly it was like a sonic boom going off in the atrium, startling the group out of their trance.

'So, what are you all waiting for, an invitation?' she yelled, louder than the clap. 'Get into position! Now!'

The agents dispersed:

Alpha Team – Casey, Jaitley and Agents Logan, Hicks and Martinez – led the way up through the service road tunnel, followed by one half of Beta Team – O'Reilly, Taylor and a stony-faced Cobb, who walked with an imperious swagger as though nothing had happened.

This left Lexa with just two agents, Nash and Kowalski, to stay and guard the Vessel. Hardly a battalion, but she didn't protest – the less there were, the less she might feel the weight of her regret. In a desperate bid to prove that everything she'd prepared for, everything her father had laboured for, the suffering and sacrifice, had not been in vain, she'd gone and tooled herself with this bunch of goons, while the one person she actually trusted had been left angry and heartbroken in a police station courtyard.

The wrong guy, Agent Casey? she thought.

The description didn't fit. Would the wrong guy have come looking for her side of the story after she'd pulverised his face and put him in hospital? Would the wrong guy have demolished half a building to rescue her the first time, and then leapt onto the back of a Firebreather in full flight the second time? Would the wrong guy have committed to staying with her, even though the last time they were alone together she had raged about what a giant mistake he was?

Lexa realised she'd rather have that mistake by her side than anyone else in the world, and every single part of her wished he were here right now.

'27

Signs of Life

*D*ear Mr. Pittman,

Thank you for entering our 'Design A Mascot' competition for the upcoming SyBall World Cup, which the DFA is delighted to be hosting next year in venues the length and breadth of the British Kingdom.

The panel of judges, myself included were pleased to review your submission 'Nutmeg'. He looks very cute and we like his smile.

But there, Mr Pittman, our admiration ends. Overall, we considered this to be a mediocre and ill-informed effort, for the reasons detailed below:

Firstly, we would remind you that the government's stance on superhero culture is that it is a construct designed to normalise violence and conflict in children – plainly not in the spirit of the Guiding Principles.

Furthermore, your assertion that a squirrel is an ideal choice for a global tournament, as they can be found all over the world, is simply not true.

You won't find any in New Zealand. Or Antarctica. Perhaps you thought of the name first and the concept second, and hoped we wouldn't notice?

Well, we did, and the panel were deeply troubled by a name which is both a footballing term and a knowing reference to a squirrel's favourite food (except it isn't – nutmeg is a spice), therefore skirting dangerously close to Section 2.23 of the Register of National Names, which stipulates that official names of the British Kingdom should not be open to overinterpretation and hidden meaning.

Which brings me to my next point.

You should consider yourself fortunate, Mr Pittman, for not all losing entrants will receive a handwritten letter from the Department, but in this case, we thought it necessary to address your baffling decision to send us, alongside your entry, your individualised crest designs for each of our Regional League teams.

Why you chose to do this is a question only you can answer. But what it entitles us to say is that the reason each team bears the SyBall spiral is to remind us of how the Great Unifier brings us together; as occasional rivals on the pitch, and as a joyful, compassionate society off it.

It is frankly horrifying that you have chosen to ignore the Principles' teachings by separating out and focusing only on local symbols which can do nothing but divide us. Your designs are so littered with endless references to historical iconography that I sit here wondering why it is easier for you, as a young man, to cling to the past rather than look to the future?

The fact is, you can't play football unless there is someone to play against. A team's name is there to distinguish itself from an opponent, and in this context is nothing more than a functional necessity of the game, much like the ball, or the pitch, or the goalposts.

So, for the avoidance of doubt, we remind you that the Regions are named for reasons of geography, familiarity and balance. That is all. Any allusion to insular pride and separatist rivalries is not only unintentional, but wholly incorrect. The Register is very clear on this point.

We consider it both a failure on our part and an insult that you see these acts of concession, mistake their higher purpose, and so in turn feel the need to foster your obsession with the way things used to be and waffle on about ceremonial counties, coats of arms, landmarks, ancestries and other things no one cares about anymore.

You have talent as an artist, Mr Pittman, but the world has moved on and so should you.

We wish you well in your future endeavours.

Yours Sincerely

Temperance Newhart
Secretary of State for Footballing Activities

Whitehall
London

***

Closer to the stadium the roads became heavier – not with vehicles, but with people. Josh had always found it curious, even with his sparse experience, how the normal rules of pedestrian conduct were usually abandoned on matchdays. Roads never appeared to close, but the cars, vans, buses and lorries always took second place to the throng of people swarming in from every direction.

The difference today was that the SyBall World Cup Final had already started. The crowds heading for the stadium would have passed through hours ago, and in their place the local residents were celebrating the day with a street party, which, although animated and excitable, existed for Josh as a static mass, blocking his path and grinding him to a halt.

He looked either side at the rows of terraced houses, all decorated for the occasion with brightly coloured bunting criss-crossing the street above the heads of the revellers. Flags of countries he couldn't name were flying from windows, or draped over parked cars, or tied around people's necks like capes. He thought back to Copacabana Beach, and the vibrant mix of Brazilian and Argentinian colours merging as one.

Behind the hedgerows, red-faced men in comedic aprons tended to their barbeques, sending thick plumes of smoke and the smells of various charred meats wafting into the air. Children ran in front of him to collect cups of juice poured from ice-cold pitchers and served over garden walls. On nearly every lawn, trestle tables had been set up with televisions perched precariously on top, their power cables trailing back through the flower beds and in through the front windows – the same way the monitor had been arranged in the station courtyard during Agent Casey's briefing; the last time he had seen Lexa.

Every screen was surrounded by a small group of people, eating and laughing, drinking and cheering, *oohing* and *aahing* with every kick of the ball.

Josh turned up the live commentary blaring through his car radio.

'North America have started this second half well… still goalless here in London… Chris Tannen, the Ontarian wing-back, has the ball at his feet… crosses it to Lamoureux… Good pass! Lamoureux has options… strike from range…! Oof! My word that was close!'

To Josh's left, a group of residents, huddled together beneath the shade of a large parasol, arched their backs and hissed like a den of snakes who'd just been trodden on. He wondered how they'd react if he got out and told them that North America were destined to score soon. Would it make the experience any less nerve-wracking for them? Would he feel better?

Josh turned the volume back down; there was a sharpness to the commentator's voice he hadn't noticed before, which rung like the referee's whistle being blown in his ear. He looked down the length of the street and saw, rising above the chimney pots, the BK Stadium, glinting majestically in the sun.

432

Even from this distance, it was hard not to be impressed by the sheer scale of the structure. Euphorivores really knew how to build. The metallic-blue exterior wrapped around the bowl and swept seamlessly up the sides of the antenna like a silk scarf caught inside a whirlpool.

Inside were 150 thousand occupants, but he could only think of one.

A set of knuckles rapped on the driver's door window, startling him out of his thoughts. A scraggly haired woman, wearing a pinafore bearing PJ Pitman's face and holding a paper plate with a hot dog and a dollop of potato salad on top, was peering at Josh

'You need a place to park, love?' she asked in an unnecessarily loud voice. 'You can use our drive! Have a sausage!'

Josh smiled politely. 'No, it's ok, thank you, I'm not stopping.'

The woman was stunned.

'You're not stopping?' She raised the plate and spoke to the space below it. 'He's not stopping! You won't find anywhere up there, my love, place is rammed!'

It was then Josh noticed the young boy cowering behind his mother, who surveyed him with an inquisitive face – a face that had been painted green with black and white swirls in the style of the spiral crest. Josh suddenly pictured the Core of the Flagship, rushing towards him as he fell.

He declined the offer again and kept moving. The car inched along the tarmac as the partygoers dawdled and danced out of his way, patting the roof and walking alongside to present him with yet more food and drink to sustain his onward journey.

On the radio, the commentator was beginning to splutter with excitement.

'Mayfield is storming down the sideline, what pace he has! British Kingdom forward in numbers, fifty minutes played... Troy Simpson has his hands in the air, looking for the pass... Pitman is behind him. A muted performance from him so far –'

The commentator cut himself off and then continued reproachfully as though he'd slipped back into a nasty habit he thought he'd kicked.

'– but forgive me, it's not my place to judge the commitment of our national players, he'll be there when we need him...'

'Let's hope not,' Josh muttered, as he turned the corner at the end of the street.

The revellers began to thin out as at last he reached a wide road lined with local amenities below some brutalist office blocks. The woman with the hot dog had been right – the kerbsides were crammed with coaches, mini-buses and cars with number plates from countries just as eclectic as the flags above the street party. If he were indeed looking for a place to park, he'd have been out of luck.

'Reuben Mayfield looks up... oh no! He took too long! Wow, what a crunching tackle that was by Símon Fuentes... the home team think it's a foul, they look to the referee... who says play on! What servants to the Great Unifier these officials are! North America on the counter... British Kingdom need to get back... here's Glover... feeds it through to Wilson, will he shoot? No! He side-steps Alex Shoreham, chips it into the box... Lamoureux's there, out comes Castle, and... oh my, it... oh my...'

From the streets he had just left and the stadium he was approaching, a faint roar of despair rose into the air, like a roll of thunder warning him of an oncoming storm. North America had scored. Everything so far was going according to the Euphorivores' plan.

Approaching a roundabout, Josh checked his phone, nestled in the holder mounted to his dashboard, and compared the on-screen map to the view outside his window. The Away Day App, another free DFA service for plotting routes to stadiums, had thrown up its first anomaly. The road leading off to the to the right of the roundabout ought to have led to a dead end but, in reality, Josh could see it heading away in the direction of the stadium – and, he assumed, the underground service tunnel. Circling the roundabout, a street sign on the far side confirmed his theory:

BK STADIUM:
Maintenance, Deliveries and Team Arrivals Only Please!
Thank you!

Presumably, all delivery drivers were Euphorivores – no human these days would dare ignore such a friendly notice to stay away. There wasn't even a gate or manned checkpoint to negotiate past.

The road sloped down through a grove of trees whose branches sheltered the passage beneath with a canopy of bright green leaves. Lock Niss had been baking in the sun all day and the interior temperature had risen steadily throughout the drive. The steering wheel had become so unbearably hot Josh was having to turn it with the butt of one hand, and so was pleased to be finally heading into some shade. If the Euphorivores were trying to make the road look uninviting, they should have held the tournament in winter.

Though the descent felt gradual, it wasn't long before the stadium was no longer visible above the thick branches. He shut off the radio, which had become a crackling echo of the faint roar of the crowd Josh could still hear from inside.

Curving in towards the noise, the trees gave way to the entrance of a concrete tunnel, lit from above by a welcoming glow of cool spotlights. Another informal signpost split the path for the service vehicles, and Josh had barely turned the other way when he spotted two enormous, gleaming coaches parked a little way ahead opposite the glass-fronted entrance to the locker rooms.

The North American coach was hard to miss, being brightly decorated with a single continuous image which encompassed the entire breadth of the continent on all four sides. Tropical-coloured cityscapes were linked by mountain ranges, waterfalls and sandy beaches, and overlooked by silhouettes of the Statue of Liberty, Mayan Pyramids and the CN Tower. Pink and orange footballs with trails of little yellow stars flew like comets across an azure sky, over the top of the vehicle and down the other side.

In contrast, the British Kingdom coach – what little he could see of it as he eased Lock Niss to a stop – was white.

Plain white.

With no decoration.

Maybe the Euphorivores thought that by adding a design similar to their opponent's coach they might end up offending people with their 'local symbols'.

Josh stepped quietly out of the car and onto a small footpath which ran along the outer edge of the road. The distant cheers of the fans, sat in their thousands above his head, were enough, he hoped, to muffle the echo of his footsteps as he crept through the narrow space between the wall and the first coach. There were voices up ahead. American, as expected, and male, which was a relief – the last thing he needed now was to run into Agent Casey.

Edging quietly along, Josh slipped across the gap between the coaches and up close discovered the British Kingdom's coach wasn't entirely white after all. Printed on the side, beneath the front passenger seat window, was a picture of Sunny, the tournament mascot. The cartoon sun, yellow with orange rays like a spikey-haired lion, was waving enthusiastically with a wide, toothless smile, wearing a football shirt with the spiral crest emblazoned over his heart. A speech bubble from out of his mouth displayed the words 'Joy and Compassion' in jaunty blue writing. Josh stared into the round, happy eyes, sneered resentfully and gave the jolly star the middle finger before moving on.

At the back of the coach the voices came into focus. He stopped again and pressed himself against the coach's side, listening closely.

'…go back to the point *just after* we left last night?'

Josh lifted his head enough for one eye to see past the edge of the coach. The man talking was Agent Cobb, his bald head facing back to Josh. He cursed his luck – that guy hated him.

'How much time would that give us – eight, nine hours? More than enough. We'd be the only versions. Problem solved.'

'Damn it, John!'

Josh knew this one without looking – O'Reilly. Assigned leader ahead of Cobb. Good at dribbling.

'Why didn't you say that back there?'

The third, unseen voice chimed in, slow and drawling. 'Ya'll keep talking about this transmitter, what about this *spaceship*, huh? She ain't said nuthin' about that! If they're really all up there, *that's* what we should be hitting. 'Cos down here it seems like we ain't doing nuthin' more than hanging up the phone... *whoa, whoa, whoa! Stop right there!*'

Agent Taylor had whipped out his dart gun at lightning speed and held it out in front of him. A second later and his two colleagues had done the same, with Cobb in particular spinning smoothly on the spot as he drew from his holster. By the look on his face, this was a much-practiced manoeuvre designed to make him feel big and clever. But it was nothing compared to the elegant twists and turns of a Firebreather in flight.

Cobb snarled. 'You!'

Josh had stepped from behind the coach with his hands already in the air. He'd thought for a moment about turning back, but then decided to offer them a chance. After all, they were there for the same reason he was; to save the world – and to protect Lexa.

O'Reilly reached for the two-way radio attached to his shoulder, his other hand still wrapped around the handle of his gun.

'Agent Cas –'

'No, please...'

Josh brought his arm down in front of O'Reilly, who winced as the radio crackled and shrieked in his ear. Cobb and Taylor each took a nervous step backwards.

'Stay back! Don't move!'

'It's ok, it's fine…' Josh said quickly, his voice soft and placating. 'The hand, I know… but last night? In the training ground? That was a bluff! I just needed to get on board the Vessel, I did what I had to do and I'm sorry. Okay? But please, I really need to speak to Lexa.'

'Ain't gonna happen, son,' said Taylor. 'Turn around, walk away.'

'No, listen to me, please,' Josh insisted, his tone of desperation both deliberate and truthful. 'Lexa is down there; she's doing this all by herself. She's all alone –'

'There are agents with her.'

Josh snapped. 'That's not what I mean!'

The agents recoiled again. O'Reilly tried once more to contact Casey. This time the call was met with silence – no tortuous feedback, but no response either. Josh could probably afford another second or two.

'She's more alone than any of us could ever imagine because she thinks this is all on her, but it's not. I need her to know that…' He screwed up his face, the sense he was getting nowhere creeping through him. 'I should have said something before now. Stupid. But it's not too late if you let me past. If not for my sake, then for everyone else's. If there's any hope left for us, you'll do this… *please.*'

Their faces were as hard as stone.

'Sir, you are required to leave,' O'Reilly said. 'If you do not do so, then we will forcibly remove you.'

A thin smile drew across Cobb's lips as he flexed his fingers around the handle. Josh opened his mouth to speak, but after thinking about O'Reilly's failure to contact Casey, he chose instead to nod with defeat and turn on his heels. As he stepped away, Josh noticed yet one more sign, a wooden one propped in front of the Tensa-barrier which stretched across the road:

WELCOME TO THE
BK STADIUM TEAMS ENTRANCE

This road leads to some very sensitive television broadcast
equipment, so we'd really appreciate it if you didn't go down
here!
Thanks for your understanding!
Good luck out there!

Josh smirked. This was all that stood between success and some inquisitive footballer blowing the Euphorivores' cover. And it was working, too.

Cobb gritted his teeth. 'Something funny?'

'No, I was just reading the –'

Josh looked up and noted how the agents hadn't moved. All three were still aiming at him even though he appeared to have given up.

'It's strange,' he said, taking a slight half-turn back towards the barrier. 'The Euphors are trying to kill me – kill us all, in fact – and a *dragon* very nearly did kill me. And yes, that's frightening, for sure, but not in the way I expected it to be. The fear doesn't feel...

debilitating. It's the opposite. It's a fear that gets your blood pumping, makes you want to fight back. Maybe it's the unrealness of it all; the whole thing seems too bonkers to let it get to you.'

Cobb shifted his feet, itching for an excuse to fire. Josh clicked his tongue.

'But when you lot pull your guns on me, twice now, I might add, there's no fear at all. I just feel sick. I can't believe I actually thought you might understand, but that was stupid, because you really are no different to them.'

Taylor's eyes widened at this, a look of resentment passing over his face. O'Reilly cocked his head slightly towards his radio, as if Josh's insult would somehow get it working. Cobb kept his focus, breathing slowly, the rising anger showing through his steely eyes. Josh was pushing the very edge of his luck.

'They have their weapons,' he continued, gesturing towards the wooden sign, 'and you have yours. The only difference is they're only doing this because they're hungry. You can't blame them for that. If you offered them an alternative, I'm sure they'd take it. But you guys...'

Josh took another foolhardy step towards them, almost surprised he wasn't yet lying on the ground with three darts sticking out of his chest.

'...you guys are just jerks.'

O'Reilly's nostrils flared. 'Final warning, son.'

'Okay, okay,' Josh said, holding up his hands defensively. The radio fizzed again. 'I'm going.'

Josh walked briskly until he passed the carnival-coloured North America coach and was sure he was out of sight. Only then did he allow himself to stop and wipe the sweat from his brow. He really did feel sick and he really had been stupid – trying to talk his way past was a chance he hadn't needed to take.

Maybe Lexa was right to leave him behind if he was going to do things like that. He pulled his phone out of his pocket and checked the match time on the SyBall App. 67:23 – eight minutes before North America would score again, only for the goal to be ruled out for offside.

Josh sat back inside Lock Niss and turned the ignition.

'No more risks,' he muttered, as he thrust the gearstick forward and slammed his foot on the accelerator.

The sprightly little car launched forward, the screech of the tyres on the tarmac echoing in the long tunnel. The distance back to the barrier was short and Josh was nowhere near top speed by the time he tore past the team coaches, but he was, at least, going fast enough to catch the agents off-guard, glimpsing their stunned faces and offering them no opportunity to raise their weapons before they had to leap out of his way. He'd been determined to drive straight at them, to show no mercy, but Agent Taylor hadn't moved as quickly as the others and instinctively Josh swerved to the right to avoid him and hit the wooden sign on his near side, which flew over the bonnet and smashed into the windshield before landing in a broken heap behind him. The glass cracked and spread like a spider's web from the point of impact. At the same time, the car caught the Tensa-barrier just below the wipers, stretching the belt until it snapped free of its mounts on the walls either side.

Two metallic thunks ricocheted around the sides of the car from the rear. The splinters of glass across his windshield obscured his vision and, startled by the sounds, Josh veered once again, more erratically this time, scraping a concrete pillar set into the wall. He looked in his rear-view mirror – two agents were down on their knees: O'Reilly was taking aim while Cobb was reaching into his pocket to reload his weapon. Josh realised what the thunks had been.

Lock Niss! No...!

O'Reilly fired again and the dart smashed into a tail light. They were aiming for his tyres. Despite his broken view, Josh was determined to go as fast as he could, using the row of strip lights in the ceiling above as a guide to follow the curve of the road. In his mirror, O'Reilly, Cobb and Taylor had stood and were giving chase.

Let's see if you bastards can do ninety.

Josh shifted up a gear and roared ahead – it felt like he was driving with a blindfold on. The cracks were spreading further, while the deeper into the tunnel he drove, the less the lights were able to penetrate the darkness. It took no time at all to disappear out of sight and out of reach of the agents, but Josh was reluctant to ease off fully; they were likely to chase him all the way.

The road spiralled down, and as the shouts of his pursuers faded into silence, Josh was left with only the thumping of his heart in his chest for company. His nose felt hot and his hand was aching again – he'd been gripping the steering wheel so tightly his fingernails were digging into the faux-leather cover.

He had no idea how deep the area beneath the antenna would be, but it was further than he expected. The road narrowed, the strip lights became less frequent and an eerie chill crept inside the car that spawned goose-bumps along his bare arms. Then, without warning, just as the spiral appeared to be tightening, the road took a sharp turn in the opposite direction. A stone wall directly ahead appeared of out the darkness and Josh tried to brake, but the momentum kept Lock Niss racing downwards and he only just pulled the wheel around in time to avoid crashing. Straightening out, he could finally see the end of the tunnel, lit from beyond by a dazzling light which sparkled and shimmered along the lines of broken glass as he drew nearer.

Josh slowed as he emerged from the darkness, his eyes needing time to adjust to the sudden influx of light and then to decide exactly what they should look at first: the atrium, with its undeniably Euphorivore-chic interior, or the upturned Core churning silently above him, or, much closer, the next set of flabbergasted ACA agents who reached for their weapons and shouted things as he drove past.

In the end, all these features fell off the scale of importance as Josh settled on a point in the centre of the room, where the Vessel stood perfectly balanced on its tip, and from where Lexa was now jumping off her perch on the Impossible Stairs and running towards him with a thunderous look of anger.

'No, no, *no!*' she screamed.

Josh smiled – it was so good to see her.

'28

Y Ddraig Goch

Josh pulled Lock Niss to a grateful stop and leapt out to greet her. He had barely one foot on the ground before he was attacked with a flurry of arms, pushing and shoving him back inside.

'Don't even think about it! Get back in! I told you to go home! Why would you even... Josh, stop it!'

Josh had grabbed hold of the door and was pushing away with his other foot against the side of the driver's seat.

'Lexa, please, I…'

'Are you going to help me or what?' Lexa barked at the agents, who were approaching with uncharacteristic caution.

Josh pushed harder, straining his neck as Lexa tried to shove his head back down.

'You think this is a game, Josh?' she was saying, 'I can't believe you'd risk your own family…'.

'It's okay,' he said, his voice muffled by her fingers spread across his face, 'I'm the one who…'

The agents closed in around him. He lurched forward, but in doing so felt the car's metal frame buckle beneath the pressure of his fingers, and in his shock, he released his grip and tumbled to the ground. Upon impact his nose seared with pain as the stitches broke and the wound reopened. Josh rolled onto his back and looked up at Lexa hovering over him, her teeth clenched, her fist raised.

'Don't make me hurt you! I won't hold back this time!' she yelled, little beads of spit shooting out of her mouth.

She pulled her arm back, ready to strike…

'No, wait! Listen! There was no mistake, PJ was never the target!'

Lexa froze, her fist hanging in mid-air. 'I'm sorry, what?'

'You got it right the first time. It was *meant* to be me.'

Lexa lowered her fist and surveyed him with an equal measure of suspicion and confusion. She raised an eyebrow.

'You?'

Josh nodded and lifted himself onto his elbows. Behind him the agents shifted nervously.

'Yes, me. I can prove it too.'

He glanced briefly back at Lock Niss.

Not yet, he thought.

There was still a risk Lexa would try to shove him inside again – or beat him with the door, whichever was easier. Instead, he looked across to where her laptop was currently perched, lid open, on the Impossible Stairs.

'The password!'

Josh scrambled to his feet and ran towards the Vessel. Little droplets of blood from his nose fell to the floor, which dissolved beneath the oily surface.

'Remember that trick I mentioned,' he said, 'the one where you choose a password by taking a memorable word and using the corresponding top-left keys? I could have said top-right, bottom-left, bottom-right, but no...' Josh stood by the laptop and raised his chin, a little more pompously than he intended. 'Look at the keyboard.'

Lexa didn't move. She was standing upright again, squeezing her fist, eager to thump him.

'I don't have time –'

'You have lots of time, Lexa, you're a time traveller.' Josh returned her steely gaze, trying desperately not to quiver. 'Look at it.'

As Lexa sauntered over, Agent Kowalski licked his lips and beamed a wide cheesy grin, while the other – Agent Nash – went to accompany her, only to be pegged back with a sharp shake of the head. They were a like a pair of guard dogs, waiting for Lexa to let them off the leash.

She watched as Josh drew his finger over the keyboard, pointing to the bottom-right corner of each key as he read them out:

'Four – nine – G – nine – Y – Q – H – E...'

Lexa looked at him. 'Robohand?'

Josh nodded. He waited a moment and then watched her face as the realisation dawned. It was clear she had never heard the name before but nonetheless understood where it came from. She took a step away from him, as though she were trying to swallow something bitter.

'No, that can't...' she muttered, 'it's not... *you're* not...'

Her face turned pale and she laid one hand on her stomach and the other over her mouth. Then, as she peered down at Josh's own hands, pockmarked with the scars and bruises she herself had inflicted, he realised in horror the thought passing through her mind.

'What? Ew, no... I'm –'

Lexa wasn't listening to him.

'Oh God, that's disgusting!' She shook her head violently. 'No – it doesn't make sense... you're not him, you're not *my father...*'

'That's–'

'You look nothing like him... it's impossible, his name was –'

'Martin!' Josh said, grabbing her arm and pulling her back to him.

She threw him off.

'Martin Bannick. And no, I'm *not* him... but I *know* him. I even told you about him. Outside the pub? He's the first-choice keeper for my team – he used to be good, really good. Even tried out for a bunch of regional teams before his accident. Fell off his motorbike and crushed his hand and they had to put all these metal pins into the bones. Not robotic or anything, but one guy called him it and the nickname stuck.'

He chanced a half-chuckle. It was not reciprocated.

'But then he had another accident,' Josh continued, gravely. 'About a week ago – much worse this time. He hasn't woken up yet. But he will do, because... he's your dad! That's how he survives through today. His wife, too. I can't remember her...'

'My mother's name was Gillian,' said Lexa.

'Gillian! Yes, that's it! Your mum and dad, Martin and Gillian Bannick. I like him. He's the only one who actually talks to me – gives me tips I never listen to.'

Lexa's eyes closed and she breathed heavily.

'You're lying,' she said. 'You never told me the man you knew had pins in his hand.'

Josh shrugged. 'Oh… didn't I?'

'No, you didn't. But you have been watching me non-stop ever since I decided, for some insane reason, to let you come along. You could have looked over my shoulder and read the password anytime. And now you've pieced together this whole story to try and worm your way back onto this mission. Why? I don't know. You want the glory? Well, you're welcome to it! You obviously know everything already, so why don't I just leave you to it and I'll just head off and go find a hole to sit in and wait for the fucking world to end!'

Kowalski muffled a laugh.

Lexa shot both agents a filthy look and screamed: 'Get him out of here!'

Nash and Kowalski burst forward and Josh threw out his arms in panic. They stopped short and drew their dart guns instead, the memory of the training ground obviously still fresh in their minds.

'Lexa, listen to yourself. That would be some coincidence, wouldn't it? I knew his name!'

'Yes, because it's written in his notebook!'

Lexa's voice echoed off the walls of the atrium. Josh quickly surveyed the scene; could he power his legs quickly enough to beat the agents back to Lock Niss?

'What, that notebook?'

He pointed to the top of the Impossible Stairs to where her father's pad was resting just below the open entrance.

Lexa gritted her teeth. 'Yes.'

'*That* notebook?'

Josh strolled briskly over to his car, summoning an illusion of calm, but struggling to disguise how shallow his breathing was becoming. He opened the passenger door, unclipped the glove box and reached inside.

'Are you sure you don't mean… *this* notebook?'

Josh held out the black, spiral-bound sketchpad from his bookshelf for Lexa to take. She didn't move.

'Really, it's more an artist's pad than a notebook,' he said, flicking back to front through the mostly-blank pages. 'I only bought it a year or so ago when the DFA held this mascot competition for the SyBall World Cup. I was mulling over art college, and I thought it'd be a nice way to get my work out there. So, I drew a squirrel. See?'

Josh held up Nutmeg's picture in front of Lexa, then turned to show the agents too, who smiled politely over the tops of their weapons.

'The judges hated it. They chose *Sunny* instead.' Josh sneered and turned the sketchpad back to himself. 'Never mind, eh? But the other thing was, back then I had this niggling obsession with how boring it was that every team in the country all had the same badge, with the…'

He pointed up at the inverted Core spiralling through the antenna and swirled his finger around.

'So, I thought I'd try and get into the spirit of this whole Grand Unifier thing, try to do something positive and create new crests, using the same shape but giving each team their own unique design. Different but equal, right? All my original drawings are in here. But again, they hated them – accused me of being, I don't know, a fascist or something. Anyway, after they wrote back, I put the pad on the shelf with all my others and forgot about it. Ah-hah! Here it is!'

Josh found the page he'd been searching for and smoothed it out.

'A brand new crest for the Welsh Regional Team.' He held up the sketchpad for a second time to show off his work. 'A *red dragon*. Original, huh? Although, looking at it now, I think it's missing something, don't you agree?'

Josh didn't wait for Lexa not to answer him and instead pulled out the pen that was clipped to the inside of the spiral binding. As he began by drawing a small hexagon over the top of the dragon's forehead, he could feel Lexa, Nash and Kowalski craning their necks to watch him. His guard was down but he had their attention.

'Extra line here,' he said cheerily, 'add a few stars and twinkles and you get…' He lifted the pen with a little flourish and showed the finished product to Lexa. '…a *lifestone*. There! What do you think?'

Lexa stepped forward and touched the page with the picture of Red staring up at her. She looked around the edges of the sketch pad and then to Josh.

'If I'm wrong, I'll leave,' he said. 'I promise.'

Lexa gave a look like she didn't believe him but said nothing as she walked over to the Stairs and picked up the Captain's old, battered notebook. Her fingers trembled as she stroked the black cover, each corner bent and frayed, and then glanced at the opening page to see it covered in thin lines of her father's tiny, frantic handwriting. After a breath, she flipped the notebook over so that the back cover was now the front. As she opened it up again, Josh saw her eyes widen as Lexa discovered that the first page was in fact five or six sheets taped together around the edges. The notebook was so full of torn pages and extra little scraps of paper stuck in with bits of yellowy-brown tape that the hidden pages at the back were almost unnoticeable.

Lexa tried carefully to break the seal, but the tape was so weak and frail with age it crumbled away as soon as she made contact. The pages fell open and she gasped as the little portfolio of Josh's designs reappeared in front of her. Josh felt overcome with a mixture of guilt and relief as she turned straight away to his badge for Wales. And there, upon the dragon's forehead, was the lifestone he had just drawn. The same strokes of his pen, the same hasty stars, the same blot of ink where he had smudged the end of one line, and the same splash of dried blood that had fell from his nose just a second before. The same scribbled drawing – only twenty years older.

Nash and Kowalski lowered their guns.

'I'm sorry,' said Josh, 'I know this is tough and I know my timing sucks, but Lexa, you *have* to see it now. Martin –'

Lexa winced at the sound of the name.

'– always intended for *you* to come back here, not him. Why would an old man send himself back to beat up a footballer when he's got a daughter who can take on anyone? And why would he

452

get such a famous footballer mixed up with someone else with no online record?' He gestured towards the laptop. 'I don't have a website, I'm not on social media and I definitely don't have a Digipedia article. In the future, I'm nothing. But PJ is everywhere, you can't miss him.'

Josh drew closer to Lexa. She had gone red around the eyes and was biting her nails. He resolved himself for one last point of revelation.

'Mar – *the Captain* – sent you back to find me because when he wakes up in hospital, I'm going to give him my sketchpad and tell him that's what he has to do.'

A tense, sickening silence fell over the atrium, lasting for what seemed like an eternity of time before it was broken by a clamour of galloping footsteps and heavy wheezing. Lexa refused to be distracted from the notebook but the others turned as Agents O'Reilly, Cobb and Taylor emerged from the darkness of the tunnel, holding their sides and panting with relief that the end of their long run down the service road was over. On sight of Josh, all three pulled their weapons, the effort a little more laboured than it had been at the top.

'Hands in the air!'

O'Reilly's voice echoed off the high walls, but with little time to recover his breath the words were followed by a fit of coughing.

'Sir – I wouldn't do that if I were you...' said Kowalski, but his words went unheeded.

With their target in reach, the new arrivals threw off their exhaustion and quickly traversed the distance towards Josh.

'I said, put your hands in the air! Now!'

453

Josh raised his arms above his head, having made sure he was still holding the sketchpad (his version of it) in his hand before doing so.

'Sir, you are under arrest!'

'No, he's not,' said Lexa, her voice low and absolute.

O'Reilly sneered. 'Begging your pardon, ma'am, but this ain't got nothing to do with you.'

'This is my mission; it has everything to do with me!'

'Tom,' said Nash quietly, taking half a step forward towards O'Reilly, 'just hold back a sec.'

Josh didn't know if it had been Nash's sincere tone, or that he simply outranked O'Reilly, but either way the agents relented.

'Goddamn pussy foot,' Cobb whispered, lowering his gun.

Josh dropped his arms back to his sides. 'Lexa...?'

'How long have you known?' she asked.

He sighed. 'Since last night – just before I came to get you from the police station.'

Lexa scoffed. 'And you didn't think to tell me?'

'I didn't know if I should, I –'

Lexa slammed the notebook shut and stormed over to her laptop to continue, furiously, with her work.

Josh persevered. 'I thought maybe I was supposed to just let things run their course and the answers would reveal themselves. After the police station I was going to tell you, honestly, but then before I knew it, we were in space, which felt like a *really* big deal, and when you didn't even stop to question how I knew the password, or how I'd even got into the Vessel without you –'

Lexa's eyes flicked up at him.

'See?' he said, leaping on the point. 'The Vessel must already be coded with my DNA, same as you – must be something I arrange with Martin at a later date.' Josh smiled hopefully. 'Maybe around the same time I share with him my password technique. All these unexplained questions and still you never said anything. I thought perhaps you just weren't meant to know. I thought –' He swallowed hard, the sense of guilt suddenly caught like a lump in his throat, '– I was just meant to make sure I survived, so I could help your dad in the future.'

Lexa shrugged. 'So, what changed?'

'Everything! Lexa, everyone in Rio is *still alive.*'

The typing stopped. For the first time since he'd arrived, Lexa wasn't looking at him as though she wished he were dead.

'They're alive?' she said, standing up again. 'How do you know?'

'Because I've seen the video! Don't believe me? Guys,' Josh turned on his heel to the agents, who seemed startled to be suddenly involved in the conversation, 'did Agent Casey say anything to you about a massacre in Brazil?'

'A massacre?' Nash snorted. 'Nuh-uh, it was the opposite, what I heard.'

Taylor smirked. 'Yeah, sounded like a few of those folks needed a bucket of cold water dumped over their heads!'

The other agents chuckled and nodded in agreement.

'There, you see!' Josh said, still slightly stunned the agents had proved themselves useful for once. 'And *we* did that. When we fell through the Flagship. *We* can change things. You and I together, we can break the cycle. Your father must have believed that, otherwise

455

why keep doing it? Why build a time machine if it won't make any difference? Because a captain knows – he knows that even if you lose to the same team, time and time again, all it takes is one small adjustment; a change in formation, a change of tactic, a little more will and desire, and it makes a world of difference.'

The atrium fell silent again. Out of the corner of his eye Josh saw Kowalski raise his arms, as though to start clapping, only to hold himself back when he saw no-one else doing the same.

Josh dabbed his nose on the back of his sleeve – the bleed hadn't been as bad as he thought and had already clotted. It was still sore though. Lexa walked over and took his arm away from his face, surveying him with a cool indifference.

'Nice speech,' she said. 'So, what now?'

The ache in his hand rose again, the little pieces of the lifestone reminding him they were there.

'Leave with me,' he said. 'You can use the laptop to pilot the Vessel from outside, right? Finish the set up and get in the car. Then we'll drive. Keep going until it's all over and then carry on forever, the two of us. Never stopping.'

Lexa laughed. 'That's it? *That's* your big plan?'

Josh suddenly felt infuriated with her. 'Martin mentions me in that notebook. Talks about how I seek him out after the Harvest. Me. Not you. His future daughter. If you were there, there'd be some hint, some clue. But there's nothing. So that's the change. I don't go to him, instead you come with me. You save the world by saving yourself. If nothing else, you deserve tha–'

'*Woo-hoo! This is awesome!*'

As loud as it was, the unexpected voice filling the chamber was almost lost against a background of static and wild cheering. With every head turning his way, O'Reilly looked down at his two-way radio as if it were a tarantula crawling up his chest. He reached across and held the respond button.

'Ma'am?'

The radio fizzed and crackled as it had when the agents were holding Josh back at the barrier, but after a few stuttered half-words, Special Agent Jen Casey could be heard again, loud and clear, recognisable only by accent rather than character:

'O'Reilly? Is that you? I've been trying to get a hold of you, man, you're missing a helluva party up here! I'm having the time of my life! Soccer, huh? Who knew?'

A chorus of incoherent song broke out somewhere behind her.

'We met these cool guys up here, say hello guys… say "bonjour"… they – they don't… ah, no, don't make me sing! God, come on!'

The singing gave way to raucous laughter.

'Parfait, Madam Cay-zee!'

'Here, here, Jaitley… use your phone to take a picture for my kids, they're gonna be so psyched when they see where I am! Ready… ready? Oh wait, ha-ha-ha! I still got my finger on the button… Agents, get your butts up here and join the fun, that's an order! Whoa, look!'

A crescendo of noise crashed through O'Reilly's radio like an ocean wave – thousands of jubilant voices merging as one and filling the atrium, whose occupants recoiled sharply from the thunderous sound.

'*Oh my God! Oh my God, we scored! We scored again! We're actually gonna win this thing! I can't believe it, that was the most incredible thing I ever saw in my...*'

The volume of the North American crowd lowered in an instant, and the whoops and cries of joy were replaced with disgruntled murmurings.

'*What? No! Come on! You can't do that! It was in! Offside? What the hell does that mean? Guys, I gotta go, catch you later...*'

A ghostly resonance of Casey's voice and the roar of the crowd hung in the air for a brief moment before the silence returned.

Josh and Lexa shared a look of horror. Both knew what had happened. Agent Casey, for all her grit and bullish determination, had stepped into a hotbed of euphoria, the epicentre of the world's mass delusion at its highest point of rapture, and fallen instantly under its spell – along with DS Jaitley and the other agents too, presumably. If the situation weren't so laced with doom, it might actually have been funny.

Josh checked the SyBall App – seventy-five minutes, the same time he and Lexa had seen Emmett Baines' disallowed goal in the Flagship. The lump returned to his throat, bigger this time, built of weary exasperation and disbelief.

'Okay, new plan,' he said, squeezing the sketchpad into his jacket pocket. 'I will go and take care of the linesman; you finish up here.'

Lexa balked at the idea. 'Don't be ridiculous – if Casey can't resist then you've got no chance.'

'I'll be fine –'

'No!' Lexa leaned into him and whispered intently. 'I don't need the linesman taken care of, it's pointless. I only said that because I needed Casey's protection.'

Josh suspected as much from the start. He shook his head. He'd been so sure of his plan until then, but now Casey's interruption had caused doubt in his mind.

'But – but what if *this* is the thing we have to do differently? What if something goes wrong with the Vessel and it doesn't work, so it has to be the linesman?'

'Are you saying I don't know what I'm doing?'

'No, of course not, but surely anything is worth a shot?'

'Or,' she said, 'what if the difference this time is *you* don't survive? You go into that stadium and die with the rest of them. You don't meet my dad, I don't get sent back... then that's it. Over.'

Josh placed his hand on her upper arm. It stopped aching at once.

'They can't hurt me. Not today.'

The muscle in Lexa's arm quivered beneath his palm and she released a little gasp of breath. Letting her go, Josh took out his car keys and stuffed them into the pocket of her hooded jumper.

'Take the car when you've finished. I will come and find you afterwards, I promise.' Josh smiled and tilted his head towards the agents. 'Bring these guys along too, if you want.'

And then, entirely without intention, he cupped her face and peeled away, leaving her frozen to the spot.

The scream came as soon as his back was turned:

'He's one of them!'

'What!?'

459

Josh spun back around. Lexa was pointing at him like as though he were some kind of abominable beast that had found its way out of a dark forest.

'He's a spy! Stop him!'

Before Josh could protest any further, five strong pairs of hands grabbed him from behind and pulled him back. He tried to tear himself free, but the more he resisted the deeper their fingers dug into his muscles. As an arm came over his shoulder and wrapped across his torso like a seat belt, Cobb broke away from the pack and reached for his weapon.

'No guns!' Lexa screamed. 'He has information!'

'*Lexa! Lexa!* Please, you don't have to do this!'

Lexa ignored him and threw his car keys at Agent Cobb, who caught them one-handed, a grisly, satisfied smile drawing across his face.

'You need to get him way from here,' Lexa ordered, 'unless you want to end up like Agent Casey.'

Her eyes flicked towards Josh, and in a fleeting moment conveyed a message of sorrow and regret behind a mask of cold indifference. She turned, picked up the laptop and notebook and ascended the Impossible Stairs into the Vessel.

'*Lexa, no!*' Josh wailed, tears rising as he watched her disappear into the chamber, rejecting him yet again to save his life.

The Stairs morphed into their liquid state, closing up the entrance, and at once the Vessel began to spin. The truth of Lexa's plan became clear – it had formed the moment they returned from the Flagship and Josh hated himself for not realising at the time. She was too careful to rely on remote operation to interrupt the antenna's signal. The only way to guarantee success would be to pilot the Vessel herself.

The speed increased, the fins cutting through the air and leaving iridescent trails of white light in their wake. The Vessel lifted off the ground. Josh writhed and squirmed and fought with everything he had as the agents dragged him towards Lock Niss.

'Come on, kid, don't fight this!' one shouted.

'Let me go! She tricked you! I'm not a –'

'Save it, buddy!'

Agent Cobb ran around him and opened the rear door. Josh dug in his heels and arched his back until his top half was almost horizontal. The Vessel had already reached the top-most extent of the walls and was nearing the whirlwind of cloud running up through the antenna.'

'Wait! Look – look at my chest! There's nothing there! Look at my head – no markings!'

O'Reilly growled. 'You got one more chance to shut your face.'

Despite this, Josh felt the hands clawing at his shirt to rip it open and he yelped as another pulled his hair back. The light of the Core above was dazzling and he could no longer see the Vessel. Anger rose inside him; fierce, bitter and unwilling. Every squeeze of the agents' hands around his arms and legs pushed him further away from a point of self-awareness, the point where he had control of his own fury, until he cried out for a final time in a voice that felt like it belonged to some long-dormant side of him he never knew existed:

'*I am not a FUCKING EUPHORIVORE!*'

Josh had smashed through the walls of self-restraint and with it came that familiar feeling of energy pulsing through his body, every nerve electrified, every hair standing on end, a supernatural heightening of his senses. In an instant he was back in the Flagship, holding Lexa's hand with the lifestone between them and then soaring down through the Core towards her...

I can reach it... I can save her...

The pulse inside his hand was like some parasitic creature trying to burst through his skin. His arm felt like it was roasting in an oven, the sizzling heat somehow painless, expanding the flesh to twice the size but half the weight. A thunderbolt shot through his muscles, his arm swung and, before Josh realised he'd even made contact, Taylor, Nash and Kowalski were flying backwards through the air.

They landed as three crumpled heaps on the floor, the impact contorting their bodies. Josh's thoughts were coming to him as fast and as sharp as his reflexes. He pondered just how far they had gone with one sweep of his arm – *ten metres? Twenty?* He was already reaching over to grab Cobb, still steadfastly holding onto his other arm, lifting him off his feet and throwing him higher and further again in a perfect arc across the wide expanse of the atrium.

Cobb crashed against one of the mangled white branches that twisted its way out of the wall like a deformed root and let out a sickening yelp of pain. The branch shook and a few broken pieces fell with him. The agent's defensive instincts kicked in and he curled himself into a ball and hit the surface on his side – although the impact sound still suggested all the air had been forced out of his body.

Cobb's gurgling, rasping breath was the moment Josh knew he had stepped outside of himself, as he eschewed any remorse and turned instantly to his final opponent.

Agent Tom O'Reilly was already taking aim. Josh leapt forward and punched the dart gun out of his hand, sending it skidding along the ground until it was completely out of sight, and then threw O'Reilly over the bonnet for good measure.

Out of the corner of his eye he could see Cobb rising to his haunches with a wince and reaching again for his holster. Josh dived behind Lock Niss and a split second later heard two dull thuds followed by a low hiss, the car lowering at its rear corner as the air escaped the tyre.

If ever there were a line to be crossed, this was it. Forgetting himself, forgetting the situation, Josh stood straight back up, incensed.

'*Stop shooting my fu–*'

Cobb fired again.

There was a blistering zip through the air, and then –

'29

Ayo

*T*he ball sailed through the air.
The perfect strike; the perfect arc; the perfect moment. Struck so sweetly it surprised even him; his legend confirmed by one flawless connection...

PJ turned off the taps and the daydream drained from his mind like the soapy water disappearing down the plughole.

Can I really give all that up?

He stepped out of the shower and buried his face in the towel, savouring the moment of privacy with nothing but the darkness staring back at him. Water dripped from his body and landed in little pools around his feet. His toes curled in the cool wetness.

The story would be believable enough; a player so caught up in the excitement he'd rushed in the bathroom and slipped over. The floor was cold and hard, all he'd need was to jump, bend his legs and land on his knees. But hurting yourself took guts, a conscious rejection of every natural instinct. PJ was brave on the pitch, yet in his solitude he was ashamed of how frightened he was. He wrapped the towel around his waist and walked into his room.

464

'You took your time,' said Evie Longford.

'Wakes the muscles up,' PJ replied, gazing into the mirror at the smooth lines of his toned, lean frame.

His dark skin was damp still, shimmering in the strong morning light penetrating through the closed curtains.

He was perfection.

Evie slid out from beneath the ruffled bedsheets. 'Well, at least one of us got to see the other topless.'

In the reflection of the mirror, PJ caught her wry, incredulous smile.

'Keep your voice down,' he said, drowning in the shame.

Despite his reputation, PJ had broken one of his strictest rules. Nights before matches were meant for focus, mental preparation and sleep. But without some form of distraction to see him through until morning, PJ knew the events of the previous evening would keep him awake and restless to the point of madness.

Josh Pittman hadn't been much of a footballer, but they did share more than just a name; they'd both been caught in a situation beyond reason and they'd both been left with difficult choices. Their little game of one-on-one had relieved some of the pressure and taken his mind off Ernie Strong and whether he ought to feel revulsion or grief at his death.

But then Josh had left, using his hand to open up the 'Vessel', as he'd called it, and telling PJ to *do what you think is right*, before diving inside and exploding into thin air.

What kind of advice was that? How was that supposed to help him? If the world was hanging on what PJ did – or didn't – do up until the end of the match, then a little more specific guidance might have been useful.

Screw it, he'd thought.

He'd already lost control of his name, and now his life's ambition had gone too. Were there any perks to being the Hitman? If he snuck Evie in, then he'd either get his release, or he'd be caught by the training ground staff and discover how indispensable he was to the team. Was he too valuable to be benched for the Final? And if so, would that mean nothing he did would stop Josh's prophecy from coming true?

With these questions swirling around his head, he'd sent his text to her less than half an hour later, as the Americans ran around blaming one another for letting Josh Pittman go.

It was late by the time the hire-car had negotiated the narrow lane and dropped Evie off behind a thicket of trees at the rear end of the camp. Everyone was still up, the players and staff long past curfew, only now they were too busy arguing with the agents over why they were suddenly all leaving to notice PJ sneaking her in. Now, hours later, Evie was standing in front of him, partially clothed, surveying him, analysing him with the tip of her tongue between her lips.

She was much shorter than PJ, with bright blonde hair still fixed in tight curls despite the night spent pressed against his pillow. For all intents and purposes, PJ had won the bet with Troy Simpson, but he felt as happy about it as he did about anything else right now.

A little part of him wanted nothing more than to drag her back onto the mattress for no other reason than to shut out the world for the next twenty-four hours; and from her stance it seemed she would let him.

But as much as he couldn't bring himself to fall in the bathroom, so again he couldn't stomach the idea of chickening out. Besides, Evie hadn't come because she was flattered, but because she was intrigued. It was clear she thought their encounter to be funny. PJ might have been physically sublime, but in all other ways he was inferior. Evie was well-spoken, intelligent, experienced; young enough to savour life but old enough to be jaded by it. And last night, when he'd changed his mind at the last second, she had stayed beside him with an ironic eye-roll for yet another of life's little disappointments.

'You alright there, Junior?'

PJ must have been contemplating his thoughts for longer than he realised.

'Don't call me that,' he shot back, finding he couldn't meet her eyes as he spoke. 'I'm fine.'

'Good,' she said, a linger of sharp regret in her voice. She slipped on the flowery summer dress she'd discarded in hope across the bed. 'You could have cancelled. Saved us both the bother. I'm not mad. Today is the biggest day of your life, the last thing I'd want is to be the distraction who becomes a 'distraction'... but if there's nothing else...?'

PJ nodded. 'Yeah, no... I've got to get going. We'll be out of here by ten. Give it an hour and the place'll be empty.'

'An *hour?*'

Five minutes later, PJ left Evie Longford remonstrating in his room, and after handing his suitcase to the coach driver, headed down to the breakfast hall. No-one registered his appearance or questioned his lateness; the lively hubbub of matchday banter was absent from along the rows of dining tables at which the squad were sat in their tracksuits. Instead, their heads were buried in their meals and the only sound filling the air was the clatter of cutlery against crockery.

PJ took a tray up to the service counter and helped himself to a bowl of porridge, a few slices of rye bread and a bottle of water, then sat at the end of the nearest row next to Jed Daynes, the Lancastrian right-back with whom he'd never had a personal conversation. That wasn't about to change.

On the wall at the far end a large BKDFA spiral crest hung above the main table, with occupants sat facing out into the hall like the bridal party at a wedding reception. George Castle was rising from his seat in the centre of the table, flanked on either side by his coaching team, his weary, sleepless expression visible from every seat in the room. Utensils were downed, heads turned, and silence descended.

George surveyed the room, looking up and down the tables until he caught eyes with PJ, his superstar, passing a message through the silence that was halfway between sympathy and contempt. PJ stared back at the well-worn face; the ghost of the manager's past glories hidden beneath the lines.

'Bloody mind-blowing, in't it?' George said out to the hall, breaking his hold on PJ. 'Last night of all nights.'

Murmurs of agreement spread along the tables. Heads nodded. PJ did nothing; something was off – small acts of vulnerability were not part of George Castle's character.

The manager took a deep breath and continued. 'So then, hands up. Who wants to know what it was that came in here and tried to upset us? Go on, I said hands up!'

Twenty arms shot into the air, elevated by whoops of pumped-up rage and resentment. The hall became as animated as usual; overlapping conversations broke out at every table, their hard-edged words piercing the air. An aggressive grin drew across George's lips, turning to a sneer as he silenced the room with his hands.

He leant forward. 'You bloody cowards. I should cut the lot of you. You wanna talk about last night? *Last night?* You should be thinking about today! You should be asking yourselves, "what I am gonna do to win? What's it gonna take? Because me, I wanna be the hero, I wanna take my place in history!" That should be the only thing on your minds right now!'

George spluttered as he spoke, his cheeks turning red, the anger burning out of his eyes. PJ recognised the manager had been robbed of a moment; this wasn't the matchday breakfast speech he'd wanted to give.

'Ernie Strong is dead! Alright?' He slammed his fist into the table. A spoon tinkled as it jumped inside his empty bowl. A glass of water tipped over. 'So, I don't wanna hear "Who was he? *What* was he?" Who gives a toss? North America don't! He's gone. The lass what killed him's been nicked, and that's the end of it. Anything else – *anything* else – can wait 'til tomorrow when we are the champions of the world. You got that?'

Jacob Terrier stood bolt upright from his seat and applauded, his dreadlocks swinging as his lone claps echoed off the high ceiling.

'Finish your bloody breakfasts. We leave in an hour.'

George Castle slumped back into his seat, picked up his glass and refilled it casually from the pitcher.

PJ's mouth went dry. Only now could he see the pair sitting further along the top table: they were Julia Castle, George's wife, and their daughter, Mary-Jane. Despite what he'd said, George appeared to have been spooked enough by the events to want his family where he could see them. PJ couldn't blame him, especially when the grizzled old bulldog had been blessed with two of the classiest women you were ever likely to meet. Even as she slurped down her porridge, Julia was exuding an air of subtle sophistication that made PJ feel guilty about leaving Evie Longford in his room, while Mary-Jane was as mesmerising as ever; though she was clearly upset about something.

She looked straight at him, twisting a strand of long brown hair between her fingers, but her gaze was lost in the middle-distance. Her forlorn expression complimented the simple features of her round face as much as her smile did.

PJ began to eat very quickly. Her sadness had spurred him into action, though part of himself was telling him not to bother. Mary-Jane Castle was off limits – another self-imposed rule. Not because she was George's daughter or Ben's sister, or because she had a boyfriend, but because she was beautiful; effortlessly, classically beautiful.

The boyfriend was an actor, or an artist, or something else just as pointless. PJ had often seen the two of them together, mostly at the Castles' enormous house, on days when the whole squad had been invited round for pizza and team-building exercises. In the evening they'd all retreat to the home cinema on the top floor and Mary-Jane would giggle as Ashley, or Ashton, or whatever his name was, sat there in his stupid hat, pointing out plot-holes and gabbing on about Shakespearean influences in modern cinema. PJ wasn't the only one who couldn't stand him, the whole team were irritated by his presence – except for Jacob Terrier, who true to form sat staring at him like an expectant puppy, hanging on every word without a clue what was being said.

The truth was Mary-Jane favoured the guy's intelligence over his moderate looks and slender physique. PJ simply couldn't match him and soon his jealousy became the driving force behind his ambitions, both on and off the pitch.

Do what you're good at, he'd told himself, *even if it puts you further out of her league.*

With every goal scored and every girl bedded those lingering thoughts of Mary-Jane were pushed further away. But now here she was again, too lost in her sorrow to eat her breakfast.

Her father dismissed the hall and PJ ducked and weaved through the vacating herd, lifting his head for a glimpse of that silky-smooth hair amid the crew cuts and dreadlocks. When he finally caught up with her, PJ was back out in the corridor, at the base of the stairwell which led to the dormitories where Evie was still waiting.

'Mary-Jane…'

He went to touch her gently on the shoulder but pulled away when she stopped and turned at the sound of his voice. Her normally bright face was paler than usual and she was red around the eyes. She was more beautiful than he remembered, even without the ethereal glow of his daydreams there to compliment her gentle features.

'Oh, Nathan. Hi.' Mary-Jane drew herself up to full height in an effort to look composed. 'I was sorry to hear about Ernie.'

'Yeah, it's a bit of a mad one, but... I, er...' PJ stuttered, wanting to move the conversation on without sounding blasé about his dead bodyguard. 'Listen, tell me to butt out or whatever, but are you okay?'

'Not really. Asher dumped me.' Her eyes rolled as though trying to cover her embarrassment. 'By text.'

The rush of opportunity flooded PJ's mind. He'd already broken one rule since last night.

'Stupid bastard.'

'Hey!'

Mary-Jane tried to look angry, though afterwards he spotted the tiniest upward curl of her lips.

'Nah, I mean it. Guy thought he was so clever; he just gave up the best thing in his life. He doesn't deserve you.' PJ paused. He was normally so cool in these situations, but today he was sweating. 'No-one does. You're too good for 'em. But that don't mean that one day you ain't gonna meet the guy, who like... comes close, you know? And that dude is gonna be the luckiest man on Earth.'

Mary-Jane turned away from him and looked out the window and across the training grounds.

'That's sweet of you to say.'

There was caution in her voice, a sense she was uncomfortable. PJ shifted his feet. He wondered if he should leave, but as he lifted his head, he caught sight of Ben Castle, the man-mountain, standing at the other end of the corridor, glaring at him through narrowed eyes. PJ felt bizarrely compelled to keep going.

'Look, I know what people think of me.' He glanced up the stairway to where the actress would be cursing his name. 'And I ain't saying it's not true... but if you ever need a friend –'

Mary-Jane retreated into herself just enough for PJ to feel awash with shame.

'I mean it… a *friend*, a proper friend, someone to talk to, then… I'm always here. I would never…'

PJ broke off – he couldn't think how to end that sentence without revealing everything he was starting to hate about himself.

'Thank you, Nathan, that's sweet,' she said.

His heart sunk. While the smile she gave him was genuine, and his friends-only offer was sincere, PJ could tell by the distance of her reply that their relationship would never go any further.

Come the afternoon, and his absolutism had transferred onto the pitch. The journey to the stadium had been like a slow-moving blur, each passing second increasing his sense of dread. North America's coach was already waiting outside the team entrance as they arrived, its brightly-coloured decoration almost like a statement of intent that whatever happened, their opponents were prepared to put on a show.

In the locker-room, as PJ pulled on his ugly blue kit, George Castle had picked up where he'd left off at breakfast with a team-talk that was heavy on platitudes and light on tactics: the basic gist was that their opponents were about the worst team ever to contest a major final and victory was certain.

And as at breakfast, PJ barely registered the words. Everything felt horrible; the rumble of thunder outside the tunnel; the walk out onto the grass and the blaze of light and noise; the height of the stands, his fearful perspective bending their shape as though the stadium were very slowly falling on top of him; the crowd, whose roars of encouragement were more like heckles and jeers, laughing at him, mocking him for his insecurities.

Even the handshake with Ray Albright felt an unbearable experience. The Prime Minister's eyes were a shimmering emerald green, his cheeks rosy-red, and up close the famed kindness of the old man's face seemed an illusion masked by the forest of bushy white hair. His little dog, like a clone of her owner's beard come to life, sniffed each player's boots as she trundled along the line-up, only to single PJ out by taking a pee on the turf in front of him.

He wondered if he should take the chance to tell Albright everything he knew, everything Josh Pittman had told him about the Euphorivores; perhaps this was the moment he *'did what he thought was right'*. But before PJ could correlate his thoughts, the Prime Minister had released his hand, given him a half-serious scolding for the Evie Longford advert and then told him to have the game of his life.

But he didn't.

Instead, PJ was having a torrid match. Mary-Jane had made him realise his fate had nothing to do with him. He couldn't do what he thought was right because his every move was being informed by the actions of those around him. It had always been this way, but only now could he really see it. Football was about tiny adjustments and quick decisions, about making your opponent play the way you wanted them to; it was an unconscious, instinctive tactic that every player employed. If your team were in control, then you felt confident and powerful, but if you were being pegged back then you became more aware of the manipulation, and for PJ this heightened the sad truths he knew deep down.

From the kick-off, whenever Michael Tannen, the defender assigned to mark him, came in for a tackle and he was forced to pass instead of shoot, it was like a new arbiter in his life – an agent, a parent, a coach, a failed actress – deciding what his name should be this week. Then, after Emmett Baines had scored and PJ had to play further up the field, away from his preferred position, the discomfort was like trying to reinvent himself as some half-decent guy in front of Mary-Jane and feeling ashamedly awkward. And when his resultant close-range shot was easily palmed over the bar by Jesper Lykke, PJ again remembered Josh Pittman, holding off the advancing agents with a raised hand and telling him to take responsibility for things over which he had no control.

Although one thing was certain: if PJ were destined to score the winner, then an equaliser would have to come first. With just five minutes of normal time left to go and the score still one-nil, he felt a glimmer of bittersweet hope that North America might actually see this one out, especially when Troy's glancing shot deflected wide for a corner off Roberto del Bosque's knee.

PJ hung around the edge of the D, dancing about in little side-steps in a half-willed effort to shake off Tannen. This was his default position for corner kicks – it gave Vincent Lyons, waiting at the flag, the option of laying the ball off to PJ, who would run to meet it and shoot from range. But Lyons, the precision dead-baller with little time for players who were off their game, opted to whip the ball directly into the crowded penalty area. PJ knew he ought to run forward and join the pack; but instead, he stayed back, either unable or unwilling to move, and watched as the ball swept into the six-yard box.

Bodies leapt like pogo sticks to head the ball in one direction or the other. Jesper Lykke, his eyes following the trajectory like a hawk, darted from his goalmouth and sprang into the air, the ball destined for his outstretched hands. The save seemed inevitable, even as Danny Holt in his last-gasp desperation shoved the goalkeeper square in the back and sent him tumbling to the ground.

The ball dropped to the grass and was knocked around a tangle of legs all lashing out to get some kind of meaningful contact. Everything was happening so quickly that Lykke was still scrambling to his feet when Chris Wilson scuffed his clearance shot and the ball trickled harmlessly into the path of Troy Simpson, who barely had to look as he hooked the ball into the roof of the net.

The explosion of the crowd merged with the muffled crunch of PJ's heart thumping in his chest. Celebrating the goal was like being forced to dance at gunpoint. His legs became disembodied from his conscious mind as he sprinted with his teammates towards Troy, who only had a second to stand with his arms folded and smile smugly into the nearest camera before they all bundled on top of him. Trapped beneath the crush of sweaty footballers and the wall of noise building up around him, PJ felt his life slipping away.

The only solace to be found as he lumbered about the pitch was in his opponents' reaction to the goal. North America were in complete control from the restart, winning back possession at every turn and engaging in some clever build-up play in the home team's half of the pitch. Yet their tiredness showed in the final third, and though the entire stadium seemed to wince as Lamoureux and Glover forced Ben Castle into a string of late saves, they had lost too much of their clinical edge to take Mary-Jane's brother anywhere out of his comfort zone.

And so the moment came.

Ben collected a low, easy shot as above him the electronic scoreboard ticked over into the ninetieth minute. He stood and bounced the ball with one hand while urging his team to move further down the pitch with the other. It was a dummy move – the North American players, expecting a long kick, had backed off too, giving Ben the space to instead roll the ball to centre-back Sam Lockard just a few yards ahead. On the touchline, between the two dugouts, the fourth official held aloft his indicator board and signalled for a single minute of extra time.

With Lamoureux approaching, Lockard looked quickly to where Glover was closing down David Barrie on his left, then turned and stroked the ball across the path of Alex Shoreham and onto the feet of Jed Daynes. Ahead of Daynes, Reuben Mayfield, was already making his run – backwards – down the right flank, screaming for the ball. Behind him Simon Fuentes was waiting and, sensing the danger, Jed lifted his head to pick out Danny Holt unmarked in the centre circle, who blistered forward.

PJ knew what was happening.

Daynes instead of Barrie. Holt instead of Mayfield. Split-second decisions were building into a picture already painted. Danny should have been sent off for his push on Jesper Lykke, and everyone knew PJ was his go-to man. They had known each other since childhood; they'd come through the academy system together and played with and against each other on countless occasions. No two players were said to know each other's game better than Daniel Holt and Nathan Pitman Junior.

It was surely then, over. There was no way Danny would pass to anyone else. The crowd believed this too and a great roar of encouragement rose like a wave and flooded onto the pitch.

90:29... 90:30...

The inevitability spurred PJ's body into life, though his mind remained frozen. He made a looping run, angling for the best interception of Danny's pass, knowing where the ball would travel before anyone else did.

Except the ball never arrived.

In a moment that lasted less than a second, PJ and Danny locked eyes. It was as though the awkward momentum of the game had broken their intuitive bond, and PJ could read the apology written across his friend's face as he twisted and cut the pass across the pitch to Jacob Terrier.

Another instant decision, but one PJ couldn't comprehend; nor could Jacob, who collected the ball with the sickened expression of a young child who'd just been given a pair of socks for Christmas. PJ realised the truth. Jacob's baleful reaction had exposed the manky idiot's true nature, a realisation sharpened by a sudden memory of that odd feeling whenever he and Ernie Strong were nearby, a heaviness in the air, a stillness. While a nifty lob over to best mate Troy Simpson seemed the best option, Jacob chose to correct Danny's mistake with a ludicrous curve ball which swept coolly around the defensive line and into PJ's path. Suddenly PJ was running with the ball at his feet, as easy and natural as it had ever been…

But then he was being crushed again, the towering walls of the stadium collapsing on top of him by the weight of expectation. His mind fogged over, unable to tell real from unreal, and as the terror embraced him his senses faltered and the screams of *'Shoot!'* faded into an impossible silence…

Defenders were closing in: if he shot now from outside the area, if he gave the world what it wanted and unleashed the Hitman, then they wouldn't get to him in time – only the keeper to beat…

What do I do…?

Help me…

PJ was gripped by a sudden desire to be in the arms of a woman. One particular woman. Not Evie Longford, nor even Mary-Jane Castle, but another who out of nowhere had appeared to him like a ghostly vision the evening before, her hair flowing as though she were underwater. He had tried to speak, yet her smile had reassured him there was nothing to be said, and all the stresses and burdens that gate-crashed his life had floated away, and he'd felt happy. A second later she was gone, and in the lingering confusion PJ had wandered out into the training pitch to breathe the cool evening air and thereafter played one-on-one with Josh Pittman. He wanted the woman to cradle him like she did when he was little, when he fell over in the playground, the place where he'd honed the skills that had led him to this point. He wanted her to sing softy to him and call him 'Ayo'.

Somewhere off to his right he heard a loud crash followed by a grotesque squeal. Out the corner of his eye, a blur of movement – a spectator had run onto the pitch. Another twist in the tale, another flush of hope: the referee would have to stop the match or, if not, then at least if PJ missed – by accident or on purpose – he could blame the invader.

90:52... 90:53...

The little figure was heading along the touchline towards the goal. Jesper Lykke hadn't noticed him, he had eyes only for PJ. Closer he came, and PJ couldn't help but look.

Oh no...

A flash of eye contact passed between them, too quick to communicate anything of value. He was moving unnaturally fast, blistering towards goal.

Screw it.

PJ planted his foot and swung his leg back.

'I love you, Mum.'

A flawless connection.

The ball sailed through the air…

90:59... 91:00...

'30

The Conservatory Group

The ball flew beneath the bar and rolled down the back of the net.

Across the world, in every country, in a multitude of languages, commentators launched into a hyperbolic frenzy – conduits of exhilaration between one quick, narrow moment and a grateful global audience, who were celebrating Emmett Baines' disallowed goal as though the British Kingdom had already won.

75:46… 75:47…

Not far from where Ben Castle was ruefully picking out the ball from his goal, Asher Bloom tried his best to look excited. In front of him people were dancing. Others were clapping in time to a guttural chant of *'Bee-kay dee-eff-ay!'* which echoed off the wide sloping ceiling. Asher joined in a little, shoulders swinging, toes tapping, but he kept his movements slight and inconspicuous, standing with his back against the wall, like a debutante waiting to be offered the next dance.

Hopefully the effort alone would be enough to deflect attention away from him. The celebrations made him acutely aware of the fragility of Felix Gently's rendezvous plan. The members of the Conservatory Group had been told to arrive at the stadium at different times throughout the day, and once there had to keep walking, indiscriminately at first, either around the perimeter or up into the tiers and out onto the stands. There they could take in the atmosphere and extract a modicum of excitement from the day. If they saw another 'Conservator' strolling about, they were to turn and dive into the nearest toilets. Consequently, Asher had taken note of the comparative sizes and hygiene standards of cubicles around the stadium. (On the whole pretty good: a clean toilet was a happy toilet). Then, with thirty minutes to go, he'd washed his hands for the final time and descended the tiers to begin circling the ground floor concourse, pretending not to notice the sub-groups growing larger with every circuit.

In the mix of the crowd, the resistant band of artists, dignitaries and sporting elite were huddled together, dressed unremarkably in jeans and t-shirts, their faces hidden beneath sunglasses and baseball caps, their minds projecting conversation to give the impression of gentle banter. Wigs, flags, and face-paint had been forbidden, as had any outlandish hairdos – beehives included. To Asher, this had only resulted in making Winsome Free appear more visible, standing out like a sore thumb as her shimmering strands of blood red hair bounced invitingly around her shoulders with each footstep.

He too felt unnecessarily naked, having been denied his hat and forced to rely on his fledgling quiff to cover his head markings. On account of his youth (and Winsome's aversion to his reckless dress sense), Asher had also been instructed to wear a replica British

Kingdom football shirt, which he squirmed around of inside as though it were an ill-fitting hessian sack.

The whole affair was becoming too much of a risk, he'd concluded. Exposure threatened at every turn; the Group had underestimated the weight of people outside the terraces and should have elected to simply turn up together at the last moment. His paranoia pervaded, and he'd become certain that with every lap of the stadium a programme seller (human, presumably, but no less devout) was gazing at him for just that little bit longer. While he could imagine worse things than being caught, it had seemed sensible to break protocol and remain in one place until he was summoned.

Less clear was whether his decision to stop so close to an imperious bronze statue of George Castle had been intentional or not. He had been blindly following the path of his unconscious mind since leaving the manager's house the day before, but now that his eyes lingered on the wobbly, ageing features staring back at him with smug disdain, he couldn't look away.

'Whatever reason it is you're doing this,' the statue seemed to be saying, 'I hope it's worth breaking my little girl's heart.'

To that, at least, Asher had his answer. Hating something was not the same as regretting it.

– Asher Bloom.

His name landed crisp and clear inside his head, as though he were being called from across an empty room. Directly ahead he saw Faith Goodwill pass without acknowledgement, her militaristic gait detached from the voice that had beckoned him. The remaining members of her cluster followed, weaving their way through the crowd, preferring to break themselves up into threes and fours rather than move forward as a single block. He tried not to wince as he pushed off the wall, but his lower back was sore from the handle rubbing against his skin.

Back in Goodwill's conservatory, Asher had been quick to place himself in her group. She had welcomed him into a home full of personal comforts that wasn't truly hers – she was an imposter, who just like him preferred the illusion to the reality. Her articulate, quick-step manner was infused with a warmth of spirit that made him feel comfortable in her presence. He wondered whether a life at sea had broadened Goodwill's horizons in the same way life with Mary-Jane had done so for him. But, moreover, he'd chosen the Admiral because she seemed the least likely to refuse him. Winsome Free would almost certainly have turned him away and Felix Gently seemed the kind of fearful lapdog who wouldn't want to upset her. Still, Asher couldn't help but wonder if a compromise had been reached between the group leaders which led to him being chosen last to merge with the pack. Was the extra waiting time supposed to give him greater opportunity to bail out?

Goodwill's flock circled the concourse one last time, passing the George Castle statue again and stopping a little way ahead where the sloping roof suddenly gave way to a low flat ceiling. There were no tunnels out onto the stands along this stretch of thoroughfare, yet he could still hear the muffled rumble of the crowd permeating through the walls.

A heavy lump caught in Asher's throat as he followed his co-conspirators towards a tall glass partition, behind which he could see a silver-plated escalator rising through a gap in the ceiling. A door set into the glass was open but its passage was blocked by a velvety red rope barrier like at the entrance to an exclusive nightclub, an illusion helped on its way by the scruffy-haired man in a pinstripe waistcoat, who stood behind a bar just inside the door pouring out glasses of champagne. The lobby was small, with room for only half the group to cross the threshold, with the rest trailing out onto the concourse. Stuck at the back, Asher noted a paper sign stuck neatly to a low wooden pedestal:

Sorry folks! This area is closed for a private event.
Don't feel sad – even the Queen's not invited!
Have a fantastic day!
#UnionJAC

The bartender looked up and beamed a wide smile, exposing a crooked set of teeth and rippling his patchy wisps of beard.

– *Admiral Goodwill! You're here! So good to see you, come in!*

The bartender surveyed his guests and waved an inviting hand over the sparkling drinks. A few obliged, draining their flutes in one go. One or two made towards the escalator, but Goodwill stopped them with a commanding shake of the head.

The bartender addressed her directly:

– *I was worried you weren't coming. I've been waiting for this chance. You might remember me; our parents knew each other.*

Asher had never thought it possible to sound quite so feckless when communicating telepathically, but this guy had it nailed. Goodwill looked at him without a hint of recognition or interest.

– *Are Baroness Free and Secretary Gently here?*

485

The bartender responded as though he'd just been asked to pilot a rocket to the moon.

– *Yes! They arrived shortly before yourselves.*

– *Jolly good, then we are the last. Be a good lad and lock the door behind us.*

The moon mission had been cancelled.

– *L-lock the door?*

Again, non-verbal nervous stuttering was a new one on Asher.

– *Yes, is there a problem?*

The bartender scanned the faces before him, looking for a smirk or a word of reassurance that this was not a serious request. When neither came, he straightened his back and spoke firmly into the collection of empty glasses.

– *Forgive me Admiral, but I've been refusing people entry all afternoon with a cheery smile and a fond farewell. I've had no problem. Surely such an impersonal obstruction on this most historic of occasions would constitute an unnecessary violation of the Guiding Principles that have been so vital to our cause.*

His eyes flicked up and then down again. It was obvious he'd been reciting a prepared line from memory. Goodwill checked her watch.

– *Yes, well, considering that in precisely six minutes and seventeen seconds we're going to kill nearly every human on the planet, I suspect we no longer need to concern ourselves with dampening their spirits.*

– *My orders come directly from the Prime Minister…*

– *…who now has bigger things to deal with.*

Goodwill paused and considered the young Euphorivore, angling her head to get a better look at him.

– What do they call you?

The bartender looked up and tried everything to avoid Goodwill's eyes without appearing to do so. A shiftiness rippled through the group.

– Chase Hope.

The director of a prestigious New York art gallery laughed.

– Who authorised that?

Goodwill scowled at the director, who slunk away sheepishly. She leant forward, resting her interlocked fingers on the bar.

– Now, listen here, Chase. I do remember you – at least, I remember your mother. As I recall she had a reputation for harbouring somewhat unrealistic ambitions for her underwhelming son. She asked me to offer him a naval commission. Naturally I refused, but it seems someone else in seniority was fool enough to allow your stupid name and position you behind this bar, wiping glasses for years in preparation for a single afternoon of responsibility.

– Baroness Free made the arrangements.

– Ah, yes. Winsome does have a weakness for youth.

At the back of the group, Asher couldn't help but feel a little reproached. Was that a dig at him? Goodwill was supposed to be cool.

– So, what if I were to report back to your dear old mum that on her little boy's big day, he purposely disobeyed a direct order from a senior officer? Hmm? We share many similarities with our human crop, including the certain knowledge that the fury and vengeance of one's superiors is nothing compared to the reprimand of a disappointed mother.

Hope audibly gulped.

– Secrecy ensures success, young Chase. As a military commander, let me tell you that it is sometimes better to hide than to disguise.

The Admiral leant in close to the bartender's face.

– So lock. The fucking. Door.

– I... I don't have a key.

– Improvise.

Chase Hope scurried from around his bar as Goodwill smoothed down her jacket, checked her hair bun and stepped onto the escalator. The Conservatory Group fell in behind her, ascending in single file with all the courtesies and 'you-go-firsts' expected of those operating in civilised society, leaving Asher to bring up the rear. He walked forward, but then was startled by the sound of nearby doors crashing open, followed by a wail of roller-coaster cheers and a rumble of collapsing bodies; the crowd outside had burst though the entrances and were in fits of debauchery.

Everything was descending into chaos.

He didn't need the display screens around the concourse or the delirium of the spectators to tell him what had happened. For Asher, Troy Simpson's equaliser brought with it a grim air of inevitability. The last of the variables had come and gone and only certainty remained.

Passing through the glass door and onto the escalator, he felt a pang of remorse shoot through him. He glanced back at Chase Hope hastily wedging a bar stool under the door handles. For sure, he was a Euphorivore on the wrong side, but nice enough, keen, and completely out of his depth – he probably didn't deserve what was coming to him.

The stairs levelled out and a tsunami of voices crashed down on him as he alighted onto the white-marble floor of a large room; a restaurant, perhaps, but with the bare tables pushed away to the walls. A few besuited Euphorivores were even dancing, though the music must have been playing over a private frequency only they could hear. Or they were drunk. One of these Asher recognised as Mark Kemp, the ex-footballer and pundit, who'd arrived as part of the first wave of operatives whose names weren't quite as obvious. He was gyrating around like the best man at the latter part of a wedding reception.

Asher crept forward and adjusted himself to the space, tuning out the unwanted snippets of conversation that flowed in and out of his head. His stomach felt hollow, the very air inside him making him feel sick. In the centre of the room, Faith Goodwill was shaking hands with the other members of the Conservatory Group as though she hadn't seen them in months. Asher gravitated towards her, mingling carefully, keeping as many bodies as possible between himself and Winsome Free, whose flash of red hair he'd noticed the moment he stepped off the escalator. It wasn't long, however, before a parting of presidents allowed her narrow eyes to catch his. Her thin eyebrows rose; a conveyance more of surprise than disappointment. A sense her estimations had been proved wrong.

– *Good luck.*

Then she turned away and never looked back. Asher gazed around, desperate to appear nonplussed by it all.

The far wall of the restaurant was taken up in its entirety by a huge window with a panoramic view of the pitch. A two-way mirror, he presumed, transparent only from their side, and sound-proof too, with the bellows of the crowd nothing more than a distant rumble, as if he were watching live coverage with the volume down.

Below him the teams were chasing each other about the grass, the match still very much in play as it entered its closing stages. In the top corner, Asher could just make out the electronic scoreboard overhanging the stands:

BKM 1 – 1 NAM | 87:32

Did it really need to be *this* tight?

– *Heavens, man! Why on Earth would I consider Rio a failure? We all got fed, didn't we?*

Asher jumped. There was no tuning out this voice; this one broadcast on all networks. Warm, jovial, and truly terrifying.

The Prime Minister stood a few feet from Asher, larger than life, decked in a burgundy red cardigan with gold diamonds across the chest, with a glass of brandy and surrounded by a few well-groomed lackeys. His white beard was bushier than ever, enveloping everything below his nose, down his chest and over the summit of his substantial belly.

He looked older than Asher remembered and seemed a little wobbly on his feet, but as usual he wasn't using his cane to support himself. Instead, he was waving the handle with its kaleidoscopic collection of tiny stones in the face of the soon-dead upstart who'd dared to ask him about Brazil.

– *Didn't we? Yes? Answer me!*

– *Yes, sir, forgive me.*

The upstart was shaking, the orange cordial sloshing over the edge of his tumbler.

– *All this stuff and nonsense about the Brazilians surviving. All I know is how bloody good it tasted! Drove them potty up there. High as kites, they were!*

– *So, you don't believe the trespass rumours?*

The second question came from a far braver source; a tall woman who much less spilt her drink than sipped it casually.

– *No, Temperance, I do not! Riding on the back of Firebreathers? Ridiculous! How the blazes would they have got up there to begin with? No, nothing but a mass hallucination – and frankly I'm looking forward to plenty more of it! Now then, how long have we got?*

– *Three minutes, Prime Minister.*

– *Three...? Confound it, Newhart! Why didn't you say something instead of letting this bunch of bootlickers blather on at me?*

Then he spoke:

'Come along, Apple Blossom'

The white-highland terrier had been asleep on a chair behind the Prime Minister, enjoying the quiet environment provided by the telepathic hubbub, but at the sound of her master's voice she sprang into life and bounded onto the floor. After an initial figure of eight through Albright's legs, the excitable pup began sniffing the shoes of those around her, only to stop and fix Asher with a frosty glare.

She knows. She definitely knows.

Apple Blossom wasn't the only one to react to the anomaly of audible speech; everyone in the room took it as their cue to shut up and turn to face their leader. By commanding the attention of the room, Albright seemed somehow to grow in stature; he couldn't see those at the back, but he didn't need to. He was front and centre inside every head.

– *Right then. No doubt you've all been expecting some stirring speech befitting the occasion. Some great oratory on our long journey to this day. Well, I'm sorry to disappoint you, but there isn't the bloody time because most of you were late. Instead, I'll give you the highlights. Today is about endings. The end of this match is the end of their world. The end of their world is the end of our hunger. The end of our hunger is the end of our exile. Salvation, as promised, is at hand. There you are. Chew on that for a bit.*

Albright downed the last of his brandy in one go.

– *Oh, and one other thing, my dearest folk. If any of you attempt to pet my dog before the final whistle, I will personally throttle the life out of you.*

Albright looked down to where Apple Blossom sat beside his feet. 'I'm afraid you've made me rather soft in my old age.'

Apple Blossom waggled her tail and yapped excitedly. Asher watched the old man's face as he realised his mistake; Albright had just admitted his vulnerability to the entire room. The cracks were beginning to show. Survivors in Rio; trespassers back home; the hidden truth of an 'alternative option' to the Harvest. Everything had been an elaborate cover-up, even amongst Albright's own people.

But with only a minute to go, lazy duplicity (*'a mass hallucination!'*) was probably enough to see them through, and nearly all turned a blind eye as the Prime Minister then kicked his dog in the stomach. She scampered away, whimpering, and hid herself beneath a chair as the Euphorivores moved towards the window in nervous unison, the rife anticipation in their voices a dizzying hum pervading the hidden recesses of Asher's mind.

In the perhiperary of his vision, he could see the Conservatory Group members moving into place. While Faith Goodwill shared some private joke with Temperance Newhart (Asher caught the words 'Simpson' and 'deluded'), Winsome was discreetly wiping her hand on her trouser leg following a sincere handshake with Massimo Fortuna, the wrinkly-faced Chancellor of the Exchequer with a near-orange tan and a pompadour hairstyle. Between them at least a hundred other pairings formed, each a seemingly casual conversation on a wonderful occasion.

As a low-ranking rebel, Asher hadn't been given a specific mark; he just had to pick someone out and start talking. With little consideration, he'd made a beeline for the junior minister – the one who'd asked Ray Albright about Brazil – and slightly hated himself for choosing an easy target whose days were probably numbered anyway.

– *Asher! Asher, my boy!*

Asher froze with fear. There was a split second of silence as Ben Castle made a superb save to stop Tom Glover's blistering shot from hitting the back of the net. A ripple of *'Oos'* rang nauseously around his head as he turned to find the Prime Minister beckoning him forward, seemingly unaware of Felix Gently's attempts to get his attention.

– *Over here, lad! Hop to it!*

That hollow feeling in his stomach was now a heavy lump in his chest. Gently persisted, his polite words a preamble to a fuller conversation to which Albright reacted like a fly buzzing around his ears. Halfway along Asher's short but horror-stricken journey, Albright snapped.

– *What? What do you want, damn you?!*

Gently recoiled, then stuttered.

– *I just w-wanted to… to congratulate you –*

– *Oh! Don't give me that twaddle, you pathetic little creep. I've got enough tongues up my backside, I don't need one as wretched as yours. Where's your wife, hmm? Make it, did she?*

– *She's visiting her nephew, just been born. But she's watching, sir, her whole family –*

– *Don't you dare lie to me! Get out of my sight! Go on, out of it! I'd rather drink Apple Blossom's piss than spend another second in your company.*

Albright's cheeks had gone purple with rage. Asher chanced a quick look behind him. Everyone was still in their pairs, enjoying the match. Could they not hear? Or were they pretending?

– *Sir, if I may, please…*

'No, you may not!' Albright blustered, showering Felix Gently in spit. They had *definitely* heard that. Albright raised his cane and with the strength of youth shoved the handle violently into the Defence Secretary's chest.

The sound that followed was a faint crunching of bones. Gently crumpled to the ground, wheezing and struggling for breath. The life seemed to drain from him in an instant. His mouth opened and closed like a fish; he lifted his head as though it weighed a tonne, stared at Asher and conveyed his final wish. Asher understood but gave nothing away as the Prime Minister led him to one side, leaving Felix Gently to die alone in the middle of the crowded room.

The numbers on the electronic scoreboard changed to red as the match ticked over into added time.

– *Now then, young Bloom. I wanted to ask you about Ernest Strong.*

A terror beyond imagination filled Asher's entire being. Did Albright know Strong was a traitor? This was a trap.

– *I haven't seen him, sir.*

– *For how long?*

Asher wished he could reply like a human; the effort to communicate his thoughts felt too much to bear.

– *A few weeks. A month, perhaps? Busy time, sir.*

– *Haha! Or he's a sullen old sod who doesn't want to talk to anyone. Always been the same. Still, I thought he'd show today.*

There was sincerity in Albright's tone; it was possible the cane would remain lowered for now.

– *I wanted to thank you both for being my eyes and ears in the training camp. Invaluable, absolutely invaluable. We wouldn't be here today without the strength of your efforts.*

– *Thank you, sir.*

– *But I had also wanted to make it clear that after today you and Strong were not to see each other again. This is for your benefit, Asher. The national team needed an aggressive streak; it couldn't be subjected to the same namby-pamby Principles inflicted on the rest of their sorry lot. That is why Ernest was an excellent choice – my choice. He is old, jaded, indignant. But that also means he has no place in our future. You, on the other hand – I predict great things for you.*

Time must have frozen. Asher was sure of it. There was no other way the match was still going and Albright was still talking. Conversation was supposed to be instant, but here every word felt articulated and drawn out for maximum effect.

– *There is a war coming. In football they talk of 'winning ugly' and 'grinding out a result'. It may be that way. We will win, but it'll be no place for the squeamish, you understand. My commanders will need to be energetic, hopeful. Bright. Only the best will lead alongside me. Only the best will never go hungry. And as it so happens...*

The tip of the Prime Minister's tongue poked out through his thin lips and curled up to touch the thick bristles of hair. His eyes flicked momentarily to where Felix Gently's body lay prostrate on the floor.

– *...a vacancy has just opened up.*

Asher thought back to the wedding photo hanging on Admiral Goodwill's wall. He remembered Gently's bride, in her full-dress uniform, beneath a canopy of flowers, surrounded by her family, her friends, her husband. A picture of joy and compassion the Euphorivores could never begin to understand. A happiness that now seemed to absorb all of Asher's fear and nerves and leave only a burning anger.

Down below, Danny Holt had just crossed the ball to Jacob Terrier, who then passed to PJ Pitman, who was charging towards goal. But so too had something *unexpected* happened.

A pitch invader.

Around the room, hands were slowly reaching across waists and into inside pockets.

– Well? Aren't you going to say anything? You've just been handed the opportunity of a lifetime!

An 'opportunity'. That, at least, was true. Asher responded with the telepathic equivalent of a mumble.

– What? Speak up, boy!

– I said…

Jesper Lykke shifted his position as PJ approached, while somewhere deep below him, a small green car carrying five agents of the American Crime Agency smashed into the wall of the secret atrium beneath the antenna. Their hysteria rose, shouting and scrambling as the driver struggled to put the engine into a forward gear.

'Taylor! What the hell are you doing?'

'I ain't never driven stick before! And the goddamn tyre's flat!'

Having already decided there was nothing they could do for Lexa and that they didn't take orders from Josh Pittman, Agent Cobb, with the keys in his hand, had declared with a grizzly authority: 'I'll drive'. But in their desire to flee the scene, both he and Agent Taylor had briefly forgotten what country they were in and opened the wrong doors; Taylor had found himself behind the wheel with the light blinding him, the walls crumbling and no time to swap places. He tried the key again, but the engine wouldn't turn over. Above them, a long, oily-white branch had broken free and was plummeting towards them.

Kowalski screamed.

The Vessel shook as it rose through the antenna, the swirl of illuminated cloud completely engulfing the fragile craft. Inside, the pulses of light were hurtling around at such tremendous speed they appeared to Lexa as a static wall of light. She was pushing the Core to its limit, far beyond anything her father could have envisioned. Lexa could feel its reluctance. The Core was in pain.

And so was she.

The distortion caused by the glitch inside the antenna was seen by many but noticed by few. As the war's first act of resistance was struck beneath the stadium, the SyBall App's broadcast appeared pixelated for a few seconds before the high-definition image resumed.

Lykke was on the ground. PJ planted his foot and swung his leg back. The ball sailed through the air, spinning, curving slightly inwards as it travelled.

90:52... 90:53...

The world held its collective breath. Billions of eyes followed the trajectory of the ball; a flawless connection spreading instantly to the shores of India, the backyards of Washington, the park benches of London, and up, way up into space, where a hungry crowd stood beneath the great domed screen, too nervous to celebrate what they knew to be true.

The linesman was picking himself out of the mangled heap of broken advertising boards as a young spectator, overcome with passion, rushed towards the goal. The US President nudged the Queen with his elbow.

'Get a load of that guy!'

Frank Pittman pressed his nose against the window and looked closer at the neighbour's spare TV, set on a picnic table in the garden, its cables trailing over the fence.

'Is that…?'

– What? Speak up, boy!

– I said…

Asher poked the dart gun through Albright's beard and nestled it against the layers of cardigan covering the old man's lifestone.

90:59… 91:00…

'I love you, Mary-Jane.'

'31

One Shot

A blistering zip through air and then... *nothing.*

Time caught up with itself. The agents ceased their groaning and stared at Josh. Yet all he could see was the tip of the dart from Cobb's gun clenched tightly in his fist, an inch away from his eye. His muscles trembled and he felt a little sick as the adrenaline drained away. He lowered his arm and let the little pencil-shaped weapon roll off his fingers and fall harmlessly to the floor. The tension in his body subsided and, in its place, came a newfound arrogance. There was no need to dwell on how close he'd come to death, because it hadn't really been that close at all.

Because Joshua Pittman could catch *anything.*

He turned his attention to the agents, who flinched as he caught their eyes.

'Stay here,' he said firmly, pressing his advantage. 'Don't you dare leave her.'

He took one last look at the Vessel disappearing into the tunnel of cloud above, then turned to leave through the service tunnel. A wavering voice pulled him back.

'W-wait…'

Josh couldn't help but grin. The agent calling out to him in such a meek and fearful manner was none other than Agent Cobb. It was very satisfying.

'If you ain't one of them,' Cobb said, 'then who are you?'

'Me?' The smile drew wider. 'I'm the Goalkeeper.'

He raised his palm and wriggled his fingers, causing the fragments of lifestone embedded beneath his skin to twinkle in the light.

'Safe hands.'

The run back up the service road had taken much less time than Josh had expected. The incline felt steeper on foot than in the car and the continual curve of the same dimly lit tunnel meant for the most part he had no clue how much further he had left to go. He'd never been much of runner – one of the main reasons Tony had put him in goal – and only a couple of minutes after leaving the atrium he'd felt his thigh muscles start to burn and his pace slacken. He'd expected it, and without knowing how – or if – it would work, he placed his hand on his leg and instantly felt of jolt of energy blast through from under his palm. He set off again, moving faster than he had ever done in his life, barely aware of his feet hitting the ground.

He tried the other leg. Then back to the first. Again and again, every touch shifting him into a higher gear, accelerating him forward, until he become so engrossed with his own speed that it was a surprise when suddenly he passed the snapped belt of the Tensa-barrier and the broken shards of the politest 'no entry' sign

501

he had ever read. Up ahead the two team coaches were still waiting patiently for its passengers to return. Sunlight cast against the windshield of the tropical-coloured North America coach. Then he winced as he leant into the final curve and burst out beneath the canopy of trees which flanked the entrance to the tunnel.

The air was still stiflingly hot beneath the greenish shadows of the leaves, and it seemed Josh's new power could do nothing to reduce the flow of sweat streaming down his face. He had half a mind to shed his jacket, but then he'd have nowhere to put his sketchpad – if he were forced to carry it, he ran a greater risk of losing it. Instead, he zipped the jacket right up to the neck, keeping the pad close to his body, then turned off the road and clambered up the muddy bank, weaving between the tree trunks.

It was only now, when his surroundings mimicked a dense and lonely forest, did Josh really notice the roar of the crowd rolling like thunder out of the stadium, every crescendo reaching its peak and then crashing down and causing a new swell of noise to grow elsewhere. Reaching the summit, Josh broke through the last of trees to find himself standing at the edge of the perimeter walkway, across from the stadium's electric blue outer shell rising up in front of him, glinting in the warm afternoon light.

He wiped his brow on his sleeve and allowed himself a moment to catch his breath. His body felt oddly disjointed – his lower half had worked too hard for his upper half to handle. If only he could reach in and place his hands on his lungs…

A thought struck him.

Josh lifted his hand and cupped his palm over his injured nose. The effect was wholly different to anything he'd felt before –

instead of a bolt of energy shooting through him, it was as though something were being pulled slowly and carefully from each of the tiny scratches and wounds, which then quietly sealed themselves up into patches of shiny, smooth skin. The little lumps of congealed blood inside his nostrils disappeared into nothing and at once the pain that had been holding the muscles of his nose in a tight grip for the last three days released at last.

He gasped as he pulled off the wound dressings, twitching the end of his nose with a regained freedom of movement until he could contain no longer contain the sneeze, which came like an instant detox. He was brought back to himself and looked quickly around to check nobody had been watching. The emptiness of the walkway on this side of the stadium contrasted with the strength of the noise from inside. Still, he wasn't alone – he could see two people in the distance, standing at a point where the walkway bent and led back around to the stadium's front, directly beneath the antenna. A muscular skinhead and a woman with long chestnut-brown hair, their faces buried in one another's and their arms writhing beneath the large *Union JAC* flag wrapped around their bodies. Like the flag behind Mick's bar, it had the spiral crest in the centre.

Josh left them to it and headed off around the walkway; above him the antenna reached into the sky as the thunder of voices came at him from every angle. He tried to focus, but the amorous couple had brought his mind back to Lexa. He had left her there, at the most fragile moment of her life, in the hands of people he barely knew nor trusted to look after her. Agent Casey's capitulation over the radio had thrown everything into disarray; he had assumed that any change, any divergence from the series of events that led to destruction, would be a moment that passed between Lexa and himself. But here he was, moving further away from her and towards a more ambiguous ending.

The path hooked around the outer edge of the stadium, breaking into its shadow and bringing Josh into the sudden company of tens of thousands of people. Instantly he was reminded of the Flagship, when he had first stood on the ledge and looked out over the excitable gathering of hungry Euphorivores. In the warm and jovial atmosphere, flags were flown like on Copacabana Beach, accompanied by hand-made banners, scarves, selfie-sticks and bits of foil-covered cardboard in the shape of the SyBall World Cup trophy.

Beyond the immediate crowds, where the perimeter walkway converged to form a huge concourse in front of the stadium, the individual faces become an indiscernible sea of colour and movement, flanked on either side by countless food and drink outlets, souvenir stalls and a live music stage, there to entertain the fans who had made the journey but couldn't get inside. Yet this was little more than a backing track to the live broadcast of the match itself, stretched out like a cinema screen across the stadium's enormous façade. The picture was implausibly perfect – crystal clear, with no shadowy interruptions or blurred afterimages trailing behind the players like ghosts trying to catch up to their bodies. It was as though the collective desire of those gathered to see what was happening had rendered the oily, blue tinctured surface of the stadium wall completely invisible so as to become a window through to the action directly behind it.

At the edge of the crowd Josh spotted a dozen or so fans decked out with coloured wigs, face-paint and plastic hooters, jumping up and down in uneven rhythm to their fulsome chanting. One of the group had a scarf tied to each wrist, dangling like enormous tassels which bobbed up and down as he swung his arms in the air. Moving closer, Josh could hear the French timbre of their accents and, coupled with their North American team shirts, made the assumption they were Canadians. As though to prove his theory, the action cut on screen to a brief replay of Corentin Lamoureux's goal, leading to thunderous cheers from the huddle. He approached the double-scarved supporter and spoke in a raised voice over the whistles and claps:

'*Excusez-moi?*'

The supporter turned to face him. He was a round, ruddy faced man, sweating profusely from beneath his curly red wig, whose initial look of surprise was supplanted by a kind, toothy grin.

'*Bonjour mon bel ami!*' he responded in a vibrant voice. '*Comment puis-je vous aider?*'

Josh was taken aback by the speed of the language, but the warmth of the reply was encouraging.

'Hello, yes… *bonjour, je… je…*'

Josh begged the words to form in his mind as he dredged through the memory of his half-regarded French lessons at school.

'Are you okay?' the fan asked, flawlessly. 'You seem confused.'

Josh stuttered again. The stilted conversation had now caught the attention of the others in the group.

'*Alain! Que se passe-t-il?*' one shouted.

'*Je ne sais pas, je pense qu'il est perdu.*'

505

The man Josh had been talking to, Alain, slapped him playfully on the arm with a chubby hand.

'A little too much to drink, eh?'

The gleeful statement was met with concurring laughter and the miming of glasses being raised to mouths. Josh could only shrug suggestively in response, but the moment had given him the chance to form his next sentence.

'*Puis-je avoir un de vos…*'

The final, key word refused to come, but since Josh had been pointing at Alain while he spoke, the message was thankfully received.

'*Mon foulard?*' said Alain. 'You want my scarf?'

Josh nodded. '*Oui!* Yes! But only to borrow… *emprunter*. I had one, you see…'

Buoyed by the breakthrough in communication, but not knowing the word for 'lost', Josh looked dramatically about himself for the missing piece of fictitious neckwear. Alain stared at Josh, the good humour seemingly depleted by the odd request.

'But you are British, *non?*'

'*Mon père est anglais,*' said Josh, '*mais ma mère est de…*' He rooted quickly around for a Canadian place name and settled on: 'Nova Scotia'.

Alain cocked an eyebrow. The moment was slipping. Time was running out and Josh couldn't afford to stand there and be quizzed on Nova Scotian landmarks. All he wanted was the damn scarf. The fingers opened without intention, and following their lead, he rested his palm on Alain's upper arm.

'*S'il vous plâit?*'

There was a miniscule pause, during which Alain seemed to lose focus, before shaking his head and breaking into raucous, red-faced laughter, his jowls wobbling happily.

'But of course!' Alain exclaimed. '*La Nouvelle-Écosse!* Emmett Baines is from Halifax, did you know? Quick, quick!'

Alain untied one of the scarves from his arm and wrapped it carelessly around Josh's neck.

'Maybe this will bring him luck, eh?'

Josh smiled his thanks but already his senses were resisting; the skin around his neck prickled in the unwanted heat of the itchy scarf and a stench of sweat drifted up into his nostrils.

Alain smiled. 'What's your name?'

Instantly Josh chose to lie, unwilling to risk the improbable chance that the comedy wigs concealed the extra-sensory markings of a team of French-speaking Euphorivores who knew their enemy by name but not by face.

'Nathan,' he said, picking the name for no reason other than the appearance on the stadium screen of PJ Pitman, who'd just been subjected to a heavy tackle by Símon Fuentes.

He thought for one blissful moment PJ had been injured badly enough he could no longer continue, but instead the player remained on his feet. PJ looked ragged as he threw his arms into the air but seemed unable to muster the energy to appeal to the referee. Then he turned to the camera with his famous face appearing resigned to inevitable defeat, as though he were looking directly at Josh, blaming him for his poor performance.

Alain's guffaws broke the illusion. 'Nathan? Nathan! Haha! It gets worse for you!'

PJ traipsed despondently out of shot as Alain swung an arm around Josh's shoulders and pulled him into a headlock

'*Tout le monde, écoute!*' he cried, addressing the group. '*Les loyautés de Nathan sont divisées! Qu'est-ce que tu penses? Devrions-nous lui apprendre ce que signifie être un véritable Canadien?*'

The final word hit like a rallying call and at once the party converged on Josh, jostling him like a ball in a rugby scrum. Shoulders and elbows caught him under the chin and heavy boots landed on his toes. He placed his hands between two damp torsos and attempted to prise them apart, but resisted putting too much pressure through his arm; his present need to be inconspicuous meant he was wary of accidentally throwing one of his new friends halfway across the concourse.

'Shall we go inside?' he said to Alain, whose round figure was rubbing uncomfortably up against him.

'*D'accord!*'

The message was relayed to the group, who greeted the idea with enthusiasm and then moved as a single entity, dragging Josh along towards the stadium entrance. Enveloped by a cocoon of noisy Canadians, where the only vestiges of natural light were filtered through the red, white and blue curls of artificial hair, Josh had lost all sense of the number and weight of the wider crowd. He caught glimpses of people through the gaps that opened between waving arms and sweaty backs and, as the stadium loomed closer, he was surprised at how easy it was to keep moving. He imagined an aerial shot of the scene and pictured a symbiosis at work – everyone lost in their own rapture, yet unconsciously aware of everyone else, swirling and moving around each other like the oily textures of the Vessel's hull as they separated to form the doorway.

Lexa...

The thought of her locked inside the Vessel, rising into the antenna, broiled an anger at himself that made him feel slightly sick. Why had he left her? Because he'd caught the *dart*? Ridiculous. Why didn't he start just scaling the wall to get her? For all he knew, Lexa could have been right – what was happening on the pitch was no longer relevant. Was the decision to bound along with a bunch of half-cut Quebecois actually the mistake that kept the world in a perpetual loop when all he needed to have done was *just stay with her?*

As he moved closer to the base of the screen, the new perspective stretching the broadcast image up towards an ice-blue sky, Josh noticed that Alain and the others were reaching into pockets and bags and each pulling out a shiny, gold-edged ticket. The horrifying thought of having made a severe error of judgment doubled down on him. It was well-known that the DFA had sold twice the number of tickets than seats in the stadium. The idea was to create a festival atmosphere, allowing people to flow freely in and out of the wide entrances as the match progressed. Yet any hope Josh had that the notion of authorised access would be abandoned by now diminished at the sight of the thin slips of card between the Canadians' fingers and the two uniformed stewards checking tickets at the door. They weren't Euphorivores – their shirts were open at the neck and their unadorned heads showed no signs of markings – but they were extremely thorough, eye-balling each ticket with precision detail.

Was this then, the first sign of jumpiness from the Euphorivores? Had the dust finally settled in the Flagship and they remembered after all the two intruders falling through the vortex?

Josh covered his face with the scarf, leaving only his eyes free. It was too late to figure out another route into the stadium, he would simply have to take his chances and hope he could slip through as one of Alain's cohorts. He reached for the sketchpad in his jacket pocket, thinking he could surreptitiously tear out a page and fold it into a makeshift ticket, but stopped short as from somewhere behind him a voice cried:

'*Come on, BK!*'

His memory jogged, Josh took out his phone instead. The match time on the SyBall App read 85:53. Troy Simpson's equaliser was seconds away.

'Stop!'

Josh turned on his heels and spread his arms wide to block their path.

'What's wrong, Nathan?'

Josh shook his head. 'Nothing, it's just…'

He looked about him, hoping some kind of plausible excuse would materialise, but nothing presented itself. He craned his neck up to the screen now towering above him; the movement of red and blue shapes in the penalty area indicated that the British Kingdom were about to take their corner kick.

'*Allons! Je veux regarder la fin du match des gradins!*'

The itchiness of the scarf was unbearable, a thousand tiny claws scratching at his skin, but still Josh kept it over his mouth and shouted through the woollen fabric.

'I just wanted to savour this moment, to... to thank you for accepting me into your group, and... I am inspired by your enthusiasm for your team and whatever happens you should be proud...'

86:08... 86:09...

Josh tried to recall the sequence of events as he'd seen them in the Flagship – *Jesper Lykke fumbling the ball, pushed in the back by Danny Holt, a scramble in the box...*

The voice from before rang out again: 'Someone, please... yes! *Yes!*'

The roar was deafening. It seemed to roll forward from the back of the crowd, gathering speed and volume, then rose like a tidal wave and came crashing down on top of the group. The noise pressed against him, squeezing him tight, constricting his senses. A celebratory dance broke out, visceral and chaotic, eschewing all previous sense of order. The ground shook beneath Josh's feet and he stumbled into Alain's wide chest. He twisted back, and through the mass of bodies he saw the two stewards hugging each other, one sobbing into the other's shoulder. The opportunity drove a tingling warmth down his arm and into his palm...

Josh raises both hands and runs forward, ploughing through the people standing between him and the entrances, pushing and shoving and knocking them to the ground without consideration. The shadow of the doorway passes over his head. The stewards' wails of joy move behind him and the floor under his feet goes from rough concrete to smooth marble.

Josh cannot see beyond those he is rough-housing out of the way. Others behind him – including the Québécois – have also rushed forward and when Josh decides to stop, he is crushed by the weight of bodies toppling on top of him and rolling off in fits of laughter.

He climbs to his feet and sees that no one has been adversely affected. Many remain where they are; lying on their backs and staring up at the high sloping ceiling – the underside of the seating bowl – and the large mural with godlike depictions of the men's and women's national teams. PJ's image is by far the largest; his arms folded, staring dead ahead with a cocksure smile.

Josh leaps over the nearest ground dweller and runs off down the wide thoroughfare. At first his progress is frustrated by the swarm of fans flowing in from outside, buzzing still in the aftermath of Troy Simpson's goal. But once he is past the lobby the crowd thins and Josh weaves in and out between them, making his way over to where the bars and burger outlets are punctuated by the gated tunnels leading out to the terraces.

But the hordes are surging forward into each tunnel and bottlenecking the gates, eager to see the final few minutes of the match.

Josh stops and looks around him. He is panicked. Time is running out. He holds up his hand; he could use it to break through, but instead he darts forward, sidestepping carelessly around the people in his way, twisting and turning...

Thump! Josh collides shoulder-to-shoulder with a man standing motionless in the middle of the busy concourse. He stumbles forward but keeps his footing.

MAN: Oh my gosh, are you okay?

JOSH: Yes, I'm fine. Sorry...

MAN: No problem! Care to join us?

Josh sees that the man is one of a dozen or so all holding up their phones in front of them.

SECOND MAN: Everybody say... 'Union Jac!'

Ahead a group of forty or fifty people have stopped to pose for pictures on and around a large bronze statue of George Castle.

FANS: *Union JAC!*

The photoshoot has left the nearest gate relatively unobstructed. Seizing his chance, Josh dashes into the tunnel. The concrete stairs are steeper than he expects, and he leaps two at a time as a multitude of distant sounds rise in a frenzy of excitement. The light streams in, filtered through the haze of a hot, cloudless sky. The heat of the day mixes pleasantly with the open breeze.

As he reaches the top of the stairs, its narrow walls fall way, transporting him from one place to another as the vast expanse of the stadium bowl suddenly blinks into existence.

Every one of his senses feels under attack. The ecstatic crowd, whose screams and cheers fluctuate with every kick of the ball, seem to cling unnaturally to the tiered stands which tower over all sides the pitch, turning his stomach as though he is watching from the top of a skyscraper.

He reaches for the handrail behind him only to be blocked by a barrage of people still flooding in through the gate.

His heart thumps inside his chest. The picture distorts and the sounds warp like a record played backwards. Heat rises in his hand; he lowers the scarf and runs his warm fingers across his face in an attempt to rebalance.

You can do this...

A feeling of becoming solid once again restores his focus. The sharpness of reality returns with a snap.

He looks up and across to where the huge electronic scoreboard hangs from a gantry above the seating blocks: 89:04. Less than two minutes. His eyes dart from one end of the pitch to the other. He is relieved as he sees he is closer to Jesper Lykke than Ben Castle. Down below him, the Euphorivore linesman is waiting on the touchline.

Josh hurtles down the stairs towards the pitch and turns along the front row of seats. He winces at the cheers bellowed from inches away, brushes past the flags waved in his face and leaps over the outstretched feet, landing in puddles of spilled alcohol.

From Josh's vantage, the linesman, dressed in his American-style black-and-white striped shirt, appears further away, hopping between each foot near the corner flag, paying no attention to the current phase of action on-pitch. Instead he is glancing nervously up at the scoreboard.

89:47... 89:48...

Josh is nearly there.

CASEY: Hey! It's the kid! Pittman! Pittman, up here!

Josh turns at the sound of his name and sees Jen Casey, four rows up with an American flag tied around her waist like a sarong, beckoning him to join her. On either side her agents – Logan, Hicks and Martinez – have been swallowed up by the mob of fans, singing, dancing and urging their team forward in a multitude of languages.

CASEY: So cool you could make it! Get up here! This is so awesome, it's gonna go to extra time! Come on! Oh wait, look, there's a TV camera – woo! Hey! Mike, Jack, Evan! I love you guys! Mwah! Mwah!

As Casey blows her kisses across the Atlantic, Josh catches sight of Vik Jaitley standing at the end of the row, frozen to the spot with an addled expression, twitching as though unsure whether or not he should be there. Josh looks back to the linesman, hesitates, but then rushes up the aisle and grabs Jaitley by his jacket.

JOSH: Detective! It's me, it's Josh, I need your help…

JAITLEY: I-I can't… I can't move…

In the distance, between the two dugouts, the fourth official holds aloft his indicator board and signals for one minute of added time. The stadium groans: it is not enough for them.

JOSH: Think! Think about your cousin! And cricket! Come on! You know this isn't right, you said so!

Jaitley flinches on the spot, as though he is about to go with Josh, but an invisible chain holds him back.

JAITLEY: I-I…

Josh throws a quick glance over to the pitch. He looks for PJ, but his attention is drawn up field. The British Kingdom's defenders have the ball. Reuben Mayfield is running backwards down the nearside flank.

JAITLEY: I need to phone Charlotte.

Vik Jaitley shrugs Josh off and reaches inside his jacket for his phone.

JOSH: *What!?*

Josh abandons Jaitley at once and leaps back down the aisle. A huge roar goes up around the stadium; down below both teams are surging towards Jesper Lykke's goal. The ball is at Danny Holt's feet. PJ is running towards the penalty area.

At the bottom step Josh grabs the metal fence along the front of the terraces and launches himself into the air, hurtling over both the fence and the advertising boards and landing feet first at the edge of the pitch.

The linesman spots Josh immediately and runs to intercept him. Josh charges forward; he is faster and stronger and he knows it.

Danny Holt slides the ball through to Jacob Terrier on the far side. The dreadlocked winger looks up for the pass and then skirts it across the grass into PJ's path.

The crowd rises and Josh feels their screams conglomerating as a tight ball of pressure bearing down on him. He lifts his arm and clenches his fist, pressing his fingertips deep into his palm. His face conveys everything: the adrenaline, the energy, the will, the anger; the weight of everything he has seen and done in the past few days; the thought of Lexa, alone in the Vessel, rising through the antenna. It burns like rocket fuel powering his whole body.

517

He swings his fist and strikes the linesman in the chest with such force that the Euphorivore is lifted into the air, his body flying backwards with an inhuman shriek, and crashes into the advertising boards. Sparks from the electronic displays shoot up like fireworks. Nearby fans 'ooh' and 'ahh' in clueless wonder.

90:52... 90:53...

Josh turns at the corner flag and runs along the edge of the crisp white line towards the goal. PJ is cheered on as he nears the penalty area. A flash of eye contact passes between them.

Don't do it, PJ, remember what I told you...

For a moment Josh thinks he has gotten through to PJ, that he is easing off, only to realise what he is seeing are the subtle adjustments of the player's body as he readies for the shot.

JOSH: *PJ! No!*

Josh pumps his arms and powers towards Jesper Lykke.

PJ plants his foot and swings his leg back.

PJ: I love you, Mum!

Time slows.

The ball leaves PJ's foot and volleys through the air, curving slightly inwards as it travels. Lykke shifts his position, his eyes fixed on his approaching target. He doesn't see Josh, who pounds the turf as he too follows the trajectory of the ball coming nearer; sailing, dipping, heading perfectly for the top corner. A gentle nudge with his elbow and Jesper Lykke is bundled into the net.

FRANK: Is that...?

Asher pokes the dart gun through Albright's beard and nestles it against the layers of cardigan covering the old man's lifestone.

The Vessel shakes violently, and Lexa is thrown across the chamber. Her possessions lay scattered and broken beneath the layer of cloud, but she cares only for one. She clutches the Captain's notebook to her chest and finally, after withholding for so long, allows the tears to come.

Josh leaps with his arm outstretched, his fingers stroking the underside of the ball...

90:59... 91:00...

ASHER: I love you, Mary -Jane.

He fires.

The antenna explodes in a ball of fiery blue light.

'32

Extra Time

There are few certainties in life, but here's one I find truly frightening: these will be my last words.

They are written, as instructed, in a space left purposefully blank on the first page of my notebook, in the hope that, come the time, you will not fail to see them and note their importance.

When I was given this notebook, it was blank except for a few sealed pages at the back which the previous owner told me contain 'a few scribblings' he'd rather I not see; reminders, he said, of a naive and gullible world, culpable in its own downfall.

Sometime later he offered me a second, less conventional gift – a vial of his own blood, so that I could code his DNA with the Vessel as well as my own. Regrettably, he seemed all too aware of his fate and thereafter told me that once he was gone, I was never to speak of him, and to mention him only in writing, on this page and on this date.

'Why only then?' I asked.

'Because time is delicate and mistakes are costly' he replied.

Salvation is an achievable but fragile goal – a point out of sequence and we are lost again for yet another turn of the wheel. We have become stuck in the loop because of the Euphorivores' ultimate mistake – underestimating our potential to love one another. Joy and compassion is all well and good, but it's a slim picking. With love as their objective, they could have collected enough food to gorge themselves until the end of time and still left plenty behind for us to carry on with our lives as though nothing had happened. (And I bet it would have tasted better too).

Love is immense, but easy to miss.

This was at the heart of their confusion. They saw so many of us struggling and so assumed we were incapable. They were wrong. Chances may be rare – even rarer these days – but still we have the potential. A second chance at love is like a second chance at time – a precious opportunity to do something differently.

As my friend once put it:

'Love is like trying to catch a tiny stone falling through the air. You can let it drop, or you can reach out and grab it, hold it tight and never let it go.'

Today's primary test of the Vessel will not go as planned – another certainty. But that doesn't mean the plan will fail. One small change, one minor, infinitesimal adjustment, and maybe when I next wake in that hospital bed I'll look out the window to a world that is still joyous, still compassionate, but where we are united by all those wonderful little things that set us apart.

Because the messy, complex truth is that we don't all have to be cheering for the same team to find a way to love one another.

Always,
Captain M. Bannick, Chief Engineer, Resistance Air Fleet

Josh's eyes flickered open and he winced at the sunlight bearing down on him. He felt strange, leaden, flat on his back with his head thumping and his senses out of sync. People around him appeared as ghosts, fuzzy at the edges, the ringing in his ears blocking out their cries. The air smelt sweet but left a sour taste in his mouth and the intense heat prickled the skin on his cheeks.

Josh…

Lifting himself from the ground, he felt as though his spinal column had been replaced with a line of rocks, one of which had migrated up his neck and was trying to pound its way out of his forehead. He rubbed his eyes and when his vision cleared, he looked out onto the scene of utter chaos unfolding before him.

The crowds on every tier were flooding towards the exits, scrambling over the seats and congesting the narrow tunnels. A few stewards, distinguishable by their high-vis jackets, were endeavouring to temper the flow of fans, while others were content to abandon their posts and join the escape.

Josh…

He looked across to where he'd launched himself over the advertising boards. Over by the corner flag the linesman had been freed of the wreckage and was lying in a semi-conscious heap under the armed guard of Agents Logan, Martinez and Hicks.

Further downfield, by the dugouts, a group of police officers were holding back the players from North America, who were aghast at the sight of their head coach, Derrick Zeus, being led away in handcuffs as he remonstrated up towards the windowed VIP lounge above the first tier.

– *You cowards! Get down here!*

Josh felt momentarily sick. He could hear the coach's silent words as clearly as Ray Albright's through the dome of the Flagship.

'*Josh…*'

The sound of his name, like a distant echo coming closer each time, brought his attention back to the pitch and the huge brawl taking place near the centre circle. Jacob Terrier was being restrained by his own teammates, fighting and snarling like a wild animal, kicking out with his feet and scraping his studs on Troy Simpson, who went down holding his leg and screaming as though it had been cut off. The dreadlocks swung and lashed through the air like a cat-o'-nine-tails attached to an actual cat, the venom of the words towards his fellow players matched by the spit flying in their faces.

At the far end of the pitch, beyond where a flurry of opportunistic news reporters came surging forward with their camera crews, Josh spotted Jen Casey, standing in the frame of the goalmouth and screaming into her radio with her eyes fixed at the empty space where the antenna had once been. Josh had caught a glimpse of the explosion before connecting with the goalpost, and he'd expected to see the antenna consumed by fire, with debris tumbling down the sides as ash and smoke billowed into the sky. But there was nothing; no flames, no smouldering wreckage, no rubble where rubble should have been. The antenna hadn't just exploded, it had completely *disappeared*.

Josh couldn't hear but every message into Casey's radio lasted a little longer each time, a little less hopeful, a little more desperate. The rock inside his skull became a lump of guilt; the world, for all its apparent descent into madness, had seemingly been saved, but at an unbearable cost. The pain of his existence in place of those left behind provided him with an unhappy clarity, and at last the voice rang true:

'Josh! Mr Pittman! Are you okay?'

The two sets of legs – shadowy poles in the perhiperary of his vision – bent quickly as Josh tried to push himself to his feet.

'Take it easy, yeah? You properly smacked your head.'

Vikram Jaitley and PJ Pitman grabbed an arm each and lifted Josh to his full height at a lop-sided angle, the footballer finding the effort easier than the detective. Jaitley smiled warmly as a piece of the stadium's roof, now missing the structural support of the antenna, collapsed into the empty seating block beneath.

'How are you feeling?'

Josh didn't really want to answer. 'A little rough.'

Jaitley guffawed. 'I'm not surprised!' He nodded over Josh's shoulder at the goalposts behind him. 'The upright's still wobbling – and that's a nasty cut you've got there.'

Jaitley was looking above his eye. Putting his fingers to the source of his pain, Josh winced as he felt the warm silkiness of his blood oozing from the wound.

'But...' Jaitley took hold of his shoulder and shook it vigorously. 'You did it! I don't know how – but look!'

Jaitley gestured around the stadium, as though the panorama of scrambles, fights, vanishing spires and the sound of sirens and helicopter blades slowly filling the air were marks of achievement.

'What about the others?' Josh asked.

The detective cleared his throat. 'Casey's on it. Okay? She's *on it*. You remember how deep that place was? They'll have had plenty of time. If they're not out already, she'll get to them'

'Yes, but Lexa…'

The image burned in Josh's mind, stealing the words from his mouth; the Vessel spinning, rising into the antenna, the relentless cloud churning around her. Had the agents waited for her like he'd asked? Even with the blown tyre it shouldn't have taken this long.

'We'll know soon enough,' Jaitley said. 'In the meantime, get yourself checked out. Team medics have been helping out with the injured.'

PJ scoffed. 'Maybe get them to check out that arm while they're at it. Think you've been working out too much.'

Josh wiggled his fingers; the stone was still in his palm, but there was no residual afterglow from his exertions. He looked around.

'Lykke, is he okay?'

PJ shrugged. 'He's fine. Hates you, though. We had to drag him away when you was out of it. He was fighting us off, but then his gaffer got nicked.'

PJ jutted his chin to where the police were losing control of the situation at the dugout. Josh recognised the broad figure of North America's goalkeeper with his head in his hands.

'I'm sorry I didn't listen to you,' PJ said. 'I mean, I did, in a way. You said do what I thought was right, and I didn't know, so I kicked it... but maybe I got it wrong? I dunno. Anyway, sorry.'

'It's okay, I should –'

Josh recoiled as the cool air inside his mouth caught him by surprise. PJ and Jaitley felt it too – the temperature had suddenly dropped and a rising wind whipped around the stadium. Alerted by the tingle of goosebumps along his skin, the sensation in Josh's arm began to resurface; far less invigorating than before, the sense of strength giving way to a subtle awareness of an external force bringing the energy inside him to life.

The gusts were coming in waves now, pulses of air thumping outwards in concentric circles from the centre of the pitch. The sound was slowly building; a kind of sonic boom that was felt rather than heard. As the intensity rose, so did his optimism, his lungs surrendering breath and filling with belief, the force in his arm willing him on, until at last his heart leapt at the sight of fiery streaks of light spinning in the air around the centre circle, leaving a sparkling array in their wake, like the tails of comets.

The metal fins were the first to break through, burning white hot as they tore at the fabric of the world. Josh crept forward, pushing against the waves and whispering her name as a canvas of light rose and fell like a curtain. Then suddenly, the Vessel was there, ticking curiously as it wound down to its eventual stop and hovering serenely over the centre of the pitch.

Nothing happened for what seemed like a very long time. Nobody spoke, nobody moved, everyone waited. Even Jacob Terrier, who had been able to project a few good swear words in the passing minutes was still and silent, breathing slowly in muffled rage.

A tense anticipation hung in the air. Doubt crept into Josh's mind. It looked like the Vessel – but it hadn't sounded like the one he knew. The tone was different. Was this the start of another attack?

At last the Vessel's rustic colours began to churn and swirl, the gentle chaos Josh recognised as a perfectly arranged sequence. He marvelled yet again as the shell split and opened itself wide, and the Impossible Stairs slid into existence. But at once he feared the worst as the cloud rolled out from the entrance into the open air and three figures – none of whom he recognised to be Lexa – stood in triumphant silhouette at the top of the stairs.

'Are we back?'

Stepping out into the natural light of the day, Agents Nash, Taylor and a hairy-headed Cobb looked around the stadium as though they were astronauts about to step out onto the surface of an alien planet.

'Agent Casey!' cried Nash, spotting her first. 'Guys, we did it! We're back!'

The agents launched into an ebullient routine of cheers, high fives and back slaps. Taylor spun on his heels and called back into the Vessel, seemingly addressing nothing but the light of the Core.

'Thank you! Thank you so much!'

Josh felt dizzy at the sound of these words, the pain subsiding, the feeling in his arm warm and luxurious. He lifted himself onto his tip toes, desperate for a glimpse, but the view was blocked by the agents swaggering down the stairs. They looked older than before, looser and less grizzled, unkempt but healthy. Strands of greying, thinning hair alluded to a stressful experience that by their manner appeared to have been overcome. Their uniforms were torn and filthy, and accessorised with obscure, tell-tale signs of passage through an extraneous place and time: a puffy white shirt and a loose cravat under an ACA-issue jacket, white spats over brightly polished shoes, trousers held up by woollen button braces and, in Agent Taylor's case, a handsome set of sideburns.

They reached the ground and strode up to Casey, dropping the smiles and standing to attention. Nash, in the middle, squared his jaw and saluted.

'Reporting for duty, ma'am,' he growled stoically. 'Sorry we're late.'

'Not a problem,' Casey said, looking from man to man with an expression of hardened pride. 'At ease, agents. Glad to have you back.'

The lowering of Agent Nash's hand was just about enough to cover the awkward silence that followed, as Casey, breaking rank with everything Josh knew about her, lurched forward and hugged each of her agents in turn. Maybe she was still on a high from the gleeful brainwashing – a hangover that might forever take the edge off her character. Or perhaps she was just pleased to see them.

Free from the embrace, Agent Cobb immediately rounded on Josh. 'There you are!'

Josh took a big step back and clenched his fist, the defensive instincts kicking into gear as the American grabbed him by the back of his neck.

'Man, I could kiss you!' Cobb shouted, inches from Josh's face. 'You know what? Screw it, I will!'

Agent Cobb planted a smacker on the injury-free side of Josh's forehead. Hard but tender.

'Your car, dude!' Cobb explained, reading Josh's confusion. 'Damn thing's built like a tank! Saved our lives!'

Josh winced at the skin being pinched beneath his collar as Cobb pulled him closer. His voice lowered.

'Listen, I know things got a little heavy back there, with the dart and the tyre and stuff, but I've had a lot of time to address my hostile tendencies, and I just wanna say… I hope you can forgive me.'

First PJ, now Cobb. Josh had never been apologised to so much in his life. If only his dad were there to see this. He smiled humbly.

'Honestly, there's no need. You were only doing your job.'

Cobb roared with laughter. 'Ha! You Brits, so modest. But hey, that dart. Hell of a catch. Maybe you should play football – *real* football, I mean. I can picture you as a wide receiver.'

'I think I'll stick to goalkeeping.'

'Suit yourself.' Cobb glanced back at the Vessel as a shadow passed across the entrance. 'You're one lucky son of a gun, you know that?'

Agent Cobb sauntered away before Josh could answer, flashing a wide grin and cocking an eyebrow before heading over to catch up with his long-lost colleagues.

'Hey there, Josh.'

Another figure had appeared at the entrance. The voice was the same, but still Josh had to look twice to check it was really her. The hoodie and jeans were long gone, and in their place were a pair of ankle-length pantaloons and thick leather boots, a double-breasted waistcoat above a high-neck blouse and fingerless gloves. He thought about asking where she'd left the eye patch and parrot; a joke to mark their reunion might make him look cool or heroic. But he couldn't – he was too happy to speak.

Lexa ran light-footed down the Stairs and flung her arms around him. Josh buried his face in her shoulder and breathed her in. Her clothes were musty and her skin smelt of carbolic soap.

'I'm so glad you're safe,' she said.

She pulled away. Her hair was longer, her face was fuller, her smile was wider.

'Come with me…' Lexa took hold of his hand and pulled him towards the Vessel. 'You have got to see this.'

'Miss Lexa!' barked Casey.

The American stood with her hands on her hips and her tongue in her cheek. Lexa turned.

'You realise you're still under arrest? And so are you,' Casey jabbed a finger in Josh's direction, 'for wrecking the station and harbouring a suspect.'

'Oh,' said Josh feebly. 'I, er… sorry about that.'

Casey scoffed and waved him away. 'Alright, alright, that's enough.' She turned and addressed the crowd. 'Clear the area! Let's get outta here before this whole goddamn place comes down on us. See you around, kid.'

Lexa beamed and climbed back up into the Vessel. Josh landed his foot on the bottom step and savoured the moment; finally he had a future to be excited about. And what's more, he had someone to share it with. At the top of the Stairs lay the possibility of adventure, of danger, a life less ordinary; either that, or the chance for the two of them to escape the world altogether, to put everything behind them and find their own, unique place in time.

The roar that erupted from across the pitch had a pathetic, humorous quality about it, and Josh didn't have to look up to know where it had come from. Jacob Terrier had wrestled free of his rear-end restraints and launched himself across the pitch towards him. Electricity shot like a lightning bolt through Josh's arm as he turned side on to Terrier, bracing for impact and wondered how far he could throw him. The middle tier perhaps? The lower?

But the chance never came. Cobb had pulled a large pepperbox handgun from his jacket and wrapped his arm around Terrier's neck, wrenching him to the ground and opening the door for every available hot-head to pile on top of him.

'Josh! Come on!' Lexa called.

He clambered up the Stairs, tripping over as he kept eyes on the scuffle, a jumble of flailing arms and legs and dreadlocks against a soundtrack of wild, guttural shrieks. Wisps of cloud caught in Josh's mouth as he collapsed inside and he was still coughing as Lexa placed her hand in the wall to seal the entrance. He watched the scene outside until the very last, his parting memory set forever by Vikram Jaitley, who cried *'Don't forget us, Mr Pittman!'* as he took off his tie and lashed the ankles of the crazed Euphorivore.

Josh's hand throbbed with pain; for the first time the pieces of lifestone felt sharp and intrusive, as though they had suddenly grown in size. He knew now what it felt like if the build-up of energy were denied a release. He didn't like it.

531

'Shouldn't we help them?'

'Nope! I am done fighting those things.' The clickety-clack of Lexa's fingers on the keyboard was accompanied by a low fizzing sound. 'Johnny will take care of it,'

'Johnny? Who's John–' Josh turned and cut himself off, stunned into silence by the Vessel's interior.

It was, much like Lexa, not quite as he remembered it. Copper wire ran around the walls in horizontal lines like a giant electromagnet, connecting here and there to a variety of heavy-set instruments bolted unapologetically into the hull – home-made contraptions built of cog wheels and pipes, oversized diodes and large tungsten bulbs which thrummed annoyingly. Thick rubber cables snaked away from the multitude of apparatus and either disappeared into the Core or found their way into the old Indian tea chest which housed the laptop, itself decked out with a brand-new brass-plated casing and sprouting even more home-spun gadgets than before, like hideous metallic growths. The desk was strewn with scrolls, ledgers, broken quill feathers and one of those tacky plasma balls Josh was certain had only been put there for effect.

'Agent Cobb,' said Lexa.

'What?' Josh had been so dumbfounded by the Vessel's upgrades he had lost his train of thought.

'Johnny. He wanted me to teach him as much as possible about Euphors. Became a sort of protégé, if you like.'

Josh did not like, instead he was cut by a childish stab of jealously. Lexa rose from the laptop and gazed around the chamber, as though recalling an old memory.

'There might not have been a Harvest,' Lexa continued, 'but there'll be a lot of them on Earth still. At some point they'll probably try to regroup, fight back. And a guy like Johnny needs an outlet, so he's made it his personal mission to… I don't know, round them up, imprison them, kill them… I was deliberately vague on that point.'

'You mean like a bounty hunter?'

'Yes, I suppose. Bill and Ricky –' (Nash and Taylor, Josh presumed) '– just wanted to get home, but he reckons he can persuade a couple of others to join him. There'll be plenty of Euphors in the stadium – weakened for now, but they won't stay that way.' Lexa shrugged nonchalantly. 'Still, I've done my bit.'

She strode across the chamber, disturbing the cloud and sending little puffs into the air, tapped the glass screen of a read-out dial on the wall and then returned to the laptop with a frazzled expression.

'What happened to the Flagship?' asked Josh. 'You said there were Euphors on Earth, so… what, the Flagship was destroyed?'

Lexa typed a final command and she let out a sigh of relief as the Calendar Application appeared in a window, dipping in and out of focus.

'No,' she replied, selecting a date.

'So what happened?'

'I sent it back in time.'

The Unique Time Signature appeared in a dialogue box in the centre of the screen. The last two characters jumbled around, running through the entire alphabet in less than a second.

'Oh. How far?'

'Really far. Can't say for certain, but...'

Lexa held down three function keys at once and, with her other hand, held in place a wire that connected to a brass button under the table, which she pressed with her knee until the code settled and the Globe Application opened. With a sigh of relief she blew hair from her face and then turned to Josh for the first time since the entrance had closed.

'...a lot.'

'What, are we talking... *dinosaurs*?'

'Hmm, maybe. I don't know. More like the stone age, I'd say.'

'How did you manage that?'

'The antenna – I used it to transmit a signal from the Vessel to the Flagship and just programmed the Signature to keep running. Ricky likened it to putting a brick on the gas pedal and jumping out the car.'

'Except you didn't jump.'

Lexa pretended not to hear and looked back at the laptop. 'The start-up sequence has been temperamental ever since. No big deal. It was worth it. They've either gone back so far they'll never survive, or...'

She broke off and left the expectation to hang in the air.

'Or?'

'They've become their own ancestors and history will simply repeat itself.'

Josh smiled. 'But history can be changed.'

'Damn right it can.'

She bit her thumbnail in a manner he hadn't seen before; cheeky and self-satisfied. With a noticeable skip in her step Lexa glided around the edge of the chamber to an area at the back where a makeshift bed, hoisted up on wooden stilts to avoid the cloud, was positioned next to a large trunk with brass fittings and a black metal clothes rail. She rummaged through a few petticoats, corsets and some restrictive-looking dresses with enormous skirts until she found two morning suits sagging morosely from wire-frame hangers.

'We got you some clothes. Second hand but good quality. No one died in them. You'll need to change before we arrive.'

'Arrive where? The Victorian period? Is that where all this is from?'

Lexa sat on the edge of her bed.

'Yes,' she said. 'I didn't plan it that way. When I was inside the antenna I thought the Signature would shoot straight into the Flagship like a bullet, but instead –'

She took hold of a pair of suspenders hanging from the rail and pulled them across herself like a chest expander.

'– it stretched, all the way along the signal, and took everything in its path with it. Only it was stronger at one end than the other. Like gum on your shoe, Bill said, and when you lift your foot there's a long thin thread keeping one small bit stuck to the pavement, until...'

Lexa let go and with a thwack the suspenders snapped against the trousers Josh was expected to wear.

'The Flagship went prehistoric because it took the biggest hit, but a bird flying over the antenna at that exact moment might only have ended up as far back as maybe... the Roman Empire, or thereabouts. And then me, right at the bottom...'

'The 1800s?'

'Twenty-third of February, 1855, to be exact. It was *really* cold; the snow was up to my knees.'

'Wow,' said Josh. 'Just… wow. So that's where we're headed?'

'No, not quite.' Lexa stood and wandered back towards the desk. 'The laptop battery, the one my dad installed, was meant to last forever, but when I hacked into the antenna's signal and fired the Signature, it blew up.'

The Globe Application was warning of a time-out due to inactivity. Josh marvelled at Lexa's easy-going approach as she refreshed the screen and selected the location.

'Batteries of any kind are scarcer in the past than they are in the future, so I had to get inventive. Literally.'

'You used Victorian technology to power a laptop to pilot a time machine?'

Lexa smirked. 'I applied scientific principles to the available instrumentation. Actually didn't take as long as you might think, we were ready for test flights in less than three years.'

'Three years?' Josh spluttered. 'You were there for three whole years?'

'Three and a half.'

Josh rubbed his face. For everything in her story, this part felt the most staggering. He responded with the first and stupidest thing that came to his mind.

'You're older than me.'

Lexa laughed. 'I was born about twenty years after you.'

Behind them the light of the Core dimmed suddenly, the needles in the dials dropped to zero and the screen faded to black with a winding thrum.

'Argh, not again!'

Lexa swept aside the litter of parchment on her desk until she came across a large brass crank with a smooth wooden handle, which she plugged into a small hole in the Indian tea chest and began turning. The faster she turned, the louder the sound of cog wheels and electronic crackles from within the tea chest became, until at last the laptop screen flickered back into life and the Vessel was once again shrouded in warm light. She returned to the laptop and began scrolling back through the error logs. Josh noticed her eyes twitching back at him, then avoiding him as he approached.

'You were meant to get in the car. You were meant to let them protect you, to let *me*...' Josh couldn't finish. 'The laptop works remotely, doesn't it? You didn't have to sacrifice yourself.'

Lexa closed the window. A new message appeared asking for a password. The look she gave him was one he recognised; the one where she was about to rage at him for questioning things he didn't understand, to remind him he was only a passenger and would never comprehend the decisions she had to make.

'I'm sorry,' she said, taking his hand in hers.

Another apology – Josh was on a roll.

'It was too risky. I had one shot and I needed to make sure it worked. I wanted you there, I really did, but I couldn't chance you getting hurt. That's why I told the agents to take you.'

Her finger rubbed against his palm and he realised he hadn't told her about the lifestone.

'Yes, but *three years*, Lexa.'

'That's nothing,' she said, the remorse fleeting. 'When I arrived the Americans had already been there *four* years. They were under the Vessel so maybe there was some kind of rebound, I don't know. I remember them, all huddled around a fire outside this little iron cabin they'd built themselves. I say 'cabin', it was more of a garage – it had your car in it.'

Josh gasped. 'Lock Niss?'

'Now's your chance if you want to see her again.' Lexa gestured to the keyboard. 'Want to do the honours? It hasn't changed.'

Josh bent down and typed in the password.

49g9yqh.

The crafty little link between themselves and the man they both knew, the evidence of their intertwined destinies.

'The agents taught me all about soccer, you know,' said Lexa.

'Oh, really? Experts, I'm sure.'

'They are in the nineteenth century. And to be honest, I really don't know what all the fuss is about. I can see how it's fun, if you like that sort of thing, but to get *so* worked up about it!' She pulled the crank out of the tea chest and set it back on the desk. 'I do understand a bit more about goalkeeping though. There's something quite courageous about it – the last line of defence, straddling the border between victory and defeat. That's when I got to thinking about you.'

She had taken a step closer to him. His arm tingled.

'What about me?'

'Oh, you know… how you dived in after me and jumped onto the back of a dragon –'

'Firebreather…'

'– when you didn't have to even be there. I kept pushing you away and you kept coming back. So, I thought, now it's my turn. And in any case, I still had to return this.'

Lexa reached into her pocket and pulled out the last thing Josh expected to see. It was his watch, ticking ordinarily in the silence of the chamber. The dial had been repaired, its clear glass face reflecting the light of the Core, and it had a brand new strap. Pure leather.

'Thank you,' he said.

Lexa searched his face. Everything had changed, but somehow it was no different than when they'd first met, in the Bovill Arms, and they had sat together on the pub wall; Josh talking about how disconnected he felt while Lexa considered whether or not to rip his heart out.

'All I wanted was to get back to you,' she said. 'And never have I been so grateful for this rotten bloody machine because at last you're standing in front of me. Josh Pittman. The goalkeeper who saved the world.'

There was that smile again, the new one that dimpled her cheeks and brightened her eyes. He could sense the ache and uncertainty of those passing years, even though it had been less than an hour since he last saw her. The subtle changes in her features served only to remind him how brave she was, how close they had come to losing one another and how deeply he felt for her.

'Are you ready?'

He smiled back. 'I'll always be ready.'

Lexa pressed the return key without looking and wrapped her arms around him. The copper wire that encircled the walls began to glow as tiny beads of light chased through its fibres. Josh could feel the beat pulsing through his chest as he reached out and drew her close to him. Theirs lips met, and behind them the Core shone, brighter and more brilliant than ever before, encasing them in their moment.

Then in a flash, they were gone.

The Fourth Dimension

Epilogue
The Replay

The killer known to police on three continents only as *The Fedora* was fond of his pseudonym.

It was certainly better than the one handed to him on assignment, the name he often struggled to remember given that he worked alone and never engaged directly with the people whose lives he stole. He liked the description because it spoke to his sense of mystique and the presumption that he was uncatchable; a phantom, hidden in the shadows, moving quickly and quietly from place to place, more unreal than real.

Always one step ahead.

Basking in the warmth of his ego and the mid-July sun, with the hat tipped over his eyes and his head leaning against the bench's wrought iron armrest, the Fedora listened intently to the repetitive crunch of a passing jogger's feet on the gravel. Birds twittered as they came into roost in the trees behind him, while over the crest of the hill two people on a date laughed awkwardly. A dog barked, a child kicked a ball and a cool breeze swept over him, whipping some nearby leaves into the air.

If he weren't feeling quite so sick, he might say that, as well as his moniker, he was rather fond of this park too. He'd slept in many over the years, in every part of the world, and this was by far the most civilised. Everyone here greeted everyone else with a cheery smile and a fond 'hello'. Warmth and affection floated on the air, wafting from person to person. There was not one scrap of litter on the ground, no evidence of vandalism nor a single line of graffiti across any available surface.

This was hardly surprising though, given he was in the homeland of the Guiding Principles, with their skewered sense of priorities. Whereas once the sight of a man lying asleep on a bench might have elicited tuts of disgust, calls to the police, or even just a quick glance to check he was breathing, the assumption these days was that he was simply a friendly neighbourhood tramp, content with his lifestyle choices, and it would be impolite to interrupt him during his nap.

Society's default position – to always assume the best and to not question otherwise – suited him just fine. It allowed him to continue his work in making sure people stayed that way, flittering blissfully about in empty-headed oblivion. But the more he evaded capture, the more he liked to push the limits of peoples' inobservance; hanging around a crime scene just long enough for the authorities to show up and dressing conspicuously with no regard to season or style. He wasn't the only operative liaising between the global factions, but he was certainly the most flamboyant; the hat, the mac and the occasional cocktail stick hanging out the corner of his mouth, like the noirish private detective out to catch… well, himself. But again, each to their own.

The real issue was his greed.

The others – and there were many – employed in long-term infiltration were generally able to suppress their appetite, but the Fedora had never quite mastered the skill. He killed indiscriminately because he believed himself too valuable to feel the pangs of hunger. He deserved his rewards because they were testament to his success. But as the death toll rose and the human agencies followed his scent, he'd been raged at by Ray Albright for being too excessive.

That fat old bastard could talk.

If the Prime Minister didn't think it was noble or courageous to starve yourself in service to your people, then why should he? There were still three days until the Final. If the others could wait, good for them. In the meantime, he was going to head off and get some dinner.

He checked his watch; a 'gift' from a recent victim that had caught his eye. There was only an hour to go. He could hold out until then. There were places to snack in the park, probably, but they'd be nothing more than titbits, when what he needed was a full meal. The ever-present bottle in his pocket was empty again, the contents a satisfying kick to boost his confidence, but without something to eat he might as well have drunk bleach.

With his remaining strength, he hoisted himself up into a sitting position. The world swivelled around and the sun bore down on his head like a tonne weight. Nausea bubbled inside his stomach and he pursed his lips together as tight as he could. Vomiting would be like taking his hat off in public.

He tried to stand, but his legs wobbled and he had to adjust quickly by spinning half a turn and grabbing the top of the wooden backrest. The edges of the tiny brass plaque felt sharp against his skin, and the thin grooves of the etched lettering encouraged him to lift his palm and read the inscription.

In Memory of
SOPHIE ALEXANDRIA CRAWFORD
1937 – 2016
She loved these gardens.

At the time, the Fedora thought only of these words as tools to help him refocus. It wasn't until thirty minutes later, when he lay dying on the alleyway's cold pavement, that the simplicity and tenderness of the words really hit him, piercing his soul, sharper than the tips of the arrow darts sticking out of his chest.

The illusory nature of his existence, his disdain for every living thing and the coldness in his heart wrenched at him in tight knots of bitterness and regret. Would anyone ever feel for him the way an old woman had felt for a big patch of grass? Would they commemorate his life and toast his name as they feasted on the Harvest he had worked so hard to provide? And what, if anything, would his own kind know of how he met his end, at the hands of the man squatting beside him now, his face in shadow, the empty gun dangling from his finger?

The questions flowed through his mind like poison through his veins. Perhaps they had seen a prediction of the man waiting there among the rats and the filth, the rotting waste and the stagnant booze, ready to pull the trigger the moment his target turned the corner; and then, for the greater good, allowed fortune to rid them of their troublesome operative once and for all.

The edges of his vision began to blur. In the murky blue light of the late summer's day, he could just make out the man's sharp features, youthful and resilient in comparison to his clothes, with their stale odour and rough textures. In the midst of his observations the Fedora had become vaguely aware that the man was talking, prompted perhaps by some fleeting eye contact only he had noted. His voice was unexpectantly sincere and laced with an air of grim responsibility. The Fedora tried his best to listen, but his pain was rubbing out the detail of the words as reality slipped further away.

'Do you know what the worst part was?' the man said. 'The waiting. Waiting for a crime to happen so you have something to solve. Heroes need villains, villains need victims. That was the way of it. But not anymore, Buddy.'

The Fedora's senses suddenly awoke, crisp and alert, the world bending and warping and then slamming back into shape with a sickening jolt.

Buddy?

Puke covered the floor. The man turned in disgust as he reholstered the gun and reached for the glove in the pocket of his long coat. Looking across, the Fedora could see the place where his hat had landed after he fell. It had come off and rolled away towards the rubbish bins and yet the man had said nothing of the exposed markings on his head. This man knew what he was. The realisation brought the Fedora to himself and urged him to resist the oncoming darkness.

– *What do you want?*

The man said nothing. The Fedora cursed. It had been so long since he'd spoken aloud and his body was weak. The effort alone might kill him. Still, it was his right.

'What do you want?'

The man thought to himself for a second.

'There is a girl,' he said. 'A young girl, barely out of her teens, but she is not to be underestimated. Honestly, you guys are screwed. You make the future so horrifying that she's coming back to wipe out the lot of you just so it'll never happen. Now I'm doing the same, except on a much smaller scale, with more...' He paused to ruminate on the right choice of words. '...*personalised* reckonings, shall we say; so I don't have the same luxury she has. Hers is one big change to prevent the apocalypse, but the consequences of my actions might have a few more shades of grey. I could make things worse. And the only way I can deal with that is to ignore it; and the only way I can do that is if I keep going *backwards*. Bury my head in the sand a little bit. I won't know if I bugger up the time-space continuum – excuse my language – or if I create any weird alternate realities, because I'm never going home.'

The man shrugged as he slipped his fingers into the glove.

'Don't worry, I'm cool with it; you lot ruined my whole life anyway. I'll start with you, then carry on, killing the killers before they kill. All the way back to Jack the Ripper if I fancy it. And before the innocent murderer is even found, I'll be gone. Off on another quest. That's my purpose now. My destiny. And it's yours too.'

He clipped the button over his wrist and ran his fingertips across the ground, the tiny blades leaving long scratches in the concrete.

'I've watched you, a few times. You pass through this alley on the way to Matthew Blaumann's flat. Sometimes you trip on that bin over there, sometimes you don't, but either way you're close to passing out by the time you get there. You wait for the final whistle and just like that –' He clicked his fingers '– you snuff out the lives of four young people.'

The Fedora's body spasmed in agony, as though the fear were strangling him from the inside out. He couldn't think, he couldn't breathe. The hunger made it worse. The man was down on his knees now, leaning over him, blocking out the last of the light.

'Except this time, Buddy, you won't.'

About the author

Sean White was born and raised in Ashford, Kent and studied theatre production at the Central School of Speech and Drama in London. He has worked in tourism for much of his career, including as a tour guide at the Elizabeth Tower (Big Ben) in the Palace of Westminster, while writing in his spare time. He now lives with his wife and son in the Cotswolds.

The Goalkeeper is his first novel.

Printed in Great Britain
by Amazon

82950340R00325